CYNTHIA SHEARER

THE
WONDER BOOK
OF THE
AIR

Cynthia Shearer was born in Chicopee, Massachusetts, in 1955, and grew up in Georgia. She
lives in Oxford, Mississippi, with her husband and
daughter, and works for the University of Mississippi as the curator of Rowan Oak, the home of
William Faulkner. This is her first book.

CYNTHIA SHEARER

THE

WONDER BOOK

OF THE

AIR

VINTAGE CONTEMPORARIES

Vintage Books

A Division of Random House, Inc.

New York

FIRST VINTAGE CONTEMPORARIES EDITION, MAY 1997

Copyright © 1996 by Cynthia Shearer

All rights reserved under International and Pan-American
Copyright Convention. Published in the United States by
Vintage Books, a division of Random House, Inc., New York, and
simultaneously in Canada by Random House of Canada Limited,
Toronto. Originally published in the United States in hardcover
by Pantheon Books, a division of Random House, Inc.,
New York, in 1996.

The following stories have been previously published: "The Sea of
Dames" appeared in *Missouri Review* (Spring 1994). • Portions of
"Flight Patterns" were published in *The Oxford American* (1992). •
"Field's Guide to Amerikan Houses" appeared in *Reckon* (Fall
1995) and in *Tri-Quarterly* as "Radioland" (Fall 1993).

Page 309 constitutes an extension of this copyright page.

The Library of Congress has cataloged the
Pantheon edition as follows:
Shearer, Cynthia.
The wonder book of the air : a novel / Cynthia Shearer.
p.   cm.
ISBN 0-679-43982-X
1. Family—Southern States—Fiction. I. Title.
PS3569.H39145W66   1996
95-31552
813'.54—dc20
CIP

Vintage ISBN: 0-679-75836-4

Random House Web address: http://www.randomhouse.com/

Printed in the United States of America
10 9 8 7 6 5 4 3 2 1

FOR SOME WHO MADE ME BELIEVE:
Dan, Leah, Lessis, Barry, Susan,
and
the late John Delafose of the Eunice Playboys,
who once made beautiful music in a nearly empty house
in Oxford, Mississippi

Orphans that we are, we make our sibling kin out of anything we can find. . . . We are fragments of an unutterable whole.

—CHARLES SIMIC, *Dimestore Alchemy:*
The Art of Joseph Cornell

CONTENTS

THE
WONDER BOOK
OF THE
AIR

MACON TELEGRAPH STOMP

I began the serious lifelong study of the lady female member of the species *homo sapiens* human being in 1931. When I wanted to be an Eminent Telegrapher. You laugh, but at the time it seemed worthy. I was sixteen. I had a good thing going with the Atlantic Coast Line Railroad—a shoeshine stand in the depot beneath the Alapaha Station sign. Alapaha, Georgia. The first thing an arriving passenger saw was *me* in my brother Carey's too-big knickers, sitting on my shoeshine stand, old Coca-Cola crates nailed together. Five feet away from me was a big waist-high cotton basket. This was the trash receptacle for the whole town's thrown-away mail. Ten feet away, the office of the postmaster, ticket agent, and local Western Union man, Hoyt Benefield.

My only competition was a little Negro kid across the tracks whose name was Motee. Motee had copied my crate idea and had set himself up across the tracks at the Negro store. But I had the edge, I had the depot.

It was a kind of found treasure, the sights afforded me by that shoeshine stand. I saw the mix and coupling of cars, I marveled at the names as they passed before me in peeling paint on rusted iron: Atcheson Topeka & Santa Fe, Chesapeake & Ohio, Illinois Central, Lackawanna, and, inexplicably once, Union Pacific. Those names were my entree to the outside world, and I whispered them to myself sometimes at night before I fell asleep.

One engineer I admired, Jim Maddox, sometimes stopped to

have a smoke with Hoyt Benefield. It was said that before 1929, he was about to be made the engineer of his own name train, called the *Alapaha Star*. People spoke of it in hushed tones when he was not around: the plans had been drawn up, and he had seen them. After 1929, plans for new trains were scrapped. They told stories of whole railroad yards turned into locomotive graveyards, with old trains being cannibalized to repair others.

One time I saw his train from Macon forced to stop, one of those big black steam locomotives the railway moguls called Mikadoes and the railmen called hoggers. Mr. Jim got off in a fury, wiping the black dust from his face with his red bandanna.

—*Where is that old son of a bitch? Where is he?*

I pointed into Mr. Hoyt's little dive of an office. I could hear their voices over the transom.

—*You got no call to hold me up! No call!*

—*Brakeman says you ain't slept in two days.*

—*Sleepin' don't get nobody from here to there, Hoyt.*

—*Well, you can kill yourself if you want, but you got no call to take others with you.*

Another time when Mr. Jim had been forced to stop, and was side-railed, I listened to them from the threshold.

—*Got a boy on my crew run off in Macon*, Mr. Jim said, rolling his cigarette.

—*Troubles all over*, Mr. Hoyt said.

—*His trouble is called the Braswell Tunnel.*

Mr. Hoyt didn't say anything. He looked at me as if I should leave.

—*He's big enough to hear it*, Mr. Jim said. —*You get in the Braswell Tunnel with a hogger and you are roasting in your own black, stinking chamber of hell. And when the crew starts cursing and crying for their wives and mothers, you're wondering if they would let you join the Brotherhood of Sleeping Car Porters if you ever make it back.* He turned his face to me. —*Boy, get some job don't have nothing to do with the railroad, that would be my advice. You get you one them jobs you just sit and count rich men's money all day.*

We could hear the sound of the other train coming through. He went over to the sooty station window and with his finger made a little circle to see through. Mr. Hoyt got the cables together for the incoming train, and I followed him out onto the platform.

It was one engine and one passenger car. An astounding waste of human effort, even to a boy like me. The passenger car looked like a throwback to robber-baron days, with TAMBURLAINE emblazoned on the side in gilt. Fresh gilt. The steps were brass, and a man in a brown pinstripe suit got off, adjusting his tie. He seemed to be the chief paymaster for the Atlantic Coast Line. He conferred with Mr. Hoyt while Mr. Jim ensconced himself back into the promontory of the black locomotive, from which he viewed us all with sooty amused contempt. I sneaked over to hazard a peek into the passenger car.

I saw the green velvet draperies first, and the fringed Tiffany lamp on a green-baize-covered table. A poker table. I saw the cut-glass decanter on the table, and the light refracting through it. I saw the white arm of a woman, bare, bone-china white, and my eyes followed the arm's length. She was milky bare everywhere that was not covered by her long red hair, and lying back on a nest of silky pillows, like an odalisque. In this manner I became an aficionado of the female form.

I jumped back from the window like I'd been burned, and maybe I had. The sight of her was burned into me, along with that word, TAMBURLAINE, emblazoned in my mind like the distant locale I imagined it to be. In this manner I learned to navigate through my life by the convincing memory of something I'd never had, attainable in some place I'd never been. The opulent car began to roll out of the station to that place. When it had passed, there was only the sight of a small sunburned local woman wielding a homemade broom made of twigs, like some horrible land-locked sea creature doomed to scrabble at the earth with an intricately brushy giant claw.

Hoyt Benefield cleaned out his office one day, throwing all manner of treasure into the cotton basket. I waited until he left for the noon break and pulled out the knapsack that my mother always told me my Uncle Artie had carried on his back at the Somme. I had written my name on it in tiny tentative India ink letters: *Harrison Durrance.*

On this day the treasure in the cotton basket was a little red leather-bound book called *Principles of Telegraphy,* and some carbons of telegrams that had come into Alapaha, in addition to the usual stale copies of the Macon *Telegraph* or the Savannah *Morning*

News, and sometimes a copy of the St. Louis *Post-Dispatch.* And a curious brass round ruler, numerals and measurements etched into it. It was a very manly thing.

As I was cramming it all in my knapsack, the train from Savannah pulled into the station, and there suddenly was this *girl,* all spaniel eyes and red ringlets, lost in a dour navy overcoat. Just in time to see yours truly in the act of scavenging with great satisfaction in the cotton basket. I paused, holding the green felt visor with WESTERN UNION in embossed letters; I had been just about to clap it onto my forehead. Instead I put it in the knapsack, slowly.

The spaniel-eyed girl was staring at my hair. Which was red, like hers.

Her mother came away from talking to the porter. There was a smaller girl, a towhead with a Buster Brown haircut. The engineer's family. I'd heard they were coming back here to live. They appeared to be waiting for him.

Hoyt Benefield appeared to be cleaning out his office, and the longer he worked the madder he got. He threw in an old telegraph transmitter with its cut wires dangling almost obscenely, like irrelevant arteries. It sank a little in the paper trash, the newspapers and circulars. After the last train from Macon went on to Jacksonville, the old Negro man would come to empty it. I was eyeballing that transmitter with considerable interest.

The red-haired engineer's daughter watched from aperch her trunk, her ankles neatly crossed in cream ribbed stockings. Agony: the exigencies of the scrounge were upon me, and I was loath to abase myself before her.

I wadded up an old shoeshine rag and walked over to the basket, threw it in, and pretended to notice the transmitter for the first time. I picked it up, and examined it. It was a man's object, possessing the quality of totem for me. The small lever was worn smooth from the touch of his fingers.

—*What's that?* the girl asked, and I liked her voice because it was a city voice.

I walked over to show it to her, and she held it in her lap, pursing her knees together somehow. She must have been eleven.

—*Come along, Marjorie,* her mother called from across the platform. —*The car's here. How many times do I have to tell you not to talk to people who are not our sort?* the mother said. The red-haired girl smiled at me, and rolled her eyes.

Their sort? I decided I hated the lady but liked the daughter. When she looked at me, I felt like somebody was *seeing* me.

When I had ascertained that there were no shoes for me to shine, I closed my stand, slid the box inside Hoyt's door, and hot-footed it home to examine my haul. My mother met me at the door to reconnoiter about my earnings and put them in a jar high on a shelf in the kitchen. My college fund. I had learned to slip a little into my shoe now and then, to cover incidentals.

—*How much did you get, boy?*

—*Dollar and a dime.*

—*Well, hand it here. What's in your sack?*

—*Books.* I slipped out *Principles of Telegraphy* to show her.

—*You steal that?*

—*No, ma'am. Mr. Hoyt threw it away.*

She grunted her dismissal, and I was free. No command today to bring in wood, weed the garden, or mind my baby brother. She always smelled of onions or mint, and I can hardly remember what it was like to see her smile. There must have been some smiles directed my way, it stands to reason. I do not remember what she looked like smiling.

That night, in the room I shared with my brothers, I took the transmitter from my knapsack, examined it by the light of a kerosene lamp my mother didn't know we had. My two older brothers never came in until late, and my two younger ones were already asleep. I looked at their heads on the one pillow.

What sort was our sort? It had never occurred to me that there was any other sort besides us. Our father was a rural mail carrier, an innocent bystander and messenger of doom, the performance of which role earned him the munificent sum of twenty-six dollars a month. He rode his bicycle out to the farms to deliver the foreclosure notices that sizzled down the telegraph lines.

There were ten of us, counting my father and mother, and we lived in a small white house. We got by with my mother's gardening, my brothers' trotlines in the river, selling eggs and milk to people who would not speak sociably to us even if they passed us on the sidewalk, and bartering with those who had no money.

There were men in my town with enough money left to lend

and foreclose, lend and foreclose, eating the small farms that lay outside town, and even the proudest of farmers had little choice but to stay on as their tenants.

I read about the amount of gutta-percha and piano wire that it would take to wire a particular pass of the Ganges River for telegraphy, convinced that such information would eventually place me among the ranks of the Eminent Telegraphers, preserved in portraiture at the back of my book between little panes of veined tissue. Jeptha Holland of Alabama. Levi Lincoln Sadler of Massachusetts. Great bearded patriarchs with flowing manes of hair.

No old woman was ever going to look at *me* again the way that woman had.

I could learn Morse code from the little red book. I could wear the green visor and tap it all out—the price of cattle, the price of cotton futures, the notices that city relatives would send when the food ran out in cities like Macon: *Arrive 3:10 with children.* Back to their parents' farms, where the vegetables and fresh milk could be counted on. In my own head I was already the one who orchestrated all the comings and goings when circumstances necessitate the displacement of large numbers of people.

I put on the green visor and practiced the Morse code.

M-a-r-j-o-r-i-e.

I tapped it down and out into some imaginary night, toward someplace where it might be received warmly. Marjorie got melded in my mind with Sheena, Queen of the Jungle from the Edgar Rice Burroughs comic strips I read in the Macon *Telegraph.*

I tapped and hammered into the night, inspired to send messages of urgent import around the swampside end of Georgia—messages divined from the carbons Hoyt threw away, my fingers impersonating his, tracing his same path:

—*Cattle futures not sound.*

—*Livestock on the track at Woodbine.*

—*Your property will be sold at public auction.*

My oldest brother, Carey, came in to the room that night and slammed himself down on the far bed, shielding his eyes from the lamplight. These were the times: grown sons sharing rooms with toddler siblings, caught in some tense holding pattern, waiting for true flight. I tried to slide my transmitter out of sight, but he saw it, then the other brass thing.

—What the hell is that?

—Mr. Hoyt threw it away. It's a sextant.

Then he began to laugh at me.

Consider that the reputations of Eminent Telegraphers might perhaps be prefaced somewhere by the laughter of others. Consider: this laughter might serve its purpose in the world.

Carey could look at the thing and see only worn brass. He could look at the transmitter and see only dangling wires. But in my mind already were vast secret archipelagoes of human mystery to be conquered, in the world in which I reigned supreme—my own head. The brain of a boy. You cast from the shore into the murk of the river because your future is out there waiting for you like a fat calico bass with your name on it.

I was just an idle angler until Uncle Artemus came back to live with us.

Just breezed into our life on the evening train. No telegram to announce it. I was the first to see him, having just slid my crate-stand inside Mr. Hoyt's door and hoisted my knapsack onto my back. He was standing there staring first at the knapsack, which had been his, and then at me. He almost knew who I was, though he hadn't seen me since I was a tyke. We had Christmas cards from him sometimes.

—You would be . . . Carey?

—No, sir. I'm Harrison.

—Well, let's go surprise your mother, son. He had only one small pasteboard valise, and he had come from St. Louis, where he was a radio engineer.

I reached for the valise to carry and he let me try it. The weight of it almost wrenched my arm out of its socket, and I only had time to get my feet out of the way before it *thunked* with a muffled clank onto the ground between us like it was full of flatirons.

—Better let me, he said, and my face fell. *—That's all right. "They also serve who only stand and wait."*

In the kitchen, my mother was standing at the sink, wearing one of Carey's old gray sweaters, chopping an onion, and I saw her through Uncle Artie's eyes: the streaks of gray in the hair, the face that begrudged smiles to anyone. She simply looked at him, and the quiet dismay broke over her face. No smiles or hugs or hand-shakes. This was the way of our family.

—Aren't you glad to see me?

—You should have told me.

—I tried to, but Western Union has cut this place off. He set the valise down.

—There's coffee, she said, and returned to her onion.

Uncle Artie took his chipped mug of coffee and walked out into the yard. This was the house and yard he had grown up in. I followed him. It was already dark. He went over to the smokehouse, which was simply a gabled roof plopped onto the ground, as if some prior storm had lopped it off some distant house and left it in our back yard. Uncle Artie knelt at the corner and picked up a little bit of dirt and tasted it.

—Ever do that? he said, holding out his hand.

—Salt. I nodded, and he smiled. I knew the terrain.

—You and I are going to be compadres, eh, compadre?

He hitched his hat back on his head, kicked in the padlocked door. We walked in, and he had to remain stooped. My sisters had used it for a playhouse. My brothers had used it for their huckleberry wine experiments, hence the padlock. Now there were desiccated centipedes in the little fireplace, and cracks in the mortar. He sighed.

—It was the best smokehouse in town in its day. It'll have to do. Any house you take is a compromise between what once was and what can be.

He meant to live there. I was very joyful. I kept thinking, *The Somme, he was at the Somme.*

UNCLE ARTIE had a degree in physics from Georgia Tech. He was an engineer for KSLO in St. Louis. Understand that it came to pass: a man with a degree in physics came home to live in a smokehouse.

My sisters brought him blankets and a pillow, and I gave him my kerosene lamp. He opened his valise: books and small tools, shirt or two, and some underwear. He took them out and laid the books in a neat row along one wall where the roofline narrowed so that he had to crawl to do it. When he turned around, he bumped his head on the low smokehouse roof.

He had a set of blueprints for a catboat. He unrolled them on the floor and weighted them with books. I looked at them, and the tiny brown ink script: *planking, strake, bowsprit, deck beam.* I was enchanted.

—*What is this for?* I asked.

—*It's something I haven't gotten around to yet.*

I was anxious to show him that I owned a book, so I brought him my *Principles of Telegraphy.* He handled it fondly in the firelight and traced the gold leaf on the spine with his index finger. I ran back into the house to get my sextant. When I came back he was still looking at the book and smiling.

—*Look here, I want to show you something,* he said, and rustled the pages. He turned to the beginning of the book and pointed to some tiny print. I peered over his shoulder. —*Eighteen seventy-eight. That's when this book was published. These were old men then. They're all dead now.*

I'd been worshiping dead men. End of grand ambition. I must have flushed crimson, because he laughed and cuffed me on the head.

—*Think "radio." What you got there?*

—*Sextant,* I said proudly.

—*Mother of God,* he said in a husky whisper. —*What you got yourself here is an astrolabe.* As he turned it over and over fondly in his hands, he kept talking. —*You don't see many of these anymore. Last one I saw was in a museum in Paris, long time ago. Where did you come across this?*

—*Mr. Hoyt threw it out,* I said defensively.

But he just barked out a joyful laugh, as if a steamboat just fell out of the sky.

—*How does it work?* I asked him.

—*I can only tell you what I know, which ain't much,* he said. —*After dark.* That dusk felt like the longest in human history while I waited to get my chores done and for sufficient dark to arrive.

—*We're going to the whirlpool,* Uncle Artie announced after dinner. My mother raised a brow. I was surprised that Uncle Artie knew about the whirlpool. But then, he seemed to know everything. I was excited. I was convinced that by the time I got back home with that astrolabe and a headful of knowledge, I'd be loaded for bear, in the cosmic sense, for the rest of my life. I would know how to get to the whirlpool, knowledge that, in our town, separated boys from men.

. . .

—*Okay,* Uncle Artie said, and the locusts were roaring around us. We had walked until the trails in the huckleberry thickets were almost impassable, and then they opened into a wide clearing. In the dark he had the movements of a boy. I could sense that water was near, as if by subliminal smell. Then a low sucking noise, which I started to hear the way a picture sometimes comes slowly into focus. The stars were brighter, scattered like cold stones.

Uncle Artie waved his arms, somehow encompassing the sky, as if the cosmos were his personal property. —*Compadre, I can't teach you how to survive plenitude. The best to be hoped for is to find it navigable.*

I had my astrolabe in my hand, but he was pacing in the huckleberry clearing.

—*What is the shortest distance between two points?*

—*Straight line,* I said.

—*Always?*

—*Yes sir,* I said.

—*Wrong, wrong.*

I didn't like the way this was going. I wanted to be moving the astrolabe, getting somewhere.

—*You know what an azimuth is?* He put a stick in my hand and held it over mine while he drew a diagram in the dirt so I was seeing through my hands. —*Suppose you need to know the distance from point A to point B. How do you find out?*

—*Measure it.* I sensed a trick question.

—*Wrong. What if it's from here to China?*

—*Just measure the straight line,* I said.

—*But the earth curves, compadre,* he said, swinging my hand in a sweeping arc. —*Always be ready to adjust your calculations. You got to account for the curves of the earth. They will set you back, my buckaroo. They will detain you. See that star?* He waved his hands at the sky like it was a black chalkboard, and the stars seemed cast up there like fireflies.

—*Yes sir,* I said, beholding thousands.

—*We used to think we could trust them to tell us where to go. But what if they move when you're not looking?*

He seemed sad to tell me this.

—*Believe it, buckaroo. Heisenberg's uncertainty principle. The Coriolis effect. Look it up. And not in those goddamn 1879 books.*

He was unlike anyone I had ever known, and therefore fortuitous treasure to me. —*If I don't teach you anything else, remember this,* he said. —*Beware the star you navigate by inside your head. It will betray you. Think about old Ponce de Leon, scrambling around in these selfsame woods looking for the Fountain of Youth. Bastard probably killed a hundred men trying to find it.*

I decided what he was teaching me about the astrolabe was that he didn't know how to use the astrolabe. But he could cast his hands and words out together into the night like some well-practiced fisherman, and I could see there the paths of Magellan and Cortez caught there, I thought.

Within days he had established himself as Alapaha's only radio repairman. No newspaper necessary, just that mainstay of American advertising, the American mouth. At first, people would knock on our door, and my mother would set the radio on the kitchen table and say that she would take it to him later.

—*Why didn't you send them around back?*

—*I thought you'd rather do it this way.* She seemed embarrassed.

—*Why?* he said. He seemed not to know she was embarrassed.

Soon there were whole radios on the floor awaiting repair, half-radios gleaned from garbage cans, and funny hunks of radios hanging from the hooks in the ceiling like ghostly hams or electric amputees. There was a black-fringed, jet-beaded horror of a kerosene lamp, and a brown wicker rocker that he had traded for. Eventually he acquired a small cot, which he placed behind a muslin bedsheet screen.

From somewhere came the waist-high butcher's block that my grandfather used to carve up the hams on, and Uncle Artie kept it strewn with the innards of radios—tubes, receptors, coils of wire. He would cannibalize old radios to fix the new at no cost, get a chicken or something else in return. Not exactly a bad introduction for me to the ways of the world. He read radio magazines to keep up, and traded with illiterate farmers, taking only what he needed. They got to hear "The March of Time"— we got chickens, venison, and sometimes odd castoffs that my sisters could wear.

He loved to present my sisters with jet earrings or peacock plumes, but his real passion was books. Within a few weeks the locals had discovered this. You can't *know* the contents disgorged from those houses, some from folks who couldn't read. Horatio Alger books from dirt farmers about to go under. I learned to watch his windowsills. He passed along some choice morsels to me: *Tom Swift and his Electric Rifle, The Motor Boys on the Border, The Radio Boys Trailing a Voice.*

I loved those books, and the times after supper when I would take Uncle Artie his plate—covered with a napkin by my mother so my father would not see how large his portions were—and I would sit and talk to him while he ate.

One afternoon I found him shaking the hand of an out-of-work carpenter who was trying to trade his toolbox—his box full of tools—to get the radio fixed for his wife.

—*I can't do that,* Uncle Artie said. —*I'll fix the goddamn radio, but I'll not take your tools from you. That's your bread and butter.*

—*Well, what about this-sheer?* the old guy said, and hauled a black Leica out of a croker sack.

—*Where'd you get that thing?*

—*Feller in Macon give it to me when I tiled his bathroom.*

—*Do you know how it works?*

—*Nope. Reckon I'll never learn, neither.*

—*Tell you what,* Artie said. —*I'll take it and hold it in escrow for you. Till you get time to learn. Hell, I might play with it myself.*

Uncle Artie fixed the radios, and built a new table for experiments. There was the beginnings of a small junk pile behind the smokehouse, but he knew it like the back of his hand and sometimes jumped up to run and rummage for just the right piece.

—*It's no way to live,* I heard my father say to my mother at the dinner table, his mouth full. —*Away from his wife, his child.*

What wife? What child? Why did he never tell me about them?

—*He is no trouble,* my mother said as if defending one of us children. —*He gave us that chicken you're eating.*

One day the carpenter's wife brought the same toolbox by to trade out service on a radio. —*I can't take his tools,* Uncle Artie said, —*but I'll fix your radio. That's his bread and butter you're trying to give away there, Missy.*

—*Not no more,* she said. —*He went to Macon and he killed hisself.*

Uncle Artie took the tools. He moved the Leica from a dark place under his bed to a more prominent one on the windowsill. I saw no evidence he ever used it. I noticed that the blueprints would sometimes replace the radios on the work table.

I went to deliver the milk to the engineer's house. The red-haired girl, Marjorie, was sitting in the front porch swing, reading a book.

—*What's that?* I asked.

—*Dickens,* she said. —*David Copperfield.* And she handed it to me. —*Take it, I've read it twice.*

I left the milk with her, and I forgot to ask for the money.

When I got home, my mother saw the book.

—*You take that back,* she said. She thought I had stolen it.

I read it first. I waited until the next delivery day for milk to take it back.

The mother came to the door. She sniffed the jar of milk. I had the *David Copperfield* tucked into my shirt. I wanted to give it to the red-haired girl. I wanted to see her. I was afraid I'd get her in trouble if I gave it to the mother.

—*Tell your mother I want fresh,* she said. —*I'll pay her when the milk is fresh.*

In this manner I was stiffed by the engineer's wife.

I took money out of my shoe stash to cover the lost milk money.

My father had said, —*We will pay as we go.* There would be no credit at either store. My mother cooked the fish and game we brought her. She must have done other things, yet I mostly remember her in the kitchen, scraping vegetables. My brothers and I developed the nonpareil of local trotlines. My sisters? I have this memory of them doing their hair a lot before dances and dates, haggling with all the élan of Mexican streetwalkers over who was going to wear which of their few good dresses. They had a red cloche hat they fought over a lot.

Some nights I lay in the dark listening to my older brothers breathing, which sometimes sounded to me like tired birds caught too long in a holding pattern, waiting for the sight of solid ground. Such nights I would wonder what was going to become of us all. There were headlines, real screamers sometimes on the papers in the depot cotton basket: about this bank or that bank failing, and though all my earnings were sequestered in a crock in my mother's kitchen—so I thought— I felt each headline very acutely.

Then Burma came to us. Just stepped off the train from the planet of the beautiful, like a jazz musician's wet dream. It was early summer, and she was wearing a gauzy gray mourning dove dress, and even Hoyt Benefield came to the half-door to look. The dress was plain and nondescript, but the body underneath beckoned a long look. I had this little inkling then that manliness had something to do with being spellbound by a set of hips that are moving out of your reach, maybe *because* they are moving out of your reach.

She walked over to me. To *me*.

I stared and swallowed.

—*I'm looking for Artemus Elliot.*

—*That's my Uncle Artie,* I said, stupefied like a mule.

She took this in with an air of irritation, like this was one more complication in her life. I was ready to bow at her feet. The little girl stepped out from behind her, dressed like a cheap knockoff of Shirley Temple. Dishwater blond hair tortured into greasy ringlets, little sailor dress, little maryjane shoes on her fat feet. But that face: a dried-apple dwarf face, ferret-like, and sharp. She was probably about seven.

—*I'm Toy,* the little girl said, fidgeting. —*It's from the French.* She reached into my shoe-polish kit and stepped on my foot, crunching the bones a little.

—*The French what?* I wondered.

I took Burma and Toy to my parents' house and said nothing about the smokehouse. For a brief instant I saw something like a look of hatred in my mother's eyes when she saw them both; the rest is lost, whatever words they spoke to each other. Memory culls out and loses what you can't use at the moment.

I remember that first night, she and Burma listening to the radio with us—the Carter family was on, one of those broadcasts out of Del Rio that you could only get on a clear night. The Carters I always envisioned as sad white trash; the plaintiveness of their voices always made me want to leave the room, the house, the whole damn *South*. But Toy jumped up while they were on and pitched right in with them, assuming the posture of a little Roman senator, declaiming.

—*That's sweet, baby,* Burma smiled, as if she was used to this.

—*What talent,* one of my sisters said. —*We must cultivate her talent.* They decided to enter her in a contest at a big fair in Macon. There was much discussion of what her "number" would be. They taught her how to belt it out like Sophie Tucker. They dressed her up like the Statue of Liberty and made her sing "The Star Spangled Banner." They put a rose in her hair and taught her a torch song, and Fran taught her how to bump and grind her dwarf ass, and how to contort the weaselish face into an unintentional parody of lust, crooning "You're the Cream in My Coffee."

Uncle Artie came through the kitchen when they had her standing on the table. Fran was coaching her on when precisely in the number to press her fat little hand to her child's chest. The effect was not all that different from that of a windup mechanical toy. The hand goes up to the chest, the eyes glaze; the hand goes up to the chest, the eyes glaze again. Dependable as a watch movement.

Uncle Artie took all this in for a minute and then he spoke. —*I do not know which is the greater calumny. To expose Toy to this aspect of the world, or to expose the world to this aspect of Toy.*

A ripple and a stir among the sisters. Burma just sat in a chair leaned back against the kitchen wall and looked wise in her womanly way, like *this too will pass.*

They waited until he'd left the room and then somebody whispered, —*We'll do it anyway. This could be her future we're talking about here.*

The word was like fat fruit in their red painted mouths: *future, future.*

I remember that I lay awake that night imagining Uncle Artie's reunion with Burma as he welcomed her into his narrow bed. I wondered if they had old tender jokes to share with each other. His touching her sweet, warm body—the *privilege* of that! The innocence of boys: navigating through your days by the memory of something you haven't had yet. In my mind that smokehouse was an arbor of romance and opulent mystery, strewn with fallen flowers like a picture of a Pre-Raphaelite painting I'd seen in a book.

Uncle Artie's household essentially merged with ours. Toy slept with my sisters. I spent a lot of time in the smokehouse.

Whenever Toy had had enough of the costuming and coaching from my sisters, she'd show up at the depot a little while before it was time for me to go home, and she'd always be sucking on a gumdrop. She was a shrewd little customer and figured out fast that she could get more candy for a penny if she'd talk Motee into spending it for her at the store for the Negroes. Then she'd step behind the door and watch through the letter slot as people came into the depot to check their mail. Toy would take it all in from behind the door, her little weasel eyes at the mail slot. I looked up one day and she was sitting on the old men's bench, purporting to read the Macon *Telegraph,* except she was holding it upside down, and it looked like a distress signal, an upside-down flag.

She couldn't read. The girl did not know how to read. I digested every bit of new appalling information about her with a pathological glee. She paraded around out in the yard dressed in somebody's old high heels and hat, with a ratty feather boa. Ferret finery. Declaiming here, bumping and grinding there, staggering and lurching as the spike heels drove into the dirt.

Then there was the time I was delivering some milk to Mrs. Lurene Browning's house, and Toy had tagged along with her incessant questions, and before I could raise my hand to knock, I could see through the filleted lace curtains into her kitchen, and there with his back to me was Hoyt Benefield, his pants around his ankles, pumping himself in the direction of—no, *into*—the woman whose faded floral dress was bunched around her waist, whose fingers were streaking flour across the back of his shirt. Mrs. Lurene Browning, a widow of two or three years and mother of various children. I put the milk down and grabbed Toy by the arm and we fled, her questions pulsing at me—*what is it, what is it?*—in much the same rhythm and tempo as Hoyt's haunches were already flashing white in my memory.

That flour on those fingertips. The woman had stopped her cooking to accommodate Hoyt. It was not exactly an arbor of romance and opulent mystery.

—*How much did you get, boy?* The first question my mother asked me when she counted the afternoon's take and understood that she'd been shorted. I couldn't do anything but stare down at my worn-out brown shoes and scuff them even more, and she slapped me, full hard on the side of the head.

The next day at the depot, Hoyt Benefield was sporting a shiner that would have done a boxer proud, and he had red, raw bruises mottled across his face.

I heard one woman tell another, —*His own sons, imagine. They told him that the littlest one needed help in the woods to get him out there, and then they teamed up on him.*

The other woman clucked and snorted. —*And well they should have. Him gallivanting around after women when his own wife is laid up in that bed. She never got over having that littlest one.*

THAT NIGHT I told most of what I'd seen to Uncle Artie.

—*They were in her kitchen, and he was—his pants were—they were standing up and they were . . .*

—*Yes?*

—*Doing it.*

He winced a little but he didn't say anything more until I had finished telling him about the cuts and bruises from Hoyt's sons. He had this way of laughing with you at your little troubles and commiserating with you on your good fortunes that was very agreeable to me.

—*Ah. Yes. My guess would be that what you were seeing there in that kitchen was the old essential transaction itself.*

—*Transaction?*

—*Between a man and a woman. Basis of all life, really.*

—*Excuse me?*

—*Those children have to eat. Forget the Radio Boys, I believe you're ready for Ring Lardner. I do believe you're ready to undertake the serious lifelong study of the lady female member of the species* homo sapiens *human being.*

Ring Lardner was a bit easier, but I despised the people in his stories. The women were whiners, or they were silly, and they always said the wrong things. They cried on their honeymoons, for God's sake. I dissolved into dreams of the engineer's red-haired daughter, clinging to me like a wispy half-clothed tendril in our arbor of romance and opulent mystery.

THE WOMEN OF THE HOUSE united against Uncle Artie. He wouldn't give Burma the money to take Toy to the Bibb County

Fair in Macon. Even my mother got into it. I'd never seen her in a church, but now she enlisted the aid of the Methodist minister.

—*Artemus, we're only talking about trainfare,* she said on one of those rare instances when she went into the smokehouse to see him. —*You owe it to them to let them try. It could mean a lot of money for you all.*

Uncle Artie barely looked up from his radios, kept working.

—*Brother, will you pray with us?* the minister offered hopefully. He was a great, glistening, sweaty maggot of a man who looked a lot like Fatty Arbuckle. He cut a wide swath in the air about town, but in my Uncle Artie's smokehouse he looked defeated. —*I said, will you pray with us?* he asked again.

—*My every breath is a prayer,* Uncle Artie said amiably, looking at him sadly. That was the first time in my life that I had seen someone look upon a *preacher* with pity, and this opened untold realms of understanding in my mind. That look. That pity. Uncle Artie was an inhabitant of a world I wanted into.

—*Are you a believer or an infidel?*

Uncle Artie began to roll himself a cigarette, tamping the tobacco from the red Prince Albert tin fastidiously.—*Sometimes the only true believers ARE the infidels,* he said, lighting the cigarette.

—*You don't want to be numbered among the lost,* the preacher said. —*Talking that crazy talk.*

Uncle Artie looked at me then, and smiled. —*We ain't lost, we is exploring.*

It was a wonderful secret, like we really were compadres.

The preacher looked at us like we were aborigines.

My mother looked at us like we were crooks.

—*Well,* she said with her hands patting at the pins that held her hair secure at the nape of her neck,—*if you can't take the initiative to do something for your family, Burma will have to do it. This could be Toy's future.*

I saw him twist the dial of the set he was working on, and the smokehouse filled with the strains of some black blues music, mournful like I'd never heard before. Could have been Bessie Smith or Billie Holliday, I'm not sure.

Toy heard it and was transfixed. This was not the nasal whine of the Carters, this was something that hit her deeper, something once, I could tell. I wanted to ask her why she would not use my name.

—*It's mine,* I stammered.

—*Give it here,* she ordered.

—*No, Ma,* I said, but she was walking over to me. I looked down and saw that it was only about a hundred. Money was missing.

—*Give it here,* she repeated. Like an automaton, I handed it over.
—*I want to teach you something,* she said, opening the door of the wood cookstove.

She threw the money into the flames and slammed the door.

—*I'm sick and tired of hearing about this money from all of you.*

At breakfast the next morning, I was ashy inside with anger and impotence. I couldn't eat. I had had a surfeit of wretchedness, it seemed to me, and it all seemed to be summed up in the miserable plate of food before me. I hadn't got up in time to get any bacon; just the leavings of it in the hominy.

—*What's the matter with you, boy?* my mother asked me. I couldn't answer.

My sister came in, wearing a new dress. Why was there money for a new dress for her and I had nothing? It hit me. Where the money had been going. The dresses, the hats, the stockings. *A woman has to make her way in the world.*

I mentioned it to my father. He was tying his shoes on the back steps, getting ready to make his rounds. He looked up at me with something like boredom, maybe a little anger. He shook his head.
—*You have to fight your own fights.*

He'd lost every fight he'd ever been in. I watched him ride off on his bicycle. Something about the slump of his shoulders as he bent over the handlebars spelled it out: he'd begun to quarantine himself from everyone. It had to do with those foreclosure papers he had to deliver.

In my times of misery I would hang out with Uncle Artie in his radio shop. I had three more days before I needed to catch the train to Rome. There was no way to earn the trainfare shining shoes in that time. I tried to read, but I couldn't be still. I wanted to smash windows, smash my mother. But when I tried to look at her, I felt close to crying.

—*Can I sleep out here?* I asked Artie. I could be a man out there in the smokehouse. Burma and Toy had given up sleeping there.

—Ask your mother. He barely looked up.

—I am not talking to her.

—Beg pardon?

—She took my money, I blurted out like a tattling child, not much manliness in my cracking voice. I told him the sordid details. *—My college money,* I added.

—There will be other bird-dog trials, Uncle Artie said. *—Every year.*

—But Ty Cobb, I said, my head already expanding with the image of him in an open field, a real man surrounded by his excellent dogs. *—Ty Cobb.*

My misery was compounded by my brother Carey's plight. His girlfriend had dumped him and run away to the railroad town of Waycross, to become a cosmopolite. He presented himself to Uncle Artie that afternoon as if he himself were some broken thing to be tinkered with.

—But I was going to marry her, he said in disbelief. *—I told her I wanted her to be my wife.* There were tears in his eyes, and I knew he would find occasion to hit me later, as payment for having seen him in a moment of weakness.

—Remember that the earth curves, Uncle Artie said. *—The earth curves.*

Toy had found Carey's old pasteboard guitar—two strings missing—and had appropriated it for herself. She aped the *whump-whump* rhythms of Maybelle Carter, but then she'd start in with that Negro blues touch. Down in the well, hollering up for help.

—Take it somewhere else, Toy, Uncle Artie said gently to her. *—Take it outside.*

—Yeah, I said sullenly, *—outside.*

—I'm going to take it to the Bibb County Fair, Toy taunted us. *—We're taking the train. We have to look out for my future.* She twitched her little lack of an ass out the door, still fingering the frets.

—Harrison, Uncle Artie said to me with new resolution in his voice, *—how much you need for that trainfare?*

—Twenty dollars.

—Dispatch that guitar, son, and it's yours.

We laughed then, compadres in the face of the tyranny of little girls and women.

I waited until Toy was asleep on her little pallet on the floor of the girls' room. I waded through a sea of stockings, dresses, underclothes, and shoes on the floor. On the floor. My money had amounted to that, things thrown on a floor. Toy slept hard, like a shot ferret, and the guitar was right beside her. I had to pry her fingers away, and her hand fell away from it like she was dead.

There was a draftway beneath the depot, great drafts of cold air that come through the wrought-iron covers even in the middle of summer. That's where I put the guitar. —*The earth curves, the earth curves,* I whispered, like an incantation.

I collected my twenty dollars, amazed that Uncle Artie even had twenty dollars. I folded the bills and put them in my knapsack.

I had slicked back my hair and was leaving the house when I heard my mother's voice. She was standing by the clothesline. She had my littlest brother, Red, tethered like a puppy to the line. He was toddling back and forth wearing only an old shirt of mine, and some blackberry jelly on his face.

—*How much you get today, boy?*

—*Not much.*

—*Well, give it here.*

I stood there frozen like *I* was the thief.

—*No, Ma,* I said. —*It's mine now.* I realized that she had been drinking. Smiling a horrible compelling smile, as if she were the sole possessor of a powerful secret. This was the first time I remember realizing she was capable of becoming drunk. She had a power to compel me, even that way. As if I were tethered to some imaginary clothesline she'd constructed and all I could do was slide from one end to the other.

I was about to the edge of the yard and I could still see her, arm outstretched over by the clothesline. Then a hot, starry feeling on the back of my head. I was down on the ground, in that kind of woozy amiable amazement, like when a beaten horse drops to its knees in disbelief that it can no longer stand. I moved my arm, and felt the piece of stovewood then. She had flung it at me.

I looked at that face that once governed me and understood: *It will happen no more, old woman. This is my penny in the jukebox. My lifetime.*

I STOOD IN FRONT of Mr. Hoyt Benefield's window to buy my ticket, but he barely looked up at me. I cleared my throat and squeaked out, —*I need a one-way to Macon.* I had heard other people say this, so I knew what to say. He came over to see my money. He looked into my face with a scowl, and walked into the little mail-room off his office. After a minute, the engineer came out.

—*Where are you headed, boy? That your school money? Are you going to that fair in Macon? I ain't give you all that shoeshine money all this time to have you lose it at some cootchie carnival.*

—*No, sir. I'm going to see Ty Cobb.*

He thought about this a minute, and then he reached in his overall pocket for a pen. —*Hoyt, gimme some paper to write on.*

I still have it, somewhere in my old box of war medals and love letters and gallstones, that blue-lined paper with that elegant In-dia-ink script: *Please permit passage for Harrison Durrance.* —*J.E. Maddox.*

—*This ought to do you in the state of Georgia,* he said. —*Nobody much knows me outside that. Well, Jacksonville, maybe.*

I folded it up and put it inside the knapsack. When I got home, there was my mother.

I took the morning train to Macon, with another ten dollars from shoeshine money rolled into the band of my cap. I had on some of Carey's old shoes, with bits of the Macon *Telegraph* stuffed into the toes so my feet wouldn't flop around in them. I was busy reading whatever I had in my knapsack, not even looking up when someone came to sit facing me in the Pullman. Somebody kicked my book, and it caught me under the chin. I heard a tinkly laugh.

Kate McLeod. My brother's ex-heartthrob. Marjorie's cousin.

Later in my life I would know how cheap her clothes were, later I would know how close to nothing she was. She had on this dress, some loose gauzy thing with bright dahlias on it. She had a purse that was a little red box.

I glared at her. I thought of Carey. So blithely she had dismissed him. He would have given her the shirt off his back. I would have given her the shirt off my back. To get her to take the shirt off her back.

—*What's in the knapsack?*

—*None of your business.* I felt embarrassed at the astrolabe and transmitter in there. Childish toys suddenly.

—*You're hurt. You've got blood on your collar,* Kate said. Instant trans-mogrification on her part. —*Come to the fair with me.*

I thought she was leaning over to whisper something to me, but she reached into her bosom for something. It was a little silver flask. She handed it to me, looking around to see if anyone noticed. It seemed so warm in my hand I almost dropped it.

That warm silver had been between those breasts. Talk about things going to your head: try some bosom-warmed bootleg whiskey. It constituted some kind of union with her—that bitter burning down my throat, warm from the silver which was warm from those breasts which were warm from her blood which was warm from the whiskey.

My first drink. Hosannas of forgiveness fanned out in my veins. I knew why my mother drank. I knew.

By the time we rolled into the Macon station, Ty Cobb was irrelevant to anything. I was following Kate around like an enchanted hound. —*I want that,* she pointed like a child, and I bought her a Kewpie doll dangling from a stick. Then I bought her a black celluloid hat with jet beading. She kept taking my arm as we walked around. I saw a playbill posted on a cattle stall: *TOY ELLIOT, child performer.* I bought Kate a ticket and we took our places on benches: planks laid across pine logs. I remember the way Kate leaned into me when I talked to her, but not what I said. I remember the brightness of her eyes, but not what she said back.

Toy walked out onto the stage in the little Sophie Tucker dress my sisters had rigged for her. It seemed all bright spangles and silver cobwebs, and she had a red celluloid rose in her hair. She was wearing new shoes, which had, no doubt, been purchased with my shoeshine money. But the real sight, the real killing thing, was to see Burma in her own silver spangle dress, very décolleté, just slightly offstage, leaning like a willow into a tall man in a pinstripe suit. As if she was saying, —*Buy me that world.* He was rolling a cigarette and watching Toy.

Toy was a big hit, bumping and grinding, an exact replica of some tiny torch singer, throwing her voice: —*You're the Cream in My Coffee* . . . It sickened me to think of what they didn't know, those dumb rubes stomping their feet and throwing their hats on the stage.

—*I've got to get out of here,* I said, and to my amazement, Kate seemed concerned about me. She was holding my hand.

There was an old Negro woman with a face like a black wax

gargoyle selling painted seashells on a little fringe-covered card-table next to the bandshell where Toy was still declaiming about the cream in her coffee. Both the old woman and her wares were gruesome. She had a row of homemade tambourines, primitive-looking things made of curved wire and conch shells. Rooster feathers tied with satin ribbons to burlap sachets that held God only knows what.

—*You got to buy your wummah a tamerlaine,* the old lady said. —*Every man got to buy his wummah a tamerlaine.*

Kate grabbed one, a spiked and spotted conch painted so gaudily blue-green that it shone like a Siamese fighting fish. She held it up to her ear like a telephone.

Man, she'd called me. I liked that. *His woman.*

—*Listen,* Kate said, and held it up for me to hear. —*If you don't shake it, it sounds like the sea.* The way her eyes smiled at me, I couldn't hear anything but the roaring in the chambers of my heart.

—*Oh, I've always wanted to go to Jekyll Island,* she said and twisted one of her jet earrings.

I said, —*I'll take you there. The seashore.*

Wasn't this what men did? I was having visions of her swirling and eddying around me all my life, like a sweet child. Women were meant to be treated to things I barely had had myself. I think it's pretty safe to say that I had no idea what I was doing. I knew enough of her story: her father had said she could never come back home. Something about being caught in a car with some boys.

I used Jim Maddox's handwritten railroad pass to get us on the train. She had retrieved a big canvas satchel from somewhere she'd stowed it. Probably all her earthly possessions.

She sat close to me in the passenger car, and there were some lovers kissing in the back. She leaned into me the way women do when they want you. She had the painted seashell on her lap, and she'd pick it up and hold it to her ear now and then, looking happily out the window.

—*You can hold my hand,* she said, still staring out the window, and I felt my face go red. I took her hand. This boosted my confidence a little. The vision of myself holding her on the shore was pulsing in my mind like a memory that hadn't happened yet. I forgot where I was, forgot she was even there, just went deeper into my own head and held her tenderly there. Instant uncomfortable pressing against my pants. I let go of her hand a minute to adjust my pants—too late—she had seen.

—*Sorry,* I said and reached to put my knapsack on my lap.

—*No, don't,* she whispered. —*I like it.* And I put the knapsack back down.

It felt like I had a telegraph pole between my legs. I watched her face while she was looking, first at *it,* and then up at *me.* I thought, *Is this what it's like to be a man?* There is a certain joy when that guilty, solitary phenomenon becomes a ponderous, treasured secret you share with a real girl. I wanted to be alone with her.

—*It's not fair, is it?* she said.

—*What?* I could almost put it out of my mind that she must have done this same thing with Carey once, possibly with others. Almost.

—*I'm having a similar problem, only it's not so obvious.*

This was a deep riddle to me, and the longer she looked at me, the more it felt like a joke at my expense. What was she talking about? Was there some anatomical fact I hadn't managed to glean through the years? I thought of Toy when my sisters were bathing her, her comic little slit between her legs. I felt my lack of experience woefully, and the situation in my pants began to subside. But I nodded, knowledgeably.

That, too, is a moment toward manhood, when you begin to despise them a little for their mysteries. Maybe they have the same moments when they begin to despise us for ours.

When we passed through Tifton, she began to cry. —*I haven't been home in a year. I want to see my mother. I want to see Grace.*

So we stopped in Alapaha, not at the seashore. Mr. Hoyt Benefield himself helped her off the train. It wasn't his way to talk, but I could tell he was curious. He tactfully waved the porter off. I was thinking that I would take her to Uncle Artie's. If she wouldn't go home, she would at least go there. She would see it as an adventure to be there in that accidental-looking house. Artie would like her, I knew it.

But the place was dark, and there was a new shiny padlock. In my innocence, I imagined that he had put it there to keep my mother out. I peered in the window. He wasn't there. There was a roll of paper thrown onto the junk pile in back. His catboat blueprints.

I retrieved them and put them in my hip pocket. I felt like a man walking along beside her with those plans in my pocket. She didn't have to know they weren't mine.

—*Walk me home?* she said, taking my arm.

We passed through the tall grass that ringed the basketball court behind her house, and stood under the tallest oak tree in the county. There her house was, lights all ablaze.

—*Wait,* she said and stopped. —*Not yet. Let's climb the tree.*

Let the record read that the first time I ever put my hand on a woman's ass was to heft Kate McLeod into that oak tree. Entirely honorable situation.

I know that because she sat astride a branch broad as a horse's back and smiled at me. So I straddled the horseback branch and smiled back.

—*You know, Carey and I were in this tree when he asked me to marry him.*

I said nothing. To pursue that subject felt like six kinds of betrayal.

She was looking over my shoulder, behind me. I turned around, and there in the darkness of the porch was her mother, Miss Lydia, silhouetted by the light from the window of the kitchen, her belly a huge and pregnant orb. She was staring down the street at her husband, Kate's father. Standing on the porch of Mrs. Lurene Browning, only it wasn't Mrs. Lurene Browning he was kissing, it was her daughter. I thought: *the essential transaction.*

That sight: that cartoon-bellied woman looking down the street, understanding that sometimes when people are telling you you're the most important is when you're the most expendable to your kind.

—*I can never go back there,* Kate said. —*Nobody can make me go back there.*

It wasn't Carey she was trying to outrun, it was something else. I leaned over, thinking to kiss her so that I could block her view. I wanted to think that I could redeem us all that way. I could begin the world again that minute. That is the way it feels when you start to sift through the falsities of your forebears: like you can, by choice, begin the whole world again, and get it *right* this time.

—*Look—who's that?* she said. She was looking over my shoulder.

It was my own mother. Leaning over in that old-lady-ass-in-the-air way, digging in one of the engineer's wife's flowerbeds. She brushed something off and put it in her bosom. She began to walk home, and my heart was pounding so loud I thought Kate must surely hear it. The world did not seem beginnable again.

−*Hey,* Kate said softly, −*my family's peculiar too.* She thought she was being helpful. She was still leaning into me like a willow looking for water, wanting to be kissed. But she seemed to think she *knew* me. In my mind she had crossed over to the side of the girl tyrants.

This angered me. But I knew I was at an advantage in the world somehow, in a way that she would never be. I wanted her to acknowledge it somehow. That's when I turned into a man; it was inked there by some rotogravure that predated me. To get her tenderest kisses, I had to slap her first. It was the only way I knew how to keep believing in anything.

THE PERSEID
METEOR SHOWER

*D*o you think that anyone will *tell* you anything in this world about men?

—*Ask your mother, Marjorie,* people were always saying. Jiminy—whatever I got, I had to learn by hook or crook. Or out of a book.

One night my mother was standing in the dark in our parlor, looking through the curtains, fuming and fizzing about something outside. I tiptoed over and looked out the window. Rose Durrance, the shoeshine boy's mother, was stealing my mother's King Alfred daffodil bulbs, right out of the flowerbeds. I froze, breathless, in shame, as if I were the perpetrator.

—*I brought those bulbs from Savannah!* she railed at my father, and my little sister and me later.

—*I'll get you some more,* my father said. —*Times are hard for everyone.*

The next day I saw my first naked boy.

I was sitting on a hassock, waiting my turn to be measured. The dressmaker had five days to produce dresses for Grace and me to wear when we sang for the bishop from Brunswick. Aunt Lydia was there with her new baby, and my mother was nervous that she was going to steal the dressmaker away to her house before she could finish with me. I was thumbing through a book my father had given me for my birthday, *The Annotated Atlas of the Known Universe*. It had wonderful fold-out plates, and I used to sit for hours with the constellations spread across my lap, and on those old ivory-paper pages the continent of Europe was pieced like a pastel quilt, roads like cobwebs. My little sister, Adrienne, was on the floor with dolls and dress scraps, and my mother held up a bolt of blue voile next to my face.

—*This is it,* she said.

—*No, I don't think so,* said Aunt Lydia. —*The blue washes Marjorie out. Use the green. Look here.* She held up a bolt of green voile, sprigged with tiny yellow flowers, and my face came into focus, my red hair, my brown eyes. Miss Adra fluffed up my hair a little, and this made Mother fluff it right back down.

—*I think we'll take the blue,* she said, and it seemed like she was angry with me, too.

—*She's going to be beautiful,* Miss Adra said, clucking her tongue a little, like this was a problem, and I looked around to see who she was talking about. She was talking about me. Mother didn't like this either. I caught her face in the mirror, and it hit me like cold water: there was some deep vein of dislike of me in her. I quickly forgot about it.

Youth is not wasted on the young.

About this time there was a whoop from Aunt Lydia in the next room, and we all went in to see. There she was, bent over her little James Archie to change his diaper, and her face was dripping wet. My mother and Miss Adra were laughing, and Miss Adra said, —*Always cover him up first. You'd think you'd have learned by now, Lydia.*

I peeped around and I thought, *Somebody move that little pink camellia off that baby boy so I can see what he looks like,* and then I realized what it was.

—*Cover him up,* my mother said to Julia.

—*But I want to SEE,* I said and infuriated my mother.

—*All in due time,* she said. —*You'll see more of that than you'll ever care to,* and all the other women laughed. I felt like they were laughing at me. Even Grace was laughing. But then, she had baby brothers, and I didn't. I only had Adrienne, a royal pest.

I didn't understand what all the hoopla was about. I sat on the hassock and hummed the song that Grace and I were supposed to sing for the bishop:

> *I come to the garden alone,*
> *When the dew is still on the roses,*
> *And he walks with me and he talks with me*
> *And he tells me I am his own.*

The little pink camellia bloomed in my mind into some warm mystery that would just have to wait.

GRACE HAD TAUGHT me a game to play during church. You find a title in the hymnal, show it to the other person, who mentally adds "under the bedcovers" to the title, and the first person to laugh out loud in church loses.

I'd point: "He'll Pilot Me." Under the bedcovers.

She'd point: "I Surrender All." Under the bedcovers.

I'd point: "I Am Coming, Lord." Under the bedcovers. Grace would snort out loud and pretend to be sneezing. I would always lose, laughing outright.

But I had no idea what was so funny. It was just . . . funny. I was afraid that Grace would find out that I didn't really understand the game.

Not long after this I awakened to a bright red stain on my sheets. Summer morning, I remember there was a blue jay carrying on outside. Nancy in the kitchen making pies, her little girl, Melvina, singing "Send Down the Rain." Red blood smeared on my thighs and a round blossom of it on the sheets. Adrienne looking at it all, wide-eyed, which made me feel like I had become a monster.

—Are you going to die?

—I don't feel like I'm going to die.

—I'll get Nancy.

And Nancy showed me what to do, not Mother. *—You ain't sick, you just got to be careful about the mens now.*

—What? How?

—You can ax your mama all that.

Nancy informed Mother, who spent the day in bed with a cold cloth on her head, as if something terrible had happened. To her. *—It's all normal*, she said, stony-faced, when she came into our room that night. She could not meet my eyes. *—It's all perfectly normal.* She kept saying it in a voice she might use to deny that a car had crashed right before her very eyes. That was all I got out of her in the way of instruction.

I thought of it as my private affliction for a long time, until Grace developed the problem too. There was a spot of blood on the back of her dress one morning, and she tried to hide it from me.

—*That's all right. I have that too*, I said in amazement.

She explained to me what her mother had told her. It happened to all women. So I walked out into the afternoon that day a changed person, looking up and down the oak-lined street, thinking of all the women closed up in their houses, sometimes bleeding, sometimes not, but always concealing from the men and boys what odd creatures we were.

And I disgraced us when we sang for the bishop, a short lizardly man who hardly noticed all the flowers in the church. Miss Willie was trying to be delicate at the piano, not her usual vigorous thumping self sliding from end to end on the bench. Grace and I were standing with our hands clasped just like she'd taught us. Grace's voice dipped and lilted like a butterfly, mine ran along like steady, dependable molasses, and my mother was actually smiling at me. But when we got to the part where *he walks with me and he talks with me, and he tells me I am his own,* I thought about the bedcovers, and my voice snagged like silk on a nail. The smile faded from my mother's face, and she was her usual dour self again, assessing and negating me with her hard eyes: *I should never have had children.*

Miss Willie looked at me: *I expected as much from an alto.*

All during the afternoon while the adults stood around in the churchyard, I felt like an outcast. I wandered over to where some boys in my grade at school were talking.

—*The almanac says tonight's the best. We can see it from the water tower.*

—*You got a real telescope?*

—*Yeah. Nine o'clock.*

—*See what?* I asked.

—*The Perseid Meteor Shower.*

—*What's that?*

—*Happens end of every August. Lots of meteors.*

—*Can I come? Can I see it?*

Silence.

—*You're a girl.*

—*Aw, let her come. We can drop her off the tower like we did them cats and see if she lands on her feet.*

To me, they were pygmies from a savage tribe. I wondered why they thought they were so important, them with their little pink camellias. They knew I had a temper, so they would often goad me into trouble. Once they followed me home from school, pulling my hair and chanting, *—Red, red, red on the head! I'd rather be dead than red on the head!*

When I got home after church, my mother was very curt with me.

—Keep your mind on music, and not on boys, she said.

Boys? I hated them. What did they have to do with anything?

My mother had black moods. A black mood could mean a rather severe critique of one's looks, moral character, or physique. Usually when this happened my father would simply get his cane and tip his hat to her, as if he were a courtly gentleman with deepest regrets that he had to go to the depot to catch the train to Waycross and play poker with the other railroad engineers until it was time for him to go on duty again. Lucky him. Adrienne and I would ride it out, trying to please Mother.

We would sit quietly and read, because noise bothered her.

We would not eat too much, because that was not ladylike.

We would not sing, or dance, because our happiness was a form of theft to her.

We would tiptoe into her bedroom where she lay with the cold cloth on her head and whisper that we would get her anything, anything she needed, but she would wave us away, after whispering aloud to some invisible witness-angel in her life we could never see, *—I just shouldn't have had children. I just shouldn't have had children.* This is the way Adrienne and I learned to hate ourselves. It never occurred to us to hate her.

On the Sunday I sang for the bishop, my father returned within an hour of leaving with his hat and cane. Grace's sister, Kate, had been found dead on the coast of Georgia.

—In a ditch, my mother wailed. *—That's ALL we need.*

Horrific memory: my mother walking around in the kitchen as if *she* had suffered injury far greater than Kate's. I also remember my father half-sitting on the table, holding a glass of amber-colored whiskey, looking at my mother like he didn't like her very much.

—If she'd done what she was supposed to, this would never have happened to her! my mother raged. *—If she'd married that Carey Dur-*

rance—you KNOW I don't like for you to do that, she said, indicating his bottle. Then she had to go close the door of her room and lie down.

I went into the kitchen to ask my father how Kate died. He wasn't even bothering to keep the whiskey decanter out of sight. *—You can ask your mother all about that,* he said. *—That is for her to discuss with you.*

Fat chance.

I knew that Kate had been turned out of the house four years before because she had been out in a car all night with some boys. I knew that she had ended up living in different places, and that my father would sometimes run into her in other towns and buy her a meal or a pair of shoes. Once he had bought her a winter coat, and this caused a loud argument with my mother, who stayed in bed for three days after. I knew that whenever Kate's name came up, my mother would change the subject.

But Kate had been put out of one of the more secure homes in town, to become a have-not. This was a deep mystery to me.

The last time I saw Kate she had been at Uncle Lovett's. She had let Grace and me play with her makeup. This was when we were eleven or so. She was lounging in a red Chinese robe, the most exotic presence we had ever been near, her black hair bobbed off blunt, her skin stark white. We walked around her bedroom reeking of her perfume, smeared with her makeup, and she made us feel like princesses. She had a trunkful of clothes that she let us inspect. She had a black feather boa, spangled purses, and dresses that certainly didn't come from the tiers of farmwife calico in Uncle Lovett's store. That was the first time I ever saw silk stockings. Our old black cotton lisle ones were always horrors to us after the sight of her translucent ones rolled neatly in their lace envelopes.

The coast of Georgia was not in my annotated atlas of the universe. I got down my father's railroad atlas, the only one in the house. The state of Georgia, according to that map, was virtually knit together by the Atlantic Coast Line, indicated by black lines that looked like dark surgical scars. Other black lines scalloped the edge of the state next to the ocean. The coastal towns, Savannah and Brunswick, were nestled into those scallops like black pearls into the flesh of a mussel. No clues in the atlas.

More likely the clues were in my parents' room, where they had

gone to talk. I could make out my mother's voice rising in her an-
guished black mood, and—this was the surprise—my father's
voice was rising too. Usually he just went along with her, humor-
ing her until he could stand it no more and would get his hat and
cane. I heard him shout at her once, *—Leila, the circumstances don't
matter! She was your brother's child!*

Most of what I knew about marriage I observed from my parents. I'd seen him come up behind her when she was standing at
the kitchen sink and try to put his arms around her, and she
pushed his hands away as if he were covered with dirt. It was rare
for them to speak sharply to each other, but I don't recall much af-
fection between them, either. So when I heard my father *yelling* at
my mother, this opened up a new vista of thought for me: that she
could be wrong about something.

That night I dreamed of Bishop Moore of Brunswick, with his
own pink camellia out of sight, being fanned and fawned over by
the ladies of the church with their gladiolas and phlox. I dreamed
of Kate lying like a pale, pearly doll, beautiful and black-haired,
nestled into the green marshes off the coast, a bright spot in her
red Chinese silk robe. I dreamed about the boys on the water
tower with their telescopes, tracking the fire-tailed meteors, and
all the other things that I was not privileged to see, like the blue
veins on the face of the man in the moon, and it was Uncle
Lovett, and he wouldn't smile for hell. The green voile dress that
Mother wouldn't let the dressmaker make for me—it was in the
dream, and when I wore it, I could sing soprano, at least until I
stained it with my own blood. Mixed-up things like you dream
when the world is slowly beginning to creak open for you like a
reluctant old oyster.

When Adrienne and I got up the next morning, Mother was
gone. Nancy explained that Mother had gone with Uncle Lovett
to bring Kate home.

—I seen it with my own two eyes, she said, amazed. *—Mist' Lovett
with his black hat CLAP on his head and Miss Leila with her black hat
CLAP on hers, driving off down the road not saying a WORD to each
other. They got to drive three hours like that.*

I asked Nancy how Kate died.

—You have to ax your mama about that.

Natch.

I went next door. Aunt Lydia was locked in her room, with the baby. Grace and her brothers were sitting on the back porch. *We can't talk about it,* Grace said. *—Mama told us we can't.*

On the day Kate was to be buried, a beautiful late summer day, there was the coffin on trestles outside, with black netting over it. People were milling around, and it seemed like a big garden party except everyone would walk over to the coffin, stand for a minute, then walk off. This was the first dead relative for me, so I took it all in, much in the spirit of a missionary newly arrived in Borneo. I watched them sign their names in a little book on a music stand. Then I decided to look at Kate myself.

That was not Kate. Couldn't be. Her face was chalky-fat, puffy, with a long bruise that started down her temple and wound across her cheek. She looked old, dressed in a dull old navy dress that I had seen Aunt Lydia wear before James Archie was born. Her middle was just a round hummock. The first thing that popped into my head was *better off dead,* and I quickly moved away. I saw Harrison Durrance walk over and look, and when he turned away his face was full of ruin. Bas relief. It was like that. He began to stand out. He went to stand behind the rows of chairs, his hands in his pockets. I could see only him. If I looked at him I didn't have to remember Kate.

I decided in my heart that Uncle Lovett was at fault, standing over at the edge of things, rolling himself a cigarette. I hated him. I don't know what I based that decision on, I just decided it, in the way that a child has some kind of radar that has not been lost yet.

Uncle Lovett was tall and lean, with a shock of startling white hair. All his children feared him. I stood there watching him light his cigarette, and it occurred to me that something in him was already dead, just like something in my mother was dead, and there was not much that either one of them liked about living.

I went to stand beside my own father, who rubbed his fist on my head like he used to do when I was small.

It did not occur to me to ask why the funeral was not in the church.

It did not occur to me to wonder why my mother took Kate's death as a personal embarrassment.

It didn't even occur to me to ask Grace if she was sad, if she missed Kate, if she was afraid. She was sitting with Aunt Lydia and

Uncle Lovett and her brothers, wearing a dress I hadn't seen before.

I sat on my little wooden folding chair in the smell of the flowers, not that refrigerator floral smell you get these days, but the smell of real flowers, and admired my own white gloves and my blue voile dress, while the minister sawed on. He asked us all to sit quietly for a moment and remember Kate, not by the soul that the world had forced her to assume, but by her one true soul. —*Think of her as she would like to be remembered as she passes into the house of silence.*

I did not want to think about the bruised, misshapen creature in the coffin. So I sat there and I thought of the red wrapper, the silk stockings in the lace envelopes. But I wanted to push at the edge of the mysteries the adults hoarded from me. Two or three bees buzzed this or that behatted head, sidetracked by artificial flowers or fruit. Adrienne fidgeted a lot, and disappeared as soon as the minister shut up and everyone stood up.

Most people lingered around in the yard, or on the porch that ran, like ours, all around the house. I went inside to find Adrienne, and she was in Grace's room. She had found Kate's trunk, and she and Grace were looking at it.

—*Have you opened it?*

—*No, Mama told me not to.*

—*We won't tell.*

We all ended up closed in Grace's room, the sunlight coming through the transom by then, illuminating the remains of Kate's wardrobe, which we inspected like seasoned thieves. Some of the things I remembered, a red sequined purse that made a perfect square cube when you closed it, and a gauzy crepe dress with pink and yellow dahlias all over it. Adrienne found the red silk wrapper, and tried it on in front of the mirror. It dragged the floor around her, even when we hitched it up with the sash.

She beheld herself in the mirror, and got very clowny.

—*Bosoms of Abraham!* she yelled. —*Get thee a behind!*

Grace and I were crowing, as she strutted around the room in the red wrapper, holding the red cube like she might be Lady Astor.

—*Maybe I will keep these things for my trousseau,* Grace said.

—*Your what?* Adrienne asked.

—My clothes when I get married.

The door flung open, and there all the grown-ups were, including Uncle Lovett and my mother. They had all come to see what the laughter was about. My mother had on her face the look that Grandmother always told her would curdle fresh milk.

Adrienne froze, and Grace took the red cube from her and put it back in the trunk. Uncle Lovett moved inside the room, and slapped Grace right on the face. Adrienne ran out, the red wrapper flapping. I followed her home.

We were confined to our room for the evening, of course. Adrienne hid the red robe behind the dresser, but Mother found it anyway.

—No! I want to keep it! Adrienne cried.

—Absolutely not!

—But I want it for my true soul! I want to keep it!

—Your what?

—My true soul.

Mother blinked, looked at me. I shrugged. Don't ask me, I'm just the monster who bleeds now and then and spoils your sheets. Adrienne's face was streaked with tears. I don't know where Daddy was, or he'd have rescued her.

—I want a true soul, she said. *—All the clothes you have when you are going to get married, and it's your true soul.*

—God! Mother screamed and snatched the red robe away from her. This was about as strong an expletive as you ever got out of her, but she could inject it with enough poison to make you wish you'd never been born. Her voice could just fizz up out of her and burn you like sulfur. *—I knew I should never have had children. I NEVER wanted you. I NEVER wanted this to happen to me.* She waved her hand and the gesture encompassed us all. Adrienne sobbed and ran to hide under her bed like she used to do when she was tiny.

Mother retired to her bed, and Daddy got his cane and ran it under the bed crooning, *—Wheeeeeere's that Adrienne?* over and over until she grabbed it and he pulled her out like a smiling little trout. There was this ritual they had together when she was upset. He would hold her in his lap in the front porch swing and speak softly to her. You could hear his deep soft voice talking about make-believe trains, mingled with her sniffles.

*—Baby girl, quit this crying. You want to ride on the Alapaha Star?
They don't let you ride if you crying. You got to have the right clothes.
What will you wear?*

—A red dress.

—And what else?

—Red shoes.

—And what else. What about your hair?

—Red bow.

—And what you going to keep your money in?

—Red purse.

On and on until it hypnotized all three of us into peace.

Later in the week we found the remains of the red robe in the
trash pile at the edge of our land. Mother had burned most of it.
Adrienne picked up a small triangle of it, scarlet banded now by
charred black edges, and put it in her pocket.

You really do come to the garden alone. You learn the little
dance of life alone. You amble off into your own curiosity and
dreams, misinformation and brutal fact. You have to.

I started daydreaming of Harrison Durrance about this time.

I'd always been *aware* of him, because people often mistook us
for siblings because we both had flame-red hair. He was always far
enough ahead of me in school that he wouldn't speak to me when
I went to get our mail at the post office and he would be sitting on
his shoeshine crate under the Alapaha Station sign. I saw him
when he delivered milk to our house, and my mother didn't like
him. His family was poor and *rough*, she explained.

—And that Artemus. You know, they had to take him away.

—Away where? I had asked once. I envied anyone who got to go
anywhere.

—To a hospital far away. His mind, it just went.

The Durrances lived two blocks down from us. You could see
their low-slung white house with the untrimmed shrubbery en-
circling it. Behind that, the smokehouse that an old man, Harrison's uncle, had once lived in. He had been taken to the state
crazyhouse. I'd heard my mother and Aunt Lydia discussing it on
the front porch.

*—Poor Artemus. He was just never the same after the treatments. They
have these new treatments, you know,* said Mother, her fingers flying
with her tatting, a lacy antimacassar.

—How does it work? Aunt Lydia asked, intent on her own needle.

–*Electrical voltage,* Mother said, and I envisioned scientists in a lab somewhere, pricking the old man's finger with an electrified needle.

In between our houses were the Methodist parsonage, and an open field which had come gradually to be covered in flowers. Daffodils in spring, chysanthemums in fall, tall, cool rye grass in summer, shaded by the biggest oak tree in the county. There was a lampshade that someone had nailed to a tall post, and in the spring the boys would congregate there and play basketball. Their shouts and the *punk, punk* of the ball on the hard circle of packed earth would bring me to the window to watch.

A girls' basketball team was organized at school, and I promptly volunteered. Not so much out of aptitude but a wish to get out of the house. We were told that we would ride to neighboring towns to play. I was a benchwarmer, and Grace was first-string. Neither of our mothers liked this new development, but there was nothing they could do. We had our fathers' permission.

When I brought my new uniform home, I put it on to show Adrienne, who could always be counted on to be an appreciative audience. It was royal-blue satin, with gold numerals. Baggy bloomers that stopped midthigh. Hideous India-rubber–soled shoes, but I loved them. I crouched in front of the mirror, raised my arms the way the coach had commanded.

–*Your legs look like rattails in fruit jars,* my mother said from the door. She had the black-mood look on her face. –*And blue washes you out. It's not your best color.*

Neither Adrienne nor I said anything for a minute. What to do? How not to make it worse?

–*You don't like anything, do you, Mother?* Adrienne said slowly, almost sympathetically, as if Mother was just now coming into focus for her. She was standing in the doorway still, dressed in one of those ubiquitous print dresses with a breast pocket, the little fake hankie sticking out. She had turned into a big floral sofa on spindly legs; her eyes were small and hard in a broad bland face. That was mostly what her life had netted her, big blandness. I was feeling revulsion, and a need to push off, set sail, get free.

–*Well, you better enjoy it now,* Mother said, directing her eyes at me standing there sheepishly in my basketball clothes, –*because it doesn't last long.*

–*What doesn't last long?* Adrienne called after her as she moved toward the stairs.

—*The fun*, Mother called back.

I put my uniform back in its box and went outside. The basketball circle was empty, so I got the ball my father had brought me from Waycross, and I went to shoot baskets. I felt silly out there, trying to control the bouncing, trying to have some influence over its foreignness, killing time in my street shoes. But the main thing was that I was out of my mother's house, doing something that had nothing to do with her way of life.

—*You shoot like a girl*, somebody said behind me.

It was Harrison Durrance, standing at the edge of the field, smoking a cigarette. How long had he been there? I stood there with the ball, feeling stupid. He crushed the cigarette under his foot and walked over.

—*You don't have a good grasp of the fundamentals,* he said, and he took the ball from me and began to dribble it. —*Shoot with your best hand, use the other to guide.*

He demonstrated, and the ball *boinged* through the bare hoop like a rocket. He gave it back to me. —*Now you.*

He laughed every time I made a basket, shook his head when I didn't. —*You shoulda gone out for cheerleading.* I didn't know why he was willing to stay out there and notice how I was shooting, but I liked this. I liked him. He was older. Somebody who would *tell* me things.

I was getting hot and my blouse was sticking to my back. He kept offering me instructions, I kept getting distracted by wanting to look at him. I saw that his hair was darker red than mine, and that his hands were squared, with short fingers. There was something about his movements that compelled me to stare—the spring of his legs when he jumped, the way his hands were suspended in the air after the ball left them in a perfect arc toward the goal.

My mind was jumping with things I lacked courage to ask: *Is it true that your brothers fight each other with knives? Did your mother really throw a hundred dollars into the fire? Is your Uncle Artie crazy?*

My mother called me back before I could talk to him much more. He tossed me the ball and I went home. She was standing on the back porch with a fist on one hip, ready to light into me.

—*Do you know that by noon tomorrow it will be all over town?*

—*I don't care.*

—Of all people! Do you know how rough they are? Let me tell you how.

And she told me again how his mother had thrown a hundred dollars in the fire one time because she was drinking. *—And in these hard times! I've heard that he listens to that nigra music, goes to those nigra places. They all do, everybody in that family.*

But it was too late. I was already dreaming: he walked with me, and he talked with me, and he told me I was his own. I didn't know enough at that point to imagine the under-the-bedcovers part. He was older, smarter, and better-looking than all the pygmy boys my age.

My school closed for good at Christmas—no money to pay the teachers. Everyone had to stay home or make other plans. My parents decided the thing to do was send me off to Georgia Southern at age fifteen. I didn't know any better than to be excited. Grace was going too, and we were going to be roommates.

Grace and I took the train with Mother and Aunt Lydia, armed with six new skirts and sweaters each. We had petitioned for silk stockings but got none. It was a condition of our admission at such a tender age that we would not be allowed to date. We had to go home on weekends or stay in the deserted dorms.

—Just remember, girls, Aunt Lydia said when we were standing in our new room, *—nobody will buy the cow when he can get the milk for free.*

My mother seemed to know what she was talking about, because she had a grave look on her face. Even Grace seemed to know, because she was nodding, and I'd seen that kind of thing pass between her and her mother too. Like some kind of inside joke that *they* knew, and I was too proud to let on that I didn't know what they were talking about. It had something to do with boys, and being wary of boys. I concluded that being female entailed either *having* a problem, or *being* one.

Fourteen, coasting into fifteen by April.

Mother just turned me loose on the world like that. Six skirts, six sweaters, and a dark suspicion that boys were somehow not good people like girls were.

I got put in remedial math, but I was so good in English that I got assigned to tutor bonehead football players I was slightly afraid of. One of them, named Axe, was always asking me for a date, and

I was relieved to tell him that I couldn't. I'd seen one girl on our hall come in from a date with him with her sweater torn at the shoulder, leaves all in her hair. She was in tears, and went home for good not long after that.

—What do you do on Saturday nights—study astronomy? Axe said to me once and reached to touch my hair.

—I'm flunking astronomy, I said, leaning back out of reach. And I was.

The older girls did not share Mother and Aunt Lydia's low opinion of boys. They lived for Saturday nights. They'd start swapping clothes around noon, doing each other's hair. Grace and I would take all this in, feeling like Cinderellas watching the stepsisters light out for the ball. There were six of us who couldn't date, and they called us The Babies.

There was this one older girl, named Adelaide, who used to tap on our window because her date would keep her out past curfew and she always got locked out. Sometimes she would talk to us a while before she went to her own room. She'd use our brushes and mirrors to get herself composed before she risked facing the housemother, a horrible old woman we called Ma. Adelaide was somewhat of a legend because she had four engagement rings. There were four young men in the state of Georgia each convinced that she was saving it all for him.

—Whew, she'd say, brushing off her clothes. *—I look like I've been dragged through the bushes by my heels. And I HAVE! Babies, I just missed getting married by a hair.*

We gasped. She made it sound like some precipice she'd saved herself from. She smelled like my father's whiskey.

—I had him on his KNEES, she'd say. *—He was begging me. He told me his daddy owns a jewelry store in Jacksonville. He said we could go to a justice of the peace on Jekyll Island.*

The next Saturday night it would be variations on the theme: *—Babies! His daddy owns a house on Sea Island. He was BEGGING me!* Sometimes she would stare at us a minute, as if she were sorry she had shared such knowledge with The Babies. *—Just remember,* she said once, suddenly serious, *—as long as you don't let him touch you with it, you can't get in trouble.*

—Touch you with what? I asked.

Adelaide looked at me, then at Grace.

—*Oh, Baby,* she said. —*You don't know, do you?*

—*Know what?* Grace and I asked together.

—*His, you know. His thing.*

I thought of tiny pink camellias, and laughed.

—*It's not funny,* Adelaide said. —*Three girls had to leave last year because they got pregnant. And not to get married, either. Or you could end up like that girl in Brunswick, the one they found in a ditch.*

—*Who?* I said, and tried not to look at Grace.

—*It was all in the papers,* Adelaide said. —*She was pregnant, and her boyfriend smashed her on the head with a liquor bottle, and tried to make it look like she fell out of the car on a curve. In a ditch, they found her.*

Grace was winding some ribbons around her hand, and she stopped. I remember her soft, small hand, the ribbon poised around it. She looked at me, and I saw that she had always known this. After Adelaide left, I tried to study for my astronomy class until I couldn't stand it any longer and I said, —*What happened to the guy?*

—*Who?*

—*The one who killed her.*

—*His father was a judge,* she said. —*Can we stop talking about this? Mother told me not to talk about it.*

I WAS GLAD that we were not allowed to date. It all seemed so scary. All those boys and girls who did not like each other, yet compelled to touch each other nevertheless. All that stealth in the pines and the palmettos. I skittered off into dreams of Harrison Durrance. The usual stuff: he would drive up and take me *away* from all this, or he would come into a room where I was holding someone's baby and he would say something like, —*You look just right like that, don't you want one of your own?* and we'd live happily ever after in some stardust-specked little cottage out in dreamland, where my soul would blossom into being. Not my current soul, which was a pool of dark molasses, full of ignorance and misgivings about the world. My *true* soul, the warm, expansive, happy one I always meant to acquire.

By April, when I turned fifteen, Grace was sneaking out of the window on Saturday nights to meet a boy. She had an ability to be lighthearted and flip, as if her soul was a soprano too. I envied this a little. She talked me into sneaking out with her one night, and I had my first date, with a friend of her friend.

I cannot remember what he looked like. I can't even remember what we did, what our excuse for being together was. I can remember that he wore a yellow sweater-vest, and that he was thin, and that he kept trying to hold my hand, and he seemed to think that the world *owed* him something because he had good clothes. Grace kept turning around from the front seat to see if he had kissed me yet. I remember that I kept wondering *why* people did this every Saturday night, and I imagined a big promenade of mismatched, overdressed human beings all over the world, completing just so many meaningless dry runs before the real event, the *real* love came along. This is what I was thinking out there in the middle of the pine woods.

Grace's boyfriend began to kiss her.

My date cleared his throat.

Grace's boyfriend's head followed hers down as he pushed her backwards, down in the front seat.

My date put his arm on the seat behind me, his fingers kneading the bones of my shoulder. I stared out the window.

Their whispers came over the seat.

—*No. . . . no.*

—*Please. Just this.*

—*No, don't.*

I decided that I wasn't ready to be kissed. I wanted better circumstances, and somebody better than the yellow vest. I didn't want to grapple in a car with a pygmy, I wanted to surrender all to someone who would walk with me and talk with me and tell me I was his own. I thought of Harrison. It was like an escape hatch I needed at the moment.

I got out of the car and walked around on this bare clay road we were on, and the yellow vest, ever hopeful, got out to follow me. We stood a few feet apart, him with his hands in the pockets of his natty white pants, me scuffing the clay with my shoes.

—*My daddy owns a boat. Want to go out on it?*

I shook my head.

—*You're a bitch, you know that?*

My problem was, and remained for all my life, that I was not capable of just necking with anyone. If he wasn't the manly knight in my head, I didn't want him to be in front of my eyes. So Grace was displeased with me that night, when I displeased my date.

—*How could you DO that to me?* Grace yelled at me as soon as we got back inside the window. —*You wouldn't even let him touch you! You're such a goody-goody.*

—*How could you do that to ME?* I yelled back at her. —*He was a pygmy.*

—*Can't you see that it doesn't matter! Can't you see we're all going to be old and married in a few years and we'll never get out of the house again!*

That night, for the first time in all the years of our life together as best friends, Grace and I parted company in some small way, though we stayed roommates for two more years. Within a few weeks it was time to pack to go home for the summer. I had flunked astronomy because I couldn't draw the Perseid Meteor Shower on the final. I blew the remains of my little bank account on a green jersey dress I saw in a store window. My mother looked at it warily when she saw it in my closet, but she didn't say a word. The dress stayed in my closet most of the summer—where would I wear it?

—*Welcome back to the house of silence,* Adrienne had said when I got home, and I came to think of it as that. She was lucky, she was still young enough that Mother let her have free run of the neighborhood. She could happily scout out everybody's business in town, running around barefooted even, without provoking Mother's fear that her daughters would be called "common."

The quiet interminable days I spent reading whatever romances I could cadge off some of the older girls I knew. Emilie Loring books: the chintz and china, the handsome hero, the spunky girl who rides in his roadster, her true soul understood *perfectly* by him as the scene shifts from their first chaste kiss to flickering firelight, to the foaming of waves. I was not aware of it but the plot was *always* the same, and only the patterns on the china and chintz changed. I ran my mind through that maze repeatedly, unaware that I had already memorized it, that the future range and repertoire of my reactions to men were being set, like slow concrete.

. . .

ONE AFTERNOON when I was reading in my room, I heard the *punk, punk* on the basketball circle, and the shouts of boys. I looked out the kitchen window to see Harrison Durrance and two of his younger brothers playing. Harrison caught my eye, of course. So fast, so deft with the ball. He truly made them look even more like pygmies to me. He seemed to fit into the spot in my mind where the Emilie Loring hero used to be. I must have watched him for an hour, standing at the kitchen sink.

—*Since when you like wash dishes so much?* Nancy asked.

As it began to grow late, the other boys drifted away, and Harrison was there alone, still shooting baskets. I walked out and stood in the tall grass at the edge of the circle. He didn't hear me. The crickets were beginning to sing in the grass. He looked up, and pretended to be startled, hands on his chest over his heart as if he'd been shot, then he snapped the ball to me so hard and fast that it slammed into my chest, knocking the breath out of me. I sat down.

—*Come shoot.*

I waved my hand, *in a minute.* I didn't want him to know that I could not breathe, much less speak.

—*I thought you were a nymph risen out of a green sea*, he said, and I wasn't sure if he was being serious or making a joke, so I just stood there speechless. He waded through the grass. —*Are you a nymph?*

I didn't know what a nymph was. I kept thinking of nematodes, blighted underground things. Was it a compliment or an insult?

—*Nymphs, the ladies that Perseus went to rescue from the Gorgon Medusa and the Gray Women?*

All I could remember was the Perseid Meteor Shower. I shook my head. —*I flunked astronomy,* I said.

—*No!* he said, all exaggerated horror, and rolled his eyes. —*What happened?*

—*I couldn't draw the Perseid Meteor Shower,* I finally got some words out of me. —*I drew the Milky Way.*

He stopped kidding around. —*What a dumb assignment. I flunked that too. Can you get out of the house tonight? I'll show you the Perseid Meteor Shower.*

—*I think I'm too chicken to climb the water tower.*

—*The what?*

—*Isn't that what you have to do? Climb the water tower?*

—Says who?

—All the boys. They go up there with a telescope.

—What imbeciles. They're not going to see much. Too much streetlight. You have to get outside town.

—Where?

—The bluff over the whirlpool's good.

—Will you take me there? I asked.

I didn't even go back to tell my mother where I would be. We started walking and realized that one of his little brothers was following.

—Go back, Red. I'm tellin' you like a friend, you better go back.

—But I want to go, Red said. I was the only other person around Alapaha who ever got called that.

—No. Go home.

It was a forbidden thing, or so I'd been led to believe. A secret, dangerous place that only boys could find. And they took bad girls there to kiss them. But all the girls somehow knew where it was. All you had to do was go down the hill away from the schoolhouse, follow the path to the river, and then let the river itself lead the way.

—Have you ever been here before? he said, and I shook my head. He seemed pleased at that.

We found an old hollow cypress log to sit on, and I hugged my knees praying there were no snakes in it. He pointed to the part of the sky for me to watch. *—They should come from that direction,* he said, and he crushed his cigarette under his foot. The frogs and crickets were roaring, and there seemed to be nothing to talk about.

—What is it going to look like?

He got up and started picking up small rocks. *—Okay. Imagine that these are the stars in the Milky Way. Here's Earth.* He placed them, and then held out three pebbles to me. *—Hold these.* He drew a series of boxes around it all, like for hopscotch. *—Now throw them.* He sat back on the log.

I tossed them reluctantly, convinced that I would not do it right.

—Well? he said. *—What did you see?*

I just shrugged and shook my head.

—Look, he said, and stood up with his arms out. *—Imagine I am a meteor, passing very fast through different spheres of influence.* He stepped

like a cat through the boxes, changing his pose for each box. —*You only get one fix on me, see? Then I'm already moved on, gone. That's why you can't draw the Perseid Meteor Shower. So that was a dumb assignment anyway.*

We began to watch as it grew dark, and he talked about the curves of the earth and celestial navigation. I was by then convinced I was about to see something special. I watched until I got a crick in my neck, thinking that probably he was seeing fifty meteors a minute and I was wondering why I wasn't. I finally sat on the ground and leaned back on the log. Nothing much seemed to be happening, and I wanted to watch *him* instead of the sky. It got late, and I kept thinking of what my mother was going to say when I got home.

—*It may be a bit early,* he said, stubbing out a cigarette. —*I haven't seen a damn thing. Late August is the best time.*

—*Can we come back then?*

—*I'll be gone.*

Sudden desolation.

—*Where?*

—*West Point. I'm leaving in a week. I can go to college there and it won't cost me a penny. I'm going to blow this burg. But now that you know what to look for, you can find your way back here when it's time.*

With the cigarette gone, he had vanished into the blackness, and I felt uneasy, and reached out. My fingers brushed his leg.

—*Just wanted to know where you are.*

—*Are you scared?*

—*No,* I said, too fast. Yes. Scared that you only brought me out here to see the meteors that aren't going to come. Scared you won't kiss me. Scared of waking up tomorrow being my same old self in my mother's same old house of silence.

—*We'd better go back now.*

More desolation. I had to hold his shirttail to follow him back along the riverbank to the path that would take us back to the schoolhouse. He walked me through the tall grass in the back field as far as the basketball circle, then he stopped.

—*Well.*

—*Yeah. See you.*

—*Yeah,* I said, and began to wade through the grass toward the yellow-lighted windows of my house. Then I heard a rustle behind me, and he grabbed my ankle and pulled me down, or it seemed that I floated down into the grass, and he caught me as I fell. I lay there a second, then laughed. He kissed me, just a peck really. I said, *—Can you do that again?* and he did, except more slowly and I had time to taste him, a warm, wet, smoky taste that made the ends of my fingers go numb. Then I became aware of this third presence below, between us, something with a power and mystery of its own. Whatever it was, it was no tiny camellia bud. I reached down to touch it, and Harrison pulled himself away from me, looking at me suspiciously.

—You're not supposed to do that.

—Why not? I could not read his face.

—You better ask your mother about that, he said, and stood up.

I laughed out loud. Natch.

He waved as he walked off.

I went back inside the house, my lips swollen, my head filled with goosedown, and my mother and father waiting in the kitchen. Probably they had seen it all from the window.

—Marjorie, Daddy started, but Mother interrupted him.

—Why should somebody buy the cow when he can get the milk for free? she said bitterly.

—Leila, that's enough, Daddy said. He was rolling a cigarette. My mother's eyes were like small brown raisins pushed into the dough of her face. She wanted answers.

—Why should I buy a horse I've never ridden? I asked her, and she stared at me in horror. I stared back with equally intense horror. She was the worst advertisement that I could see for anyone's buying the cow. All she needed was a ring through her nose.

I won the staring match; she had to go lie down.

—Give me one of those, I said to my father, and he rolled me a cigarette and lit it for me. His hands were shaking a little, and I felt like the world creaked open for me then. God only knows what he was thinking. I was thinking that if I smoked one of those, I could keep the taste of Harrison in my mouth a little longer.

THE SEA OF DAMES

*T*he army sent Durrance and me to speech class at West Point, to wash out that cracker drawl of his, and to modify my Bronx Irish, so we could sound like we'd gone to radio school in Rahway. We had this other roommate and erstwhile buddy, Saxon Van Cleve. His speech was Ivy League and Main Line Pennsylvania horse farm, all portmanteau with imminent eminence, so he played polo while we had speech therapy. He was a good sport about it.

—*You guys have it lucky,* he said into the dark one night after taps. —*You get to sound like you're from nowhere.*

—*Why'd you come here?* I asked, though I would never have confessed that I did not understand the sequence of events that led me there. I imagined him growing up insulated from the rest of his species by several thousand acres of greener pastures than the second-floor apartment my brother and I had grown up in. —*When did it occur to you, I mean.*

—*When I was fourteen,* Van Cleve laughed almost bitterly, but not too bitterly, because you never knew if someone would report you for lack of authentic patriotism or reverence for the army. —*Folly. Mere folly. I wanted to get away from the money. I wanted to be in a place where I was like everyone else.*

—*You are such a horse's ass,* Durrance said. —*I wanted to get women. Herlihy, what's your story?*

I thought of Therese. —*I needed to get away from a woman,* I said. —*She was married.* To my brother, I didn't add.

Catcalls in the dark from them. Whistles. Curses down the hall, silence, then sleep.

There would be other confessions to come. Those confidences that come forth after you have survived things together. There was the time some upperclassmen had smeared our shoes with fresh horseshit sometime between taps and reveille.

—*There's something on my shoes,* Saxon said.

—*Aw, CRAP!* I said, looking at mine. We had maybe twelve minutes to get out to the drill field. —*There goes the weekend pass. CRAP!*

—*Exactly what it is, gennamen,* said Durrance. —*In the immortal words of my Uncle Artie, the earth curves. The earth curves. But you are blessed to be in the company of the former heavyweight champeen shoeshine boy of the Alapaha Territory.*

We got through it—after we'd survived other hazings, everything from term papers burned the night before they were due, to almost being drowned in the showers by some sophomores we'd beat at tennis.

Everything was competitive, even between us. That was the thing they used to make us chant during the physical conditioning, —*Competition and coercion.* Which means that even if you sit down to have a drink, to relax from the competition, you compete.

Collectively we comprised what Durrance referred to as a *ménagerie à trois* made in heaven. An interesting cross-pollination, one of those situations you get in the storefront democracy known as West Point. Going to West Point was for him like being let out of a great white jail, though he said he'd first begun drinking when he was nine. This confession into one of those early plebe's darknesses of the night made Durrance and me speechless.

—*How old were you when you first got laid?* Durrance demanded of Van Cleve, like an inside pitch meant to make you question your innate right to stand at the plate.

—*Fourteen,* Van Cleve said. —*She was the trainer's daughter. Her father worked for my father. She was nineteen.*

Durrance whistled softly. —*Splendor in the GRASS, you horse's ass.*

—*Not exactly.*

—*So where was it?*

Van Cleve was quiet.

—Where was it, horse's ass?

—In a loft in one of the stables. It just happened. Annelise, her name was.

—So how long did this go on? I had visions of a plump peasant girl getting it from him repeatedly, like so much noblesse oblige from him. I resented not just his speech but the fact that he had big invisible wads of money bankrolling him, no matter what happened.

—Just the once. Never again with her.

—Why not? Durrance asked.

—I lost her to somebody else a few days after, he laughed.

I began to think of him as human then, though I resented the ease with which he laughed.

—Who? Durrance pressed. *—Somebody richer than your old man?*

—A veterinarian from Germantown. The funny thing is, I know exactly when I lost her. There was this mare that was having trouble dropping a foal, and the guy came out, and my father was out of the country, so he decided on his own to put the mare down.

—You mean, he killed her.

—Yes. An expensive decision. That was the thing. We were all in this stall for a few hours, and it was rather gruesome. The guy put her down, and that was that. I mean, I saw it happen. He put that horse down like he was God himself, choosing. Annelise had eyes only for him after that. I used to see her sneak out to meet him. He was married. I had this dream that I would go away and come back a general and she would choose me. That's when I began to think about coming here.

I resented any humanness in the rich. I even resented the subtleties of the rich. That he had time to be so experienced and perceptive, even at fourteen, while the rest of us were merely scrabbling for some toehold on life, drowning in our dreams of greener pastureland.

—The earth curves, horse's ass. Durrance laughed.

The women always noticed Harry Durrance's red hair and freckles and interpreted it as earnestness of the wholesomest American kind. The expression on his face was like milk-fed honesty. He never had any problem finding willing women.

And me, I had no particular talent except for mathematics.

Van Cleve usually got the best women. It was a given. Harrison and I would meet our Brooklyn or Bronx girls at Penn Station, but Van Cleve would usually vanish for a while and show up later with some pale blonde that you could smell the money on. Some girl that would fix her icy blues on the view outside the cab window *just so,* and ride all insulated by her nickname and her good fur. And the odd thing: Van Cleve never appeared to like them much.

And she'd pointedly not speak to us—or even to Van Cleve—which never seemed to matter much to him. This would be standard for the entire night as everyone got drunker and drunker. Durrance's girl would be in her cheap rayon dress fresh from her job at a five-and-dime and my girl would have on some fierce fire-engine-red lipstick that she wouldn't be allowed to wear at her bookkeeping job.

They ought to name that shade of red "1939" and restrict its use to girls twenty or under, like our girls were then.

Especially would Van Cleve's girl not speak to Durrance's girl or to my girl. And it would get to Durrance. You could see him itching to get revenge on the society girl in some way.

The thing that Durrance never noticed was that Van Cleve did not particularly enjoy the women whose company he kept.

But we'd all dance, and only if Van Cleve was feeling mean toward his girl would he insist that she dance with his good friend from the Deep South, Durrance, or with his good friend from the Bronx, yours truly. And on those occasions his piece of ice would just stare over your shoulder and wait for the song to end, and Durrance's girl or my girl might dance like a frostbit rag doll with Van Cleve, with a look of fear or worship on her face, depending on the intelligence level.

I'll never forget one time, Durrance had dragged us into this dive of a place in Harlem. He had a knack for that. That son of a bitch could ferret out some of the best music you ever heard, and not always in places you could confess to your mother. This one time he insisted that we go to this little joint in Harlem, and we get there, and there is this enormous black man, Sgt. Joseph Caliban, playing the trumpet. Caliban was the trumpeter for the 367th Infantry out of Fort Riley, and he was home on leave, playing a few sets with his old buddies. One look at that body and you knew that it was the trumpet that got him past the Army physical. The music was like nothing I ever heard before, better than what you'd get on a record, some white boy's wishful thinking.

Van Cleve when he was whistled was not much different from

Van Cleve when he was sober, and he was sitting with his lanky legs crossed, his face looking like it was all some grand anthropological expedition he was making. Like he was just passing through this lower life on his way to great statesmanship. And Durrance was sitting there slightly whistled, with his head cocked just so, like he always did when we were being briefed before takeoff, like it was some serious flight instructions he was receiving.

And Van Cleve's date that night was a Bryn Mawr girl, and she was sitting there more than a little miffed because she had wanted to go to the Village because she knew that that was where the clubs were if you wanted to drop names later like Thelonius Monk or Bird Parker. She knew that much about music, the right names to drop. And the other two girls, our girls, were probably wondering why in the hell they were wasting their time on guys who wouldn't take them to the Rainbow Room. Or they were worrying how the hell they were going to powder their noses in the black chicks' lavatory, but basically enjoying being in a place that they couldn't tell their mothers about.

The funniest time was that night when we were at that nowhere dive to hear Joseph Caliban, and Durrance, in the presence of whatever piece of ice that Van Cleve had saddled himself with for the evening, asked Van Cleve what his latest Wasserman score was.

And Van Cleve choked a bit on his drink because Durrance had caught him off guard. A Wasserman was a VD test.

And the girls are all sitting there smiling, like they are in the ballgame too, like Durrance and Van Cleve are doing this bit about intelligence tests.

—*Adequate*, Van Cleve says.

And even the piece of ice was feeling good, being seen with West Pointers, and she's had enough drinks by now so that the stares of the black chicks are not getting to her anymore.

And the piece of ice would be sitting there *just so*, with her Wellesley or Smith diploma in her head, none the wiser that the hick from Georgia has just dealt her a major dig.

We noticed a pattern in Van Cleve's amorous life. There was no amour in it. None of the private, desolate need to forget someone, as in my case. Not even the gregarious democratic rutting of Durrance.

There was this thing he did, repeatedly. We saw him do it. The modus operandi: woo the girl for weeks, always the same ice-queen types. Give him two weeks and he could effect a most impressive thaw. Two weekends of dinner and dancing and hansom cab rides, long conversations always conducted at a slight distance from the rest of us, and you'd see the dame begin to exhibit some humanity, a bit of cleavage, and a lot of frustration that he hadn't made his move. Then, just on the night when she thought her prince had come, he'd call a cab, put her in it, send her away, and never call her again. This mystified Durrance and me a bit.

—*What a waste,* I said one morning when Durrance and I were shaving. I couldn't stop remembering the eyes of this one girl when she realized he wasn't taking her home, he was sending her away. This after some weeks of cultivating her, teaching the girl how to go all liquid on the dance floor, sick with lust for him, then dropping her just when she wanted it the most. —*Why does he do that?*

Durrance thought a minute, and his eyes met mine in the mirror. —*Maybe it makes him feel like he's putting down mares.*

It was swing time, the time of the women, 1940. We could walk down Park Avenue and the women would follow us, or just stop and fumble with their packages, or do whatever they did to get us to take off our hats and help. It was a different time. The three of us never really bought into that bit about finding a good little woman your senior year and getting serious about her.

We used to walk around Times Square at three in the morning singing "Love Her and Leave Her on the Lava." Durrance would appoint himself Officer of the Day in the Middle of the Night:

—*Gennamen, gennamen. Assume pursuit formation. There are females in the world, languishing. I can't teach you how to survive plenitude. The best we can hope for is to find it navigable.*

And we'd cast our lot with the swabbies for what always turned out to be not loose New York girls but grain-fed lovelies from Des Moines or Wichita or somewhere. The kind that never quite comprehended what she was meant to do with the male of the species once she had dressed in her tight sweater and put on that 1940 lipstick. The kind who can pass, at forty paces, for a slick New York girl with her own place but when you get right down to it, she's only got a cot in somebody's spare room.

I would stay away from my own neighborhood. On those summer nights that seemed to last so long, I would prowl with them anywhere but where I wanted to be: back in my parents' apartment, where I slept in a room next to the one my brother's wife Therese slept in with the baby. My brother was a submariner, somewhere in the North Sea, we were told.

Her own parents, Italians who barely spoke English, had turned their backs on her when she married my brother. He left for the navy, left her big-bellied with his kid, and left me to pace in his place in the hospital waiting room. Later I had to cope with the sounds of her movement in the house, the rustles in the hall, her cooing to the child, the clank of her pots and pans in the enamel sink, the rush of the water for her own bath—intimacies I had no male right to be hearing. No right. It was my brother's right to hear those things.

Up on the roof of the building was the only place to get cool. Like Old Testament dwellers. I went up there to drink a few beers alone, and there she was, watching the sun go down, drying her hair. And to give myself credit, I did curse a little—*DAMN is there nowhere I can get away from her*—but she smiled when she saw me, good Catholic girl so glad to see somebody to talk to who wasn't fourteen months old like her baby, or sixty, like my parents.

Good Old Testament girl so glad to have some other hands on her swollen breasts besides a baby's that I thought she would tumble us off the roof. I moved out the morning after the accidental night on the roof. She wrote me one letter after I left, full of the little intimacies that did not rightfully belong to me: *The baby is walking, your mother's arthritis is so bad this winter, your father lost his glasses, I will never forget you. Never.*

I'll never forget this: Durrance came in drunk one night and threw a woman's garter across the room and stared ceilingward and said, *—Thank you, Adolf Hitler, for making the world a safer place for debauchery.*

On the day we threw our hats into the air at graduation, nobody from Durrance's family could make the trip from Georgia, and there was no special girl there trying to catch his hat.

They had special roped-off rows for Van Cleve's entourage, including the congressman who had appointed him. Did anyone catch Van Cleve's hat? I don't remember, but I doubt it.

My parents were there, looking startled and scared, as if the sun on the drill field were a big flashbulb nobody warned them about. And Therese and the baby, which drew some puzzled looks from Durrance and Van Cleve later.

—*Please come home*, Therese whispered to me, the baby on her hip. —*Please*. It was as if she existed in some neighborhood of need I didn't want to enter into again. Where she existed, all love was lamb-like, white, soft. Even after what we did on the roof.

—*Think of my brother*, I said bitterly, as if she were the sole culprit, and it felt like the massacre of the innocents, some kind of irreversible slaughter. —*I have to report to flight school in one week*, I said with all the officiousness a twenty-three-year-old stuffed with his own importance could summon.

I would rather remember her as tempestuous, angry with me. Worse, she wasn't. She looked me in the eye a moment, and I saw the light leave her eyes.

It was as close to putting down a mare as I never hope to get again in my life.

We headed for flight school. We continued to learn from each other. Durrance taught Van Cleve and me how to *belly* a Vultee trainer down over the trees and top off a few, to indicate to a green flight instructor just exactly who was in control. Van Cleve taught Durrance and me *altitude*: how to sit in a room full of old colonels who'd never flown planes and *lift* oneself up to skim along just above the protocols, to establish just who would be in control. The old men needed us more than we needed them, and it was a tactical advantage. It's not like that now, pilots are a dime a dozen.

We used to refer to the brass out of their hearing as the ground-hoglings. We were respectful, but we had the edge; we felt it. It was before they gave the whole works to Hap Arnold and named it the Air Force. And even then you had planes and pilots subject to big brass who didn't know a snap roll from a Post Toastie.

Later, after Pearl Harbor, there were flying schools all over the country, cranking out what Durrance always called jackleg pilots. Hell, before it was all over with, they had the goddamn Chinese learning to fly out in Phoenix, and the black cats out of Tuskegee talking over the radio like they had their very own code. And Navajo code talkers. But at that time, we had the edge.

Consider the day that we got our first assignment. It was June of 1941. Randolph Air Force Base, Texas. They had just shipped in a

crop of grease monkeys from Chanute Field in Illinois, and we figured that crew assignments were being worked out. All us young
glamor boys were there in the briefing room, and the air was tense
and snapping. They were sending us to the Boeing plant. But we
were to take full dress uniform.

We flew cross-country to Fort Ord, with Durrance threatening
over the radio all the way to the Grand Canyon to stop and pick
himself up an Indian maiden. Those old radios were horrors; you
had to fill in the blanks yourself.

—*Big ditch,* Van Cleve remarked affably over the canyon.

—*Who you calling a son of a bitch?* Van Cleve asked.

Ménagerie à trois, cross-country.

A groundhogling drove us to the aircraft plant, a long, low,
sand-colored building that seemed to rise out of the horizon like a
moss-covered dock out of standing water. Closer look: camo and
netting. The whole building was covered, as if someone had tried
to hide several city blocks under a woman's hairnet with leaves
stuck in it. Durrance had a smirk frozen on his face, and Van Cleve
simply cursed his elegant Main Line curses, and the groundhogling
never knew that it all had to do with the dubious-looking factory
of war before them.

They were taken by the colonel into a meeting room, where
there were other pilots. Full dress. Atmosphere all asnap with too
many males of the species confined in one space. Long tables with
red tablecloths, and the steel Silexes of coffee. Doodle pads and
Boeing fountain pens. All the accoutrements of the ground-
hoglings, standard stuff. One of them stood up and began to speak,
and he was smiling.

—*Gentlemen,* he said, —*thank you for joining us today*— and we all
laughed, as if we'd had any choice. —*I'd like to recognize the officers of
the 41st Bomb Group, the 101st, the 82nd, blah, blah blah*—he's running through this whole bit, and Van Cleve zooms up to his own
private altitude by simply staring pointedly out the window.

—*We've been having some problems with the bomb bays, and with the
de-icers. Not design problems. Personnel problems. I'm sure you gentlemen
understand the speed with which we feel we must work now, yet we must
not sacrifice quality for speed. It's your lives at stake.*

He paused officiously then, as if he *understood* the thing it was to
have nothing but forty thousand feet of air between your ass and
the earth.

—You are the cream of the crop, the finest examples of American military intelligence and know-how that we can present to our personnel. We want them to know you all well by the time you leave here. So that when every rivet is driven, they think of you, remember what you look like. We're going to ask you to each make a brief speech, just a few minutes is all we'll have time for. You'll address all three shifts, then you'll be given a short time to frater—uh, socialize with the personnel.

Van Cleve let out one of his noblesse oblige sighs, but Durrance nodded. Of the two, Durrance always took the army with utmost seriousness and respect. He was probably thinking of all the men from his hometown who would only know the war from some foot-square piece of floor they stood on to do the same boring movement with the same small tool, day in and out. And he's the type to think that they might think of him in such moments, and wish to see him alive again. I heard in later years that even after he had a family, he kept his doors in the house angled at 45 degrees, just like at the Point.

When we were taken down a narrow hallway at this munitions plant, through some double doors, a little guy from the 41st said, *—Jesus!* when he looked in. *—It's all dames!*

It was a veritable sea of dames. You saw the white faces first, startling against the brown uniforms. The hair was all netted or pinned as if to disguise the state of damehood, but the lips were all that 1940 fire-engine female color, and looking much like a cartoon of the female genitalia. As if what had been covered in the lower regions by the uniforms and the ugly shoes had rebounded with a vengeance in the lips.

Some were seated, but there weren't enough chairs, so most were simply standing elbow to elbow, with the shorter ones jostling gently to get a better view. Not your highest class of dame, either, and not entirely an array of petite nubility. You wondered where these Amazons had come from.

It was the first time any of us had ever spoken over a PA system. And it was a bit of a bum ride to be sitting there knowing that you were not *quite* going to have the same feeling when you flew a Boeing, ever. The little dark guy from the 41st went up first, and asked if there was anybody else present who hailed from the cornfields of Nebraska besides him, and told them about his wife and their baby that was coming. They clapped their hands for him, and smiled those red smiles. There was this gallery that ran around the circumference of the room, and the women up there dropped all these slips of paper that fell all around us, and we sat there racked back in those chairs like we were not going to be put at ease anytime in the next century. Later we were told they were sales receipts, laundry tickets, chewing-gum wrappers, with names, addresses, and phone numbers on them. In some cases, measurements.

I don't even remember what I said. I think I was numb.

Durrance said, *—I come from the part of Georgia where the beautiful women are outnumbered only by the alligators,* and there were all these catcalls and cheers, and he flushed to the roots of his red hair. When Durrance flushed, his freckles turned green. He relaxed a little, and worked some charm with his words. *—And I have always been, in the words of my immortal Uncle Artie, a serious student of the lady female member of the species homo sapiens human being. Rest assured that every time henceforth that I step into the cockpit of a Boeing aircraft, I will remember you,* and they did the bit with the slips of paper again. Durrance reached out and caught one in midair, tucked it into his pocket, and saluted the general area of the gallery it had come from.

Van Cleve sat through this with those lanky legs crossed, and he was the last one to speak, but I've never seen him so discombobulated. The dames knew he was the last one, and things were getting restless and rowdy. He kept sweeping his eyes across all those faces out there like it was getting to him, to be not only outnumbered but *surrounded.* I'll admit: it was not an easy thing to think about—that B-17s, those big, elegant planes, forgiving as your mama in her Sunday dress, were put together here in the Sea of Dames. It was a major newsbreak to Van Cleve, to think about what was holding him up in the air besides the principle of lift: these hands, some plug-ugly, some red-painted.

He didn't present himself well, for the first time that I'd ever seen. He mumbled something about understanding now the grace of the machine, that it was due to the grace of the ladies who'd assembled them. He might as well have been speaking Ubangi, but it didn't matter. They smelled the old money on him, and saw him standing there like a piece of Greek statuary in Army Air Corps full dress, and they screamed and cried like for Sinatra, like for every wish they'd ever had for their ship to come in.

It was quite a phenomenon to watch. You had to understand:

this was the only big chance they'd ever have at anything in life, to get on the bus and go to the aircraft plant and work, and unless they snagged some bastard with a better future than theirs, it would be back to the hometown and the old Lou Hoover of a mother. Durrance and I knew this, and could forgive it. We were from the lower echelons ourselves. Nothing wrong with a woman trying to better herself, it just made dating a bit trickier.

You had to remember these things, and remind yourself not to get too carried away when you didn't know quite what a woman was seeing when she was looking at you all starry-eyed and wet between the legs and ready to go anywhere with you and do anything, even if it was only around Central Park in the back of a cab.

Hell, the whole world was a wet sea of dames in those days if you walked around in uniform.

But anyway, Van Cleve was stammering that he hoped the ladies would remember us all when they were at their jobs, and he was talking down to them, probably sounding in his own head like he was already a five-star general hopping onto Hirohito's front porch. And about this time this big Clydesdale of a woman from the gallery who'd been waving an enormous garter belt threw it down and it cut him on the temple. Right about here.

Some of the smaller ones rushed up to the podium and the next thing you know he's got lipstick marks on his face, and somebody has ripped his wings off, and the civilians have these tight smiles on their faces like they're trying to figure out when is the right moment to stop it. Van Cleve had this tight smile through it all too. But I'll hazard a guess that that was some pivot point in his life. Durrance and I stayed in pretty tight formation for some years after that, but Van Cleve just seemed to peel off by himself right about then. I used to think it was because we went Pacific Theater and he went European, but it wasn't that.

But the thing that really got to *me* was when they bussed in a load of hired girls from one of the movie studios to pose with us for the magazines. The girls looked good, don't get me wrong, and there were more than a few phone numbers passing around between shots, but it wasn't soldiering. It wasn't much of a buzz to be swinging your legs off the wing of a B-17 next to some stage cutie with the fire-engine-red mouth when she's not really hot for *you*, she's hot for any pair of pants carrying a camera. And she's not really going to remember you, she's going to be remembering the guy with the camera. And then the real women who made the planes, the plug-uglies, were standing behind the fence watching it all like forlorn denizens of the dog pound. The situation did not exactly have the makings of true romance.

I remember this one particular woman looking at me through the fence while this Hollywood dish was squirming around on my lap trying to please the photographer, and this one woman over behind the fence was looking like nothing would make her happier than if we'd all drop dead.

We walked on the beach at Monterey that night, abuzz with scotch and more than a bit blue at the prospect of the next junkets to the other plants, North American, Lockheed, Martin Aircraft, Consolidated. For once in our lives we didn't want to see women. Durrance kept insisting it was his turn to be Officer of the Day, and that we were to walk down the beach in a staggered line formation, which any sober mind would know you can't really *do* with only three aircraft. Van Cleve kept trying to talk about the women.

—*We observed sharks and barracudas in their natural habitats today, gennamen. Sharks and barracudas.*

Durrance, big-hearted and forgiving as a B-17 himself, tried to horse around with Van Cleve and fall back into that hick talk of his. —*Naw, man. You just don't know your way around the taxonomy of dames. Those were just salmon swimming upstream to mate. It's the essential transaction. Why for you want to mess with those little Vassar pan-fish when you could have you a REAL woman, like that Brunhilde that got your wings? Ain't no field manual when it comes to the dames, man. Talkin' about the lady female member of the species homo sapiens HUMAN BEING here.*

Van Cleve was getting sore.

—*Duty! Honor! Species!* Durrance yelled out on the empty beach, sounding just like this old bastard that taught ordnance back at the Point. The bluer Van Cleve got, the more Durrance would make like the cheerleader. The man could take a joke into his teeth and shake it until it was dead.

—*Those women are not of my species, you southern son of a bitch,* Van Cleve said. I could tell that Durrance wanted to hit him, but naturally you don't hit unless you're in the mood to pay the piper.

We hit all the other places and gave the same speeches before we got real assignments, and it was never all women again for Durrance and me, but Van Cleve had to go to the Willow Run Bomber plant, this thing that Ford was running in Illinois, to help recruit women workers. The last time we were all together was in Atlanta, and we'd heard each other's speeches enough times that we no longer listened.

Durrance tried to telephone some hometown girl to talk to before he shipped for New Guinea. It was typical of Durrance. Not to say one word about this girl as long as we had known him, then suddenly to get this idée fixe that he's got to see her, and *only* her, before he ships out, standing in a hotel lobby saying, —*I want to see her hair, I want to see that red, red, Pre-Raphaelite hair. And I want to say hello to my Uncle Artie.*

It was an interesting phenomenon of those times. You could be a free man, free in your own head, but when the sorties became more than field exercises, you needed to believe that some lithe lovely might be thinking of you while you were gone, and not confusing you with all the other dates she'd had, and hoping you'd get back with all your parts in working order. It was like an insanity that could come over you suddenly, a very necessary insanity.

We understood this and humored him, knowing full well that the insanity would more than likely strike us too, as time to ship out came. But this was well before Pearl Harbor. After Pearl Harbor you had guys going on innocent dates and coming back married. Like lemmings: over the cliff, over the cliff, one after the other.

On this last weekend he gets this bee in his bonnet that he's going down to the south end of the state to look in on this girl. And the immortal Uncle Artie. So I went with him. Navigated by the rivers, for chrissakes. Found the Alapaha River and followed it. Put the plane down at Moody, and they looked at us like, *Dr. Livingstone, I presume?* and he talked the base commander into giving him a jeep. So we took the jeep to this town of his, only we had to stop off at a crossroads juke joint and drink a bit.

He pulled the jeep up in front of a roof on the ground. Just as it's getting dark.

—*This your house?*

—*No. Uncle Artie's.*

There was a light on. We went in.

—Hey, compadre. How you doin' down here in radioland? Durrance said in the gentlest voice I ever heard him use. My eyes began to focus. Sitting near a green-glass kerosene lamp was a thin, white-haired man with gold spectacles on his nose. There was this butcher's block thing he was leaning over, and as we got nearer I saw that it was covered with bottles of all sizes. What the man did was, he carved little boats out of softwood, and put them in the bottles. Only this was not the first-rate stuff, like you might see in a museum. This was crude stuff, joke boats. In Ovaltine jars or whatever he had at hand. A skiff in a brown snuff bottle, that kind of thing. I saw that they were everywhere, mixed in with old radios, spilling out of bookcases, lining the floors.

A nut case. The immortal Uncle Artie was a nut case.

—Hey, buckaroo, he said to Durrance, and his eyes filled with tears. *—They got Red too.*

—Who got him? Where did they take him?

—To the war, Artie said. Then he looked at me with these eyes that I have never forgotten, lucid-blue animal eyes that lacked the capacity to conceal that he had been profoundly wronged, some-how.

Turns out the brother Red is only sixteen. Enlistment by lying.

What was interesting is that Durrance did not go to his own house. He didn't want his parents to know he was in town. Next stop, the girl's house.

We stood on the front porch, knocked. While we waited with our caps under our arms, he adjusted his tie three times. The door opens and there's this matron with white hair there, the flesh all blousy under the chin. Your basic garden-variety Lou Hoover. She said not one word. She came close to the screen, frowned a little.

—Carey?

—No, I'm Harrison, he answered, the faintest tinge of embarrass-ment.

—Well come in, then, she said.

We stood in the foyer. I felt like we should be dripping rain or mud. She didn't know what to do with us. She was looking at us like that.

—Toy delivers the milk now, she said.

—Mr. Jim here? I wanted to say so long for a while.

Why was my heart beating for him? Get on with it, man. Say it.

—I am here for your daughter. I'm going to love her and leave her on the lava. You owe me this, you owe me this. The sight of you, madam, is not much talisman to take up in the air with me.

—He's in Waycross, she answered. *—The trains run day and night now.*

—The girls? he asked.

Progress. I figured at that rate she'd offer us a chair by sunup.

—They are fine, she said. *—Thank you for asking. Do you think the war will last long?*

—No, we said in unison. *—No.*

There was this noise from the back of the house, or up the stairs, and then we seemed to be back outside again, and that was that. Standing there on the sidewalk as if we'd been forced to get off the subway a few stops too soon. We walked a few steps and there was this girl outside a window, only she didn't have red hair, it was brunette. The body was one that would have stopped traffic in Times Square. She looked about sixteen, seventeen. She had on this pink dress, made of that stuff with the flowers embroidered on in pink thread, with the holes in the centers of the flowers. Eyelet, they call it.

—My god, Harrison, she said. *—You scared me to death. You're supposed to be at the war.*

—Adrienne? he said. *—What are you doing, trying to sneak in? Last time I saw you, you had a skate key around your neck.*

She laughed. *—I'm not sneaking in, I'm sneaking out. I have a date.* Then she looked at me. *—Who are you, soldier?*

Soldier. I came to hate the sound of that word in a girl's mouth. *Soldier.*

—A Yankee friend of mine, but don't hold it against him. We're looking for Marjorie.

The girl's face contracted, not frowning, just drawing in the welcome mat a bit. *—What's it to you?*

—Well, I wanted to say goodbye, he said.

—She's not here, Adrienne said.

I'm standing there, shifting from foot to foot, thinking, *Come on, come on, you've seen one swamp girl, you've seen them all. Let's get this thing done and get airborne again, man.*

She came out on the porch and you could smell this tropical floral kind of perfume, and I thought, *How odd, how many, many times I'd smelled that same perfume in New York on the hard-eyed acquisitive chicks I seemed to end up with*. I thought of truckloads of that bottled scent traversing the continent, like what they call pheromones now. Pheromones of love? Pheromones of war? It affected us deeply, those sweet odors, and there were guys who held on to scarves or scraps of lingerie or something with that smell on it. I remember a guy from Louisiana, slit your throat in your sleep if you called him a coon-ass, but he had this pink lace garter lining the brim of his hat, sewn on the inside. Called it a love-fetish and said it protected him. I thought of him that moment and wondered if I'd ever see him again. The first recorded instant of any misgivings I felt about what was coming in the war.

He went down off the coast of France, the coon-ass and his garter.

But Durrance. The girl in the pink dress. We had that one whiff and then she ran off toward the trees. Before I could even think how extremely odd it all was, Durrance lit out after her, and they both seemed to know where they were going. Nothing to do but light out myself, cursing a bit because I didn't know the terrain, and I heard that the people in these parts could wake up some mornings with alligators or bobcats in their backyards.

We must have crashed through a couple hundred yards of brush, and there were these star-shaped fans that rustled and cut at my hands. Palmettos. I could navigate by the rustling ahead of me, and the sound of Durrance's boots.

—*Hey, we ain't lost, Herlihy,* he called back over his shoulder. -*We is exploring.*

Then there was a clearing, and there she was, stopped short, chest heaving, not an unwelcome sight.

A low sucking water noise.

A river.

—*Whirlpool,* Durrance explained to me, slipping back into that hayseed accent. -*The illustrious and venerable Alapaha River. Don't go any further than that log or you'll get sucked underground and surface tomorrow in the Suwannee.*

But he was looking around for someone. The sister.

—*Nobody's here,* Adrienne said and sat down on the log.

Durrance lit a cigarette, passed it to me.

—*I want one,* she said, a bit petulantly, and some alarm went off in me. This kid was much younger than the body indicated. Some good pilots had done tours of duty in the guardhouse for fraternizing with the wrong mens' daughters. Statutory rape.

—*Let's go, buddy,* I said to Durrance. He raised his hand.

—*Where is she?*

—*What do I get if I tell you?*

—*My continued patience and high esteem for you, Adrie. Which is on thin ice at the moment.*

She got up and circled the log, and she swept her hair up off her neck.

—*Hot. You know, this whole town has dried up to nothing. The only boys left in town are humpbacked or crippled. Everybody's getting to go to the war but me.*

He walked over and grasped the twist of hair at the base of her neck and pulled it tighter and tighter, forcing her to sit back down on the log.

—*Ow! Okay, I'll tell you, but you have to give me a kiss. Both of you.*

The absurdity of it roared into me right about then. We had spent some time hedgehopping around the country in flying machines. Looking for one dame in particular, like looking down on an ant bed, trying to find the one that held meaning. It is all so democratic, looking from the air. Munitions factories, museums, same configuration from the air. We were trained to wipe them out. For what? These females in these flounced dresses who would probably be on the phone to the humpbacks the minute we took off from the cornfield.

I kissed her first, Durrance still holding her hair tight enough to tether her. It almost *meant* something to me, I could feel something like sentiment welling up in me—*What will there be to remember if we all are going to die?*—and I fought it back like vomit. I didn't know for sure whether I wanted to fuck her or kill her there in the palmettos, the bare legs like a taunt, they were so long and so at ease. I walked away and wouldn't look at her.

There was this confusion in me. The woman I needed to kiss was far from me, but it wouldn't have helped if she had been six inches away. I would still not have that right.

I had no talisman to take with me, not even a garter. Just the memory of Therese that night on the roof. The memory of her eyes when I put her love for me to death.

—*Not like that,* the girl in the pink dress said to Durrance. —*For real.*

—*Since when do you know what a real kiss is? Where's your skate key? Your mama know you're meeting dates down here?*

She snorted, a snotty child's pout.

—*I need to remember you and that skate key, Adrie. You can't know how much I need to remember you like that, with that skate key around your neck.*

She began to cry.

—*Fuck it,* I said, —*let's go.*

—*She's in Atlanta,* the girl sniffed. —*She teaches guys to talk on the radio. She has to get into the nose of the plane sometimes. But it's not a real plane. They're teaching her to talk like she's from New York. She lives at the YWCA.*

—*Link trainer,* I said. —*We'll find her.*

—*Don't,* the girl said. —*She's engaged.*

—*You stay right here till we're gone,* he said. —*You don't need for your mother to hear that somebody saw you come from the river with us. You hear me? You don't need that.*

The pouty snort was the last we heard from her.

The minute we hit the hangar in Atlanta, Durrance was on the phone. I knew he'd found her when he came back with his eyes soft and his hat shoved back on his head.

—*You're at liberty for the evening,* he said when he walked back.

—*And you?*

—*I'm taking liberties for the evening,* he grinned.

We agreed to rendezvous at the YWCA in the wee hours before we flew back to Randolph. Durrance deemed himself most likely to end up actually sharing a bed with a genuine female for the night, so he made a big deal out of getting his girl to arrange for a ground-level window in a vacant room to be left open for us. That was the backup plan. We could sleep there if we had to.

Van Cleve went off to find some people he knew from the upper echelons of local society, and spent the evening in somebody's living room playing bridge. Being respectful to some daughter of a general who could pull some strings for him later.

He knew wiser ways of soldiering than we did. It seemed bred into him.

I wandered around Peachtree Street, necked with a girl I sat down next to in the Roxy Theatre for a while, and went to the YWCA around two in the morning, climbed in the window, and there's Durrance, sleeping all lamb-faced and innocent on a bottom bunk.

I climbed into one of the other beds and don't even remember falling asleep, but I dreamed of reaching into the clefts of bosoms, looking for skate keys, and the next thing I know, Van Cleve is slinging his long legs over the windowsill as the sun is coming up. We talked a little, and he stretched out on a bed across the room. Durrance was still dead to the world.

Then we heard this rustling from behind him, and up sat this naked girl, and she had red, red hair. It fell in ripply waves down, like she wore it braided into what the women called a coronet under normal circumstances but she had let it down for Durrance, or probably he had taken it down, and it was indeed Pre-Raphaelite. She had no makeup on, and I had just about forgotten how a woman's lips really look, that pink shell color, that purity. She had small breasts, and an elegant collarbone. Van Cleve and I quit breathing, just *froze* there, looking. You couldn't *not* look, even though it didn't seem sportsmanlike. Maybe Durrance wanted witnesses.

She rubbed her eyes, reached for a cigarette and lit it, took a deep drag. I can still see in my mind how her breasts were when she leaned over, like milky apples. She reached for Durrance's hat on the bedpost, and put it on, took another drag off the cigarette. She didn't know we were there. There was a silky green dress, jersey or something, in a tangle on the floor with crumpled nylons, green sandals.

Van Cleve was thoroughly smitten. Over the cliff, right before my very eyes. Like he was pinning up that image of her on some corkboard in his mind. But Durrance had got there firstest with the mostest, and the moment seemed to require some serious re-arrangement of Van Cleve's pride. Neither of us could stop looking at her, and he sat up and cleared his throat as if he felt the urge to effect a proper introduction, even if he had to do it himself.

There was something very civilized going on, or very primitive. Maybe they are the same phenomenon.

The girl just looked back at Van Cleve like he was some lowly pedestrian she was passing in the street. She had spaniel-brown eyes, and when she looked at us, it was like the uniforms didn't cut any ice with her. Like she could take you or leave you, and most likely leave you. It was that feeling that she would leave that was the pull.

She tamped out the cigarette and lay back down behind Durrance and covered herself with the sheet, and that was the last I saw of her.

When we woke up a little later, she was gone. Durrance was smoking, doodling on a notepad.

−*It must be the uniform, has to be,* he said, and his voice had a bit of wonder in it. −*She never let me go that far before.*

I didn't know what to say. I was thinking of Therese, remembering the sounds of her in the morning, cupping the memory of her to my ear, like a seashell. The rush of the water, her voice on the other side of the wall talking to the baby. If there was any talisman I took with me after that, it was the memory of love like an accident on the roof, dress coming off like a burden she couldn't live with anymore, the growing knowlege between my legs that she was taking a risk, for me. For *me.*

That was the moment I chose to remember, rather than the moment when I put her down like a mare.

−*That was the first time she let me in the foyer,* Durrance said, for once without his fake film-star bravado.

I stared at him a minute. Was that some southern expression? In the foyer?

−*Before, when I delivered the milk, she made me come to the back door, and she would hand me the money through the screen door.*

−*The girl?*

−*Hell, no,* he said, his voice still soft with amazement. −*I'm talking about her mother.*

ACROSS THE ATLAS
FROM THE ALAMO

*T*he first time I ever thought of leaving Harrison was in Toms River, New Jersey, in 1954. We were living on one of those Air Force bases where it's all nothing but rows and rows of flat little ugly houses. And no trees, just identical driveways in the front and barbecue grills in the back. You couldn't walk outside without feeling like a voyeur and a victim of someone else's gaze at the same time. You could always see into everyone else's life. It was a Saturday, and the kids were watching Roy Rogers. I had locked myself into the bathroom to soak in the tub, smoke a cigarette, and try to read the *Saturday Evening Post*. Field was nine years old and Allie was eighteen months.

I was listening for when Roy Rogers would be over and then I would come out and face them. I looked down at my name on the subscription address, *Marjorie Durrance*, and rubbed my thumb across it. I do still exist, I thought. *I am still me.* And then I thought I must be crazy to think such a thing.

On this day I felt that it was going to get bad. I felt it coming, because Harrison came in mad from the base the night before, drank himself to sleep, and got up to start building a shed. The undertaking of a new project always tipped me off—I had learned a little by then. So when the sun was straight up and he was out there with that hammer and those other old tools of his Uncle Artie's, I knew it would be a bad day. He was never very good with tools, and he'd just get madder and madder as he worked.

I lit another Viceroy, and the doorknob rattled a little. *–Marjorie!*

—*Just a minute*, I said. I thought it was Field, to get in the bathroom. —*I'll be out in a minute.*

The next thing I know, Harrison kicks in the door, and he's standing there with a wrench in one hand and a scotch and soda in the other and he's yelling at me that I'm a terrible mother and I should go fix lunch for everyone.

Which was absurd, because we had Melvina.

—*What are you doing with that?* he said. He had seen the magazine.

—*Just looking at it*, I said.

—*You waste too much time reading.*

I had to keep him away from the kids. So I got him to go back outside and show me what he was making, and I was telling him what a wonderful job he was doing, and that it was a good idea to do it, when he just fell silent and stared at me. I felt the hair prickle on the back of my head, in the pits of my arms. The overture for the tempest that would follow.

I HAD LEARNED THAT IF YOU JUST WENT LIMP, just *inert,* he would feel silly and stop. And I hoped there was no one else watching. That's a reaction you don't ever lose, no matter how often it happens.

Melvina had learned a lot by now, too. We had worked out this little system, without ever even talking about it. I'd keep him away from the children so he couldn't do anything to them, and she'd keep them busy playing so they wouldn't see anything.

But it was only some sore ribs that time.

In the beginning, we were novices. I didn't know any better than to hit back. The first time, I ended up with a broken nose. He didn't know any better than to tell me it would never happen again, and I didn't know any better than to believe him. He had put his arms around me, and whispered, as if he had been genuinely worried, —*You and me are compadres, eh, compadre?*

Do you know what it was about? I had cooked, for three months, on a hot plate. With two burners. That's what it was about. It was when Field was a newborn and we didn't have Melvina. I was sick of trying to sterilize bottles on that stupid little hot plate. I told him that I was not going to do it anymore. But I didn't know any better than to tell him when he was drunk, and in front of two other majors. He had brought them home at three in the morning. They were all drunk, and he woke me up to tell me to cook them something to eat. I wouldn't do it. He had unrolled that old set of his Uncle Artie's boat blueprints on our excuse for a kitchen table, and they were all poring over them.

He waited until they had left, of course. And he just came up behind me when I was hanging up some nylons in the bathroom and jerked me around by the arm.

I started screaming at him, fishwife voice fizzing up out of me like my own mother's. —*You've changed!* I felt duped, tricked. Other men had been to the war and hadn't ended up so mean. Why couldn't he be more like them?

—*Ever since the war,* I cried later when it was over and we were lying there, strangers who've discovered they've mistakenly booked the same berth on a runaway train. —*Ever since the war.*

This brought such a chilly silence from him that I never brought it up again. I was too afraid of him by then.

And we were so naïve we didn't get our lie straight before I went to the base doctor to get my nose seen about. *I* said I'd tripped running in the dark to get to the baby; *he* had already told the nurse that I had hit the dashboard of the car when he braked. The doctor didn't believe either one of us, and we made him uncomfortable, you could see it in his face. He wanted us out of there, as if we were a contagion. And I didn't know any better than to feel ashamed, as if *I* had done something wrong.

That's the way it was then. You couldn't talk to anybody about anything. Especially *that.* It wasn't done.

It was like a huge bubble of a secret that kept getting bigger and bigger inside me. I used to leaf through the *Saturday Evening Post* or *Newsweek* and look closely at each woman's photograph and try to read there if she had a husband who was capable of what mine was. I used to lock myself in the bathroom and wonder how my life had come to this pass.

We got married in 1947, in San Antonio, with two of his Air Force buddies as witnesses, at a justice of the peace near the Alamo. It seemed like the right thing to do. We started our married life at Ft. Leavenworth. Field was born in Dallas, and when I went home to Georgia on the train to show off the baby, I cried when we got into Louisiana because it had been so long since I had seen real trees.

I had thought that being Harrison Durrance's wife, being an *of-*

ficer's wife, was going to be all parties and fun, but I never really bounced back after Field was born. Nothing was the same, ever. I was always tired, and the red in my hair faded flat.

We moved so often, there was no time to make any friends anywhere. Twenty-two times in ten years. Nobody much was willing to invest much in friendships, it seemed to me.

This time in Toms River was the first time I ever talked to Saxon Van Cleve on the phone. He'd been behind the scenes all along, I found out later, bailing Harrison out of one scrape after another. But this was the first time Harrison just vanished, and nobody knew where he was for more than a week.

He was a flight instructor then, no longer a pilot, and he had removed some student's name from a list of volunteers to ferry some B-49s over to Holland or somewhere—I can't remember where—and signed in his own name. Then he disappeared. He did this on the Monday morning after our little fracas in the backyard.

Saxon Van Cleve called from Bermuda at the end of the week. He was base commander at Kindley then. They had known each other at West Point. Harrison was supposed to refuel at Kindley and stay a night with him, but he never showed up. Saxon checked around, but nobody had seen him.

Van Cleve's voice: imagine having someone who sounds like Edward R. Murrow call you up and ask, *—How are you and the children? Do you have everything you need?* For a few moments I closed my eyes and couldn't speak, it was so humiliating. How much did he know? Were we the subject of gossip? I had an arrangement at the PX and I could get groceries. Harrison had left me some cash, not much. Another thing you couldn't talk about then. It seemed to me that there was a relationship between whether or not we had food and how happy he was with my behavior at home.

But I told Van Cleve everything was fine. He found Harrison in Alapaha.

—It's his uncle, he said to me, as if that alone would explain.

—Artie? I asked.

—Yes. He . . . passed away. Harrison will come home in a few days. It would probably be better if you don't talk to him about it.

My first thought: that I would somehow pay for this. Just like I paid when anything at the base went wrong. I imagined Harrison in Uncle Artie's smokehouse, playing cards with him. I felt bitterly resentful that his life was so much freer than mine. That he could just appropriate a plane and go where he wanted to go.

Harrison brought me back a present from his little escapade. He handed me a bag from Rich's when he walked in the house, and I thought, well, he's *trying* to be nice, and there was a green paisley cocktail dress in it, with spaghetti straps and rhinestones. It was the kind of thing a twenty-year-old girl might wear—this peplum ruffle thing around the hips. And in the bottom of the bag, the receipt, with another dress listed on it, to be shipped to a woman in New Mexico. Probably some floozie he met in a bar.

A few days after that, we got transferred to Kindley, probably so Saxon Van Cleve could keep an eye on him.

Bermuda has to be the most beautiful place on God's green earth.

We moved into a pink sandstone house with a field of lilies behind, and a rocky path that led down to an inlet in the harbor. Melvina and I took turns seeing after the children and unpacking, and she did all the cooking and cleaning. Field had a room upstairs with a view of the bay, and Allie had a small room off our bedroom.

We had Cruiser with us, a border collie that Field got from my father. He used to ride shotgun in my father's car, hence the name. Soon after he got out of quarantine in Bermuda, he learned to ride the bus around the base to get where he wanted to go. The Hamilton newspaper did a story on it, with a picture of him sitting at the bus stop with some airmen. A few times he missed the bus, and someone would always bring him home.

I used to envy Cruiser. He could get up in the mornings and go where he wanted to go. I couldn't even drive there. If you got a learner's permit, you had to have a big red "L" on the side of your car. It took forever.

Saxon Van Cleve and his wife, Bunny, wanted to do a party for us the first week we were in Bermuda, but I was "indisposed" with blue and brown bruises on my arms and back. And by then, I was always nervous when I went anywhere. I hated happy people. So I spent most of my time at home.

I would go into Field's room while he was gone to school, and Melvina might be feeding the baby or pressing Harrison's uniforms (I could never get the starch or the creases *Air Force* enough to suit him), and I'd sit on a broad flagstone windowsill. You had to move the seashells and other little-boy things, and the room always smelled faintly of sea rot. Sometimes I'd just sit there and smoke and look out at all the oleander and hibiscus, and other flowers I'd never seen before, just growing wild and spilling out of the old stone wall that went down to the bay.

I loved those times in his little room when the house was quiet. I used to sit there and look out at that blue water, those other pink houses, and all that beauty, and wonder what it might be like to live there with someone who would be *sweet* to me.

Oh, I'm not saying that I was perfect. It was always my mouth that got me into trouble.

One time I walked into his office to ask for grocery money and I didn't know it was one of those times when they do an alert and an inspection at the same time, and he yelled at me in front of some officers to get the kids off the clean floors, and I said, —*Well, if the Russians DO invade, do you think they'll notice if the floors have waxy yellow buildup?*

He was infuriated, but held it all in until he got home. Then all hell broke loose.

So at this point in Bermuda, I was trying to be a better wife, to be what the Defense Department pamphlets called "the key partner."

A chaplain at Toms River had discussed the matter with me, and had brought me little pamphlets. When I remember this now, I think that man knew. I think he *knew* what I was living in, this alleged man of God.

Everything in our house had to have its place. The teacups were in symmetrical rows, the books were alphabetized by author, the towels were folded to his specifications. Shoes in neat rows in the closets, the whole nine yards. We had a big fight one time because I made up the beds without mitering the corners. I overheard Harrison tell someone one time that I ran a tight ship at home. Can you *imagine*?

We had these conversations, eerie moments.

—*I think you should redecorate the living room,* Harrison might say. And I would even understand what had set it off: my reading a book.

—*But it doesn't need it.*

—Yes it does. You have to accept my judgment, Marjorie. You know, there's a reason why I am in command and you are not. His voice would take on that timbre that terrified me, and my mouth would suddenly taste metallic. Too much disagreement from me and I would be without money to feed the children for the week. He had his ways of making me acquiesce, even if he couldn't make me *agree.*

I didn't much like the room Harrison and I slept in, because even when he wasn't in the house, there were his things, so neatly in rows, reminding me of all the defects in my organizational skills, as Harrison referred to them. Field's room was organized: all his toy planes and battleships in labeled rows on the shelves. But it was my favorite room in the house.

Field had little copybooks that he kept. When he filled one up, he'd start another. He filled a whole one in the first week in Bermuda. Little-boy stuff that grips your heart so. Pencil and crayon drawings of sea horses or amberjack or bonito or whatever. He'd sit up in the window at night, in his little pajamas with the cowboy lassoes on them, trying to be careful about his handwriting because his father had once made him sit at the dining room table for three hours working on penmanship. He had a whole notebook of sketches of each house we had lived in that he could remember, all the way back to Leavenworth. He could remember the house we'd lived in when he was three. He had penciled across the front of the notebook: *Field's Guide to Amerikan Houses.* It ripped my heart so to see it, to think: *This is an extraordinary boy. This boy will be a great man.* Field's handwriting slanted stubbornly back the wrong way, and Harrison was always attempting to right its course:

Bermuda is in the Sargasso Sea.

Bermuda is perhaps the most isolated inhabited place in the world.

You are an unofficial ambassador of the United States of America.

That was from a pamphlet they had issued to us before we came. These were the years when the Strategic Air Command was the thing. And Kindley was a busy place when we were there, because they were doing all these experiments with how far a bomber could fly without refueling, things like that. The British were very glad to have us there, but in such a way that they never let you forget that we'd all started out as indentured servants or whatever.

I once took the children into Hamilton to see the governor in a parade, and it was incredible. —*This is marvelous pomp and circumstance*, I said to an Englishwoman next to me, and do you know what she said back to me?

—*Then why did you people throw it all away?* she said. Those people hated us.

I finally met Saxon at a party at the American consul's house in Tucker's Town, which was swanky, so Harrison had drunk a good bit by the time we arrived there, trying to fortify himself. Harrison would never admit it, and I would never have had the nerve to talk to him about it, but he was dreadfully shy in situations where he had to stand around and make small talk with people who came from money and good backgrounds.

Twenty-eight missions against the Japanese, and got the Silver Star for bravery, but put him in a room with snotty people, and he's got to drink before he can face it.

And I always felt that he hated me at these times, because of all I knew about him—the way they went after each other with knives in his family, the way his mother was the meanest woman in town.

It doesn't matter if your heart *does* go out to someone like that. You still can't talk to him about it. You can't be truthful about it. He'll break your nose.

Harrison and I arrived at that Tucker's Town party not speaking, and he headed straight for the bar, just leaving me out there in the middle of the floor by myself. I was looking around for somebody to talk to. Didn't know a soul there.

That's when I saw Saxon coming toward me. I knew who he was because of the silver hair. His hair had gone silver a couple of years into the war, and I had seen pictures of him standing behind FDR at Yalta. He said, —*You must be Marjorie*, and found me something to drink.

He walked us out into this beautiful garden—riotous flowers I've never seen anywhere since but in magazines—and he said, —*I feel like I already know you*. It was an odd time, walking down that flagstone path with him in his dress uniform, loping along like MacArthur probably did when *he* was thirty-nine.

I did not understand why anyone would choose to talk to me about anything. It had been a long time since anything I said or thought had mattered to anyone.

—*Thanks for your help with everything over the years,* I said, and then the first thing that popped into my mind was that Harrison would hit me if he knew I'd said that. He said I always accentuated the negative.

—*This man you've hooked yourself up with,* Saxon said, grinning at me, —*I could tell you some stories about him.*

—*Don't tell me stories,* I said. —*Tell me how to live with him.*

He looked uncomfortable, like military people do when you bring up honest human topics. —*It's going to be different here. This is a wonderful place.* And he told me about how Mark Twain had come here a lot, and that there was a house nearby that Eugene O'Neill had lived in.

—*Oh, God,* I said. —*What I mostly read these days is Winnie the Pooh.*

Then he picked some leaves off a tree and crushed them for me to smell, and when he did, his fingers brushed my lips. —*I bet you've never smelled allspice,* he said, and I felt a little panic coming over me, like when you talk too long to someone, and you might have to pay for it at home later on. But this was worse.

It had been *so long* since I had heard anyone say my name in a kind way. It had been a *long, long* time since Harrison had touched me in a kind way. So it was like what happens when somebody touches some stray puppy that's hungry. It homes in on the soft-ness, and decides it belongs to you.

I felt like I was in the presence of someone who was still a real human being, for the first time in a long, long time.

I decided I belonged to him, in my heart.

And I was afraid that I was going to cry, or feel sorry for myself, or turn into one of those awful military wives who pretend to be drunk so they have an excuse to curl up in somebody's lap beside their husband's. But that was the moment it happened, when I got hooked on Saxon Van Cleve.

—*Come, you have to meet Bunny,* he said, and we went back to-ward the patio where some women had come out. Bunny was a tiny woman with a good tan, and she wore a yellow linen sundress that almost hurt your eyes to look at it, not just the suggestion of the sun, but the idea that anybody could be my age and still look *that* good, and be married to *this* man.

She hesitated a moment when she looked at me, and I had the feeling that she knew the story of the Toms River debacle, but

Bunny was all business. She introduced me to all the other wives, and by then I'd been through this scene so many times before I didn't *feel* it when their awful eyes inspected my shoes, my dress, my hair, my earrings, my purse. And I remember that my clothes were all wrong. The other wives were all in bright sundresses that show everything you've got, and I was still in New Jersey clothes to cover some places on my arms.

They knew we were from Georgia, so they were expecting some Mammy Yokum or Daisy Mae type who can't read or write. They seemed so amazed that I owned shoes. And some of *them* didn't even have high school diplomas.

But Bunny gave it the old college try, making friends with me. She was the president of the Officers' Wives Club, and she made an effort to include me in all their little wretched to-dos. The first function of theirs I attended turned out to be a pool party. There all these women sat, drinking and tanning and gossiping. Queen Elizabeth was coming in a few weeks, and there would be high tea at the American Consulate, and so they were all in a swivet about what to wear. Hats or no hats.

Bunny had little finger bruises on her thighs, the kind that husbands' hands make sometimes in bed. And I was sitting there in this long-sleeved thing.

They were talking about where to buy lingerie on the island, and Bunny seemed to know where to get the best things. One of the other women was teasing her about a nightgown she had bought from an old Englishman in Hamilton. —*You should have seen his face when she asked him if he thought the buttons were too complicated for an ordinary American soldier to undo. You should have seen that red face!*

—*Oh, when you wear that gown, you can get anything you want out of him.*

—*Hmmn. Maybe those earrings I saw in New York.*

I kept watching Bunny, as if I could learn something about Saxon by knowing her. I didn't like to think about the difference between how she got her bruises and how I got mine, and how your whole life seems to hinge on the right kind of man. I had married the wrong kind.

Once I was a girl who had her own illustrated atlas of the universe, and I could look at it any time I wanted to.

Then I was a twenty-year-old woman who took planes and trains to places, and paid her own way.

But in Bermuda I was a woman who had to ask a man for money to buy her own Kotex.

I used to try to figure out how I had got from one point to the other in nine years. This line of thought always led me back to the afternoon in my room with Harrison in Atlanta, shortly before the war.

It was the first time we made love. It was the first time *I* had made love. I lay beside him tracing circles in the semen that had spilled on my thigh. His eyes were closed, and I thought of the textbook pictures I'd seen of sperm, like little comets with fiery tails I'd seen in my old annotated atlas of the universe, and it began not to matter to me that I'd never seen real meteors or comets. He was more important. I had no understanding what a pilot's life was like: I imagined him in cold, wet foxholes, and held him tighter. It seemed to me that he touched me because he *needed* me, and this seemed like the craziest, holiest, *best* thing I'd ever been privy to.

—*Will you regret this night?* he had whispered to me, binding me to him. They always think it is their heroism that does it. But it's their wretchedness that does it. Hooks you.

—*Never, ever,* I'd said. —*No regrets.*

There's no way you can know that you're marrying the wrong kind. Or is it just that they change, once they have you where they want you?

MY THING ABOUT SAXON VAN CLEVE was a little secret thing, something harmless going into it, just a little something to get you through the day. It usually started with my remembering the smell of the allspice, and the feel of his fingers brushing my lips. I racked my brain to remember anything Harrison had ever told me about him. After a few hours of thinking about Saxon, of *imagining* what it would be like to talk to him some more, I felt good. I could be nice to Melvina, I could look at cookbooks, I could stop yelling at the kids. I could quit walking around the house like a zombie.

That's pretty much what it was like before I met Saxon: sundown comes and you can't tell anybody what you did with your day, and if you're lucky the house looks clean and you have stacks

of clean laundry to show for yourself, and you dread the night.
You feel very dead inside.

So I thought of Saxon often, too often, and wondered what he
was doing.

There was not much between Harrison and me by then. In the
bedroom department, I mean. I guess it was pretty much like
everything else between us: unpredictable, and subject to surprise
attacks. No warning, and not much way to take precautions, no
time to get ready. That's just the way he was. After a while you
don't feel much like a woman anymore, you just want to survive.

There was this spate of magazine articles during that time. How
to tell if you were frigid or not. That was the big word of that
decade: *frigid*. Harrison left one of those articles on my pillow one
night when he went out without me, not long after Allie was born.

Some women are frigid for religious reasons.

*Some women are frigid because they have never explored their own bod-
ies.*

*Others are frigid because they have not received the proper instruction
from their husbands.*

There was even a photograph of the military doctor who had
written these lines, with his arm around his wife. I stared at the
picture, prurience like a vested interest in me. I imagined them in
bed together, him barking his proper instructions to her:

—*You will feel pleasure when I touch you precisely here. I command it.*

—*Yes sir.*

Another thing you couldn't talk about—it wasn't done then—
how the men had their truths, and we had ours, and *theirs* were always the ones that made it into print. I read a few lines more and
fell asleep, which is what happened to me anytime I had a few
minutes to myself, and my own mind managed to speak some
truth to me: *Some women are frigid because bed has nothing to do with
need or crazy holiness anymore.*

IN 1955, THE B-52s came into being. It was when everybody in
the country was in love with the Strategic Air Command. There
was this one weekend when five B-52 B's were going to refuel at
Kindley on the way to Europe. Stratofortresses. Everybody was all
excited about it, and they built a special little grandstand for all the
wives and children to go watch. Melvina took the kids; I didn't go.

I loved being alone in the house, and I heard the B-52s coming but I didn't go out to see. You've seen one bomber, you've seen them all, as far as I'm concerned.

That was a Saturday afternoon. Harrison didn't come home after this, and I covered the dinner table with a cloth—covered his cooked dinner the way he said his mother did on Sundays to leave it all out for whoever would wander in.

At dusk I went down to the water and smoked, and watched the little fishing boats with the gold lights strung all over coming home to roost for the night. And I let myself go all dreamy about Saxon Van Cleve, wondering if he could see the same beautiful thing from across the inlet in his house. I began to think about his long, beautiful hands, his voice that always still remembered how to be deeply human. I sat there long enough, thinking of him, until I had the wherewithal to go crawl back into my life.

Harrison did not come home until one or two in the morning, but then he was up early on Sunday, drinking again. Something about the B-52s was getting to him, but of course there was no way to talk to him about it.

He was walking around the house with an old Stearman propeller, something he had gotten when they phased out some old trainers, and he was trying to show it to Field, explaining that that was the first plane he ever flew solo in. I followed him around, watching his glass. He was proud of our mahogany furniture, but anything would make rings on it. I was afraid he would think that the children and I had made the rings and go after us. But it was risky, even to pick up his glass off a table, because he might decide he was being *handled,* and come after me.

He decided he was going to hang it on the wall over the head of Field's bed.

Two problems here. One: the walls in that house were stone with plaster over that. Two: that propeller was very heavy. I had visions of the things crashing down in the night, splitting Field's head open. But I couldn't say anything. It was an instinct by then, not to say things like, *Bunny says you have to get a special kind of nail for these walls,* or, *Don't you think it might look better over there, above the bookshelves?*

That was when we were in the most danger. When I told him the truth.

So I said nothing. Field could sleep with his head at the foot of the bed, or on the floor. While Harrison was up in Field's room, hammering and cursing and throwing things around, I made the children stay downstairs. It was Melvina's day off.

We had a new hi-fi that Harrison was very proud of, an RCA. You don't see them anymore: real burled walnut on the front doors. Field turned it on to the base station, and the pilots of the new B-52s were speaking. They were young and cocky, of course, and there was a lot of joking. Their voices filled the house as I was trying to cook Sunday dinner and watch Allie at the same time, then I heard Harrison yelling at Field: —*You are NOT to touch that radio. Do NOT touch that radio.*

I walked in then, hoping that Field would know how to go along with him. But a child doesn't know how to reason with an adult who's been drinking. A child only knows how to tell the truth.

—*You don't want to listen because you can't fly anymore,* Field said, and I understood that I did still love Harrison—no man should have to bear such a thing from his child.

There was this little sound that Field made as Harrison moved toward him, a mewl of animal fear. It is an atrocity to hear it come from a little boy, all snips and snails and toughness at that age. There is a little dance that children do, to avoid being hit. I don't remember the rest of it clearly. I do remember that I went into the kitchen and turned the stove off and put Allie in the playpen. I remember that I faced Harrison with an iron skillet and I think I was screaming at him not to touch my son or I would call the MPs. Something like that. I must have sounded like a real fish-wife.

Well, you can just imagine. Field saw it all: me in a heap on the floor, my arms covering my face, waiting for it to be over, and Harrison standing over me yelling at me: —*Call 'em! Pick up the phone and call 'em! I'll court-martial 'em and ship 'em to the Azores!*

It helps, in such times, to pretend that it is happening to someone else, not you.

It was horrible to have Field see this. As if he had seen us together in bed. The same loss of dignity or privacy or whatever, the same regret that you can't hide things from a child.

The two acts were very similar, now that I think about it: you know every move he's going to make, right down to the last thrust, the last grimace, and then it's over. Except, during fights he would say horrible things, that I was unstable and he was going to have *me* put away, things like that. That he would take *my* children away from *me*.

Needless to say, after the Sunday of the B-52s, I didn't make it to the tea party for the queen.

Field could never quite look me in the eye after this. School was out by then for the summer, and he would leave the house in the mornings and head down to the bay with Cruiser, and I wouldn't see him until suppertime. I would go up into his room sometimes, and open his drawers, and just the sight of all those little folded striped T-shirts would make me weep. He would always rearrange his socks in the mornings, so that they'd be in rows, because he knew his room was subject to random inspections by his father.

His little copybook changed. He would draw pictures of B-52s, and the SAC shield. His handwriting changed—his letters were ramrod straight, and I don't know where he got these things:

—*Gain control of the environment.*
—*Survey, assess, command.*
—*The enemy is entrenched and intractable.*

I was losing him. To *them*.

I felt like if I got him and Allie back to Georgia, we could be ourselves. Without worrying about someone hitting us. I knew that my mother would gloat over the failure of my marriage, but I figured that saving my kids was worth this.

I needed an atlas to figure out where we could fly to have my father or Adrienne meet our plane. All I could find was one of those old textbook things from West Point, not a real atlas. You opened it up and all the great battles flopped out in your lap like paper accordions. The Somme, Waterloo, the Alamo. Marks that looked like turkey tracks or circles or whatever, and a legend to explain who was who. Absolutely useless.

I had some Bank of Alapaha stock, and I wired my father to sell it and send me the money. I didn't say why. And I didn't want Harrison to see the call on the phone bill. I sent Melvina into Hamilton with a note. Adrienne wired back: *Will not sell. How much do you need?*

One day, while I was waiting for the money to come, I was out in the sandbox with Allie. God, I can still see her standing there with sand on those fat little knees. She had an old colander on her head—it looked like a doughboy's helmet—and she was little enough that it was a big deal when the bombers would pass over. She'd stand up and wave her hands and yell, *—Ep-pay in da kye, Mama!*

She was doing that when Saxon Van Cleve walked up with Cruiser.

—He missed the bus again, he said, and he was smiling until he got closer and saw me. I had no time to run into the house. I wasn't that bad, really, just some faded brown places on my arms. There had been worse times.

It was dusk, and Harrison wasn't around.

—How long has this been going on? he said.

I just sat there in the sandbox, ashamed, holding Allie. I couldn't talk. I was imagining that he was going to call the chaplain to come see me, or that somebody was going to take the children away from me.

—Please don't tell him you saw me, I said. *—It'll just make it worse.*

I told him where I thought Harrison probably was, at a tavern in St. George. I'd seen matchbook covers from there. He turned to go, then turned back around as if he were going to reach out and touch my hair, and I jerked my head away. He probably thought he had scared me. It wasn't that.

If he had touched me, I would have begun to cry, to feel sorry for myself, to make a fool of myself. The last thing that I needed under those circumstances was to *feel* anything.

So off he walked, hat under his arm, and Melvina watching from the window. And I sat there trying to teach Allie not to eat the sand, but my dreams of Van Cleve blossomed bigger.

I wanted to touch his hair, I wanted to hold his beautiful hands. I wanted to see him out of uniform, walking on a beach some-where, to me.

I found out later that he found Harrison and took him home with him. And Saxon must have gone back in to work, because by nine the next morning, Harrison was presented with his orders for one of those ninety-day rotation things that all the SAC people had to do. He would be away from us for three months. He had one day to get himself together, and then he was gone. He would be back in time for the big reunion of Eisenhower and Eden and Churchill.

There's a sense in which the wives and children got rotated out, too, even though they stayed behind. People stopped inviting you to things. It was understandable. There were some wives who just went crazy before their husbands were even out of radar range.

There was this one officer's wife who had preceded us by a couple of years, and they were still talking about her by the time we were stationed at Kindley. The husband, a full bird colonel like Harrison, had come home and found his wife cohabiting in a Quonset hut with an enlisted man. Nobody seemed to care that she had wrecked the homes of two different sets of children—the big thing to them was that she'd ruined her husband's career.

A man who couldn't control his wife was seen as somebody not to be trusted with military authority.

But I remember one woman saying at a party one time that she had seen that woman on the day the chaplain and a social worker came to get her children and take them away, that she had run out into the street barefoot and in a black lace slip, screaming.

So my Van Cleve dreams were secret ones.

I wondered if *frigid* simply meant not wanting one's husband to touch you.

I wondered if perhaps *marriage* wasn't the most isolated inhabited place in the world.

Harrison's rotation out was the happiest time of my life. The house was quiet. Field drew page after page of B-52s and taped them to his bedroom wall, and they fluttered like pennants when the sea breeze came in the open windows. The towels were crooked in the linen closet. We had an ant farm in the kitchen, and the hamster had babies in my lingerie drawer. After my children were in bed, I could read any books I wanted to.

I saw Field down at the edge of the water with some other little boys one day, and they were shooting marbles, and all the little English boys had this way of wiggling their fannies when they got down to shoot, and it seemed that the love I had for him at that instant would burst me open. There is a pure intrepidness that little boys have. When it's one of your own, it's breathtaking. Allie's hair grew long and coppery and she began to talk more.

I let myself go all dreamy about Van Cleve whenever I wanted to, and it made me happy. Sometimes after I got the children to sleep I would walk across the field of lilies and down the rock path, and sit alone at the edge of the water, dreaming of long talks with him in Eugene O'Neill's old house, or of long, slow dances in English gardens hung with Chinese paper lanterns. But once you start that kind of thing, it's not like you can just stop on a *dime.*

Slow gauzy thoughts came unbidden in the shower, bathing my breasts, while Allie was asleep. And I would touch myself in the ways I wished he could, but ashamed of the ripples and shudders this caused, ashamed like I had been when I learned to do that as a child.

Once I took off my dress and waded out into the inlet in my slip and thought of hurricanes that wiped everyone else off the face of the island except *us.* And I dreamed of making love to him in beds of Bermuda lilies, in rains that would wash all the tarnish off me. And I stood there in that water like a deaf-mute, like an idiot, with the water up to my chest, fanning my hands around me, and understanding that the world was still a beautiful place to be, mostly because *he* was in it.

And I was always a little ashamed, walking back to the house. But who did I hurt with it? I could have done worse things. I could have become a drunk. I could have become a homewrecker, or one of those wives who vamp the base doctors to get drugs, but I didn't. And I may have burned a pot roast or two, all dreamy with hearing Van Cleve's voice in my mind, *wanting* him, feeling alive again.

Being alive had its risks. I wanted sometimes to go back to that old safe zombie life, where you don't let yourself want anything from anybody. But I couldn't. The dreams of him were so much a habit by then, and I couldn't get away from them.

The worst I ever did was stay so long down by the water one night after the children were asleep, watching the lights on the water, that Allie woke up crying and couldn't find me. I could hear her screams as I got closer to the house, and Field was holding her. He said, *—Daddy called and you weren't here,* and we all held each other and rocked and cried.

But who did it hurt? Nobody.

During those months I might catch sight of Saxon somewhere just even a moment, just crossing the street, and I could feel happy for days. That familiar walk, that wave. When it was almost time for Harrison to be back, Field came in from his little explores one day, scratching red welts all over him. By midnight, I was at the base hospital with him, and he was all swaddled up from the top of his head to the tips of his toes. Poison ivy. Bunny had met me there to take Allie.

I felt so strange around her. So traitorous.

They put Field in a ward with six airmen with various peace-time ailments, and he loved being in with real soldiers. I felt very awkward being around them, but Field was really too young to be left alone.

By the next night, we had a private nurse, a Wac from Kansas, to stay with him. Saxon brought Allie back to me at home and she had a huge lollipop stuck in her red hair. He stood watching while I washed her hair at the kitchen sink, and she seemed dreamy about him, too. He made himself a drink while I put her to bed.

He seemed to want not to go home, and he said he hadn't eaten, so I scrambled him some eggs. I could feel him watching me while I cooked.

—*Why is it that he hits you?* he said, and my knees almost buckled with fear. It was almost a kind of mutiny against the marriage to translate it all into language. I wanted to hit him, cry out. How dare he speak true things to me?

—*He hits me when I tell the truth about things*, I said after a few moments. I wanted to ask him what he did when Bunny told the truth.

He rolled up his shirtsleeves to eat, and said, —*What are you going to do when Harrison comes back?*

—*I'm not sure. I have to see what the situation is.*

—*It's the flying,* Van Cleve said. —*He misses the flying. He hates being a desk jockey.*

—*So? Let him fly again.*

He shook his head. —*It's not like it used to be. The planes now— they're not very forgiving.*

—*What does that mean?*

—*They don't give you a big margin for error like the old ones. And once a man gets past thirty, reaction time increases, eyes start to go, you can't check out. I can't check out on jets either.*

I sat across the table from him in my stocking feet, and it was very quiet in the house. I was thinking that this must be what it is like in normal families: the children asleep in their beds, and the man and the woman talking together, and they can say to each other that they are getting old, and it does not necessitate his hitting her.

—*Do you remember seeing me in Atlanta before the war?* he said. —*You were . . . you had on a green dress.*

—*Where?*

—*It doesn't matter,* he said, and waved the subject away.

There was a night when all the girls at the Y helped me dress for a date with Harrison when I borrowed a green rayon dress, when they found out my date was a pilot. That night, that whole *time,* there was camaraderie in the world. That was *my* finest hour. To think of Van Cleve milling around in that same sea of people, and I hadn't even known it!

There is so much they don't *tell* you and what they *do* tell you is often wrong. My mother's only guidance to me during those years was a clipping from an Emily Post column, something about etiquette with a man when there was a war on and your parents were not around to chaperone you. Something about *let your conscience be your guide, since he will be risking his life to save you and your country.*

What they don't tell you: he can save you from everything except himself.

Then the front door opened, and I could hear whistling, Harrison's whistling, a Bob Wills song, "Across the Alley from the Alamo," something about a pinto pony and a Navajo. He had an airman behind him carrying his bags. He dismissed the airman, and stood in the doorway looking at us, and then at my shoes under the table.

—*So kind of you to stop by, Van Cleve. Did you know I was coming? Ain't it funny, compadre, how the earth has this way of curving on you?*

That's when I knew he was drunk. The smooth talking, the confidence. All I could think about was what a mess the house was in, and that the hamster babies were still in my lingerie drawer and he would be able to hear them. And he was going to *get* me when he found out about Field's poison ivy. My heart began to beat too fast, and every pulse beat was some scream that nobody else could hear but me: *Saxon, don't leave, Saxon, don't leave.*

Harrison just went over to the refrigerator and looked in, then remembered that there would be no beer there. Allie was asleep in our bed; I had let her sleep with me whenever she wanted to.

He began to pull food out of the refrigerator, piling it on the counter. It was ten at night, and he wanted me to cook for him, and mere scrambled eggs would not do. I began to broil some lamb chops.

He was at the table with Saxon. He pulled an old photo out of his wallet to show to Saxon. It was the one I gave him before the war.

—*Who'd have thought it, Saxon?* he asked. —*I seem to have married Crabapple Annie. We seem to have homesteaded on the Boulevard of Broken Dreams. Got a light?* he asked Saxon in a mocking way. Saxon handed him his sterling-silver lighter.

He put the photo in the ashtray, and lit the corner of it, and the edges curled. Another mess for me to clean up, I thought.

SO, OF COURSE, Saxon got up to leave, in the way that visitors prefer their own homes when a tempest begins.

I tried to act as though everything was normal. "Normal" meaning as it would be in some other house besides our own.

—*Do you know,* I said gently to him as I set the lamb chops down in front of him, —*I'm sorry I will never see your Uncle Artie again. I had the funniest dream about him—*

—*What do you care what happened to Artie?* he snarled at me. —*You've never asked. You've NEVER asked.*

You can't speak what is in your heart in those moments. You'll pay for it.

—*He opted out. He made his own electric chair. He even made a timer to turn it off, so whoever found him wouldn't get hurt.*

—*Who found him?* I gasped.

—*I did.* The food was cold and ignored in front of him. —*Take down your hair,* he said, and my fingers shook so I spilled the pins on the kitchen floor. I was thinking of how there was no train anywhere that could take me home to my father. No trains. Harrison reached across the table and coiled my hair around his fist, around and around until his hand was fast against the base of my neck. In this way he made me stand.

—*Why do women lie to men?* he asked, and his voice was so tortured, like a child's.

—*Because you hit us when we tell the truth,* I said, and my own voice broke, and I was thinking, *This is a tempest, and it will pass. It will pass if I can ride it out.*

He pushed me so hard away from him that I fell halfway across the room. We didn't know a baby was on the way. I knew several days later: nausea so great that I could not stand.

—*I have tickets to the Army-Navy Game,* Harrison said, ominously, one morning.

I waved the topic away, unable to speak. The smell of the bacon cooking made me wish I was dead. I couldn't begin to tell him what was wrong. It would give him too much leverage.

I visited the base doctor. —*You have to help me. I cannot bring this baby into my home.* He looked at me as if he hated me, the way men look at women when we disappoint them. As if somewhere, elsewhere, there were only pure-hearted, generous, soft-spoken women, never critical of anything around them. He wanted to get there soon, take his shoes off, put up his feet and have one of them serve him a martini. He was writing something on his prescription pad. I didn't look at it until I got outside. He spoke not a word to me.

It was a street address in Hamilton. Maiden Lane.

I couldn't drive, couldn't ask Harrison for help. I knew no one. I called a cab to take me there. The lane was so narrow that the cabbie had to stop three blocks away. What was I supposed to do? Ask him to wait? Take me to the base morgue if anything went wrong? What would happen to my children if they only had Harrison? While I was watching, I saw the doctor go into that place with his little black bag. He was a black man in a white linen suit and a panama hat.

—*You wait here,* I told the cabbie. —*I will be back. I will pay you.*

The Negro doctor spoke softly to me, fairly crooned to me in his impeccable English, and I wanted to crawl up into his lap and weep.

—*You have to help me,* I said. —*You can't make me go through with it. Please. Isn't my life worth anything to anyone?*

—No, dear lady, you have to help us, he said.

He said it so coolly that I wanted to scream at him and throw a child's tantrum: *Who do you think you are? You are a black man. I am a white woman. You have to do what I say!* But I sat there meekly. I was wearing a hat and white gloves. He was so goddamn British.

—I cannot do what you ask of me, madam. Because your life is worth something to me.

He reached over and laid his hand on mine, on those stupid white cotton gloves. As if it were high tea. I was even wearing a white straw hat. He patted my hand and I pushed his away. I was filled with rage at him: *I am a white woman. You are a black man. You are supposed to do what I say.*

I went home and locked myself in the bathroom. I took my clothes off and looked down at myself. It all looked like some cruel atlas to me, the blue veins crisscrossing me. Roadmap to the rest of my life.

On the day that Churchill and Anthony Eden and Eisenhower landed at Kindley Field, I was standing on my white chalk mark on the tarmac, wearing something that was too warm, something that covered me in the right places. There were two chalk marks separating Van Cleve and me. Bunny's mark and Harrison's mark.

When Eisenhower stepped through the door of his plane and waved, and looked down for his red chalk mark, where he was supposed to pause for the photographers, I wanted to turn and look at Saxon, to see his lovely face, but of course I could not.

He wouldn't have looked back, anyway. He and Harrison were at attention, looking not much different from scared West Point plebes who'd been told to *rack it back.*

Eisenhower came first, and put them at ease. Churchill and Eden walked toward him. You had to be there to see it: the way these men looked into each other's eyes, remembering those other, finer, hours.

Eisenhower went first to shake all our hands. When he shook mine I understood all those soldiers who were willing to die for him. In the presence of a man that great, your knees turn to jelly and your heart goes *wild.*

We were different people in those other, finer hours. Camaraderie was possible then.

Churchill paused for the photographer, and then turned to shake our hands. He remembered Saxon from Yalta, and cuffed him a little, the way big bears do cubs. And I thought of Winnie the Pooh. By the time he got to me, my eyes were brimming, and he looked at me suspiciously, wondering what was the *matter* with me.

RIGHT DOWN SANTA
CLAUS LANE

*T*his is *my* dime in the jukebox.

This is the way it went down.

Career, family, the entire *contretemps*.

I accidentally married Crabapple Annie, and we got beached on the Boulevard of Broken Dreams.

Only she wasn't Crabapple Annie when I fell in love with her, she was a nymphet in a borrowed green dress and green sandals, unpinning her hair and her heart for me in Atlanta. I had already said what felt like goodbye to her in the lobby of the YWCA, then climbed in the window of the room she'd arranged to be vacant for me. Then there was this voice at the door and it was hers.

—*It just seems so wrong,* she said, —*for me to be upstairs and you to be down here. It seems wrong not to be where you are.*

Then she was in my arms, fragrant with some jasmine scent that made me drunker than any liquor had before or has since, and whispering love to me, crooning to me like you'd croon moony words to a drowning man reaching for the life preserver. There was a war on somewhere outside the walls of that room, and that fact governed our every caress and whisper.

—*What does that mean?*

—*It means everything, silly. It means nothing else matters but you.*

—*Will you regret this night? I'm not good at promises.*

—*No regrets,* she had said. —*Never, ever.*

Where do they go, the girls we marry? That was 1942. By 1958, after some years of marriage to her, I would drive past my own driveway after work, pause down the curb, stare at my own house, which was like all the other houses, reliquaries of other long-ago moments of never-ever and no regret, other onetime nymphets. These houses were in fact museums we were all maintaining for each other's edification. You invite the neighbors over for drinks, give them the tour of your life, temporarily on exhibit the way we all once imagined it was meant to be.

Since Bermuda I had fallen into the habit of an ongoing crazy dialogue with the imaginary nameless faceless Japanese kamikaze who had shot me down in 1942. He had begun, I noticed, an acerbic running commentary on the state of my life since we'd last met, when his bullets were meant for my ass.

—*Do I have to go home? This place has the potential to kill me.*

—*Yes, you have to go back there. Only the kamikaze is privileged to understand the meaning of true flight.*

—*Says who?*

Then I might drive on to one of those ubiquitous bars that cling to the edges of military posts like a blight of barnacles. I called it core sampling. To explore the deeper terrain by looking at a small part. I could talk to other men in those places, bear witness somehow to their stunned, ox-like amazement. We had brought the Germans and the Japanese to their knees, understand. But had been brought to saidsame position at home by the lady female *homo sapiens* human being of our species. You could have bored down to the core of me and found two spirits: the one that wanted to live and the one that was sick of being punished for trying to.

Where did they go, the girls we married?

I embarked on the great expedition of marriage with a girl who worshiped me.

I came to, some years later, and she was screaming at me, in her mother's voice, —*You've changed, you've changed,* like she thinks maybe she will take me back to the store and demand a full refund.

There was an old reel-to-reel tape of Saxon explaining to me that I would be transferred from Bermuda to MacDill in Florida. The base needed attention, he said, because some officers were writing their own effectiveness ratings reports, that the situation had run amok under the previous commander. And on that tape were my quiet responses, and the moment when I halted the proceedings.

—*Tell me the truth. They're trying to wash me out. No. You. You are.*

—*No, it's not that,* he said. —*You've been through a lot. It'll be easier closer to home.*

I had a new baby, which brought the head count at home up to five. I'd had a little bureaucratic skirmish with the SAC command, and I was forty-three.

Eisenhower was going around saying things like the Western World need never worry again. We had fought the war to end all wars.

The Joint Chiefs of Staff were warring among themselves, which is what is left to war against when there is no common enemy.

I got sent to MacDill while Marjorie and the children packed our things in Bermuda.

A cleanup operation could entail any of several things. You had your undesirable elements, your malcontents, your homosexuals, your suspected fellow travelers. Apparatchiks of a clear and present danger, so we believed. Then you had your very desirables, your steely doves who frequented the club in hopes of snagging some officer, a different clear and present danger, especially to the pilots. Not necessarily your streetwalker-caliber of woman. Sometimes they were the same faces you saw in the Sunday paper's society pages, the orchid over the ear, the strapless dress, the party girl face maintained to specs that matched Dorothy Lamour or Elizabeth Taylor or whoever was on the cover of *Photoplay* that month.

I liked to arrive incognito whenever I was transferred, give myself time to case the joint before all the shucking and jiving starts in the lower echelons. First night: a drink in the officer's club, and there was this hombre homesteaded at the end of the bar like this was his main haunt.

Clark Pomerantz. Thin lieutenant from one of those nowhere towns in upstate New York, which didn't keep him from feeling entitled to endless myopic critique and commentary about the rest of us. An alien chirruping out inept descriptions of the indigenous flora and fauna. Such creatures have their uses. Feed them a drink or two and the can of worms begins to open right before your very eyes.

He was working on this chick who he discovered to be an officer's wife, then he retreated. Then he tried to talk to the bartender, a guy in a white coat, a dead ringer for Xavier Cugat, only taller. No dice. Then he fixed his eyes on me, easy prey sitting there in my civvies and my regulation haircut, looking harmless.

The man had a demeanor like a bad breath. No other way to describe it. He gets near, you get the instinct to draw back.

—*Passin' through?* he asked, comradely.

I shrugged.

—*Welcome to the armpit of the Stategic Air Command*, he said. Materiel, he was in. —*We're between commanders right now.* Then he arched his brow. —*We ran the last guy off. We get the dregs here. We get the guys nobody wants anywhere else.*

I stirred my scotch and soda, clinked the ice companionably.

—*Ominous detente,* he shrugged. —*The whole country.*

—*You talking about my marriage or yours?* I joked. It was a common way of establishing trust.

I saw him file my joke and what it told him about me, lay it aside for future reference. I saw that he was the kind to traffic in the personal, to stockpile the domestic secrets of others against some future threat to himself. I filed that away for future use.

—*I'm not married,* he said, flip. —*Marriage is an outmoded institution.*

Another lieutenant came in, and Pomerantz perked up, alert. —*Be right back,* he says. He has this confab with the other guy, they look at the watches, an enlisted man appears at the service entrance to the club. Enlisted man is anxious. They go over, some money passes hands, into Pomerantz's. He comes back over to finish interrogating me.

Loansharking?

—*Lemme buy the next one,* Pomerantz says, and I hold my hand up, no. —*Well, lemme show you around,* he says. —*I have errands to run.*

It was the hangar at the edge of the tarmac. Always it is the hangar at the edge of the tarmac.

—*As you were,* I said to the pilot, out of reflex, when he saluted Pomerantz, and this was the first tip-off, the first warning buzzer to him. He ignored it. He took me further.

Officer out of uniform inspecting the contents of a wooden packing crate, Air Force issue. He signed the pilot off, logging up some expensive flight time in America's vigilance against the threat of Russian communism in the name of the Strategic Air Command and the *use,* fully "authorized," of a B-25 to make a run to the Eastern Seaboard to pick up a *running board* for a 1926 Ford touring car.

In this way Pomerantz delivered unto me the Director of Materiel of the 306th Bombardment Wing. Vincent Casbeer. West Point, 1933. Wholesale premium-grade clown.

—*Napier made his payment,* Pomerantz said to him.

Casbeer nodded at him, then at me, fondled the board. He motioned us over to a steel cooler, the kind used for the transport of explosives, encased in Air Force wool blankets. He opened the lid, and there was a load of two dozen steel-grey New England lobster, on ice.

—*Catch of the day off Cape Ann,* he said, then straightened up to assess me. —*For the Moonshooters party tonight. Like to join us?*

—*We may be the armpit of SAC*, said Pomerantz, —*but we are not without our vestiges of civilization here. We employ only the finest.*

I filed it away. Secondary purpose of the jaunt. Moon-asshole-shooters.

—*The commander lets you do this?* I asked, acting impressed.

—*What he doesn't know won't hurt him*, Pomerantz says, Puts his thumb into the moment and pulls out a plum and says, What a good boy am I. —*We have a strong working relationship with the pilots and ground crew. In a manner of speaking.*

One more stop before I am delivered back to the BOQ. Quarters of the enlisted men. Pomerantz's errands. Quonset huts. You had Quonset huts divided by plywood, families in each quadrant. As if that was what a couple hundred years of pushing the Indians off the land had netted us: the right to bivouac our own in similar squalor. Damn Quonset huts.

We pulled up in the jeep in front of one where a woman in a cheap rayon dress, the kind a pert New York secretary might have worn in 1942, sat nursing an exceedingly ugly child. That was what it had come to: the Okies and the Appalachians and the Alabama coal mine trash, living in steel teepees. The officers were like landed gentry compared to the enlisted men.

This was an increasing problem with me in 1957. It was in me like some bad seed, some awful black growth that would not stop: my inability to muster the old reverence for the Air Force.

It was Napier we had come to see. Alabama coal-mine trash. Napier was the senior sergeant of the ground crew, at the ripe old age of twenty-four. Red hair like mine used to be. Lean, earnest face, like mine used to be. He had a patch of grass six by six to call his own, temporarily, in front of the end of the Quonset hut assigned to him. A wife, a baby: all the accoutrements of the American life of the gentleman of the species. He was using the patch to build a little catboat. He had it flipped over on steel drums, sanding it tenderly.

—*The men say to tell you they're not interested.* This from Napier. There is no dignity like what those miners' sons take with them when they leave those hills.

—*You can tell them I said to get interested.* This from Pomerantz. —*There will be no leaves granted until they get interested.*

—*Interested in what?* I asked, casually. Ever so casually. Come to me, you son of a bitch.

—*Weekend work.* Pomerantz was irritated. —*Sons of bitches expect overtime pay every time they fart.*

I could already see it all, how each new transferred officer had contracted the same infection, so that no matter who was there, the basic malignance of the place had remained the same for years. My hand was itchy to excise. If thy right-hand man offend thee, cut him out.

I met Pomerantz for dinner at the club. You could not exactly say it was entrapment. I never lied to him. He just never inquired who I was.

—*You look like you could use a good fuck,* he said.

I shrugged. —*Can't everybody?*

He was scribbling names on a napkin. Phone numbers. —*You have stumbled into the happy hunting ground,* he said.

—*Are you a hunter?* I asked. —*You seem to be an all-round Renaissance man.* Open unto me, Shylock. Bloom like the black flower.

"—*So much depends upon a red wheelbarrow, glazed with rainwater, beside the white chickens,*" he recited. He liked that. —*We live in an age of moral decadence,* he said. —*Thank god.*

—*So what are you?* I asked. —*Are you one of these bohemian beatnik types?*

The veil came down, but not before I saw him file that question away for future use. He shook his head. —*I think of myself as a con-*

noiseur of good times, good women. Arbiter of moral taste in a tasteless world.

We were joined by a Col. Weber and his wife. Weber was a dyed-in-the-wool tightass. You could see that it went back for generations. There was this discussion of something, I can't even remember. The wife, a small and plump blond woman, weighed in with an opinion. It's a blank in my head what she said; I just remember the way the colonel somehow clicked his fingernails, just the merest gesture of irritation with her. She fell silent, spent the remainder of the meal with eyes on her plate or lap, and we did not hear her voice again. Though I discovered that I wanted to.

I knew that game, I'd played it myself. Survey, assess, command. Gain control of the environment. Keep the wife quiet, use your body to threaten her with from across four feet of white linen tablecloth.

That was on a Friday. On Monday morning I reported to my command. Pomerantz and Casbeer were among the welcoming committee, along with a burly one who looked like he escaped from a navy brig. Cappie Duncan, the base chaplain, face etched with tiny blue veins that read like a roadmap back into every drink he'd ever had in his life. My secretary was a Lt. David Raven, from South Dakota.

Let the shucking and jiving begin. Their jaws were a little slack when it hit them who I was. Pomerantz squirming in an agony, a veritable halo of ineptitude surrounding his head. Casbeer friendly as a three-peckered dog all of a sudden.

—*Colonel Casbeer,* I said, —*my first official command to you is that you circulate your log of all flights and their purposes through this office within twenty-four hours of the requested flight.*

—*Yes sir.*

—*Pomerantz.*

—*Sir.*

—*You will circulate through this office photostatic evidence of all goods and materiel received.*

—*Yes sir.*

There was this brief, brief moment of silence.

The last grace period I had in my military career, really. The few weeks they spent trying to figure out if this was merely my way of trying to get a piece of the action, to deal myself into the game.

Sleaze only knows how to translate all it sees into more sleaze. Honor is a language incomprehensible. They walk around it, scratching their heads as if it is some old wrecked fuselage encrusted with vines.

—*Chaplain.*

—*Sir.*

—*You will spend three days among the men at Wherry Housing and write a status report. Title: "The Morale of Enlisted Men and Non-Commissioned Officers at MacDill Air Force Base." Your primary contact will be Sergeant Wycliffe Napier.*

—*Yes sir.*

—*Raven.*

—*Sir.*

—*From what pothole in the universe do you hail?*

In this manner I delivered myself unto them. Wholesale. The gauntlet was down.

Then my wife and children arrived a few days later and the potential for holocaust was real.

I went shopping in Tampa before their visit. For *her*, I bought a green dress, a lovely thing that I wanted to see her in. For Field, *The Wonder Book of the Air*, a boy's encyclopedia of flight. For Allie, little red-haired dervish and delight of my life, a pink tutu and tights. Ballerina time. I cannot remember what I got Phoebe. I got Melvina a red petticoat, as per the Margaret Mitchell book.

Marjorie accepted the new dress with the kind of apathy that she lived in. I knew she would not wear it for me. She said, —*Why do you always think it will fix everything if you buy a woman some clothes?*

Field ran away to seclude himself with *The Wonder Book of the Air*, dream his boy's dreams of dirigibles and zeppelins.

Melvina did not get the joke but smiled in spite of herself at the red petticoat.

Allie was entranced with the pink tutu and hugged my knees, and I knew that if I wept before them I would never command them anymore. So I walked outside. Stared out at the ordinary Florida horizon and thought, *It will work this time. I will make it all work.*

It was some days before I realized the tutu had vanished.

—*Redheads can never wear pink*, Marjorie said when I asked about it, that petulant voice she had when she was a college girl. —*You think every female can wear Mamie pink?* she added in that older voice that reminded me of her mother.

What ensued was not one of the finer periods of my life.

This had a lot to do with why I sometimes bypassed my own house after work. There had been some times before when I had hurt her. There were some things she said I did that I do not remember.

The first time, in Leavenworth, I could not believe it had happened. More amazing was the tenderness it brought from her later. It was real, the tenderness afterwards. That first time. After that it was pure theater. Stage productions to belie the fact that what we had in our little museum was nothing. Nothing. What was different about this time was that we had entered a new phase—we were tired of the little theater of the boudoir, in which she played the wronged woman and I played the penitent man, pestilential in the things I needed from her.

She sat smoking at her dressing table, eyeing me in the mirror. We had learned to conclude the little dramas with silence. There was nothing to say, no emotional promises.

—*You know, I used to pray sometimes that you would die,* she announced in this raspy whisper. —*Up there. I used to pray that you wouldn't come home. What do you think of that?* she asked. —*How will you punish me now for thinking that? What is there left to do to me?*

—*Well, I wish you godspeed,* I said. The script seemed to call for bitterness, but I didn't feel any. I didn't feel *anything*, and that was frightening.

The nadir of your life is the holiest. There is a point at which you will opt for life you don't even understand yet. Something guides, something takes over and navigates because you are temporarily *hors de combat*. This is the true wonder book of the air, the secret flight manual tattooed inside you, brought into blossom by clear and present dangers to you. The best to hope for is to find it navigable.

So I had too easy an excuse to frequent the officers' club. And I wanted to observe Pomerantz more.

He wanted to buy my drink. I bought my own.

—*To a state of ominous detente,* I raised my glass.

—*A state of ominous detente,* he parroted, held magically in abeyance by the differences in insignia on our uniforms, my magic stars, my little fierce bird. I drank for pleasure. He drank for information.

—*To the continued stellar service of the 306th Bombardment Wing*, he said.

—*To the continued loyal apparatchik-hood of your class, genus, phylum, and species*, I said. That word rattled him. The A-word.

Here's the truth. I knew better. I knew better than to goad him. I did it anyway. I did it the way the man alone in the mountains puts the bullet in the chamber and spins. Always it had been like this, that I would reach the point of no return. I had reached some kind of interior altitude so dangerous that you don't care anymore if there are survivors.

—*Where do they go, the girls we marry?* I did not know that I had said this aloud until Pomerantz offered once again that marriage was an outmoded institution.

—*You know what the biggest security threat to this country is today?* He was in earnest now. —*Take a guess. Sir.*

—*What.*

—*The wives of the officers of the Strategic Air Command.*

—*Brief me, Lieutenant.*

—*They are lonely. They need people to talk to. If you want the skinny at this base, you don't talk to the personnel, you talk to the wives of the personnel.*

Then he was off to enter without knocking the conversation of some wives. Quisling par excellence. Growth potential as an officer extremely limited. There could be no greater service to my country than to take this man *down*.

This is soldiering during peacetime. I had met the enemy. He was *us*.

These were the things you could not utter then.

Cappie the chaplain reported to me that the enlisted men lived without meat most days. Fatback in the greens, maybe. They lived without hot water, they lived without heat. There was a baby that was scarred for life from playing too near a kerosene stove. There was a wife who had died from septicemia; the baby was anemic. There was more. These are the things I remember. The upshot of it was that MacDill had the lowest reenlistment rate in the United States.

Sooner or later it always came down to this. What we referred to as the chickenshit factor.

I formed a committee. The chaplain, the flight surgeon, the Air Provost Marshall. The president of the officers' wives auxiliary, Olivia Weber. Our Lady of the Downcast Eyes at the Dinner Table. I directed them to draw up a plan to, in short, fix Wherry Housing. Fix the food situation, the heat, the women, the sick babies.

The woman lingered after the meeting. She looked like something you would see carved on the prow of a Swedish ship. She looked at me like she wasn't afraid of me, and like she'd never spent a moment of her life shucking and jiving, and this was pleasing to me.

—*They're calling you the Estes Kefauver of MacDill.* She laughed. —*They say you're taking names and numbers in the club.*

I blushed. She laughed again, but it didn't bother me. I had knocked my wife down for lesser laughter. This woman could put me at ease. Then she got serious. —*You won't win, you know. They will. This isn't Hollywood. The baddies always win.* And thus she began to deliver herself to me, though it was months before I understood the package had arrived.

I had Raven infiltrate the base newspaper and publish the regulations concerning weekend work, mess hall standards, entitlements of dependents receiving medical care. Like flares tossed to the enlisted men to light their way out.

I met with the MPs to persuade them to quit beating the airmen who ended up in the guardhouse.

—*You don't get a guy to quit drinking and report to work by giving him reason to drink more.* I said this as they sat in dress uniform. They scratched their heads, tried to interpret. I tried another tack. —*You beat a man under my command and I'll ship your ass to the Azores.* Instant increase in comprehension, one hundred percent.

I knew it would begin anew the moment I was transferred to a new post, but for my tenure there, the beatings ceased.

I revised the purchasing and contracting procedures. I neutered Casbeer. He counteroffered with an invitation for me to join the Moonshooters.

I declined. Fatal error number one. I have never had the inclination to belong to purely social claques. I do not require an audience like some men do. I have always gotten by. Mostly on the faith in me of one good woman at the time. Or the *illusion* of said-same.

Wherry Housing yielded up a cartoonist, a kid from Oregon. Lovely pictures of bosomy women, like Vargas girls, but emaciated from BX shopping. He did one of a platoon of lobster goosestepping across the tarmac: *Anything to protect our native soil.*

Fatal error number two. I could have stopped that.

Fatal error number three. When I befriended Napier.

Understand: it wasn't *done*, fraternizing with enlisted men.

Understand also: it was a kind of narcissism I had. As if he were the key to my raising those reenlistment rates.

There was this kid in the guardhouse who had stolen food from the BX. Some ground-crew lowlife. Money in his pocket to pay, yet he stole. They take him to the guardhouse, he pulls out a knife, he cuts the MP in the face.

The *face.* Over a can of Spam, some olives, cheese.

—*Napier,* I said, —*you got to talk to this boy. Your assignment is to find out why.*

—*But the chaplain—*

—*No. You.*

The kid owed Pomerantz three months' pay. Blackjack losses.

—*Tell him those debts are forgiven,* I said.

—*It's not that easy,* Napier answered. —*I owe him some myself.*

A matter of honor? That kind of honor is coercion. The monkeys see the little dots on the dice, the monkeys get fearful. Totem is the basis of honor.

The Renaissance man himself was in the club the next time I was. I was there to talk to Olivia about the women. You might say she had the obstetric detail in regard to Wherry Housing. Only she had no children herself, so she was relating the details to me secondhand.

That pristine quality of the mind they have when they have not given birth. That is the charm.

—*So why the problems with the women?*

—*They don't know . . . how not to have babies,* she said delicately. —*The Waves at the hospital haven't been much help.*

—*The Waves probably don't know how not to, either,* I said, thinking of all those mannish goonlike creatures. —*You sound like my wife.*

Having babies is the root of all evil at Wherry? I said bitterly. It just boiled out of me without warning.

—*No,* she snapped at me. —*You think a baby is the only reason a woman has to be alive?*

Historic moment there. Like two creatures in adjacent harnesses stopping sullenly in their tracks: *You are like me.* Candor was a rare commodity in those days. We looked at each other across that table like we were compadres. That was probably the first time it ever occurred to me that women have different reasons to be infidels.

—*The doctors don't care.*

—*So the solution is to make them care?*

She nodded. —*They'll lie about the stats. You have to do your own stats.*

Partners in crime. Peacetime skirmishes. Memo wars. You fight for what there is to be fought for.

I saw her again after that at a large party at the club. Marjorie had stayed home. I was standing talking to Casbeer and I could see her from across the room. She was wearing an azalea-colored dress. I saw her husband come up to her, take her drink from her hand, and push her into a bathroom, locking the door behind them. The way her heels had clattered, the way that women are doll-like when they are being shoved around. Some women like being actresses in the little spitfire tragedies performed for the benefit of others. She didn't. I saw her later, and she had been crying.

—*Are you okay?*

—*Please don't talk to me,* she said. —*It will only make things worse.*

—*I just asked you if—*

Pomerantz enters the conversaton without knocking. Some snide-assed remark about the condition of the steaks in the officers' mess.

—*Pomerantz,* I said.

—*Sir.*

—*From this day forward you will maintain a distance of thirty feet between yourself and me at all times. You are an oaf, and a boor. There is an MP in the hospital with a gash on his face for the sole reason that you are a poltroon, and I require you to pay restitution to him in the amount of three months of your pay.*

They both looked at me as if I had stepped out on the edge of

somewhere, and I had. Altitude of the kamikazes: white, holy
rage, like fire in a fallow place.

—*We are not without our vestiges of civilization here, Pomerantz.*

Fatal error number four. The bullet was in the chamber, spinning. What else was there to fight for in my life?

—*You've got one month in which to complete the physical exam,* the
flight surgeon said to me one morning. —*Orders of Brigadier General
Van Cleve.*

—*Let me see it first,* I said. This was pro forma. Lose a few pounds.
Quit drinking for the weigh-in. —*Let me go over the goddamn form.*

It was the form they used for new pilots. For the kids.

I was forty-three.

I drew this to his attention and his slow, careful shrug told me
everything I needed to know: *But this is war, sir.*

There was a notice, standard, in the base newspaper that tests
would be administered on a Saturday to screen those men interested in a transfer to a new terrain: military advisement of civilians in a little, unheard-of place in the East called the Republic
of Vietnam. Passing score required, with recommendation from
commander.

Napier came to see me one morning, cap in hand. I was looking at a calendar some joker had sent me: itsy-bitsy-teenie-
weenie-yellow-polka-dot bikini as kind of an afterthought to the
girl in the picture.

—*I need to go,* he said. —*Onliest way to make something out of myself.
I wasn't born part of no aristocracy.*

We both knew it was his only chance. He'd come back, enter
OCS, emerge the other side of it a first lieutenant, and world trav-
eler to boot.

—*Bullshit,* I said. —*You see this?* I threw the calendar down on my
desk. —*That is the only aristocracy in this world, compadre. Lady female
member of the species homo sapiens human being. And she only gets to
have it for a little while, for the little while that belly remains firm. All
other forms of aristocracy are negotiable.* Pyrrhic thing, to utter to the
young what they have no wish to hear. You feel like you're giving
with one hand, taking away with the other. —*But I could be wrong,* I
added, searching his face for his future.

I ran into Olivia one day downtown in Tampa, her hair softly
blown, a long loaf of French bread under her arm.

—*This year's fashion accessory,* she said. —*De rigueur. It says so right here in Vanity Fair.* And made me laugh for the first time in days. We talked a little while about stupid things.

—*Let me buy you a drink,* I said, and it caught us both off guard. Her eyes narrowed a bit.

—*I am engaged in a serious research project vital to the national defense,* I said, and the grin that spread across her face warmed me somehow.

—*And that is?* she asked.

—*The serious lifelong study of the lady female member of the species homo sapiens human being,* I answered.

The smile faded from her face. I remember looking at the wisps of hair at her temples, trying to read them like hieroglyphs that might contain some mention of me.

—*Is this going to be one of those conversations where you talk about how your wife doesn't understand you?* She was only halfway irritated with me. —*Do you get it all on the table quickly, what you want, or are you the kind that likes to take his time? Maybe we will get all the way up to the place where you ask me if I am happy, and I say no, I am not happy, and you say sorry, there's not a damn thing you care to do about it. Look: I can save us both a lot of trouble: I am not happy. And if there's nothing you can do about it, if you are just a voyeur, then no, I do not want to have a drink with you.*

That was the way she was. Even the protocols of infidelity were meaningless to her. It made me a little frightened for her. I wanted to see tears in her eyes, real ones. I wanted some reason to go forward toward her. I wanted her to need me. She seemed only angry.

—*I have it on good authority that every sixty seconds is a second chance to start over,* I said. —*And get it right this time.*

—*Says who?*

—*My immortal Uncle Artie,* I said. —*Now deceased.* And she laughed.

—*Maybe sometime.*

One night, one other loveless night in my house, I lay on my back, contemplating the fact that I could not remember the last time a woman had loved me, and I felt like some parched, scorched creature. I thought of Olivia. I *thought* of her. My mind would spin these little lies to myself, that her hands were touching me. That her eyes were for me alone. And there was not a damn thing I could do about it.

Every sixty seconds is a new chance to stare at the sameness of the layout of all the ceilings you've ever lain under, at the pattern of the rivets that wall out the sky from you, nail heads like parodies of constellations made to march in single file. I wondered if I would ever sleep under bare sky again in my life. I thought of the river, in Alapaha, and wanted to be there. But *alone*.

Marjorie said she never saw me. She said the children didn't know me. This was in part true. Phoebe would wail whenever I came near her. So I stopped coming near her. Somewhat like the relationship I had with her mother.

—*You worry more about the trashy women in Wherry Housing than you do about your own family,* my wife sniffed.

No. You got that wrong. I worry more about Olivia than I do about you. This was the unutterable thing. It was as if the only way to save myself from what was happening at my house was to envision saving Olivia from whatever was happening at her house.

Which at this time was still secondary to the detritus of the Strategic Air Command, the day-to-day skirmishes and memo wars.

The memo, mine, stating that there would be no more seven-day shifts for the ground crew. No more night work for the boys who'd worked all day, no more pulling them from the hangars to drive the Buicks for the visiting brass of the Strategic Air Command.

The memo, Casbeer's, which Raven kept from me, requisitioning fuel alcohol.

The second request for fuel alcohol. Casbeer's. Also kept from me.

A memo, Cappie Duncan's, reporting on the death of the guardhouse kid. *Self-inflicted gunshot wound.*

Self-inflicted. Nice touch, that.

A memo, Pomerantz to Van Cleve, describing me as pugnacious evidence of the moral decline in the officer ranks: I had begun acquiring for my own personal use the names of ladies who frequented the officers' club without escorts. The suggestion that if I could overcome my "difficulties in dealing with his fellow man," there might be some hope for me.

A flight plan, filed by me. The unauthorized use of a transport plane to pick Field up in Georgia and ferry him to Montgomery when he blew his eye out with the cherry bomb. Aircraft checked out by one Sgt. Napier.

The memo, Van Cleve's, warning all that during the month of November there would be widespread unnannounced alerts, inspections. Also kept from me.

A memo, mine, explaining that while ultimately the proper mix of water-alcohol in the tanks rested with the base commander, there were extenuating circumstances.

A memo, mine, hat in hand, requesting the convening of a committee to effect my separation from the Air Force.

I handed Marjorie a copy of the last one.

She sighed. —*We can go home now,* she said, the smoke from her cigarette curling around her. —*We can live in my grandfather's house.* As if she had been waiting for this moment all along, to take me back home in my dress uniform, fresh from the taxidermists, and didn't I look natural?

THERE WAS A CLASSIFIED AD in the base newspaper, with photo: Napier had put his boat up for sale. *Seaworthy catboat, never been used. Must sell, owner transferred East.* I put down the paper and drove to Wherry.

—*Don't sell your boat, man. A man needs a boat. How much cash do you need?*

He shrugged. I gave him three hundred dollars. I couldn't spare it, but that boat. That sweet boat. Handmade. The green trim. The brass lanyards.

I took out a piece of paper, a receipt from the base laundry and began to scribble on it. —*This is not a bill of sale, Napier. This is an escrow agreement. I am holding that boat in escrow until you bring your ass back to the States to get it.*

He grinned at me. —*The boys are throwing me a party Christmas Eve at the Blue Azalea. I'd be honored if you could come.* His face had this tic, as if he knew that he'd gone out on a limb here to show any wish, hope, desire for anything in this world.

I'm telling you: we were all these tight compartments of fear.

—*Bob Wills is playing,* he added.

—*Jesus, Napier*, I laughed. —*You are talking to the original Texas swing aficionado. I heard him in San Antonio in the forties. Son of a bitch caused my ass to get married, him and his music.* But I didn't commit to showing up for his party, or anything. I'd left that world behind after the war, after my brother Red was shot in Montgomery.

Sixteen, he was. AWOL, too. Red hair like mine, earnest face like mine. Digging the sounds of some black cats with clarinets.

The scenes would come to me some nights when I tried to sleep. How my mother would tie a rope around his waist and tie the other to the clothesline while she weeded the garden. Then my mind would start making up scenarios, the MPs always looking like Hitler Youth.

—*I ain't goin' back there.*

—*Yes, you are, buddy.*

—*But that is WAR, sir.*

I towed the boat home. It was a week before Christmas and there was that false feeling that that brings in Florida. As if it's not winter, it's just business as usual, with poinsettias and tinsel the only indication that time is passing. She was sitting in the living room with Melvina, and she was looking into a box of German blown-glass Christmas ornaments, the best Neiman Marcus had, as if they were some new insurmountable obstacle in her life. Like me. It occured to me that a man ought not to have to pause in his own driveway and talk himself into the completion of the rest of his life.

—*I ain't goin' back there.*

—*Yes, you are, buddy.*

—*But that is WAR, sir.*

Every house we'd lived in had virtually the same driveway, it seemed to me.

—*We're overdrawn at the bank*, she said, in lieu of hello.

I looked at her and went upstairs.

—*Christmas is one week away*, she called up to me. —*I suppose we could give the children a boat ride for Christmas morning. Or sell it.*

I came back down. —*You touch that boat, you'll regret it.*

I remember the way Allie and Phoebe would clutch at her skirts. Her the port, me the storm. I remember the way Field would just vanish. I remember the way Melvina would keep on with the laundry, the dishes, the cooking, as if nothing were going on. I told myself I was assessing the state of affairs. I told myself that if I said nothing, did nothing, I'd force her into kindness to me.

One afternoon I took my son out in the boat. I was not a sailor. It was calm on Tampa Bay. I didn't know what we were doing out there. How we had come to be there. The father-son bit. All I knew was, it had something to do with driving. You set out to pick up a lady female member of the species *homo sapiens* human being; you wake up years later with a little boy with your own face, sitting in the stern of a boat, judging you.

—*Let's paddle*, I suggested. —*We ain't lost, we is exploring*. But he kept turning the boat. We kept turning, and turning, and turning, and others were looking at us.

—*You're drunk,* he said, the little hanging judge.

I watched him, his bent head. I'd seen a piece in the paper about a man in Michigan who murdered his whole family, sons and daughters, dogs and cats, and, most importantly, the missus. Then turned it on himself, like a proper Sunday-dinner patriarch, waiting until everyone else has been served before he fills his own plate.

—*You don't know how to do this, do you?* Field said.

I slapped him then, seeing my own hand come up before my eyes like some foreign thing that had nothing to do with me. There was nothing to call me back, no reason to stop myself after that, other than the reason that one more slap could turn the boat over. It was that that called me back.

—*All right,* I said. —*Let's see you do better.* I held out the paddle. He stared at it, the red imprint of my hand on his face.

—*Take it, goddamn it,* I snarled at him. —*I want to see you do as well, compadre.*

He began to cry as the paddle dipped into the water feebly and he could hardly raise it from side to side. The boat lurched and wobbled, began a horrible comic circling, my voice booming, —*Do it, come on and do it. You don't know how to do this, do you?*

I understood the dead man in Michigan more than I understood anything. He was a holy man. He had committed a profound act of mercy. The only way to get ground clearance from God to kill himself was to kill his children first. It was cost-efficient risk management, as the military might put it.

The clarity, the logic of it all. The loneliest form of understanding in the world. Didn't anyone understand this besides me? I drank until I passed out that night.

On Christmas Eve the missus came to me with a tear-streaked face. The radio was full of that Gene Autry song, *Here comes Santa Claus, here comes Santa Claus, right down Santa Claus Lane.*

—*I need to do the Christmas shopping.*

—*Come on, come,* I said. —*A little kiss is apropos for Santa Claus. Let me see you whore for your children. I'll give you the money, but you'll work for it. The essential transaction, my Uncle Artie used to say.*

When the going got too rough for her, she had this way of summoning Allie. She had this instinct that Allie could charm me, hold me at bay for her. I have read that Arab terrorists do the same thing with children, use them as shields.

She was her own compartment of fears.

Memory is about as controllable as prop wash. Sometimes you just have to stay out of its way. My memory of the rest is like that. Turbulence of the unseen thing that can buffet you. I went down into the basement to try to put together a little red tricycle I had bought before. It wasn't going very well, and I was still drinking. There was a fisted rage inside me, a gnarled, clenched thing. But I wanted to surprise Allie. I wanted to see the wonder in her face.

I forgot to lock the basement door. I didn't hear Allie come up behind me, but suddenly I sensed her there.

—*Dada?* she said.

—*Get out!* I screamed at her. —*Get out! I said get out of here!* It was not my voice I heard boil out of me. It was someone else's. Like I was listening with perfect ironic detachment to someone else's life come apart at the seams.

By three in the afternoon, Marjorie had put the kids in the car and driven off to shop. I was drunk. Melvina had gone home. Even Cruiser, the dog, sat on the kitchen floor and rebuked me with his baleful eyes, and I wanted to kill him. By seven I was at the Blue Azalea. I didn't want to see Napier sail off into his life with that same earnest face I used to wear.

Napier was there with the ground crew. His wife was a frail-looking thing with bad teeth. She would go back to Gadsden, Alabama, when he shipped out. They were all there with their women. I was already beginning my reentry into the world I had come from.

Bob Wills was in fine fiddling fettle. —*This is a song I first started thinking about back in Limestone County, Texas, before the war. Now, you may be thinkin', Which war, Bob? Okinawa? Korea? It's all the same war. And I don't even know where the gal is now that I wrote it for. Maybe I don't want to know. And so this song's for you, boys. But you gotta get off your butts and dance. You ain't even kicked up a good dust in here yet.*

I looked at Bob Wills standing up there playing for the enlisted men, felt the pull of that bass backbeat, felt the pull of the years like gravity yoking his shoulders. But here he was, and he was in his spangled Texas dress, exhorting us all along the path of life, describing it to us in a lanky drawl. Bob Wills was forever after for me what the ticking alarm clock wrapped in the towel is to the new puppy.

> *Deep within my heart lies a melody,*
> *A song of old San Antone.*
> *When in dreams I live with a memory,*
> *Beneath the stars all alone.*

The guys got up with their women, like bears exhorted to schottische to the "Hoopaw Rag."

It can make a God-fearing man of you. That sight: the same lummoxes who can load the bombs into the bomb bays, humbled by a fiddler. The women, all with that pale-dregs-of-Britannia skin we all had. Like displaced persons spat out of wherever they came from, trying to make the best of the new terrain in the cheap dresses. They couldn't afford nylons. Napier could move his woman around, controlling her every turn with one hand on her neck, one on the small of her back.

This made me exceedingly surly about my life. I didn't need to hear the rest of the song, I'd lived it: *It was there I found beside the Alamo, enchantment strange as the blue up above* . . . The beat was like a swift river current, and the bodies jostled a little and finally stopped, hands clapping in collective thunder.

Don't give me no bohemian beatnik poet in Greenwich Village.

So much more depends on those who don't give a flying fuck about a red wheelbarrow glazed with rainwater beside the white chickens.

Give me Bob Wills on a buckling pine stage, one leg slightly ahead of the other, tapping that steel-toed cowboy boot to some metronome inside himself.

You could say that music is the culprit in my life, always has been. I felt like I needed to get out of there. But I felt a need to acquit myself with Napier. I got a paper cocktail napkin and began to write on it. What I could remember of The Cadet Prayer.

> *O God our Father, Thou Searcher of men's hearts,*
> *Help us to draw near to Thee.*
> *Suffer not our hatred of hypocrisy and pretense ever to diminish.*
> *Make us choose the harder right instead of the easier wrong.*

I rolled it up and walked over and tucked it in Napier's breast pocket. I thought the fool was going to stop there in the middle of the dance floor and salute me.

—*As you were, fool,* I laughed. —*Don't ever drop my name anywhere. They'll ship you to the Azores.*

—*My grandaddy had this sayin'*—this was Napier's way of trying to acquit himself of me. —*"Who you are has tuck you this far, and who you are will take you anywhere you want to go."*

—*Well,* I said, —*I'm giving serious thought to putting my application in with the Brotherhood of Sleeping Car Porters.* Even as I boxed him gently on the shoulder, I felt this fetal tremor of fear, the suspicion that all my trafficking in the world was no longer based on anything human, it was all based on the barbaric silver bird on my uniform, the primary purpose of which was to conjure fear and respect among subordinates.

I was going to leave. Then I saw her, Olivia, over with some of the other officers and their wives. No husband. He wasn't there. I watched for an hour from the bar. She seemed more like the type to want Handel's *Messiah* for Christmas, and she looked out of place in the Blue Azalea, red sequin dress, black orchid on her wrist. For whom?

I moved across the room toward her. She had moved toward me. We met in the middle of the dance floor, and neither one of us knew how to two-step, so we just held each other a minute. I looked over the top of her head to the stares of the other officers of the Strategic Air Command, and I'd like to think that my eyes issued some sort of invitation to them: *Make it swift, soldiers. Shall I draft your memos for you?*

We stopped out on the porch of that place, and there was a fine, generous rain coming, and I could not remember the last time I had smelled warm rain on a tin roof. I could not remember the last time I had felt such plenitude.

—You know what the greatest threat to the security of the Strategic Air Command is?

—What? She was as breathless as a girl for me. But I saw the little lines at the corners of her eyes. She was no girl, and I was both frightened and comforted by this. *—What is the greatest threat?*

—Me, I said. *—I am lonely. And I think you are too. And I'd like to do something about that. Or try to.*

She put her arms around me and put her forehead against my chest like she needed to steady herself. Like I was what she needed to steady herself. Me. It was a novel feeling, something I'd not had in years, respect and need from a lady female member of the species *homo sapiens* human being.

—Will you regret this night? I said into her hair.

If she said, *Never, ever,* I would walk away.

She didn't answer.

—I can't make any promises, I said.

She shrugged. *—I no longer believe in them anyway.*

—I'm flying on instruments, I said, and I knew somehow that here was a woman who could take my teasing. *—Visibility is poor. I got no compass, no chart. I got this way of totally forgetting about how the earth can CURVE on you.*

—That makes two of us, she laughed. It felt like it was going to be different this time, this woman. It felt like we were going somewhere, embarking on a big trip. She ran out in the rain and I felt lost a minute. But she was tucking the black orchid under a windshield wiper on Bob Wills's bus. She ran back and huddled against me, warm woman in a wet dress. I heard the voice of the kamikaze, my imaginary counsel, my enemy, issuing me some flight plans:

—You got the fear of death?

—Check.

—You got the love for every living thing?

—Check.

—*You got the warm woman in the wet dress? Lady female member of the species homo sapiens human being?*

—*Check.*

—*Only the kamikaze is privileged to know true flight. Flight clearance granted.*

I was already saying goodbye to my children, wishing them godspeed without me.

This is the lesson of war: the enemy's blood is red and salty like yours, and time will negotiate peace, with or without your consent. You may not live to see it.

This is the lesson of love: the beloved's blood is red and salty like yours. You have to negotiate your own peace. Or you may not live to see it.

These things are nigh unspeakable in any ear. You want the regret, the guilt, the remorse?

That is not within your purview.

This is my dime in the jukebox. I like my scotch just about the color of the water in the Alapaha River, and I ain't even kicked up a good dust in here yet.

A TRUE EXPLORER IS
NEVER LOST

*T*he afternoon that I got my degree from Baylor, I rode all night home, to my new job. To my next man trouble.

Austin Collins. Now there was a *man*.

Hired me sight unseen over the telephone, straight out of Baylor in 1959, partly because his wife Grace was my second cousin. —*Is this Adrienne?* he said. —*You ready to come to work?*

That was the personnel interview. He was building one of those Hill-Burton hospitals, little forty-bed thing. He needed a director of nursing. I could have taken better offers.

My mother had died, and there was no one to take care of my son, Jim, at home but my father, who was too old and sick since he had retired from his railroad job. My sister, Marjorie, could not be counted on to do what needed to be done, even though she and Harrison had come home from the Air Force, over some kind of woman trouble she wouldn't talk about.

I arrived in at the Alapaha Station depot at five in the morning. Sun barely up through the pines. Mailman waiting with the red wagon for the mail to be thrown off the train. —*Your daddy used to DRIVE that train, Adrienne,* he called to me. Miss Lil out in her zinnia beds with her ass up in the air. Got to get the jump on those weeds and everybody else's business. Old Cruiser sleeping in the middle of the highway like it was his road and he was very pleased not to be in Bermuda anymore. Business as usual.

I felt more of an oddity than ever. Before, I was just the only divorceé in town, and the only nurse. Now I was the only divorceé nurse with a master's degree. I had the makings of a real pariah.

I glanced over at my grandmother's old house when I walked down the sidewalk carrying my bags. No lights on. Marjorie and Harrison were living in it with their three kids. He'd left the Air Force. "Retired" was the euphemism Marjorie was using. I did a double-take when I saw the huge vegetable garden in the field behind the house, the old basketball circle still right out in the middle. An odd homemade sailboat parked out back about where Aunt Lydia used to grow her vegetables. Weeds growing up around it.

When I tiptoed in the back door, I wasn't carrying anything but my train case, and all I wanted was to go fall in my bed. I wanted to peep in on Jim, my son, then I wanted to go brush my teeth and lie down.

I heard Harrison's voice in the kitchen. I went in, and there he was with Field and Jimmy and three other little boys I didn't know, and they all had on Cub Scout uniforms—those little yellow bandannas around their necks—and he had this big map unrolled on the table. All these little towheads bent over that map, and my little black-haired one. I just stood there a minute, drinking it all in like a deep drink I hadn't had in a long time. Home. My home.

Harrison was teaching them to read the legend on the map.

Field was playing with his compass, his head canted differently. The artificial eye. But Jim was listening. My little black-haired joy. He didn't look like his own father, he looked like *my* father. There is no gift greater than the sight of your own son.

Harrison looked up about then.

—Adrie, he said. —*I've commandeered your kitchen for my troops.*

He didn't have to explain to me why he would need my kitchen at this hour of the morning rather than his own. I knew my sister well enough not to ask.

—*Well, carry on, then,* I said and sat down with them. Nothing compares to the smell of little boys with the sleep still in their eyes.

Harrison had a detailed aerial photo of the Alapaha River, but the map was hand-drawn, and I recognized his handwriting all over it. *Lucy Lake, Sheboggy, Glory.* He had drawn the whirlpool on it, the place where it goes underground before it gets to the

Suwannee. He was letting them take turns holding an old astrolabe he'd got from somewhere.

He knew that river by heart. He was going to teach it to my son that way, by heart. Why had any of us ever left here, I wondered. What had impelled us away to founder on other shores? I knew that by heart: the war.

—*To resume*, Harrison said, tapping one of those stubby fingers on the map. —*The honorable Alapaha River. Our objective is Lucy Lake. Location of the last remaining artesian well in these parts, and the finest huckleberries you will ever put in your mouth. Ever drunk from an artesian well, Fisko?*

Fisko looked entranced, and passed the astrolabe to Jim.

—*Jim*, Harrison snapped. —*Tell your mother our motto.*

—*"A true explorer is never lost,"* Jim grinned at me, top front tooth missing.

—*That's not the way I taught it to you, boy*, Harrison growled.

—*"We ain't lost, we is EXPLORING,"* Jim shouted and grinned. The astrolabe in his hands had the power to make him sit up straight, like a little man.

—*Now repeat after me*, Harrison said. —*The earth curves, the earth curves.*

Merciful God, it hurts to remember that morning, that little black head among the towheads, and his ice-blue eyes. How I couldn't see down the road, the way I'd lose him.

I'd forgotten how Harrison was larger than the ordinariness of Alapaha. He was like that even as a kid, snapping that shoeshine rag in the depot, stringing all those old farts along with his various tidbits from the Macon *Telegraph*. Just biding his time until he could leave for good.

And now here he was back home for good, forty-one years old, and it had come to this: a West Pointer leading the Cub Scouts. I could look at that map, and think about the hours he probably spent on it, and I knew it wasn't going to work.

After I'd slept an hour, I reported to the old clinic where Austin Collins's office was, and he wasn't there, but Mattie, his cleaning lady, was. She started showing me around. I was standing in the examining room behind a shirred dressing screen wondering why in the name of God a licensed physician would keep three nasty tackleboxes in his examining room.

I didn't know then what I was in for; I mean, you were just as likely to find an old dead cigar in the autoclave as a suture.

Then I heard the door thrown open, and that rusty voice:

—Mattie! It's a goddamn beautiful day. I could frig 'em standing up today!

Mattie froze, bottle of Windex in one hand, rag on the window in the other. Then I stepped out from behind that screen with one of those damn tackleboxes, and that was the first and last time in my life that I ever saw Austin embarrassed at anything.

—Grace didn't tell me you were pretty, he said, and it made me feel like a hunchback.

I couldn't think of anything to say to that, so I said, *—The tackleboxes have got to go. This is a hospital.*

We were off and running from that point on.

It was a long way from Baylor, let me tell you. The patients were always stacked like cordwood in the waiting room. He was building himself a hospital not a minute too soon. Merciful God: the farm injuries, the nigras and their knives, the white trash and their runny-nosed offspring. The Mississippi pulpwooders were the worst. They'd cut all the trees in *their* state and they were on us like a locust plague. Ignorant as the day is long.

No incubator. First thing I did was try to talk the board into getting me one. I'll never forget standing in the John Deere dealership talking to that owner, rich as Croesus and couldn't recognize his own name if you wrote it in boxcar-size letters in the sky. President of the school board, no less, and some big secret deal in the Ku Klux Klan, if you could gauge it by the way the nigras feared him. I was wasting my breath on him.

—Well, do I care if they's a few little nigras lost? You be doin' them a favor, Miz Adrienne.

Saturday nights it was "Katie, Bar the Door." Austin, me, three LPNs. Couple of orderlies and Mattie. There wouldn't have been any money to pay other help, if we could have found any other help down there in the middle of nowhere.

—Missionary work, Austin used to say. *—Hill-Burton, hell. We should just rent the old hardware store across the alley from the pool hall,* he said. *—Then they could just roll 'em across to us.* This was one time when he was putting some stitches behind a nigra pulpwooder's ear. His name was Motee. Sitting there like a patient old hound, head cocked.

—Motee.

—Yassuh.

—You are temporarily hors de combat. You got to get your women under control.

—Yass. Suh. Sho do.

All members present knowing full well Motee is going to be there with *bells* on come Saturday night next, reeking and bleeding. And some gal would be in there birthing a new one, welcoming some new little wretch into the whole grand mess.

—Reekin' and bleedin', Austin used to say cheerfully, passing me in the hall, white lab coat flapping. *—Reekin' and bleedin' and lambin' time! Is the moon full, or what? I haven't had time to look.*

One Saturday night the place was really jumping. Hoyt Benefield was about to breathe his last on one end of the hall, and a little nigra gal was in labor on the other. November by then, raining to beat the band outside. Austin comes flapping in in his old mackinaw, dripping all over Mattie's clean floor. The damn cigar in the mouth. The orderlies had a poker game going in the supply room, and he wanted in on it.

—Look, you can't do this, I said. *—It's like Grand Central Station here tonight. We got one going out and one coming in.*

He gave me a look like, *—Not now, lemme finish this one hand.*

I went back there, and there was nothing I could do for Mr. Hoyt except wait. The blueness had all settled toward the bottom, gravity being stronger than the force of his heart at that point.

So I kept watch over the girl, who was all of fifteen.

When the baby's head began to crown, I went back to the supply room.

—You better get in there, that baby's almost here.

He waved me away.

—I'm not coming in here again, I told him. *—I got better things to do than be your damn air traffic controller.*

So I was sitting in what we called the OR, holding a warm towel against that girl's perineum. She was in twilight, and I felt like some kind of horse doctor out in the barn. My shoulders hurt, and I was wishing that gal would get up off that table and let *me* lie down on it for a while. The head was through. I felt somebody come in behind me, and I knew from the cigar smell who it was.

—*Well, look at you go,* he said. —*They didn't teach you that at Baylor.*

—*Nope,* I said. —*I learned that from a midwife in Savannah.*

You don't get any tearing that way, see. I almost got kicked out of the program at Candler over it, too, when I bounced into my instructor's delivery room and laid that piece of news on him while he was stitching up a patient he'd let rip from stem to stern.

Austin, God love him, was not like that. His curiosity always got the better of his ego. Like watching me deliver that nigra baby. I thought he would take over when the shoulders were coming through, but he just stood back, like he was daring me. I thought, *Damn you, I'll just DO it.*

And I did. Cut the cord, clamped, the works.

—*You know that's against the rules,* he said. As if he had ever given a damn about the rules.

—*You broke the rules, buster, not me. Just sign the certificate. Or do you want me to forge your name?*

—*Why didn't you just let her tear? You could have kept her out of the pool hall for another month or two. She's just going to be right back in here ten months from now.*

I just looked at him. —*I was once a sixteen-year-old in labor.*

That was the night something changed between us.

We got too aware of each other, watched each other too much. I got to liking going to work too much; I got to liking the sound of that rusty voice too much. But even then, I could keep my wits about me, just watch him from a distance, keep his clinic running the way he liked it, keep it all strictly business. Just try to make him feel loved from a distance.

I always felt a quiet kind of astonishment at him. He had this way of closing out the whole world—nothing in it but him and his patient. I used to think that somebody could have test-dropped an A-bomb in the parking lot and he'd not even have looked up. He was one of the best surgeons I'd ever seen, and it all seemed inconsequential to him.

When we opened the new hospital, after the speeches and the ribbon cutting, I was standing by the empty punchbowl feeling stupid to be wearing high heels in a hospital, and the president of the hospital board was bending my ear about what a crime against nature it was for a fine-looking woman such as myself to go to waste, and *blah, blah, blah*. Me knowing full well that his wife had just been in to see Austin the week before, and he'd referred her to a surgeon in Jacksonville. Lump in the left breast. Everybody knew what was coming, including him.

I was tired that night because I'd been packing at the clinic all day, and I had taken off my mother's pearls and was fingering them like some kind of rosary. Austin walked up to the board president and said, *–You'd make better time with her if you'd buy her an incubator.* Then he reached over and pulled that string of pearls through my fingers slowly, as if he had all the time in the world for me, and dropped them in his shirt pocket and walked off.

He might as well have reached into me for my secret heart and walked off with it in his pocket. Next thing you know, I was standing there flushed and about as inconspicuous as some alleycat streetwalker on a corner, holding a hundred helium-filled balloons. All colors.

And my cousin Grace standing not even ten feet away.

Merciful God.

Monday morning I said, *–Where are my pearls?*

–You can have them back when you get that incubator out of old Atlee.

–You can go to hell, I called after him as he walked, laughing, down the hall, and Mattie looked at me like I'd lost my mind.

But I got my incubator. A few months later, Harrison worked some kind of shady deal with the Air Force surplus, and the Boy Scouts presented it to us in the newspaper office. That was when Harrison met Austin, when they had to stand together for the picture. Fast friends, inside of ten minutes. The drinking, the fishing, the cussing.

–I'll take my pearls back now, I said. Austin just laughed, and patted his pocket.

Harrison raised his eyebrow and gave me a look: *Watch your step, Adrie.*

I tossed my head and shot him a look right back: *YOU'RE a fine one to talk.*

One afternoon I looked across to Harrison and Marjorie's backyard, and there were Austin and Harrison, with that old boat of Harrison's upended on sawhorses, and that odd little old toolbox that used to be Artemus Elliot's. They were sanding away, making big plans. I wanted to think of Austin free to just get in a boat and go sit in sunlight and pleasure, somewhere away from the sick, the dying.

I walked over to inspect their work, and tease them a little. They had decided to name the boat and have a christening ceremony at the river.

Alapaha Star. There on the side in Austin's prescription-pad script. It made me dizzy to see it, that handwriting that I never *meant* to love so. It made me remember too much the time when I could sit in a man's lap and dream of wearing a red dress on a make-believe train, one that never made it off the drawing board.

Then there was the night I walked into the hospital kitchen because it smelled like something was burning in there, and there were Austin and Harrison, sitting on high stools they lifted from the lab. Austin with the big leather ledger in his lap, ripping pages out, throwing them in the big stainless steel sink. Had himself a small bonfire going in one side, a right good mess of fish in the other. Harrison cleaning the fish, supervising the burning. A fifth of scotch between them.

—*Look! You can't do this. This is a hospital.*

—*You watch me,* Austin said. He tore out a page, read it. —*Johni-ette Exum. Appendectomy. Two hundred dollars.* Then he threw it in the fire. Looked up at me with a face full of grief. —*Adrie, if I died tonight, you know what would happen?*

—*What?*

—*Grace would try to make all these people pay.* He ripped another page. —*There go your new drapes, Grace.* Rip. —*There goes your next Chanel suit, your Cartier watch, your Florida room built on the foundation of human misery.*

I reached over and turned on the water. —*Mattie's going to get you for messing up her kitchen,* I said over the hissing and stinking. He was drunker than I thought, because he just smiled at me. I smiled at him, not quite knowing what to say that would help him. —*No rest for the weary, is it? There's nobody in Thirteen. Why don't you go back and get some sleep?*

—*Only if you come lie down with me.* He didn't care if Harrison heard or not.

—*Don't start with me, mister,* I said, but the thought of it made me almost fall down. Lying with him.

Austin went to lie down.

Harrison just looked at me. —*Adrie*.

—*What*. I had wet paper and fish heads in my hands. But I was smiling.

—*You are building your house upon the sand*.

He was like that. You'd think he was moon-drunk, just *out* of it, and he'd lower the boom on you, see right *through* you.

—*I know this flight instructor at Moody Field*, he said. —*Divorced guy*.

—*I don't have time for that*.

—*But what is going to become of you?*

—*Why don't you tend your own little patch, Harrison?*

I will say this of Harrison. He was the one you want in the foxhole with you. The man would stand by you, even when he was doing good to *stand*, period. Daddy used to say to me, —*You've got to do something, that's your sister over there, you've got to go give her a helping hand*.

—*But it's also a man and his wife and it's not really my business*.

But of course it was. You talk about missionary work. Every night Phoebe, the youngest one, would run away from home as soon as everybody was asleep good. Like a rat trying to get off the sinking ship, I guess. Nobody locked any doors then. She'd just come crawl in bed with Daddy. Half the time they wouldn't even miss her till the middle of the next morning. I'd stop by over there sometimes on the way home from work, take Allie and Phoebe some little things I picked up in the dimestore. It would be almost night, and Marjorie would be sitting there watching the six-o'-clock news, like there's no need to get a meal on the table for those children. Harrison would be off somewhere. I don't know what she did all day. Smoked, I guess. The house was a mess. Melvina came one day a week. I went over there one night in February to take Phoebe and Allie some little red Valentine nightgowns, and they were running around in their panties and no slippers, and it was cold in the house. Marjorie acted like she didn't have a care in the world.

—*Marjorie, let's take the train to Savannah Saturday. There's a sale at Levy's; you can get these girls some things. Get you some things*.

—*No*.

—*Why not?*

—*Then I have to ask him for money*.

—*What's wrong with that?*

—It makes me feel like his prostitute. It makes him think he owns me.

They had their big last blowup not long after that, and he left for good. Came over to say goodbye, and left a box of things for me to give Jim, because he knew it was Jim's ambition to be a soldier one day. Old flight manuals, textbooks, the old astrolabe, and junk like that. He'd been staying over at his mother's for weeks, and everybody in town was on some kind of alert to see what his next move would be. He said he was headed for Savannah.

—I got a job offer from Embry-Riddle. I can't sit here and fish the rest of my life. I'm not ready to be retired. She doesn't want to get out and explore the new terrain. She just wants to lollygag around in the wrecked fuselage, being her own cause célèbre.

People are going to do what they are going to do. Savannah was where that other woman was. The one that caused the trouble. He drove off, towing that boat, which seemed to be the only constant he had left. *Alapaha Star.*

Austin lost his drinking buddy, and I lost the closest thing to a big brother I ever had. I found myself missing some of those funny nights at the hospital. Like when the two of them would show up in a blind rain with fine strings of fish, and sweet-talk Mattie or Eula into frying the fish at midnight. Two men, each married to women who didn't have the time of day for a string of fish, so they showed up at the hospital full of the infirm, the newborn, the down-and-out. Mattie and Eula would fuss over them a while, then they'd fuss *at* them.

They came to the hospital because they felt loved there.

When Harrison left, it was like somebody cut the lights down too low. Even Austin felt it. He didn't like to drink alone. One Saturday night he came down to the nurse's station and wanted me to come have a drink with him in the kitchen.

—You know I can't do that.

Or he'd just blurt out, over somebody's open entrails in the operating room, *—I'm just a wallet to my wife.*

—Don't start with me, mister, I'd say.

—Why couldn't I have married somebody like you?

—WHY? I said, slapping a clamp into his outstretched hand. *—So you could be telling some other woman how I'm just a wallet to you? This way, I get to be your friend and not your adversary.*

He shrugged. *—What happened to your husband?*

—Not something I talk about. Water under the bridge.

I held it in the road like that, joking and bantering, for about two years. Jim went off to military school. Then everything seemed to conspire to catapult me into some hard times I had no clue how to live through.

My father died after a stroke, convinced that he still had to rise up and get to the train station to make a run. I sat with him for three days; Marjorie didn't have the stomach for helping others. I watched the blood settling into the earthward side of his flesh and was so confused I tried to dial the funeral home at two in the morning. You get that way when it's one of your own. There's nothing holding you up for a while. You need sleep, but sleep won't come. You need food, but it all tastes like cardboard. I had dialed to tell them to come, and I just blanked out. Nobody would answer and I was standing there trying to remember who I was calling.

—It's two in the morning, Austin said. *—I'm driving you home.*

The house was so quiet. The little metal TV table was still up-ended by my father's chair where he had fallen. Somebody, proba-bly Mis Lil, because Marjorie wouldn't have noticed it, had got my sheets in off the line for me and they were folded on the foot of Daddy's brass bed.

Austin was poking around in the kitchen for something, clink-ing things in the pantry. He had found a decanter of Melvina's peach brandy.

—This is the best we got, he said. *—If this doesn't work, I can give you something.*

Innocent days. When I would try drink first. Which only made me blurry and lonely, opening up whole dark corridors of need in me.

—Should I call Marjorie? he said.

—God, no. I said. *—I'll tell her in the morning.*

He was unlacing my shoes.

—What are you doing?

—You've got to lie down while you can still walk.

—I can still walk. Watch me. Just a little tired in the cranium, is all.

—Good. Now where do you sleep?

—Up there, I lied. Jim's room was upstairs. I wanted to be up un-der the gables in the room that was mine when I was a little girl.

Even if it was all bunk beds and model airplanes now. I wanted to forget that I had been born downstairs and I was probably going to die downstairs alone.

—*That's the ticket,* he said, going up the stairs. When I sat down on Jim's bed, he looked around, set the bottle down on the night table. —*That's a girl. Now just lie down—*

—*Only if you lie down with me,* I said.

You could have heard a pin drop in all the neighboring counties.

—*Don't start with me, mister,* I said, —*unless you intend to finish what you start.*

—*Adrie, I don't want to do something that is wrong. Would it be wrong?*

I didn't care, I didn't care. I thought a minute and then I said, —*Only if I'm just some more of your damn missionary work.*

Which is how we came to be lying side by side on our backs, naked under Jim's sheets a while later, covered to our chins. Afraid to look at each other, as if he had not just rammed himself into me in a way that I was not likely to soon forget. God, *that* was like being mauled by some wonderful bear.

Men always think you want the big fireworks display, the grand paroxysm. When what you *really* want is what comes right *after,* when they've spent themselves. You've got a few moments there before they revert to the wild creatures they are and it feels like you can *know* them.

With Austin, what you got in those moments was very much like coming across the wild creature in the woods, but he looks right back at you, and you've got a few moments to know that he's just as wary of *you* as you are of him, before you both bolt.

I wanted to look, to *see* him, to trace his lines with my finger like I'd seen him do with newborns. But I just lay there with the sheet up to my chin, too shy to even put my head on his shoulder. I was afraid I had filled him with regrets, in my need to feel close to life again.

—*Adrie, I don't even know what—*

I just put a finger over his lips. —*Don't start with me, mister,* I tried to tease. —*You don't have to make a speech to me now.*

—*No,* he said, —*I will say this.* He seemed upset. I was imagining that some awful confession was ahead, something he thought I should know about him. Some needless operating-room loss, or some misdeed that was burdening him, the deed we had just done.

—*I have never understood what love is.*

—*What?*

—*Love. I have never understood.*

—*I love you*, I volunteered.

—*DON'T.*

—*Bit late to be telling me that, don't you think?*

—*Don't take me on like some kind of raison d'être.*

—*Speak English.*

—*Some reason to be.*

I didn't know what to say next. When the wild creature is still and quiet, you are, too, before you scare it off.

—*I always thought it would be*—the words all seemed to stick inside him. —*I was a little boy and I saw this*—*there was this place I used to run away to, an old nigra man's farm*—

I put my head on his shoulder.

—*This was up at Rabun Gap*—*and in the fall, he would be grinding cane. Had this old albino mule.*

—*I saw one of those one time.*

—*And the man would rig up this thing off his harness, a carrot on a stick, or a turnip, or whatever.*

—*I've seen that, too.*

—*And it always seemed horrible to me to fool the mule like that. A horrible thing to see, that mule going around and around with his eyes blindered so he could only see straight ahead. I tried to give the mule some sugar one time, and the nigra stopped me. He said it would be better if I didn't. The mule would work harder if I didn't. So I just stood there holding the sugar, and that was the last time I ever cried as a child.*

I was trying to understand what he was telling me. I was trying to think not so much about the sugar that he had just fed me. He kept talking, and the way he could not lie to me made the love in me more hopelessly strong.

—*I've always felt like it's something you never get, it's just the idea that keeps you going.*

Dear Austin. We weren't lost, we were *exploring*. Like children, like shy mice.

Me lying there with the tightness in my chest so hot I thought I would burst. It wells up in you, it feels like it's going to do you *in*, then it just disperses into your veins like a deep red-orange righteousness: *I will build my house on this sand, I will build my house on this sand.*

—So love is like the turnip on the stick? I said.

—Yes.

—But what about the little boy with the sugar in his hand? What is that? Who is he?

He didn't really have time to answer. We heard bumping downstairs. Phoebe. Four in the morning. Time to run away from home and crawl into bed with Grandaddy, except Grandaddy isn't there anymore, and never will be again. I found my robe downstairs and went to see about her.

She was walking in her sleep. Little thatch of hair just wild.

—I have to find my grandaddy, she said. *—Where is he?*

—He's not here, baby, I said, grinding teeth. Could there never be anything in my life that happened for me, for my own joy, or would it always be this kind of missionary work toward my sister's family because she couldn't be bothered? I got Phoebe settled in the big brass bed, and I went back upstairs. Austin was gone. He had dressed quickly and vanished. I went down to sleep with Phoebe, my thighs still sticky from him.

Melvina came to clean at sunup and didn't say a word to me when she came down from upstairs with the messy sheets. She had found my pearls under the pillow. She patted me on the back. Fussed over me all day until I just told her to *shut up* and go home.

After all the confusion of the funeral—everybody asking Marjorie where Harrison was now, her crying and saying that she'd lost her last friend on the earth when she'd lost her father, I fed her children. Austin was always around, but keeping his distance. He came up to me in the kitchen, and my pearls were on the windowsill.

—Can I have those back? He seemed a little sorrowful.

—Yes, I answered him, the breath caught in my chest as if the pearls were trapped in there. And he put them in his shirt pocket.

When I went back to work, it was hard to talk. I felt like a big wart on the landscape. Then I got a note from him in the mail one day telling me I could retrieve my pearls at a certain house. Even had a map. I got out there and it was the McCranie brothers' fishing camp, this old two-story log house down on the river near the whirlpool. The whole second floor was just a bunch of beds, and it was like being Goldilocks sneaking into the three bears' house, trying to find one that was not just squealing rusted springs.

He was a very playful man, and I liked to imagine that this was a secret only *I* knew about him. He was a sometimes fierce, sometimes tender lover, always baffling in his generosity. I'd lean into him sometimes and whisper —*Why do you let me do this?* but he would just hold me tighter, saying, —*Hush, hush*. If I closed my eyes and imagined that my arms were around him, and his children, and even Grace, I could convince myself it was not a shameful thing I did, but a holy one. I enabled him to climb back into his life.

This went on for two years or so. He'd leave the pearls behind, always. I'd say to myself that each time would be the last time, and then I'd slip the pearls back into his lab coat or mackinaw pocket when I couldn't stand it anymore. I was always hoping to get back to that first tame moment there in the dark, when I had had a glimpse of him, when I felt like he was letting me know him.

He took me down through the woods once, to a part of the river I'd not ever seen before. It was early summer, Sunday morning, and so there were no little boys swimming. They were all in church. The rose mallow was blooming, little pink stars cropped up on the old sandbars. I was following him through the tupelo trees and thinking that I was soon going to be too old to be out in the woods somewhere for the reason that we were out there.

I even drove across the country with him and Grace one summer, me in the back seat with the children. Jim was in Germany then. A Green Beret.

It was Grace's idea for me to go with them. Her in the front seat singing with the radio: *Silks and satins and linens that shows, and I'm all yours in buttons and bows.* Tracing her finger on the back of his neck. I almost think she knew the grief this brought me.

Me in the adjoining room with the children while she had him all to herself next door.

Even when we were girls she was at her happiest when she could hoard something no one else could share.

In Texas, she had to be outfitted like Dale Evans. In the Ozarks, she had to have six baskets. In Tucumcari it was all silver and turquoise. It was enough to make me ill. I was looking at the Fiestaware in some store, and Austin came up behind me softly, almost made me drop a pitcher.

I wheeled around and he reached for my arm but I snatched it away. —*What's wrong?* he said.

—*Why have you done this to me?*

—*Done what? What have I done to you?*

He looked puzzled, lost for a minute. Dear Austin.

In Seattle I sat across him—across from *them*—in a Chinese restaurant. He read aloud the fortune from my cookie: —*Alas, you are the apple of my eye.* I began to gasp for air and sob. He folded it up and put it in his pocket, cool as a cucumber. In the ladies' room, Grace came to comfort me. —*It's probably the change,* she whispered. —*It comes early in our family.*

I was glad to get home. It felt like there was *nothing* holding me up, nobody. The summer was over, the light seemed thin.

I was thirty-six and I was getting old. I wanted the old bright red-orange righteousness filling me again. Not just a few furtive kisses at the hospital just to send him home to Grace all hot and bothered. Not just the once-in-a-blue-moon pearl swap. I wanted that chest-bursting love for every living thing. I swear, I would have dealt with the devil for one entire night alone with the man in my own bed. Or just to go to the movies with him—a deep dangerous hunger that welled up in me out of nowhere. I could make myself perfectly miserable imagining all the dinners I would have cooked for him if he were mine.

Jim had volunteered to go to Vietnam, and I had one week to visit with him at home before he shipped out, except he had spent almost all of it running with that Christy Wakefield. Out all hours of the night.

Volunteered to go to Vietnam.

I said, —*Son, do you WANT to die?*

All he could say to me was that he was a soldier.

BUT IF I COULD GO BACK IN MY LIFE and put my finger on the point where things went wrong, it would be that afternoon that I stopped by the Rexall pharmacy. It was raining, and the storekeepers had begun to do their windows for Christmas, and I felt balky about going home to nothing. I felt like somebody should attach guy wires to me to keep me upright.

Austin had given me my pearls back for the last time. I just found them in my purse at work, and he could hardly look at me or talk to me. —*I can't do this anymore, Adrie*, he said. —*It hurts too many people.*

It would be years and years before I could think up an answer to that moment.

Don Avery told me at the pharmacy that I looked like I could use a cup of coffee and I took it.

—*I know it's hard for you,* he said. —*A woman alone.*

He didn't know the whole of it. Hell, he didn't know the *half* of it. I began to cry. —*It's just so hard,* I said.

—*I know it's hard.* Before it was all over, I'd cried all over his shirt. He offered me some capsules, and I took them. And it got easier.

—*That's Miltown*, he said, teaching me.

Before it was all over with, I had married him, and I had all the little capsules I wanted. Did I love him? I thought so at the time.

I woke up one morning to see Don looking through the curtains out at the street with an odd look on his face. A black government car from Fort Benning.

He told me I had to let them in. They were nice boys, about Jim's age. He wasn't killed for sure, they said. Just lost.

The things you think: that you can just pack your bags, get on a plane, and go find him out in the middle of the jungle: *Excuse me, generals, stop the shooting for a minute and let me find my boy and take him home.* The dreams: he needed water or food in his bamboo cages, he feared the tigers and bullets. It would have been easier to know he was dead. There was nothing holding me up those years but hatred of Ho Chi Minh.

I had a letter from a boy in Germany who had run into somebody who'd been on the last mission with Jim. Told him that one of the other guys had been dead and that Jim was dying.

Was dying. I wanted to fly to Germany and stand in the bar where those words had been spoken, as if that would be some starting place that would lead me to the very spot, his very bones, so I could bring them home.

The army sent me a box of his things, after six months. Medals. Letters from Christy: *I love you because you are so brave I will never forget when you took me to the whirlpool.* A Vietcong flag. His dog tags, his dress beret. And a Kalashnikov he had captured, one of those Russian-made ones. I put it all upstairs in his room. Hung the flag and the gun on the wall where I knew he would. It got all over town that I'd gone crazy and gone over to the other side, was pulling for Ho Chi Minh and the Russians.

The Methodist preacher came to see me. The new ones always tested the waters with me. I usually sent them away like scalded dogs, and this one was no different.

—*Miss Adrienne, you are not serving the Lord well when you let yourself be like this*, he said, the jackass.

I gave him the baldest stare of hatred that I could muster. You have an instinct when you are in the face of the enemy. It raises your hair on the nape of your neck.

—*Son*, I said, —*my grandfather put that church up, and I can take it down. I've got a hand grenade*, I said. —*All I have to do is pull the pin.*

There was nothing holding me up. No turnip on the stick in sfront of my nose, no *raison d'être*, not even the one that wants love. There was only Don, and that was when we got into the Demerol.

—*It's just so hard,* I'd say.

—*I know it's hard,* he'd say, and help me do it. —*Atta girl.* Then he would hold me.

—*It's just so hard*—I'd start out, but there it was again, the tightness in the chest, the bright red-orange righteousness. I recognized that pleasure from somewhere before, and tried to recall the place. —*Austin?* I said, blurting it out in the air.

Surely if there is such a thing as love it is like that red-orange righteousness.

Sometimes I'd sleep for four days; sometimes I'd not sleep for four.

I have a memory of Austin coming to see me, sitting at the edge of my blurriness and holding my hand in both of his, saying nice things to me that I couldn't hear. I sat dully, and my mouth was dry. I wondered, in some secret little red silk-lined chamber of my heart, what had ever become of that little piece of paper that said, *Alas, you are the apple of my eye.*

—*Look,* he said. —*You can't do this.*

—*You watch me*, I slurred my words slowly, angrily, my tongue too fat. I wanted to slap his lovely face for thinking I had any reason left to live, but it was too much effort to lift my hand. All I knew with any clarity was that I had lived an errant life.

I had ignored a secret the world had always been whispering to me: *Love is not the thing.* Those little bottles were the thing. Keys to the kingdom and the mercy of God. That red-orange righteousness in my veins felt like the mercy of God. There was another secret: I was no longer exploring, I was lost.

THE SKIDAWAY
ISLAND SCHOOL FOR
WAYWARD GIRLS

*Y*ou know that old question they always ask: *What were you doing when you heard that Kennedy had been shot?* Where were you the day after? I was trying to reason with a nasty little tart in my office. All I really wanted that day was to listen to my transistor radio. I wanted Kennedy news. It was the day after he'd been shot. November 23, 1963.

But the PE teacher had harangued me for ten minutes in the teachers' lounge, –*Olivia, Olivia, that new girl reeks of men again.* I called the girl into my office. She was thirteen, a pale, scrawny little thing, a real scrapper in the dorm fights, and she had been with us two months. You could tell how much her hair had grown in the months she'd been with us by the dark line of demarcation: she had about an inch of black roots showing, the rest was old peroxide.

Marilyn Monroe. They all wanted to look like that, and the results were always pathetically mixed. The pout, the whisper voice.

I was the headmistress at the Skidaway School. I hired and fired teachers, ordered supplies, books, and called the parole officers when any of the girls failed to return to us from weekend furloughs into Savannah. I also explained on the phone that no, we weren't exactly a finishing school for the well-heeled, that our student body came from the Savannah City and Chatham County juvenile court dockets.

Forty or so castoff girls who'd been exposed to far more of the world than I had, and all I was armed with to help them was secondhand outdated textbooks purchased from a Binghamton, New York, system, and free "health and hygiene" kits from the Sisters of Mercy: shampoo, toothpaste, sanitary napkins, tracts with the intentions of God explained.

—*How did you spend your weekend?* I asked the girl, and she shrugged.

I hated those shrugs, that hard-shelled indifference.

—*Well, how are your parents?* I persisted.

—*Fighting all the time,* she said.

—*What do they fight about?* I said.

—*He's always after her,* she said, picking at the nubs of wool in her sweater.

—*After her?* I said

—*To fuck him,* she said.

The language, I never got used to the language.

—*Janelee, we call it intercourse.*

—*Well, we call it fuckin', Miz Landon.*

She, of course, relished the moment. The discomfort on my face, how she loved it. I was trying to think of some delicate way to ask her about the smell, when the door opened and somebody brushed past my secretary.

And there Harrison Durrance was. I hadn't seen him in three years. Not so much as a phone call, then there he was right before me.

I waved Janelee out of the room, speechless.

—*Olivia, I came to invite you to dinner at my place,* he said, and jingled the change in his pockets. After three years.

The last time I had seen him was in a hotel room in Tampa. Me trying to find my way out of a bad marriage; Harrison heading straight into a maelstrom. I'd heard he'd been court-martialed, I'd heard terrible things. And then he just vanished. Now there he was, standing hesitantly inside my office, with that smile. Civilian clothes. Odd to see, that. It was the first time I had ever seen him sober, and it was almost frightening. As if there were no barrier of fear anymore, no further excuse not to love him abjectly.

All I could think was, *My God, he's here, he's here where I am.*

But I was still back in that hotel room in Tampa, remembering how I'd come out of the shower to find him gone, and how it took me weeks to figure out he meant for that to be the last time.

—*You didn't even tell me goodbye*, I was all poised to say, but I had already melted a little inside and was smiling like a real trouper.

—*What time do they let you out of this place?* he asked. —*I want to take you out in my boat.* I heard the wisp of hoarseness in his voice, the slight rasp his voice took on when he was beginning to be aroused. I remember the first time I'd ever noticed that, those short life-times ago, before I had turned into the headmistress, the half-spectacles on my nose.

—*Four,* I smiled, and my heart was like a fistful of doves wanting out.

—*I'll be back to get you,* he said, and he was gone.

I was wishing I'd worn a better suit. My shoes were a brighter pink than my suit, and this bothered me. We all wore such odd clothes to work in: the soft wool suits like Chanel uniforms, the dagger-toed shoes in matching shades.

He was still the Harrison I remembered. Always in command of the situation, and capable of rendering me wordless. There is that moment, early on with men, when the capitulation is good, when they can make you *stop* filling your brain with everything that is a substitute for them, like canasta and Toastmasters and whether or not this year's shade of plum-colored lipstick is going to look decent on you.

—*Where do you live?* I asked.

—*On Skidaway,* he said. —*Couple miles down the road.*

That made me laugh.

—*It won't be so funny, girl, you don't catch us some supper,* he said.

He had rented a cottage on the other side of the island, but I had driven past it every morning on my way to work. We had martinis on a little dock behind it, and watched some shrimp boats chuffing back for the night. It began to rain, so he decided to just show me his boat, not take it out. I noticed the boat had a name now: *Alapaha Star.* That was his hometown.

Also her hometown. But he'd been here two years, I reminded myself.

Too cold to be out, but he loved the water so much he didn't even feel it. The terrible clatter my heels made on the dock—he loved that—the ridiculousness of me in the pink high heels with the crab basket. He was grinning, and the grin warmed me.

—*Nice. Negro pink.*

I flushed.

—Do you know what you're doing?

—I was catching crabs before you'd ever seen one, I said.

—Wanna bet?

—How much? Don't push your luck. Remember that I'm older than you.
And I was.

I leaned back a little to lift the basket to the rail, and my heel
snagged between the boards, stuck. I slipped my foot out of it, and
we both looked down at it like it was a little dead animal.

—Wardrobe needs some major modifications, schatze.

I felt the tears in my eyes then, at the sound of that word. Is it
deliberate, the way men balance the hurt with their odd off-key
tenderness? First the one, then the other? Is that the way they
make us theirs?

The last time I'd seen him I'd told him that story, the night the
people were shouting outside my father's bakery in Savannah in
1917, screaming for us all to go back to Germany. My parents
locked me into a trunk at the foot of the bed so I couldn't hear the
bottles and glass breaking downstairs. The next day my father held
me all day long on the train, crooning, *—Schatze, schatze, we had to
put our little treasure somewhere so we put you in the little treasure chest,*
as if that would bring my innocence back to me.

This I had confessed to Harrison, in a Tampa motel room in
1957, neon filtering through the cheap slats of the blinds. He'd
made a confession about the scar on the back of his head. It had
seemed to me that night that we lay for hours confessing things to
each other, as if there would never again be a chance to utter these
things to anyone.

Harrison moved over to hold me on the little dock, and murmured, *—My shoes keep walking back to you.* I moved away from him,
pulled at my broken shoe, and threw it off into the water. He suggested I try out for the women's Olympic shot put, and I took off
the other shoe and threw it at his head and missed, thank God.

*—Every sixty seconds is another chance to start over. Lemme see if I can
get it right this time.*

There was no saying no to him. There never had been.

He made me an omelet, later, much later, after we'd had a
chance to get caught up with each other in his bedroom.

—How did you know where I was?

—I have always known where you are.

—You could have called, you know.

—I didn't think you'd want that. I was having . . . a hard time.

—Well, a hard time was had by all.

Later I was trying to find my stockings in the dark, and I remembered that I had no shoes. I shook him awake.

—Where are you going? he murmured out of his sleep.

—I have to go home and dress for work. I had visions of myself showing up for work no fresher than Janelee.

—Skip work today, he said. *—Kennedy is dead, baby, and I have loved you for years.*

That sweet governance men have over you at first—he pressed me to the wall in the shower, bruising me and pleasing me, then washing my hair for me. I stumbled back into my apartment late that evening, stunned at my good fortune, and my phone was ringing.

My whole apartment seemed odd to me because my eye had begun to judge it from Harrison's point of view. It all looked silly, the "French Provincial" furniture, the violet moire drapes. I had lived alone for four years.

—Where were you last night? my sister, Sloane, snapped at me. *—I called and called, and Fontaine called and called, and for all we knew you could have been in a gutter somewhere with your pockets picked.*

I was part of this loose affiliation of unattached women. The Canasta Disastahs, Harrison later named us. We were in the habit of phoning each other at bedtime to make sure everyone was safe. Downtown Savannah was changing. My sister, Sloane, alone like me, had been knocked down on River Street one night, but had held onto her purse, and—I swear—I don't think she was going to be satisfied until the same thing had happened to the rest of us.

—I was seeing a friend, I stammered, and felt three years old. Already my mind was looking at her through Harrison's eyes, and I knew that they were not going to like each other much.

Sloane had a studio in the south end of the Cotton Exchange, with huge palladian windows overlooking the river, a onetime warehouse, so large she had to screen off a little cubbyhole of living space to live in. She rented it for a song, which was just as well. She was so poor she didn't pay income taxes. I could imagine her sitting cross-legged on her army-surplus cot, her brow knit in judgment of *me.*

—*I cannot believe you would do that.*

—*You'll understand when you meet him.*

—*"She who lives by the sword, dies by the sword,"* she said to me.

She had decided before I ever left Tampa that I had broken up Harrison's marriage, and nothing would disabuse her of that notion.

Sloane had never bothered to marry. She therefore had no idea what it was like to find yourself gasping for air on some summer afternoons, feeling like if you don't find absolution from your own captive loneliness soon you are going to end up in some white room with soft walls and nurses bringing you pills on a tray.

—*OH, IT'S ALL SO WONDERFUL,* my good friend Fontaine said. —*You see? I told you your fortunes were going to change.* She was part of the canasta crowd—the only married one of us—all women in their forties. —*And he's younger than you? God.*

We were having lunch together, she preening happily at what she thought to be my good fortune. Fontaine's grand scheme for world peace was to have everyone happily paired off. She had needlework pictures and cushions all over her house, of creatures that we all believed mated for life: cardinals, Canada geese. The canasta group fluttered around me, it seemed, when we were together, as if I were the one whose star was suddenly ascendant—*A man in your life, a man in your life*—fussed over by the ladies-in-waiting.

BUT I WOULDN'T MARRY Harrison at first. I didn't like what marriage had done to me before. Turned me into somebody's crippled quail, required to flutter through the house, through the *world,* like I'd been winged. Being an Air Force wife was like that. He gets flight clearance; you get winged. You have to agree to go through life with both hands tied behind your back so you don't make him look bad. You start out as a real person with a job and a credit rating and then you wake up one day and that's all gone and you can't even go to the movies without asking permission first, and you're not likely to get it. It took me a number of years to figure this out, and then I left.

I liked making my own money, paying my own bills.

I liked my pink sofa, my ruffled lampshades, my African violets, and my Persian cat.

I liked the feeling that I owned only what I needed: car, clothes, books, *self*.

I even liked sleeping alone, sometimes.

I had no nostalgia whatsoever for military wifehood.

This was fine with Harrison for a year or two. You have to be a woman to understand the joy of having all one's pastel sanctuary invaded by one very real man and to know that it's *finite*. Monday morning comes and you are in control of all your life's boundaries again, even though you are already longing for the moments when he will come back, using your best towels first to dry you, then himself, and then to spread out all his fishing lures on.

We took turns, his place one weekend, mine the next.

One Sunday night I got out of his bed, and he said, —*Schatze, don't go tonight.*

—*You know I have to.*

—*I am tired of sleeping alone. It's unnatural for a man my age.*

—*It's unnatural for me to get up at four in the morning to go home and shower.*

—*Well, I wish you godspeed.*

Two weeks later, when he hadn't called or answered his phone, I understood. It was his way of saying goodbye. This was the first time that I noticed the pattern: tell him the truth, he disappeared.

FOR THE BETTER PART OF A YEAR, I didn't know where he was. The cottage on Skidaway was rented to someone else within weeks. I drove out there at dusk one Sunday night, feeling like I'd settle for the sight of him, even from a distance.

—*You know what your trouble is?* Sloane advised me. I had got so lonely I got in the habit of dropping by her place for a drink on the way home from school. —*You have no real ambition. You have always let the love of men be your goal.*

I was sliding into that zone where you go to the movies with other women more than men, and you all bore each other with incessant artificial good cheer and gossip.

I started my secret vice around about then.

I would check myself into the Manger Hotel, top floor. Order a pitcher of martinis, and sit by the window facing Bay Street. What did I do there? I watched the Savannah River, the lights of the docking ships, the cars moving in the street until dark came, and then the cars were like golden beads sliding along on an abacus made of light. I had loved high places since I was a little girl.

It was a great comfort to me to be up somewhere where I could *see* things clearly. I could *think* clearly in high places. The first thing I'd do, as soon as I got into the room was look straight down at the sidewalk. And I'd think about what state of mind someone would have to be in to jump, and how terrible it must be for them to have to do that. Then I'd drink my martinis and watch. It was the watching that always saved me, and I was always aiming for that moment when the cars were like gold strings, and I could make up stories to myself about how they were all going home to their little assigned niches in town, and I had had enough martinis that I went gold inside, like I was everybody's mother, even Harrison's— Harrison, who was out there somewhere practicing love for every living thing. I did this three times in that year.

—*Oh, honey, there are other fish in the sea*, Fontaine said one night, just blurting it out over the canasta table, in front of the rest of the Canasta Disastahs. I'd been lost in my own thoughts, and they'd all been staring at me God knows how long. My star was no longer ascendant with them, and I was making them sad. I had gone out a few times with a man who taught at Georgia Southern, but he could do the slightest thing, like make a big ritual out of how dry his martini was, and I would have this irritable flash inside me: *Who do you think you are? Do you think I am in the public domain?* and things would go no further. I didn't *want* things to go any further with anyone.

After almost a year, Harrison showed up at my door one night, soaking wet, with a shoebox under his arm. I let him in, trying not to be angry, trying not to let my pride ruin everything. He had a shoebox under his arm. It was a pair of pumps. Negro pink, my size. One of his hands was all cut up. He'd taken one of his socks off to bandage it. He wasn't much in the mood for joking. I remember the way he leaned into me when I toweled his hair dry, like some lost child.

—*You were right*, he said. —*The baddies always win.*

—*Thanks for the shoes*, I said. —*Negro pink.*

—*Not so fast there. You have to marry me to get those shoes,* he said, his hands remembering their way around my body. He sensed this was not enough. —*Baby, lissen. Who we are has taken us this far, and who we are will take us anywhere we want to go.*

Later between my eyelet sheets: —*I need only you, I need only you.* He whispered that to me, and I bought it wholesale, and the joy blossomed in me like big red peonies. Nothing that can help you to live like that does: *I need only you.*

I met his red-haired daughter Allie at our wedding. The other two children could not be bothered. Sloane stood up with me, Allie with him. She cried, and I sensed some sorrowful bond between them, and he reddened in the face when she cried. It's all there in the wedding pictures. Her eyes are glistening with tears, his eyes look angry at her for that, and I look like I need to check into the Manger Hotel once more for old times' sake.

I was forty-eight. He was forty-two. I'd slept happily naked with him for more nights than I could count, but on my wedding night I felt clumsy and old, a wife now and not a lover, safer in my clothes than out.

—*I want you to wear only the pink shoes.*

—*Not so fast there,* I said, stalling for time.

—*Pardon me?*

—*You have to pick up your socks to get those shoes. And is the cat in or out?*

THERE IS THAT SWEET, utter ownership a husband has over you at first. I loved to cook for him, and I wanted all the buttons on his shirts to pop off so I could sew them on again. You're all gold-filled when he is the one thing you are alive for. You measure time by how many hours until you see him again. You measure space by whether or not he is in the immediate vicinity. That nice little envelope of intimacy before circumstances necessitate that he begin lying to you.

THREE YEARS INTO THE MARRIAGE, we got a new neighbor across the courtyard from our apartment. She was alone, it appeared at first, with a baby girl of around two or so. Harrison watched from the kitchen window as she was throwing empty cardboard boxes out the back, the packing excelsior strewn around the steps.

—*Messy. Not a good sign,* he said.

I came to the window to watch with him. She was very young, a brunette with a pageboy hairdo and a good figure. The word *gamine* came to mind.

What was her story? I watched her play with the baby in our little excuse for a courtyard, three days in a row. Where was the father? These were the days when the Huntley-Brinkley report was all Vietnam, all helicopters and gunfire and maps. The war had not touched me. I was spinning a grandiose history for her: the father had died in Vietnam, probably. Two or three days of this imagining and it felt like the war had touched me, and I could *do* something.

I took some cookies over.

Her name was Leslie. The little girl was two.

Leslie was trying to hang some pictures. She wanted to know if I knew how to find the studs in the wall, so she could hang up her father's picture for the baby. —*I think she needs to see other faces besides mine. She doesn't have a daddy.*

—*Excuse me?*

—*Her father was someone I didn't know very well,* she said. —*And I didn't want to be married.* She shrugged as if it were nothing.

—*Is that bad?* she asked, taking a drag of her cigarette? —*Is it like, you know, ancestor worship?*

I blinked, couldn't figure out what she was talking about.

—*To have my parents' pictures up? They've never seen her. They've practically disowned me.* I told her I thought it was a good idea, and that Harrison could find the studs for her.

—*Can you take your toolbox and help her?* I said to Harrison that night at dinner. —*She really needs some help over there.* I figured he'd find out the rest soon enough.

—*Schatze, that baby has no daddy.*

—*So she told you.*

—*Her parents don't even know about the baby.*

—*Well, we have to help her, I guess,* I said. —*A woman alone like that, she might just walk off with the first pair of pants that shows up at the door.*

—*You're right.*

It seemed to give us something new in common, instead of just the Sunday papers and the bed. I rather liked it at first. We were co-conspirators. He got out his old toolbox and walked across the courtyard. He wasn't gone long, but when he came back across, he seemed taller than I remembered.

We had them both over for dinner a few nights after that, and ate in the kitchen at the little table, like a family would. She had dressed up a bit for the occasion, a little green sheath with a paisley scarf, and she ate heartily, as if it had been a long time since she'd had a home-cooked meal. There was something a bit waif-like about her. She had a part-time job as a secretary, and she was giving ballet lessons.

—*We eat out a lot,* she said.

I got up to make the coffee and get out the mousse, I turned around, and her scarf was on the table, her dress unbuttoned, and the baby was at her breast. Little smacking noises. Two waifs in my kitchen, it seemed. Harrison was enchanted, trying not to look at her. He was looking at his hands, at his spoon, at everything except the thing he wanted most to look at. I dropped the coffeepot and broke it. A little more life than we were used to, that night in our kitchen.

I WAS HANGING SOME FRESHLY IRONED SHIRTS in his closet one afternoon, and that green chiffon scarf fell to the floor. Leslie's. In our closet, like treasure Harrison couldn't bear to part with. He might as well have slugged me with his fist.

I felt like I was on thin, thin ice. How many other stupid assumptions had I made about things? What were all the things that others knew that I didn't? I didn't know which of his clothes the scarf fell out of. I put it back on the floor, in the back.

I never mentioned it to him.

I quit doing his shirts and suggested that he take them down the avenue to the laundry. I balked at sewing on buttons that Leslie's hands might undo. I didn't feel like anybody's treasure anymore. I felt full of worthless currency.

I watched him eat his dinner each night, and tried to think of what to say. We were having baked shad one night, and he loved the way I cooked the roe with it. It was one of his favorite dishes, and I felt desolate watching him eat it.

—*Are you happy with me?* I finally just blurted it out.

He paused, napkin at his mouth, lowering it to his lap slowly. He didn't like this kind of conversation. *—What a question, schatze. I'm here, aren't I?* He was angry. *—What a vote of no confidence.*

—I need to know. I felt very close to tears, to breaking. I felt very acutely every flaw in my skin, my hair, my body. I was fantasizing that he would get up and come around the table to hold me. But he didn't. He was annoyed with me.

—You're still the queen bee. There is no one else for me but you. You know that.

It isn't the other woman that puts a marriage asunder. It's not the forbidden fruit that boots you both out of the garden for good. It's the *lying* about it that un-mates you. You start wondering what else he's been fooling you about over the years. Out of tenderness? To keep the good meals and the clean shirts coming?

A few days later I found a package under my pillow. A pair of pearl earrings.

—You're still the queen bee, he whispered into my hair when he made love to me, like someone trying to soothe a spooked mare.

The next time I went to lunch with Fontaine, I wanted to tell her. She knew that something was wrong and seemed to lean forward in her chair, much too solicitous for my taste. She had a jewelry fetish, a way of armoring herself to go out in public with all her good jewelry, and I found this irritating that day.

A man stopped at our table, somebody who worked with her husband.

—How's Al? he said.

—You tell me, she said, with a bit of a bite in her voice. *—You see more of him than I do.* And she poured herself more wine. *—Ask him how he is for me, will you?*

He sat down with us. I thought, *What have we here?*

—Have you met Elaine yet? he asked her. *—The new secretary?*

I saw the little tremor on Fontaine's lip. Just the little flicker of muscle, very telling. Just the little flash of fear in the eyes: *So it's true, so it's true.*

—So this is middle age, I thought to myself, and for a moment it was supremely funny. Bless us and save us and batten down the hatches. Not that thing you have when you're young: true love is just around the next bend. Just people prone to wrinkling, sitting around being wry about it.

—Fontaine, I said, when the man had left. Then I froze up.

Should I tell her she was going to live through this bad time, or ask her if she was missing a green scarf?

—*Oh, it's nothing,* she said airily but I felt that she was like cold wax under all her jewelry and makeup. —*After a while, you get so used to it, it doesn't even matter anymore.* She twirled her wine glass around and her rings clinked against it. —*Who knows? Maybe I'll get that watch I wanted out of this.*

I felt uneasy. She was spreading out her hands, looking at them.

—*See these?* she suddenly touched her earlobes, the diamonds there.

—*They're gorgeous. Leave me those in your will,* I joked like we always did. She was supposed to say, —*I plan to outlive you,* and we'd be on track with our usual little comfortable laughs. But she wasn't smiling.

—*These were Dodie Alexander,* she said quite seriously, touching them again.

—*They were hers?*

—*No. These were what I got when Al was in love with Dodie. One summer. Six whole weeks.*

I said nothing. I wanted the waiter to bring the check. I wanted away from her.

Fontaine was still staring at her hands.

—*I can always tell,* she said. —*He feels so guilty when it's over and the smoke in his head clears—he always buys me jewelry. Pays me off, so to speak. Oh, don't look at me so holier-than-thou. I have to think about my children.* She wriggled the fingers, pointing to some of the rings, and some of them were stunning. —*Carole Nichopoulous, Helen Drake, Fran Ellis, and . . . your sister Sloane. That was his artsy phase.*

Sloane had made that ring. Her silversmith phase.

I'd been sitting there like some fool in my new pearl earrings. I wanted them off. It felt like they were burning me.

I checked myself into the Manger Hotel and ordered my martinis. I phoned Harrison from the restaurant and told him a lie. I told him I was going out with the Canasta Disastahs. My heart was beating so fast, and I was so scared, I thought, *How does he do it so easily?* And I began to watch, waiting for the golden time to come. Only this time it was different. It seemed to me that everyone was tired, their faces were sad. The men and women in their cars were on their way home not to the cozy little niches I'd imagined, but to try to pull their marriages around themselves like dry husks they were expected to live in the rest of their lives.

The things your eye will select to remember: I saw a girl, a waif, could have been somebody from my own school. Sixteen, seventeen, maybe. In a car with someone who looked like a banker, and they were sharing a cigarette. *Don't they have two?* I thought at first. And then I saw: the whole point was the sharing. Some years later I realized what they were smoking when I saw a documentary on TV about hippies.

They kissed a while, then he got out of her Volkswagen, put his suit coat on, and got into his Lincoln. Drove away. I couldn't imagine anything colorful for him to be driving back to, just a dry husk of a marriage to wrap around himself. Not to mention the orderly drawers of clean socks and underwear, the adoring wife. I couldn't seem to drink myself to that gold state of motherhood where I loved it all. I felt like there was no connection between me and the rest of the people milling around down there—they seemed to know things I couldn't get the hang of. They seemed to know how not to care.

I thought of all the adulterers out there. How did they do it? They must have hearts like tough leather to be able to hold each other in the harsh light of day, without even the comfort of night for cover. Each caress proof of one's basic untrustworthiness. How could they learn to trust, when what they had were little purloined scraps of each other? How was it worth it to them? They'd have to be tough, or in the shape I was in that long-ago Christmas Eve when Harrison first took me to bed. Needy beyond words.

The whole earth had lied to me about love. All the elders, all the books. All lies.

I was thinking of some movie title I'd seen—*Stop the World, I Want to Get Off.* When I looked straight down at the sidewalk, I wondered what people found to think about on the way down, once they'd left the windowsill. Was it bliss? Was it awful? Did they have terrible moments of regret on the way down? *Wait a minute, I want to get back on?* I opened the window and threw one pearl earring out. I was trying for the street, so a car could smash it, but it only landed on the sidewalk. After a moment, I saw the doorman walk over and put it in his pocket.

Here's the thing. Marriage is predicated on ownership. *I will only agree to love you if you let me be the queen bee.* It invites lies, does it not? It required that Harrison squelch in himself the very thing that attracted me to him in the first place: love for every living thing.

Oh, the gold-filled trust business, it goes by the wayside. I sat in the Manger Hotel and felt it go irrelevant. When I left, I tipped the doorman, even though I had no bags—pretending to be more drunk than I was—with the other pearl earring rolled up into a bill. He smiled indulgently at me, like I was an adulteress.

FOR THE FIRST TIME SINCE I WAS A CHILD, I began to go to church again. The same Unitarian one my parents had attended.

—*Come with me,* I would say to Harrison, thinking that this would piece us back together.

—*You know why God quit showing his face and departed the earth?*

—*Why?*

—*He finally finished making his golf course in heaven.*

—*You're hopeless.*

—*No, it's just that the relationship between him and me has always been adversarial. You go on to church, just don't use my name or he'll ship you to the Azores. I usually have to implore him for his mercy on the ninth hole by that sandtrap. He never hears.*

FONTAINE HAD A NEW DIAMOND PIN, little stars and baguettes. She saw me looking at it across the canasta table, and later whispered when we were scraping the plates in the kitchen: —*Marsha Taylor.* The lines in her face were like a brittle net that held it all together. I felt the irritation surge in me, oceans of anger. Would we live out the rest of our lives scraping the same food into the same bins, different house each week? I thought that Fontaine was about to tell me more, but Jane came in, waving recipe cards. She wanted to give me the same chicken-salad recipe she'd given us all twice before.

—*It's a good recipe for a man,* she said, almost wistfully. —*Hearty.*

-*Ooh, Jane, yes,* Fontaine cooed at her, comforting her in that tone of voice that married women use to comfort those who've coasted into menopause still being maidens. Fontaine was capable of that cheerful kind of whoredom that so many wives seem able to manage. I was not.

I wondered where Robert went, imagined him downtown scouring around for young girls. There were so many of them on the streets then, their long straight hair parted in the middle, no bras, tight jeans. Girls from good homes *choosing* waifhood.

I was walking through the science lab one day to get to the home ec room. The girls in there were watching one of those nature films, the old ones where the color is bad, and the music warbles as the projector whirs. I wasn't even looking when I went through, but the words QUEEN BEE seemed to shout at me, and I looked at the screen. The queen bee was a wretched, white, glistening thing, so bloated as to be immobile. Repugnant. I looked away. I was on my way to get one of the girls out of the home ec class to tell her that her brother had been killed in Vietnam. I made my way through the tables, and one of the teachers had a little chart out—very scientific—showing how to sew on the various types of buttons. This was what we were arming these girls with to face the world. How to sew on a button.

Our clientele at the Skidaway School shifted a little as 1969 came. The waifs were coming out of some of the good neighborhoods now. They were just about as recalcitrant as their counterparts from the row houses, not as streetwise, but just as likely to mouth off. One of the more frightening days of my life was the day they brought in a pale blond girl from Savannah Country Day, somebody the Savannah Civic Ballet had been cultivating. Father was a realtor. I got her after she'd had a detour in a hospital to get off heroin. Natural blond, no roots. Scandinavian blue eyes. Chip on her shoulder a mile wide.

I wasn't afraid for *her*, I was afraid for the whole country. The news was full of kids like her. I had begun to understand that my job entailed more than dispensing cello-wrapped packets of toiletries, and had taken a counseling course.

—*Bonnie, we have to set some goals for you to work toward.*

—*Goals?* She had honed her sarcasm to a fine sharpness.

—*What you are going to do with your life.*

—*You mean as in marry, have kids, stay home, get fat, spread my legs upon command? Not me.*

—*You make it sound as though everyone is doomed, and that's not true.*

—*Do you have a good life?* She flung it back at me.

Did I have a good life? Harrison and I had a marriage that worked like a Swiss watch. The gears were engaged and turning, but no real heat to it. When we made love, I froze up, self-conscious, feeling old. I was there in body, but my mind was always distracted by the memory of that green scarf, wondering who he was probably wishing I was, feeling apologetic for the softness of my own flesh, my mind skittering off into odd morbid thoughts that I could confess to no one.

I read somewhere that old Eskimo women just walk off into the tundra and die when it's time, and wondered how they knew when it was time, wondered if the men were relieved.

The lie had turned things maternal between us somehow. Sometimes I would look at him as he lay asleep, wondering, *Are you my friend or my foe?* and trying not to think about the Manger Hotel.

Middle age.

So I went on Sunday mornings to church. It was the place I could go where everything didn't seem like a dry husk rustling around me. Sitting in the sound of the minister's voice leading me into some better promised land. It was like being held captive by a shaft of sunlight. His name was Michael Keyes.

—*A bitter heart will kill you*, he said simply one morning. I squirmed a little. It seemed he was reading my mind, that his words sailed out across the heads of the other listeners and were aimed at me.

I prayed to be blessed with a better way to see my life. I prayed not to be bitter, but I still was. I hated going to my job. It all seemed hopeless to me, my work. During the gold-filled times, when Harrison loved only me, I could work all day, buoyant throughout the day.

When Harrison loved only me. The pride and folly in that statement astounds me now.

The minister stopped me in the foyer of the church one day as I was leaving.

—*I want to visit your school.*

So he came to talk to the girls. It wasn't what I expected, and it certainly wasn't what they expected. I was dreading it a bit—there was a little clique of seasoned prostitutes—fourteenish—in the back row of the gym. The last time we'd had an assembly, they'd booed some nuns who were trying to teach them to sing madrigals.

—What kind of woman does a man fall in love with? Michael asked, bluntly, hands in his pockets, and the Skidaway girls were all his. Even the whores with the gila-monster makeup stopped smacking their gum in anticipation. He had them right where he wanted them. He really had them hooked—their favorite subject—males.

—What does it take for you to be that kind of woman?

No one could answer him. He answered himself.

—A man falls in love with a cheerful giver. It's that simple. A man falls in love with his sister in the sight of God. Now how can you work to be his sister in the sight of God?

I was not such an easy touch as the gila-monster whores.

I believe a man falls in love with a fantasy. Just like a woman falls in love with a fantasy. Then they spend the rest of their lives punishing each other for being real.

But you do not say such things in front of the young. You do not say such things to a man unless it's one you trust very well. You shove your hands deeper into your own pockets, and go along with it all, complicit in the same lies once perpetrated on you.

Later I showed Michael around the school. He walked with his hands in his pockets. I felt cantankerous. *—You didn't tell them the rest,* I said. *—What comes after the cheerful giving.*

—And that would be . . . ?

I felt ridiculous, an irritant in his eye, pursuing some schoolmarmish point. I was very self-righteous in those days. Always in that state of sputtering *but-but-but* that he could reduce me to.

—The hurt.

The next Sunday his words shot across the heads of the others to me: *—We can drink from the cup of bitterness, or we can drink from the cup that tastes good. We can walk around in misery because of how diminished we are in the sight of God, or we can CELEBRATE how diminished we are in the sight of God.*

He had the habit of patting my shoulder when I shook his hand leaving the church.

—I want to show you something, he said one morning as I was leaving.

I met him on a Monday morning at a little Catholic school I'd never heard of. It wasn't in the school directory, and it was hard to find. It was an old clapboard boardinghouse, and the gingerbread on it was fairly rotting, but there were geraniums on every windowsill. I was a little startled when a little nun in a navy skirt and white blouse opened the door and called him by his name.

—*Let's go see the boys,* she said, and led us into a sunlit yard behind the house. There were twelve or so boys playing, some shooting marbles, some reading comic books. They looked at me with curiosity for a moment, then resumed. He watched them later from the school's kitchen window while the sister made us tea. Michael was watching them, still, when she put the teapot in a linen cozy and put it on the table before us.

—*Now which one was it whose mother tried to drown him?* he said.

I clanked my spoon against my cup and spilled sugar on the table.

—*The littlest one,* the nun said. —*We call him our littlest angel.*

I walked to the window to look. A little mop-haired boy was building a tower of blocks.

—*And show me again the one whose mother burned him with cigarettes.*

The nun looked quizzically at him, and then said after a moment, —*The one in the pear tree. He wants to be a soldier.*

Michael turned to look at me. I lifted my teacup wordlessly, a secret toast: *Touché.*

We had to walk through a little park to get to our cars. It was mid-spring, and there were some groundsmen setting out geraniums, huge buckets of them, and they had spaded up the path to our cars in the time we'd been at the school. That fast. We stood at the edge of a little sea of pink blossoms.

—*So, what did you think?* he said.

—*Oh, it was impressive,* I answered in my hard-candy headmistress voice that I hated now. I nattered on about schools as we backtracked around a little duck pond to get to our cars.

—*If you think you can retrieve me, then have at it. Let me see you call me back into the fold.* I said this to him rather nastily.

As we rounded the far side of the little duck pond, there was a pair of black swans, mating. In broad daylight, very noisily. You couldn't miss seeing it. We both stopped in our tracks, long enough for me to see that the male had nipped at her neck so much that the feathers were gone, the skin was gone, and the cords of her neck muscles were showing, red, bloody, obscene. Neither of them was having any particular pleasure from their coupling, it was just something beyond their control.

An awful moment to share with a man, as if all life is predicated upon ugliness, like there is no gold-filled time, just some haze that comes and goes in your head.

It always comes down to that, doesn't it? You are with some man and some little brutality you see together spells it all out for you: he's a man, you are not. He could destroy you if he wanted to, and you don't understand why he doesn't. And all you can feel at the moment is something like shame.

I was thinking of the Manger Hotel. I was thinking, *This is it, I can't go on*—when Michael turned around to face me, putting himself between me and those terrible swans. Blocking my view on purpose, like the gentleman throwing his cloak over the mud puddle in the old movies. The way he was looking at me, for a minute there I thought he was going to kiss me.

I wanted that very much.

He reached up with his hand, the one with his wedding ring on it, and he brushed my cheekbone softly.

—An eyelash, he said, and my face was burning.

He might as well have kissed me. The effect was the same. We turned our backs to the swans and walked on. We parted on the sidewalk. I, not quite gold-filled, but not ever the same again.

I pretty much started measuring out my life in sabbaths. I was lonely enough that I began to imagine that Michael spoke to me, not the others, in his Sunday-morning musings. This went on for months.

I stayed away from the Manger Hotel, and my smile muscles were in good working order. But I had begun to want more than Michael's avuncular pats on the back when I left church. One evening in late summer I was passing the church on my way home from work and saw the light in the study on. On an impulse I stopped, and I wanted to tell him that if he needed to say something to me, then please say it to *me* and not just cast it out like bread upon everybody else's waters.

I was going to say impassioned things about men and women, about how I thought marriage was the biggest hoax to come down the pike since that bit about the tree of knowledge. I was going to tell him to explain to me, since he seemed to know everything, why it was that my husband was capable of being somebody's trashy secret and I wasn't.

The hall was carpeted and my footsteps made no sound as I neared his office and saw the open door. About the time I looked in, I heard a woman's voice, and then I saw her. Soft wool suit, legs crossed, handkerchief in hand, teary eyes. A moment frozen in time: queen bee sliding backwards into waifhood: *Oh, I am so broken, can you please fix me?*

Michael looked up when I was standing in the doorway. Bored, really, looking past me, barely recognizing me. As if we were all interchangeable—queen bees, waifs. The man was running his *own* school for wayward girls, and it was to him what the Manger Hotel and the martinis were to me. I felt like he had just handed me my diploma. Next waif, please.

I could still taste a bit of the old bitterness, whole underground streams waiting to well up in my throat. I drove around a while, not wanting to go home.

I checked into the Manger Hotel. I sat with my pitcher of martinis by the window, and drank from the cup that tasted good, and set sail for the golden time. *Hey, Michael,* I thought a little ruefully, *I want to be your main waif, I want to be the wretched refuse on your teeming shore.*

I sat and looked down at the cars turning into gold beads, and at the freighters in the channel, and it began to seem to me that I was up in a watchtower. It was coming, the motherly time, when I was watching over everyone. It was coming. I could make it this time. One martini more.

I thought of all the men and women, of holy matrimony.

I thought of how it was all just a big planetary dance.

I thought of all the alleys with the waifs.

Why ever should a woman *be* anything? Be something and your man will turn away to a new partner. Be a waif and your dance card is full. The doctors, the lawyers, the middle-class chiefs looking for absolution in the waifs' eyes. The waifs looking at them and making them feel loved. The queen bees, glistening and white and immobile, and bitter to the taste, probably.

It had all been going on too long. Long before I ever hit the scene, as Harrison would say.

I could only save myself. I could be something other than a queen bee.

· · ·

—*WHY DON'T YOU GO see Leslie?* I suggested to Harrison when I got home. He looked at me over the newspaper. I'd already seen her carving a jack-o'-lantern for Lucy out in the courtyard. I'm sure that he had, too. He was eating tuna out of a can, and I felt guilty. It wasn't any particular largesse that made me say that to him. I felt like the big lie was still there between us, like some unwanted old mother-in-law keeping us apart. I didn't want to be the queen bee. I wanted to practice love for every living thing.

—*What?* he was staring at me. Suspicious.

—*Why don't you go see her? You don't have to lie to me. Just go see her.*

—*You're crazy.*

—*I'm not crazy. The Lord loves a cheerful giver.*

—*Is it a bad time of the month? What? You don't know what you're saying. Have I ever given you reason to doubt me?*

I couldn't speak for a minute. —*Yes. Yes, you have.*

I thought for a minute he was going to hit me, but he didn't. He went out for several hours.

That night I tried to explain myself to his back as he turned away from me to go to sleep. —*I'll not be your jailer, Harrison. I won't do it. So don't use that to fetch her. You can attract her on your own.*

He was silent with anger. I tried again.

—*It's my way of not being the agent of your inward death.*

—*Go to hell. You don't love me.*

—*Remember when you said that every sixty seconds is a new chance to start over?*

Neither of us slept well that night, and I felt bad for forcing the issue. But how could I not? What future was there for me in this life? The awful imprisonment of concealing from everyone the fact that you know what they were concealing from you. The next day was Halloween. Sloane dropped in on us like she was prone to do on holidays, when she felt like she was rattling around the Cotton Exchange like a BB in a tin cup. She wanted to be at the door to hand out candy. Our first customers were Leslie and Lucy. Lucy was dressed like a little mouse, and Leslie had painted little whiskers on her with an eyebrow pencil: Leslie had started wearing jeans, and looked waifish. She glanced at Harrison, and I saw it all in her look. She wanted his approval.

Harrison hung back, Sloane fussed over the baby.

—*Why don't you go with them, Harrison?* I said.

He made a face. *Is this a trick?* he was wondering. *Am I being tested?*

—*We cannot let her go around with that child alone,* I said. I wanted to grab him by the lapels and tell him: —*You can't just draw her out like that and then abandon her. She's given you something, and now you have to give something back.*

So he sailed out into the warm autumn night with her, and my heart felt like the big blooming red peony again, only I wasn't sure if it was bursting or breaking. Sloane and I dispensed M&Ms to all comers. A rather steady stream of witches and pillowcases with eyeholes, and princesses and Robin Hoods and such. Such a big dance it all was. I smiled at them all and felt like I was back up in my watchtower again, without even having to check into the Manger Hotel and drink the martinis. My head was making up its own madrigals: *We are all interchangeable, we are all interchangeable.*

—*I don't think you know what you're doing,* Sloane said when Harrison wasn't home yet by eleven.

—*Of course I don't know what I'm doing,* I opined over our grandmother's Limoges teacup. —*That's the pleasure of it. Why shouldn't I share him if I want to?* Something about that word, *share,* sounded sexy, gave me that old low want between the legs. Something I had not felt in a long time.

—*Why not step out in front of a moving bus for the pleasure of it?* Sloane said. She needed me to be the white pale queen bee, trapped, immobile, and unhappy. So she could feel free and eccentric, living among her paint splashes. This had been our habit since childhood.

—*He's lovely, lovely in the sack,* I tormented her. —*Maybe you could benefit from* . . . Here I trailed off, sensing I'd gone too far, then my mind just went off into whole fusillades of unspeakable thought: *Harrison was shot out of the sky one time. The summer that you and I taught swimming lessons at the club, and danced the nights away. We slept until noon and painted our nails and stole the nylons from Mother's secret stash, while Harrison was trying to get out of New Guinea alive, and he came through it with something that neither you nor I have, and all I know is that it makes women want to live.*

It no longer made sense to me to try to own Harrison. It only made sense to practice love for every living thing.

Maybe my little plan backfired. When he came home, he'd been drinking, alone, for hours.

Sloane made some Christmas plans that year, so she wasn't with us. Harrison's son, Field, decided, after years of not seeing him, to come for New Year's. I dreaded it: they would be in an argument within five minutes of seeing each other.

We had snow, unusual for Savannah, whole puffs of it in the courtyard on the day before Christmas. I could see Leslie's windows, the reflection of her Christmas tree lights bouncing off her kitchen wall, starbursts of red, green, blue. Where were her people? How could anybody be so self-sufficient?

Harrison was wandering around the apartment at loose ends. Christmas had always been hard for him. There were some Christmases when his children did not phone, or even send so much as a card. Sometimes he would start drinking a few days before Christmas and not stop until after New Year's.

I looked out the kitchen window at Leslie's lights. No signs of visitors, family. I thought of her over there waking up alone on Christmas morning, and I couldn't stand it. It was Christmas Eve, and the snow made it seem that the whole world was waiting to begin. That some *good* could begin. I put on one of Harrison's old coats and went over there.

The baby was asleep and Leslie was trying to put together a tricycle. The parts were scattered all over her kitchen floor, red and chrome. She tried to hide it, but she'd been crying. I sensed that she was on thin, thin ice in the world. Christmas has a way of making the ice even thinner.

She made us some tea, and I took off Harrison's coat and laid it over the back of a chair. That she could just *choose* to have a baby, and just do it without depending on anyone for help. This was mind-boggling to me. I looked at her mug with the psychedelic designs on it and wondered what was important to her. She looked tired and discouraged, like she knew she would pay the rest of her life for that one little act of bravery: *I wanted to have a baby but I didn't want to be married.*

—*I envy you,* she said. —*You have a wonderful husband.*

In my mind I was already up in the top of the Manger Hotel, seeing everything, watching over everyone, understanding how interchangeable we all are.

—*Most men are wonderful*, I said carefully. —*If you get right down to it. They have something we don't. They're real fighters.*

She was fingering the threads in Harrison's coat. Her face softened when she did this and I saw that she knew she had met one. At the moment, he was fighting his wish to drink, in spite of the fact that his kids had spurned his invitation to spend Christmas with us.

—*Come have Christmas dinner with us*, I said.

—*But your family . . .*

—*Harrison's son isn't coming until New Year's*, I said. —*It's the first time he's seen him in seven years.*

—*I think I'm going to have to give up on this trike. I can't figure it out. I just wanted Lucy to see something big under the tree when she wakes up*—she trailed off and seemed near tears.

—*You need some help. I'll go get Harrison. He'll have it together in no time.*

Maybe it is the function of Christmas to make even those with hard-candy hearts holy for a little while. One day of the year you can be a cheerful giver even if you can't bring it off during the other 364.

—*SHE NEEDS SOME HELP over there*, I said to him when I came into the kitchen. He had been looking morose and bored, but he brightened up a bit at this. —*She's trying to put Lucy's trike together, and she doesn't even have a wrench. No pliers, either.*

—*Why didn't you take her mine?*

—*Why don't you take them? I have to stuff the goose. I invited them for Christmas dinner. I have to make that baby some Christmas cookies.*

He had that tender, needy look on his face. He was at an age where he wanted no upheavals, just for life to proceed on an even keel: meals on time, clean clothes to wear, my presence a sure thing. On the other hand: the longing looks out the window. That age where he understands the finitude of his own life.

I wanted to see him in love, one more time in my life.

—*That baby has no father*, I said to him in my headmistress voice. —*She needs help.*

—*I have to change*, he said. He changed clothes twice, and I ironed his favorite shirt, the one that I'd noticed would give him power when he was nervous about something. I kissed his temples where the gray was coming.

—*Come with me,* he fussed.

—*Too much to do. And don't just fix the trike,* I fussed over him a little. —*She needs somebody to have a drink with her and talk to her.*

I watched through the African violets while he checked the tarp that covered his *Alapaha Star,* then crossed through the puffs of snow with the toolbox. I saw her let him in. I could see the colored light of her Christmas tree, those aluminum ones we all had then, with the revolving colored wheel that splashed light on it. She'd pinned her hair up, and put on some makeup. Good.

I imagined her fixing him a drink. Not too heavy on the soda, I forewarned her in my mind. He doesn't like that. I imagined them sitting together on her kitchen floor and how he'd make her laugh about the trike parts. *Foot bone connected to the—pedal bone.* Maybe he'd put his arm around her, probably he'd be too shy.

My head was leading them on. I told him in my mind: *You have to make the first move. I felt so discouraged and ugly when you took so long to touch me.*

For insurance, I told her in my mind: *You may have to make the first move. I'd thought he'd never kiss me at first.* I was dizzy with an odd communal desire, not a lonely one. The love I felt for him felt credible again, not just some habit I had.

—*Then again,* I reasoned. —*What if she's predatory? What if I'm mistaken about her and she's not worth this.*

I put my hand on the phone.

No. He survived *me,* and all the ways I failed him, didn't he?

What if she isn't good to him?

Hand on the phone.

No. If so, I am here to hold him. Until the next one comes along.

I was rinsing dishes at the sink not much later and saw him walking back across the courtyard. There came this lump in my throat, a kind of rage, really. *And why should he not have what he desires? And why should he have only my old paper white narcissus skin to hold? Who decreed that it would be this way?*

He paused in the door and put the toolbox on the counter.

—*You would not believe the cheap metal they make those trikes out of,* he said.

I must have been staring at him dumbly. —*What?* I asked.

—Ran into some problems, schatze, he said, smiling.

—What's that?

—My shoes keep walkin' back to you. She's no treasure, baby.

So it was going to be more difficult than I had thought. He was walking toward me, but my head was dizzy with a different possibility. *Procure* for him? No. Just put them in his path. Be the agent of his inward life. Make the world new for him every day. Make *him* new for *myself* every day. We could have our own school for wayward girls.

But we needed some rules.

They'd have to be waifs.

They'd have to be tough. Anything could happen. Or not. To *have* him was just as tough a fate as *not* to have him.

They'd have to be cheerful givers, sisters in the sight of God.

But mostly, they'd have to *adore* him. They'd have to *adore* him as he taught them to pass up the cup of bitterness by letting them drink from the cup of himself.

FIELD'S GUIDE TO
AMERIKAN HOUSES

*F*our summers after the Summer of Love, I got a notice from the Selective Service, forwarded to the University of Georgia by my mother. *Report to the induction site at Jacksonville, Florida, for the physical examination.* I flipped the envelope over, thinking maybe there had been some mistake. I was 4-F. But it was my name on there, all right: *Field Durrance.*

I had sight in only one eye, the other having been blown out by a cherry bomb my cousin Jim and I were trying to set off when I was eleven. So once I got over the initial fear, I got curious. I was about to make a little sortie into Pig Nation, otherwise known to us in the antiwar movement as Amerika. I figured the field trip to the enemy camp would only better equip me to train others how to flunk their physicals. Part of my job as a draft-resistance counselor at the University of Georgia.

I made it all the way up to the eye exam. Stripped to my shorts, standing in line with other guys. You could sort us by looking at us: who was ready to kill some gooks, who was not. Then the sergeant guy covered up my one good eye, glanced at the piece of paper that pertained to me, and said, —*Okay, Durrance. Now.*

I squinted and pretended to parse it out: —*It says, "I . . . will not . . . serve . . . the emperors . . . of Pig Nation*—"

—*You READ that fuckin' eye chart, you asshole!* he hissed at me.

—*I can't,* I said. I took out my glass eye and held it out to him in the palm of my hand. —*Read it yourself, motherfucker,* I said. —*Read it yourself.*

Just the smell of that man, a combination of aftershave, starch, that self-serving, self-righteous attitude—I had traveled many miles and years away from my father just to come back to the place where he was. Operant conditioning: the mouse in the maze remembers the fear. I was twenty-one. I felt real terror there, that by some fluke I could be thrown back into that long-ago world.

Where you are nothing but a piece of meat to be commanded by some other piece of meat who has bluffed his way into acquiring the requisite medals and scrambled eggs on his shoulders that give him the power.

—*I'm sorry, son,* the sergeant said, and he saw the 4-F then on my paper. There was this thing in his eyes, a terror of his own—*It's gone too far, it's gone too far.* Then it was gone, the façade came down, and he was safely a patriot again.

I stopped by to see my family before I went back to school.

I went to the river with my cousin Jim. Sentimental journey home, mosquito-peppered night, honeysuckle smell, as if I could crawl back into the time when I played Roy Rogers in the river bottom. Half our history was in those woods. He was a Green Beret. He was between tours in Vietnam. There were things we could no longer talk about. Like the day he had to carry me on his back out of those woods, my blood streaming down his shirt front, after we blew my eye out with the cherry bomb my father had given me for my birthday.

—*How many tours is this now?*

—*Third, coming up.*

—*Third time could be the charm,* I said. —*Look, I could have you in Ontario two days from now. I know some guys there, Quakers. You'd have to help them harvest tobacco, though.*

His eyes flashed at me. This was seditious ground. He didn't say a word, just took out a joint and licked the end of it, before offering it to me with raised, quizzical eyebrows.

—*Mr. Nixon know you smokin' that shit?* I asked him, grinning.

—*Mr. Nixon don't 'low no shit-smokin' 'round here.*

—*I don't care what Mr. Nixon don't 'low,* he laughed. —*Do women like long hair like that? Is it easier to get laid like that?*

—*Like you would not believe,* I said. His own hair was cut to a coaly burled softness; he was an officer, so he didn't have to have a buzz cut. I couldn't tell him: it wasn't the hair that brought the women to me. It was the clothes, the political talk, the feeling that we were fighting some common evil. Him and his type. I couldn't tell him.

We stared at the stars separately that night, the locusts roaring like a wall of noise that kept the world away from the river.

—*This is not a REAL war*, my mother decreed, on the front porch in Alapaha. —*In a REAL war there is camaraderie, there is purpose. But don't ever tell that to your father; he'd break your jaw the way he broke mine. That was when I was in the most danger. When I told the truth.*

You know you are a man when you refrain from telling the truth to your elders. Vietnam was meaningless to my mother for one reason. I was 4-F. It did not exist for her. Those lines of boys who came out of the system in Jacksonville with shaven heads and hands clasped over genitals, like the pictures in that old book on Auschwitz she always thought she had hidden from us. We had our own camaraderie. We had our own purpose.

—*So how is your drafting class?* She asked. She always had this plan that I would be an architect. I didn't tell her that I had stopped attending the class after two weeks: it was full of budding emissaries of Pig Nation—would-be engineers with the plastic pocket protectors, the locust horde waiting to go forth and pave all nations.

In Athens, I lived in an old falling-in Presbyterian manse with a gambrel slate roof and more rooms than I and four other guys in the movement could fill. So we held "sessions" there in a sunroom in the back. Four summers after the Summer of Love, after Nixon's goons had gunned some of us down to the ground at Kent State. How to make a Molotov cocktail. Where to take your girl for a legal abortion. I did the sessions on what to do when your number came up in the draft lottery.

I had the attic room, an unfinished cupola that smelled of pine in hot weather. Mullioned windows all around. It was like living in a tall turret on a stationary ship, from which I could see the neighborhood was changing. I loved those old houses. Some not quite Tudor, but the bald aspiration to it. Others not quite French colonial, but the coveting of it. The little dowagers who lived in them would come out in their straw hats and tend flowerbeds, oblivious to the marijuana smoke and motorcycle exhaust of their new neighbors. After a while, some didn't come out anymore; you'd see nurses come and go. Then the realtors' signs would appear, and the houses would pass into another incarnation—a boutique, a barbe-cue place, a rabbit warren for more students.

The Phillips 66 station on the corner had become the Treasure Heart Truth Temple, wherein beehive-headed white-trash matrons raised their fat-wattled arms heavenward on Saturday nights. The old Presbyterian church down the block was a boutique where the girls we dated sold psychedelic posters, beads, scented candles, Leadbelly, and English madrigals side by side. I watched the sun go down over the housetops, opening the windows to let music out, releasing anthems like carrier pigeons to the sky—

> *Find the cost of freedom,*
> *Buried in the ground.*
> *Mother Earth will swallow you,*
> *Lay your body down.*

On the Sheetrock wall of my room I sketched out the kinship patterns of the Ik, a loveless society I was fascinated by in my anthropology class. They had no word for love. Didn't *need* it. I used to try to figure out if we had evolved from them, or maybe if they had evolved from us. The first time I did acid—I was alone, up there—it seemed to me that my soul was a black wax flower in closed corridors of kinship scribbled in black, no love to be found. But when I closed it into a red fist, I could release a gold haze of good intent on the neighborhood.

I would hole up in my attic tower and write:

The enemy is entrenched and intractable.

There are different forms of fighting.

Everything must be willing to adapt to some more habitable way of life.

I had girls like music; play them over and over until you can't stand to hear them anymore because it reminds you of some old self you had shed like snakeskin on your way to Nirvana. That, too, felt like freedom: wake up with a girl whose name you didn't get.

We had our own mimeograph machine, which somebody lifted from the Admin Building and deposited at the manse like a bagged trophy. At some meetings we chanted the names of political prisoners who had died, and Vietnam was some fragile lily that our fathers were trampling.

Someone would read the names of the Vietnamese dead, mingled with the Resistance dead, and we would answer in Spanish.

 —*Le Duc Thuong.*

 —*No se lo olvide.*

We will not forget you. Why in Spanish, I don't even remember. We had this thing about Che Guevara, maybe. We did not call out the names of American military dead. I did the workshops on draft resistance, using materials supplied to us by groups at Berkeley and Chicago. One of my roommates had some murky ties to the Weather Underground, some Emory guy who would introduce us, there in the Presbyterian manse, to the art of Molotov cocktails.

There was a book in the library I aspired to get my hands on, a Defense Department bomb manual. How to make them. We called it the cookbook. But it was checked out to some girl named Madeira Webster. She hadn't given an address, and she wasn't in the phone book, and that made me a little in love with her, thinking maybe she was a bit like me. I wouldn't consent to have my name listed in the phone book. To do so was to participate in Pig Nation. My number was secret.

I answered the phone one time and it was this kid from Watkinsville.

 —*They got my number,* he said. —*Shit, man.*

 —*How much time before you report to the induction site?* This was the drill.

 —*Two weeks.*

 —*Do you want to explore the options? Are you a student?*

 —*I'm nineteen,* he said. —*I ain't even got high school. I ain't got no rich daddy to buy my ass off. I ain't got no daddy, period.*

 —*Well, I'm here, man, and we are going to take care of your ass.*

Rodney Screvens, his name was. I remember it because it is now etched in black marble in D.C. I remember him because we climbed out the mullioned windows together onto the roof of the cupola and got stoned. He was supposed to take a bus to Detroit the next day. We had a party and passed around a bedpan somebody lifted from the university infirmary, and collected just enough for his bus ticket and a few meals.

 —*Canada, man,* he said. —*I ain't even been to Atlanta.*

That was when I knew he wouldn't do it. I closed my eyes a

minute, and was just about to tell him about the Ik. How they have no word for love, how they have no *need* for the word for love, and I couldn't. I wanted to stop thinking—and I couldn't.

He had a girlfriend.

It was a given: if there was a girlfriend, you would lose him to Pig Nation. You could bank on it. The girlfriend would give him the illusion that there was something personal at stake.

It was hard to tell sometimes when a new party had begun, or if it was just an extension of the one the night before. Even when it was nothing but six or seven guys sitting in a room getting stoned in honor of the inductee, the sacrificial lamb. I woke up one night and there was someone in my room. A couple, I thought. The thought crossed my mind that the human instinct for privacy was a bit superfluous at this point.

—*Go find somebody else's bed to screw in.*

—*I just need a place to hide,* came a girl's voice in the dark.

I rolled over. She was alone, she was in a long white lace peasant dress, and she had brown hair down to her waist, and wire-rimmed glasses. She was fumbling around the bodice of the dress.

—*Oh damn, he's peed on me.*

I stared. She shucked her shoulders and the dress fell down and a little tortoiseshell kitten fell out with a mewl.

—*They were getting him stoned,* she said, not self-conscious, not calculated, and her lace bra showing. These were the times. —*They were going to castrate him. Somebody's father is a vet, so he was the one who was going to do it.*

—*That makes him eminently qualified doesn't it?* I said, dryly, and this earned a slight smile from her. Already there was something subliminal between us.

—*Nice dress,* I said. —*Is it ruined?*

—*It's a Mexican wedding dress,* she said. —*Washable.*

—*So that means some Mexican woman probably worked a month for five dollars to make that dress,* I said, half-teasing. The knee-jerk thing we all did then, the instant translation of everything around us into oppression of the huddled masses by some sinister force we vaguely associated with our parents.

—*No, you asshole,* she said, laughing. —*It means three Filipino women worked one day for probably ten dollars. And split it three ways.*

—*What's your name?* I asked, and took the kitten.

—*Madeira Webster.*

The cookbook girl. How to keep her there.

—*You're missing the party.*

—*I'm sick of the party,* she said. Then she stared. —*You're not stoned.*
She sounded almost suspicious. One could never be too careful;
those who didn't indulge were suspect.

—*You're not, either,* I said.

—*I have never trusted the people around me enough to do that.*

I gave her a T-shirt that came to her knees and left her and the
kitten on my futon and went to the Waffle House and nursed a cup
of coffee, along with the instinct not to go back and sleep with
her. That would have been the end of it.

At a session on the *Upanishads* I saw her again. This guy from the
Philosophy Department wearing his black turtleneck reading from
a tattered paperback:

—*"Who sends the mind to wander afar? Who first drives life to start on
its journey?"*

Madeira smiled at me then, as if to say, *What utter fucking bullshit,*
and all the other people in the room peeled away to an extraneous
blur. Later I wanted to finish that semaphore conversation. —*Do you
still have that bomb book checked out? You going to teach the girls to make
bombs?*

—*I don't just talk about peace. I am really into it. That book is at the
bottom of the Oconee River,* she said, and walked away.

—*See you around,* I said to her back. And didn't see her for weeks.

My father and Olivia invited me to come see the New Year's
Day parade with them. I hadn't seen him in seven years. He lived
in Savannah in one of those old walk-up apartments overlooking
the river. It occurred to me that his building was, like him, always
trying to overcome its origins. Even assuming that you could pry
off the layers of "improvements" you'd still have a façade forced
onto something basically crude. That was the year that downtown
Savannah had something like the highest per-capita murder rate in
the U.S. and the urban renewal attempts seemed to be mostly nostalgia for when the white people were in charge.

It must have been a shock for them both to see me. My hair was
down to my shoulders and I had a beard. I wore an old army-
surplus sergeant's jacket, shoulder patches still intact, on which one
of my girlfriends had sewn *my* patch, a red fist. Across the back,

"Amerikan Dead" with a plastic credit-card window that I would slide a number in, sort of a spoof on the McDonald's signs claiming how many millions of hamburgers they'd sold. When my father answered the door, he actually looked over my shoulder, as if the real me, the boy he used to know could be found standing behind me. Then he decided to break the silence of seven years.

—*You did not earn those stripes, son. You have no right to wear them. It just isn't done.*

I smiled gamely, tense in a way I had not been since the *last* time I saw him. But there was a difference, now that I was grown. I wanted to have it out with him.

—*Come in, come in,* he said impatiently. —*We are not without the vestiges of civilization here. I think a little aperitif is apropos. We'll get your bags later. Lissen, kid: every sixty seconds is a chance to start over and get it right this time.*

What largesse. I only made it through dessert and coffee. Olivia moving around like the world would be fuckin'-A if only everyone would simply obey Emily Post and dress like Republicans in polyester. This damn record on, "Silent Night" farting through a saxophone, like what you would get if the Virgin Mary were a stripper in a riverfront dive.

—*Fortissimo!* he shouted, as he turned up the volume. I hated them both a little. I told myself this was not a visit of filial piety; this was an excursion, an anthropological expedition into the generation that believed it had an inalienable right to develop its hometowns into Bayonne, New Jersey.

I had infiltrated Pig Nation.

—*About that coat,* he started. —*Do you know how those coats end up in those places, those flea markets? The wives throw them out. They don't want anything to remind them.*

I thought for the first time about the previous owner of the coat. Maybe he was six feet under in Arlington, maybe he was a pile of bones in some mass grave in a jungle. I liked the idea of wearing his coat. I could carry on the fight, and do it right this time.

I had a joint in my pocket. I had the not-so-wise idea that I would turn them on. They certainly liked to drink. The joint was rolled in stars-and-bars paper.

—*Get rid of that. I never want to see you do that again.*

—*It doesn't hurt. It's not as bad for you as scotch, even.*

—*You are an embarrassment to your nation. You are an embarrassment to me. Why do you choose the path that closes doors for you?*

—*It's a meaningless war. It has no meaning, no purpose.*

—*That is not within your purview.* He stared levelly at me. —*Meaning is not always within our purview. Schatze,* he called into the kitchen, —*come out here. I'm daft, and I'm playing to an empty house.*

—*I have curaçao, crème de menthe, brandy?* Olivia offered helpfully.

—*He used to keep these little notebooks*, my father said to Olivia. —"*I am an unofficial ambassador of the United States of America.*" *He wrote that. He used to have a mature appreciation of the use of military force in the management of freedom.*

I looked around their place. There were no traces of us. It was as if we did not exist. There were some photos of other people's children, none of us. He had laundered us out of his life.

The management of freedom.

I excused myself, left by the back door—*I will show you a closed door, old man*—drove back to Athens, imagining the two of them checking in all the rooms, bewildered, wondering where I'd gone, if I'd be back. I was looking forward to more years of silence, welcoming seven more years of silence. I turned the music as loud as I could stand it:

> *Tin soldiers and Nixon comin'.*
> *We're finally on our own.*
> *This summer I hear the drummin'.*
> *Four dead in Ohio.*

I drove through bleached-out wintry fields, bare trees, towns so small that the police would tail you from one city limits sign to the other, just to be on the safe side. I looked hungrily at the stark, empty farmhouses in the fields: *I could live there, I could live there.* This was like a reflex, a throwback to my childhood. It was a simple matter, my management of freedom. It was a form of power, to leave. It felt good.

I thought about the last time I'd been on those back roads, the last time I'd seen him.

Once I came out of school and there was my father's car, lined up with all the moms in the stationwagons, and I walked over to see him.

—*Long time no see, compadre,* he had said, and I felt this odd stab of love and annoyance: *You, you.* I sat in an enraged pygmy silence as he drove through back-country roads, and talked about my coming to live with him. He stopped at a shoe store and bought a pair of pink stiletto heels and had them gift-wrapped, after having the salesgirl model them for him. It began to rain as we got nearer to Savannah. I looked at all the tidy farmhouses, and thought, *I could live there, I could live there.*

Before it was over, he had driven me to Fort Stewart for intelligence testing. He did this because there had been an article in the newspaper about me, how I'd broken the local records for achievement-test scores, and they put my picture in, glasses and all, like I was the very thing to save us all from the Communist threat. My father sat outside in the hall while a skinny lieutenant tested me. Then there was this brief time when I sat working crossword puzzles in the Chatham County sheriff's office with a black dude named Hosea who was in for forgery. The sheriff came in with my father and said, —*Boy, where do you want to BE?*

—*At home with my mother.*

Then my father vanished into the rainy night without a word to me. And then my mother was there to get me.

After the intelligence-testing fiasco, there were seven years of silence from my father. He showed up for my high school graduation, then disappeared into the May night, while I went my way to a party with my friends, who would soon not be my friends anymore after I went to college and got radicalized.

I GOT THE CALL ABOUT JIM from my mother one night when there was a party on at the house. I could see this black chick dancing naked on the kitchen table. Somebody was waving the phone receiver and pointing to me. I could barely hear my mother's voice, but I remember that I sat down suddenly on the floor when she said it and it registered: *Black car from Fort Benning parked by the curb at dawn, waiting for Adrienne to get up and open the door. Missing in action. Jim.*

It was exam week and I was doing a lot of speed, and my first instinct was to start walking. Anywhere. Asia. All night. I would just go *find* him. Carry him home on my back. I don't remember hanging up the phone. I remember some people standing around, the music stopped.

—*My cousin is missing,* I explained, beginning descent, dangling like some stage mannequin on a rope, feeling the ground get very flat beneath me, but still out of reach of my toes. Everyone's faces seemed flat-nosed and foreign, like the Ik in a paler color. —*In action,* I said, and there was this bad silence. —*He carried me out of the woods one time when I was hurt. On his back.*

Someone opined as to how his misfortune was the price of serving the emperors of Pig Nation, and I took a swing at him. They got me upstairs into my own bed. Then they all left me, except Madeira, who sat in a chair embroidering something with a little gold hoop in her lap. I was coming down from the speed, like a ravaged old sock, full of holes. And the oriental spirits were coming through the holes to torment me: the name of every Vietnamese soldier I had chanted, like some kind puppet jerked by the momentum of the antiwar movement. There was a blank notebook in my head, and an enraged child that did not know the logic of real time scribbled things there:

Let us go backwards, to the river. Every sixty seconds is a chance to start over and get it right this time. I will carry him on my back to fucking Canada—

I put the pillow over my head and curled up. The scribbling stayed inside me. I wanted to have fierce nightmares, call out for help, have some crisis. Anything to get Madeira to cross the room and hold me together.

—*You know, this happens all the time,* she said. —*They find most of them. Do you want me to call your dad?* she asked into the dark.

—*Nope,* I said, emphatically.

—*Wanna tell me about it?*

That thing that women do, to get you to turn yourself inside out just for them, the better to darn the holes.

—*Nope,* I answered. She let it alone.

—*I feel . . . very much . . . the ravaged sock that needs darning,* I spoke toward her. Let me not die. Let me not be dead. Let me die. Let me stop thinking.

—*It's the speed,* she said.

—*No, it isn't,* I answered.

—*I'm going to take you home with me,* she said, and my heart got all syncopated, bumpy ride, oriental ghouls trailing my every good thought of how she looked to me.

It was a cottage in front of the Spinoza Salvage Yards, where she lived. Board and batten white frame, green-shuttered, like the house in Alapaha, that face-on austerity that doesn't try to be anything more than what it is: hopelessly American, on the right of way of the confluence of two highways. There behind it was an array of old Ford Galaxies, Mercury Comets, Studebakers, and Ramblers, smashed flat and stacked like fading pastel lozenges. Lesser piles of stoves, refrigerators, boat motors, bedsprings. The house seemed to yearn for downhill, toward its brethren of similar vintage, things that no one had any use for any longer. The detritus of Pig Nation.

The tortoiseshell kitten was grown up, meowing for its dinner. No roommates. The bathroom had a picture window, claw-footed bathtub—she had painted the toenails pink, its sides paisley. Hulking Victorian bordello sofa, a quilt on it. There was an empty bedroom in the back, full view of the stacked cars in the salvage yards, nothing left in it but a poster of Janis Joplin in her chorus-girl clothes.

We watched the sun go down over the smashed pastel cars—this was the spectacle there was to be shared. Warm with cheap chianti, we could see Mr. Spinoza walking through the lanes of his magnificent junk, followed by a retinue of cats. Beneath that warmth in me, black glutinous guilt, slow oil spill going down inside me. How to keep going. How not to just run out in the street and kill someone, blow up a building.

—*So, what are you thinking about?* Madeira asked.

—*I'm thinking that I wish I could stop thinking. About the Ik.*

—*The ones who don't have a word for love?*

I nodded. —*I feel like . . . they make perfect sense. That's bad, right?*

—*It's the speed, still,* she said.

—*Yes,* I assented. —*Maybe, no. The speed, I mean.*

—*There is one other thing we can try,* she said.

—*Yes.*

She had this old iron bedstead that she had painted yellow, and a mattress that had two dips in it, as if some long departed couple had broken it in for us. We could hardly look at each other as we undressed and got beneath the quilt, and she hid her face in my chest.

She cried out at first, and then I understood. She'd never gone this far before.

—*Do you want me to stop?*

—*God, don't you dare stop,* she laughed, and I smiled into the dark, for what this told me about her. —*God,* she said again, and made me feel like I was one.

Later, she said, —*Give me Field lessons.*

—*What?*

—*Lessons in you. I want to know it all. Every bit.*

I'd worked too many years at having a mind like a strongbox. She wanted lessons, I offered a test.

—*My father left us on Christmas Eve.*

She didn't cluck, she didn't gasp. She got astride me, nuzzled her face into my neck.

—*Why did he leave?*

—*He got kicked out of the Air Force.*

Her eyes widened. So. The secret was out.

—*So . . . he was, like, a radical, if they didn't want him?*

—*I don't think so. It was so mixed up when he left, my mother forgot it was Christmas.*

—*She forgot?*

—*She forgot. I noticed that she wasn't doing anything to get ready. My sisters were too little to notice. And then Christmas Day came, and there was no food.* Take that little hole in my heart and darn it.

—*No food? Nothing?*

—*Well, Rice Krispies and stuff. Those little individual boxes.*

—*So what did you do? What did your mother do?*

—*I raked the yard. She sat by the window by her bed and smoked.*

—*I know why you raked the yard,* she said. —*So you could feel normal.*

In the morning the air was full of cinnamon and coffee. It was Sunday. She was in the little kitchen, wearing only my shirt and her earrings and she had this little brown crockery bowl with a blue rim, beating eggs. Aromatic thing cooling on a bread board, like a tricorn hat with cooked apples in it.

—*What is that?* I mumbled into her hair.

—*Dutch baby,* she said. —*I need to cook for you.*

This was my introduction to how she would pull ethereal things out of the ordinary shelves. With the passing of each night, we bloomed for each other, private flowers in our shared darkness. Nothing in my life like it, before, or since. Mr. Spinoza's splendiferous jewel-like salvage was somehow of no consequence to me or to our whispered confessions, when I held her near to me.

—*I have always wished I'd been born Amish,* she confessed into the dark one night.

—*Why?* I asked her, stroking her hip. The tortoiseshell cat was purring on my feet.

—*Because they let the men have dominion. That is very sexy, don't you think?*

—*I can top that. I wanted to be a soldier.*

—*Why?*

—*I dreamed of outranking my father, so I could—*

—*Could what?*

—*I don't know. Make people do what they were supposed to do?*

End of lesson. I used to fantasize about calling the MPs to take him away.

We had a couple more weeks of food and love, love and food. And music. She pored over my records like she was making some serious inroads into my soul, and I liked to watch her do this. She wrinkled her nose at the Benny Goodman, the Doors made her want to make love.

Then one night I reached for her and she wriggled away from me, sighed. —*This isn't a good time.*

—*Why not?*

—*I might get pregnant.*

I stared at her, the light from Mr. Spinoza's utility light a silver band across her face. Not entirely a bad thought to me, pregnancy. That in itself is a way station of the journey. You see the mile marker and smile secretly.

—*You mean you're not taking the pill? Are you Catholic?*

—*No, I just don't believe in poison.* And she looked back at me like some animal beseeching me.

Blessed and cursed I was, all the while imagining the big sexual picnic, the one that I always seemed to be missing. She was this white lily my touch might leave brown marks on. That was what manhood felt like to me.

I came into the kitchen one night and she was writing into a notebook.

—*What's that?* I said gently, but the thought was like a razor: *She is tired of me. She will leave me.*

—*Oh, nothing,* she said. I put my arms around her so I could look over her shoulder. *Chocolate biscotti.* There were other recipes in the pink notebook. *Profiteroles. Steak with Stilton sauce. Zuppa di cozze.* I had this stab of love for her, and thought of how maybe we could afford these things some day.

I did not attend my college graduation, though my father did. Maybe he thought I was there somewhere in Sanford Stadium, in the sea of faceless black mortarboarded heads. Some of my buddies from the movement wore red-fisted armbands; I was driving a forklift for Anaconda Wire and Cable. Madeira was waiting tables at the Steak and Ale. Sometimes we'd meet at midnight in the paisley bathtub, the water as hot and soapy as we could stand it, and she'd nestle herself back into me, and we'd stare out at the stacks of cars, and I would knead the calves of her legs. She always had shin splints from standing on concrete.

Sometimes on rainy nights when we had the windows open and I could hear the tree frogs peeping in the junkyard, I would feel so rich that I would get a strange inability to breathe deeply, like the moment when you first learn to balance on a bicycle, afraid your breathing will disturb it all. So you hold your breath, but what you really want to do is call out, *Look at me! I'm doing it!* There was this one night we were lying together in the water, listening to an old Blind Faith record:

> *I have finally found a way to live*
> *In the colors of the Lord.*

I watched the water play around our legs. —*I think I was made to love you,* I murmured into her hair.

I had a letter from my father, tickets to the Masters Golf Tournament in Augusta enclosed. —*Bring a date,* he said. Right, and my raccoon coat and my little flag that says "UGA Bulldogs."

So when I didn't show, he got drunk and drove over to Athens. The Winnebago, about the size of two Brink's trucks end-to-end, was in front of the little cottage when I got home from Anaconda. I had a sense of doom, afraid she would leave me after this.

But he was in the kitchen with Madeira, contrite as a child while she was beating something in her little crockery bowl. She had him peeling potatoes at the kitchen table, and I was suddenly enraged at him. I knew him when he would have taken a woman's nose off for such an offense.

—I propose a toast, he said to Madeira, raising a nude potato. *—WHEREAS, you have got yourself mixed up with a real Durrance, and WHEREAS, saidsame Durrance has a good eye for women, and WHEREAS in another incarnation he would write things like "I am an unofficial ambassador of the United States of America," THEN, let us band together and wish him good fortune and a better barber next time.*

He was looking at my steel-tipped boots, my yellow hard hat under my arm. You would have thought I was his long-lost son or something. All was right with the world, Nicklaus was having a good year, if not as good as Arnie's. My father had comandeered the television, of course, and Lawrence Welk was there in his plastic tuxedo and teeth, and there were these women in bouffant hairdos and fake Scarlett O'Hara evening gowns, singing "In the Good Old Summertime." Madeira went out to get some scotch— I rarely drink—and I was alone with my father. He leaned over, as if he had very little time to work with: *—I can get you a job at Embry-Riddle in Atlanta. Public relations. You could get out of here.*

The thought flashed into my mind: *You are an unofficial ambassador of the United States of Pig Nation.*

Madeira could handle him and me at the same time, amazing feat. She packed him off in the Winnebago with some periwinkle clippings for his new yard in his new house with the swimming pool in Florida.

—I'm twenty minutes away from Disney World. Logistics, logistics. And you need to bring this gracious lady to see Namu the Killer Whale. I'll pick up the tab.

Years of silence and he's ready to pick up the tab. I broke a windowpane with my fist when he was finally gone. Madeira was pinched and white. *—He was just trying to be nice,* she said. *—He doesn't know how. You have to help him.*

She had this way of taking me to bed, riding me down out of whatever untenable place I had gotten into in my mind. We married not long after that night, without any parents present. My mother had little to say to me on the phone when I told her I'd married.

—I don't give advice, she said. *—Especially about that.*

My father was ebullient, drunk when I called to tell him.

—Remember this: every house is a compromise between what once was and what can be.

Tory was born in 1974. Lamaze, the whole bit. Madeira insisted on staying at home in the big deep bathtub, up until the last possible minute. I was afraid the baby was going to be born underwater.

—Read to me, she demanded.

The Upanishads. There it was, right next to the *Rubaiyat of Omar Kayyam*, right next to *Portnoy's Complaint.* I sat beside the bathtub while she lay in the water. *—"Who sends the mind to wander afar? Who first drives life to start on its journey?"*

I could see it in her eyes, the need for the deep narcotic of these words, and I read on. *—"There are two birds, two sweet friends, who dwell on the selfsame tree. The one eats the fruit thereof, and the other looks on in silence."* Madeira, we have to go now.

—No. Read.

I read to her of the rivers of life, wherein all things live and die, wandering like swans in restless flying, thinking that God is afar. *—"This is the truth: As from a fire aflame, thousands of sparks come forth, even so from the Creator an infinity of beings have life and to him return again . . ."*

Hours of this, and I was getting hoarse.

The nurse at the hospital looked at me like I had committed the ultimate atrocity, to postpone the intervention of Pig Nation in the beginning of my child's life. And God was very, very far from me.

That was when I began not to know Madeira. She did it without drugs, eating of the fruit of some horrific tree of knowledge, while I looked on in silence, but her screams left me with a hunger for oblivion, and a mental resolution to go get stoned as soon as this was all over. As if that would restore to me the girl who lay in my arms and asked for Field lessons.

No happy grandparents waiting in the hall for the first glimpse of their immortality, red and wizenend and thoroughly pissed off at having been born into the whole catastrophe. They were all relieved not to take part, as if they'd had their similar struggles long ago, and had no wish to participate in ours. We named her Tory Vientiane. They put her in my arms within moments after weighing her, and I understood that I was no longer free.

Madeira would sing to her when she thought I was not there,

and I would stand eavesdropping, voyeur in my own home, while
she inducted the baby into the ways of our people, her voice like a
hoarse bell:

> 'Tis a gift to be simple.
> 'Tis a gift to be free.
> 'Tis a gift to come down
> Where we ought to be.

Sweet, scary, raw time, when the baby sometimes cried between
us in the bed at night, and nursed at Madeira's breast as if she could
not quite have enough of her presence. It felt like they no longer
required my presence. I organized the first known labor union at
Anaconda Wire and Cable, and I helped start a new newspaper.
We stayed on in the cottage hovering over the Spinoza Salvage
Yards, and the baby began to toddle. My father would mail her
postcards of Minnie Mouse. Disney World was booming. We mailed
him pictures of her, but that was all.

There was one rainy April night, you could hear the peepers in
the salvage yard as if it were some nearby exotic woodland.
Madeira was making marzipan leaves at the kitchen table with
Tory, teaching her her colors.

—*Red?*
—*Weh.*
—*Green?*
—*Geen!*

Tory got a bite if she repeated the word. Madeira would knead
it into some small animal and pop it into her mouth, upturned like
a little bird's.

—*Magenta.*
—*Moninna!*
—*Fuchsia.*
—*Footchie!*
—*What's that?* I asked, and she blushed.
—*A marzipan tree. The baby is learning her colors.*

That night I read over her shoulder: *The real Madeira is a little island with all these rain forests, and orchids, and bananas, and they have pools
big as football fields there. There are paintings by the old Flemish masters
in the museums.*

She put her hands over the page. It was the first time in my life I felt shame for not having more money. I worked for the wire and cable company, and wrote columns for the newspaper.

Every few days I would look at her notebook.

I looked at it the next morning when she was bathing Tory.

I have not seen the ocean in five years. She had drawn a line through that.

This is the house that passion built. A line through that.

This is the heart that harbors the hardness, that lives in the house that passion built. A line through that, too.

It was the first inkling I had that we had outgrown, somehow, the cottage at the edge of the Spinoza Salvage Yards. I took a job at the Atlanta *Journal,* so that by the time Tory was old enough to play outside, she would have a yard to play in, in one of those neighborhoods I swore as an adult that I'd never live in, the kind where they hustle parcels of land just ahead of the bulldozers, with big signs saying "If You Lived Here You'd Be Home by Now." Everything was new.

One night I stood in my own quiet foyer, and got goosebumps at all the quiet normalcy. Meals were on time in my house. Clothes got laundered, bills got paid. It was the kind of house I had always wanted to live in when I was a child.

We lived in a little cul-de-sac, at the end of Nightingale Lane. Our house was a split-level Dutch Colonial, with a fake stone and pressed-wood façade. There was a great field in back that had not been developed. We shared common fences with the neighbors. In the Mock Tudor on one side a man who worked at something called Diversified Dynamics lived with his family. *—Extrusion,* he said to me convivially over the fence when he met me. *—If you're thinking of investments, think extruded food. Fish that you would swear is Alaskan King Crab, cheap. We developed that process at Diversified Dynamics.*

On the other side of us, in the stucco Spanish Mission house, lived a brilliant man who ran a research lab at Emory. *—I design simulations of the human condition,* he explained, as if that explained anything. *—Devices that reproduce, under test conditions, phenomena likely to occur in actual circumstances. What do you do?*

—Work for the newspaper.

—Hmmn, he said. *—Property line runs along here,* he said, pacing it

off like a big zoo cat. *—All sewers are united into a common one right about there, in the middle of the road. I have an easement for my driveway.*

I covered the slow, petty passions of city politics, the methadone freaks in the Henry Grady Hospital Emergency Room, the sting operations at the local S&M parlors, the urban-renewal scams. I sometimes stepped out of the house at night to walk off my own land lines, inside the common walls of the fence, surveying the southern variants of the single-family dwellings, spaced at decent intervals over the landscape. Very little true lumber or stone, but the persistent *memory* of houses of real lumber, real stone.

I noticed that the widow in the mock New England saltbox in the next cul-de-sac had planted arcs of flowers like outstretched arms toward the bachelor across the street—*Come to me*—and my soul was again like a loosened fist that dusted the gold pollen of good intent upon the neighborhood. One night, I found the Emory lab man alone in his garage, reading pornographic magazines, still in his chair as if strapped into a flight simulator. In the photos a middle-aged man in diapers writhed in torture, the expression on his face infantile and pasha-like, as beautiful women whipped him, reproducing under test conditions the sexual cosseting and shame unlikely to occur under actual circumstances at his own house.

So what? I thought. *So what if we are only squatters here, with our prefabricated fanlights, our board-and-battened souls?*

One night I watched, like a curious voyeur, my own wife through her kitchen window, intent on learning to cook something exotic, like candied violets. Sometimes, alone beneath a benign moon, I held my breath, like balancing on the bike: *Look at me: Colors of the Lord.* One night I went to her in a fever of love for us all.

—We could have another baby, I said. *—Maybe a son.*

She smiled at me like I was daft, and left me in the dark with the remote control to the TV in my hand, as if this was my appointed task in the house, to be the man watching the TV. Housewives sang passionate arias to their toilet-bowl cleaners, danced with cans of dog food. A man's chest exploded from a gunshot on one channel; medicoes rushed into the mountains to save a baby condor on another. My soul resumed its fistlike position, and I turned the sound down, and saw felled trees, no, the bodies of dead boat

people from the Caribbean floating off
prayed their souls would find someplace
rest.

When my mother began to die from
to go help her.

—*Might be a feature in it,* my boss said.
*Think about it. Fresh angle, of course. Deatl
got to get the different perspectives.*

So I drove the four hours down
shanked woman sitting in her chair in the kitchen. Did I come
from that little, wizened body? How was she ever a force in my
life? I knew the end was near when all she could do was show me
the age spots that had bloomed like wine-colored asters on the
backs of her hands. Her eyes said it all, but calmly: *Can you believe
that I am this old?*

I drove her around on the country roads. She seemed content to
drink it all in through her drugged eyes: the metal house trailers
parked in front of the old abandoned farmhouses, with black steel
satellite dishes cupped and poised to snag whatever was up there:
Australian cattle drives, Japanese commercials for Italian leather
shoes, Scandinavian commercials for Japanese cars. At one point
on some old river road we paused for a sea of dominicker hens to
part, and my mother gasped with pleasure. I put her to bed in her
clothes that night: she was unable to bathe herself, and I was too
shy to do it for her.

—*How you doin' down there in radioland?* Phoebe said softly when
she called, using my father's voice.

—*I ain't doin' so hot,* I said.

—*I'll be there in eight hours,* she said.

Three months after my mother died, my father showed up at my
house, towing the little green boat with a string of glassy-eyed
bream floating in a Styrofoam ice chest.

—*Catch of the day from the Alapaha River,* he said.

The little green catboat. It gave me a sweaty-palmed nausea to
look at it. It had a name now, the *Alapaha Star.* How like him to ro-
manticize the town that had repelled him. Or had *we* repelled him?

He wanted to take the boat out on a lake nearby. I shook my
head. I was sullen. It would be like some of those other Saturdays.
His jackass will exhorting me.

*lighten up. All you kids need to lighten up. You get this
other, not me.*

had a hard life, I said, baldly. I didn't mean it as a rebuke, but
me out that way. I was thinking, *Father of mine, I am down on my
ees to you today.* Because her life was so hard, and I seemed to be
somehow inadequately clothed in this universe as a result. I seemed
to want some responsible male adult to be marginally interested in
my well-being and give me something, some words to clothe my
naked soul in.

—*Take a lissen to this, Field,* he said, waving a tape, an Aaron Copland tape, *Fanfare for the Common Man.* —*It's all here. Everything you
need to know about life. I'm out there on the lake, and the fish are biting,
and I got my own soundtrack here on my Walkman. This man, Copland.
A genius. Lissen to it when you drive to work. I came up here to give you
this boat. I want you to have it.*

I stared at him, waiting, no clue what for.

—*I'm getting old,* he finished lamely.

—*Don't want it,* I said. —*Try Allie.*

I listened to his Aaron Copland tape one day, driving home from
work. It seemed as though it was no longer a gift for Common
Man to be simple and free, Common Man required fanfare as he
tooled home on the freeway, manacled to his briefcase, the music
booming like big Wagner: 'TIS . . . A GIFT . . . TO BE . . . SIM-
PLE . . . 'TIS A GIFT . . . TO BE . . . FREE.

I began to dream of my own son, the one I always meant to
have. I told Madeira about the dreams, how he called to me at
night. *Daddy, Daddy.*

—*Can't we try?* I asked her. —*I am not too old to be a father again.*
Silence from her. —*I am too old to be a mother again.*

A few days after that, I saw what she had written in her pink
notebook: *I will not serve the emperors of Pig Nation.*

She underlined this in a cookbook: —*To understand foie gras, you
must visit Gascogny to see the plucked and cleaned geese, which have been
force-fed corn to fatten their livers, arranged on long tables covered with
clean white cloths.*

There was this one recipe I saw that haunted me. *Songbird pâté.* I
dreamed at night of thousands of small, sweet birds slaughtered for
their tiny livers, and Madeira could see only them, not me. There
was this stab of something new in me: *Madeira, you could take a*

lover. There is still time to save you. But I couldn't say it. She would have cried and hated me. One night I went into the kitchen late, and she had made a marzipan tree.

Weh, geen, moninna, footchie—I joked, but my eyes were wet and I was maudlin. *No se lo olvide,* I will not forget us, whoever we were. I reached for it, not to eat, but just to touch, to remember, and she slapped my hand.

—*That's not for you,* she said. —*It's for Tina's party. I'm catering it.*

Slapped my hand, and I smashed the tree into the floor. The air was full of the smell of almonds, and my mouth was acrid with something that felt like hate for my life. Steroid-fed chicken in every pot. Two cars in each garage, standard. Two TVs and at least 1.5 VCRs per house. Every man a paladin of Pig Nation beneath a benign moon, pacing within the confines of his common wall. *I don't know you! I don't know anyone!* flashing in my temples like some kind of warning buzzer.

Later I tucked a tendril of her hair behind her ear in bed. Her little pin money she was trying to earn. I was touched. Apology has never been easy for me. Making love is as close as I can get to that.

—*Madeira, let me love you. I want to.*

There was the silence. There was the sigh. —*This all feels pretty incestuous to me,* she said finally.

—*What in hell is that supposed to mean?*

—*It just feels weird,* she said. —*I mean, I cook, I wash your clothes, I iron, I send the two of you out into the world in the morning. I don't feel like your lover, I feel like the resident mommy.* She began to cry. —*We had more love when we had no money. I miss our old house. I miss us, Field.*

I thought: *I could snap that neck of yours. I could snap it. I own every board in this house, every rag on your back. I paid for these things. I worked for these things.*

I said: —*Baby, you have to let me love you the ways I know how.*

At nine that night she started another marzipan tree. I slept badly, and seemed to have the dream of the son I wanted first, but then a man was hitting a little boy. I could hear the little boy: *No, Daddy, no.* I could hear his little heart beating in the distance, or was it my own? Then I faded back into my troubled dreams, whole corridors of doors closing as soon as I came near.

—*Field. Field.* Madeira had shaken me awake. —*Something is hap-*

pening next door. I followed her to the window and looked out. The dovecote in the backyard next door. Mr. Extrusion was dragging his son out of it, and they began a little dance of fists and ducked punches that was so familiar to me —*No, Daddy, no*—until the boy just impersonated a sandbag on the ground. Then the father walked away, hitching up his pants like a vindicated gunfighter. He spoke over his shoulder to the boy, who scurried inside after him.

—*What are you going to do?* Madeira asked into the darkness. —*What are you going to do about it?*

The next morning I went over to see Mr. Emory. He was attaching a thatcher to his mower, fresh as a flower from his night of simulated guilt and pain. —*What's up?* he asked. It is unusual for one paladin in our neighborhood to cross into the kingdom of another.

—*Guy on the other side of me beats his kid,* I said. —*And I won't have it. We have to come up with a plan.*

Mr. Emory's face went concave like worn-down suet. —*Touchy situation, there. A man's family. His . . . personal situation.*

—*I won't have it.*

—*Just a minute,* he said, and rummaged in a little box behind some paint cans. He pulled out a little bottle and handed it to me. Blue pills.

—*Xanax.* He said, affably. —*Anxiety inhibitor. I can get them by the boxload for my lab animals. It's the coming thing.*

I blinked. Was I supposed to poison my neighbor? Give them to the son? What? I looked quizzically at him.

—*Go ahead, take one twice a day. Takes a day or so to really work. You'll feel like a new person forty-eight hours from now.*

—*I prefer to undergo life without benefit of anesthesia,* I said coldly.

This enraged him in the quiet subverted way of the suburbanite. —*Anesthesia?* he repeated. —*You don't get the picture. Works on a different principle, different types of inhibitors. Lemme give you a little pharmaceutical guide to your neighborhood.*

He looked over my shoulder at the other houses. He pointed at the new gingerbread Victorian in the little knell beyond the merry widow's outstretched arc of flowers. —*That house: Mellaril.* He pointed to the bachelor's house: —*Valium.* He pointed to the merry widow's saltbox: —*Halcion.* He pointed overhead to where his own bedroom would be. —*Xanax.* I noted the lack of explanation. His wife?

—In the old days, it was alcohol. Too destructive. We know a lot more about how the mind works now, what the mind can tolerate. Sentience, that is the desired effect. To get rid of the anxiety and have the subject remain functional.

I sat down on the lawnmower, tired. Every house a compromise between what once was and what could be. We seemed like just so many geese in these houses, force-fed to fatten us, but to what end?

—But eventually the woman's nightmares would have stopped, I said. She did, after all, plant those flowers like the outstretched arms, beckoning Mr. Valium.

—It's not just simulations I'm into, he said ceremoniously with a sweep of his hand toward the United Sewer of the Cul-de-Sac. *—I'm into futures.*

That night, it began again. I saw the pattern: Mom is drugged into submission to the rigors of life in the plenitude of Pig Nation, while Pop watches Pig Nation on TV, drinks his beer, kid pays for Pig Nation's sins out in the yard.

The moon was no longer benign, I noticed when I crossed to the common wall, dreaming what I would do before it even happened. The moon, when you get right down to it, is a gibbous, humpbacked, slobbering witness, itself drugged into submission. Something throbbed in my head: the Upanishads in neon: *O lovers of the true: this is your path of holy action in this world.*

Chain-link fence, but I jumped over it from atop the toolshed. When I landed I had that guy's polo shirt crunched up tight around his neck, and I was whispering in his ear, tender like a lover, *—You hit that kid again in my presence, and I'll cut your balls off, buddy. I'll extrude them to your wife in her granola.*

The boy was more terrified of me than of his father, and I understood that dance, too. He might possibly have to pay for this sin of mine later, when I was no longer there to protect him. *—Go inside,* I told him. *—Your dad is coming home with me for a while.*

I had begun to feel silly, but he came willingly. I kept my hand on his arm, like a father's. I banged on the other neighbor's door. No answer. We went around to the garage, and there he was, resplendent in his padded headphones watching his porn videos in near-perfect solipsism.

—Give me the fucking Xanax, you asshole, I mouthed, and the bas-

tard read my lips, took off the headphones, and went straight to the stash behind the paint cans. —*Whole bottle,* I said. When he handed me the bottle, I passed them to Extrusion. —*My advice, which you probably should not follow, is to take them all at once. Spare me the messiness of putting a gun to your head. But you could probably get through the week better if you take them one at a time.*

Extrusion was scoping out Emory's lair. —*What you reading?*

—*Leather and Black Lace. Take it. I have others. You know, I got this buddy has a condo in the Caribbean. Fix you right up. Take a little break.*

I left them. Sat fuming in front of my own TV like a camera panning my own nation. Floods in California, firemen rescuing a dog. An old black woman gunned to death in her apartment in Chicago, the remains partially consumed by some sixty cats left behind. Enthroned on a gilt and red velvet bordello background, a man in a Minwaxed hairstyle peered into the camera and inquired, —*Are you washed in the BLOOD or just in the WATER?*

—*Have you noticed that the neighbors don't speak to us anymore,* Madeira asked at the end of the next week. It was not a rebuke. She sounded relieved.

She was never without her notebook: *Lessons from the Field,* she wrote at the top of the first page. *The male of the species weathers well as age advances; the coloring and confidence of the female fades. His dominion in bed is heaven; dominion at the bank is hell.*

She published a poem, and I had a sense of dread. That kind of woman, standing at a podium, declaiming the injustices of the female world. We were not like lovers anymore. I felt like her parent. I paid the bills. What did she do all day? I found a scrap of paper on the kitchen table once:

> *A red dress, a feather boa, to catch the eye of a man?*
> *And begin the old catastrophe of love again?*

What catastrophe? I could hardly speak to her for days.

—*I'll be gone all day,* she said the next day, Sunday. She had arranged for Tory to stay with a baby-sitter. She was unusually well dressed to be delivering a confection.

I followed her. She drove to Athens, past the fields where the farmers' chemicals do their quiet killing, past shanties where the indolent white trash kept their old cars on cinderblocks in the front yards, like commemorative old relations sleeping in the sun. The

Treasure Heart Truth Temple had become ensconced in a big brick church, like Tara with a thyroid condition. In the place where a steeple should have been, a satellite dish perched, ready for transmissions to radioland.

Madeira paused at the familiar confluence of the two highways, and my heart raced, about three car lengths behind her. *Sentimental journey home*, I thought. Nostalgia for the house that once was ours.

But the Spinoza Salvage Yards had become a mini-mall, mostly an asphalt parking lot. An earring emporium, a record shop, and something called the Women's Cooperative, a storefront for an abortionist. All built on fill, and I could only assume that beneath it all was our little house. There was a small circus tent there in a patch of field that had not been built over, red and white striped.

There was a protester with a sign: "More Have Died from Abortions Than Ever Died in Vietnam." It seemed to me that I was walking on glass, like those experiments where the puppies panic because they don't know what's holding them up. I had this instinct to crouch low, as if hugging the ground would steady me. Madeira parked her car and got out, and the protesters spat at her, copied her license-plate number, and snapped her photograph as she and several other women entered

I was dumbstruck. I thought of the Upanishads: *This is the truth: as from a fire aflame, thousands of sparks come forth, even so from the Creator an infinity of beings have life and to him return again.* I got out of the car and ran inside, pushed past a nurse who seemed to be saying, —*You can't go in there*—

I was going to carry her out. I could make things right again.

But she was sitting behind a desk, talking on a pink phone, wearing a little plastic badge. I blinked at it. *Madeira Durrance— Counselor.* I blinked at her. She covered the receiver and mouthed *Just a minute* to me.

—*How did you get our number?* she asked softly into the phone. —*How much time do you have to work with? . . . Are you interested in exploring the options? . . . Are you a student? . . . Well, I am here to help, and we are going to take care of you.*

—*Why didn't you tell me about this?* I shouted.

—*You wouldn't have understood*, she said. —*Obviously.*

The proprietor of the clinic, a small Vietnamese doctor, came to the door. —*Jesus, they're doing it to US now!* I screamed.

—*Please go now,* she whispered to me. —*We can talk at home.*

Catastrophe, she had called it in that poem. What *catastrophe* of love?

This is a Field lesson, I thought, as I drove past the road where I should have turned to go home. I started toward the apartment of a girl who worked at the paper, the one who had looked up the old FBI files on me—*You were really something in the movement, weren't you?*—then turned into the street she lived on. I could already imagine it. The *Cosmo* on the table—"You Deserve an Orgasm Today"—the pill and condoms and coke in the medicine chest, all the amenities for your sortie into Pig Nation. The eyelashes made from emu feathers, the lipsticks of pig fat, pigskin gloves.

I drove past her apartment. I drove the back roads, hungrily staring at the abandoned houses, succumbing to my old habit: *I could live there, I could live there.*

Ten hours later, after I'd fought my way out of the Disney World-bound traffic, I turned onto my father's street, a benign-looking neighborhood, much like my own. Same old gibbous and humpbacked and slobbering moon, just like at my place. It took them by surprise, to see me.

He answered the door in old clothes, the first time I'd ever seen him without the armor of good clothes. He seemed smaller than I remembered, and I was secretly astonished at the tiny red veins that had covered his face like a subtle root system. He was watching a bass-fishing tournament on television. —*Nothing else on worth a damn,* he explained. —*Let's get your bags in. Tomorrow I'm going to take you to Disney World.*

I had no bags. This caused him to be, for once, without words. He went over to his liquor cabinet. —*Name your poison, compadre. You drink scotch, gin, what?*

I took a scotch. It tasted like what I remembered him to smell like when I was a child. I remembered that I had left my keys in my car. The scotch made me not care about that. He found me a toothbrush and some pajamas. Olivia fussed around me, using her let's-pretend-everything-is-normal voice. I was grateful to be in a place where no one was interested in asking questions. One more scotch, and I was beginning to stop thinking. Insentience, that was the desired effect.

—*Take a lissen to this,* he said.

—Benny Goodman. I nodded. *—"Sing, Sing, Sing."* This was my cloistered secret. That I had always loved big bands.

—You know this stuff? You got a good ear.

I nodded. *—Fortissimo, maestro,* I laughed, and he pumped it up. Olivia watched us from the door to the kitchen.

The next morning we headed out for Disney World. *—It is a primer in the American experience,* my father explained. *—It will reassure you, it will terrify you. I am always dumbstruck with awe when I leave there. You cannot imagine the efficiency. If Roy and Walt Disney had run the Vietnam War, we would have won.*

The first known instance of my father offering the slightest critique of anything military. I looked sidelong at him, tooling down the interstate in his old straw fishing hat with the green plastic visor. This was the first known instance of my taking a car trip with my father and not being filled with anger.

—Mind if we make a little stop first? he asked. I had never been anywhere with him that he had not stopped somewhere to get a drink and chew the fat with someone he claimed to know. The actual destination would never be met. I knew we would not make it to Disney World, but this time I was relieved.

The stop was something billing itself as the Seminole Nation Salvage and Flea Market, what seemed to be acres of rickety wooden sheds spilling with Confederate flags and Marilyn Monroe beach towels, paintings of Jesus on black velvet, a Mona Lisa made of dried black-eyed peas and navy and kidney beans. We both stood transfixed before it. My father cocked his green-visored hat back on his head, grinning. *—I can never resist this place,* he said. *—Olivia won't let me come here.*

Since when did he take orders from a woman? I looked sidelong at him again and had an odd understanding: that he was *finite*. That he would die in the near future. How had I ever imagined that he had been a force in my life?

—Good stuff's always in the back, he said, pulling my arm. *—You got to wade through forty years of kitsch to get to the treasures.*

He chortled with delight every time he could haul something out of a bin or off a table that I couldn't identify. *—Perfectoreno casting reel,* he said loudly. *—Kid here doesn't know what a tobacco cutter is.*

—Fishing pole, I said helpfully when he picked up the next item that caught his eye.

—A little correction in the nomenclature is apropos here, he said gently.

—Fly rod. This kind came out the year you were born. They don't make them like that anymore.

—Me or the fly rod?

He laughed. *—Kid's got a sense of humor. You didn't get that from your mother.*

He bought an old lens cap for his old Leica, some molly bolts, an old router that didn't work. The old guys seemed to know him. I found an old fountain pen, encrusted with mud; under that, inlaid with mother-of-pearl. Two bucks.

—You got a good eye for this, my father said. *—You never know where this stuff comes from. They got Spanish galleons lying in the same mud with space debris off Cocoa Beach. They got the Haitians digging in the Miami city dump.*

We had turned down a new aisle and he dismissed it all. *—Domestic surplus. Women's stuff.* He picked up a red pillbox purse made of sequins, mused over it, threw it down. He grabbed a fringed lampshade among some aluminum Christmas-tree limbs and garish crocheted toilet-seat covers, and clapped it onto his head and did a few samba steps like a drunk Shriner, his orotund belly leading the way.

He paused over a bin of books. *—Close your eyes,* he said. I complied, felt something pass in front of my face. *—Sniff.* I sniffed.

—Grammar school, I said, and opened my eyes to see him smiling, holding out a worn copy of an old reading book. I opened the book and the sentence leapt off the page at me, taking me back to Bermuda: *Some day you may go to Friendly Village.* The houses in the illustrations were the essence of *house* to me, the kind to which I always aspired: not the memory of stone and tile, but real stone and tile.

—That is the smell of your boyhood to me. What was the name of that aviation book I got for you? What was it? I bet you forgot.

—The Wonder Book of the Air.

—Whatever happened to it?

—I don't know. I guess it didn't survive the movers.

It occurred to me that my father was wooing me somehow. Pulling me to himself in the meager ways he knew how. Then something caught his eye. Baby stroller, a familiar-looking one, blue metal with a white wicker back, colored wooden beads across the front.

—Taylor-Tot! he said. *—You had one of these. I bought it in Dallas the day you were born. Man, they don't make 'em like this anymore. Indestructible. Lasted through you, Allie, Phoebe. Shock absorbers on the thing. Look.*

I felt the old habit of rage curl inside me, as afraid to speak it as when I was a child: *But you weren't ever there.* As if there was a censor inside me that my mother left operative: accentuate the negative.

—Did you know, he offered me in a whisper, the fringe of his lampshade quivering, as if he'd waited all his life to tell me, *—she had two abortions? One between you and Allie, and one between Allie and—I bet she never told you that,* he said simply, and there was this tremor in his bottom lip. *—Look, I never was a believer in defaming the dead. It serves nothing.*

I stared across the flea market tables to the traffic whizzing by. Was this us? Standing in normal daylight, having a normal conversation? It raised goosebumps. *—Madeira is working at one of those places.* I said. *—Those clinics.*

He shrugged. *—Sometimes that is the arena in which a woman casts her ballot. And sometimes the vote is "no confidence."*

—In whom? I said. I wanted to add, *I make a good living, I am a good father.*

—Does it matter? he said. *—Could be no confidence in herself. In the future. Hell, in America. The women, they have their own ways.*

—How did it make you feel when she did that? I asked. I needed to know what we were to him.

—Your mother, he mused, *—was the the sole sovereign authority in her own arondissement of bitterness. But I don't believe in regrets. They serve no purpose to the species. End of subject, ancient history. So why are you here? Does Madeira know where you are? Is she worried about you?*

—I don't know, I said dumbly. *—I don't know what she thinks anymore.*

—Lissen, compadre, he said spinning off into one of his maddening airplane bromides. *—Sometimes it's hard to tell what's drag and what's lift. Only the kamikaze is privileged to know true flight.*

We made one more stop before returning to his house, not Disney World, and I didn't mind. Fresh amberjack and lemons. Back at his place we got into the scotch once more.

—WHEREAS— my father declared a toast, and held my antique pen aloft, and Olivia raised her glass too. *—Whereas this boy has*

come to see us, and WHEREAS, *he is possessed of a good eye, and* WHEREAS *he has a good ear . . . and* WHEREAS *. . . .*

—*Whereas, we have fresh amberjack and lemon,* Olivia offered.

—WHEREAS *we got fresh amberjack and lemon, we drink to the health of this boy and his home,* my father finished. —*Upon the condition that he telephone saidsame home while still in a condition to do so.*

Later, he continued to woo me to be his son, played his Harry James for me.

—*Fortissimo! Maestro!* we shouted together. —*Perfectoreno!* I called to him.

WHEN I GOT HOME A DAY LATER, Madeira was making a marzipan tree and didn't hear me come in. Or pretended not to hear me come in. I felt lucky to have gotten off so easily; the visit with my father had left me only with a hangover. Tory took her Barbies into the little meadow behind the house to play in the sun. I watched her from the window as she pressed the flowers down to make a place for her dolls. The boys from next door came over to talk to her, brandishing their battery-powered plastic laser wands that glowed. They played a separate game just beyond the little circle she had made for herself.

I got confused for a minute. I thought of Jim. He would have been forty-seven that year, if he had lived. Two birds, two sweet friends that dwelt on the selfsame tree. He ate the fruits thereon, and I looked on in silence. There are different ways of fighting for nothing. The grief ripped me like fabric tearing. *No se lo olvide, Jimmy. I will not serve the emperors of Pig Nation.*

—*Field.* This was Madeira. Standing in the doorway.

—*I need to check on Tory,* I said.

—*She's okay. She's playing with the boys next door.* I could sense in her movements and restlessness that she had an agenda and I had somehow made it to the top of the list. —*What's wrong?* she said.

I stared up at the ceiling. I couldn't say it, the thing in my heart.

She started unbuttoning my pants. —*Vee haff ways of making you talk,* she teased. I pushed her hand away. I didn't feel like being kidded.

—*You have to talk to me,* she said. —*You have to tell me everything.*

I thought of how I had lived in so many different houses, so many, sometimes they melded together, the memory of the saltbox in Chicopee, Massachusetts, with the prairie house in Ft. Leavenworth, all the way back to the conjoined apartments in Dallas where they knocked the wall out so Melvina could be next door. I became a student of houses at an early age, the secret hidden places, even as the military movers were rolling the cartons down the planks off the moving vans. In Dallas I was three and could fit myself in the linen closet. In Leavenworth, Kansas, I was four, and I could still fit beneath the kitchen sink, if I had to. In Toms River we had a basement, and I could fit behind the hot water heater, in a place where the light did not reach. In Bermuda, Allie lay in a white lace bassinet with a skirt that reached to the floor, and I could conceal myself safely beneath it if I had to, in the terrible tropical storms when my parents began to fight. Anywhere near Allie was safe because he loved Allie.

But when it was warm, I would slip outside into a vast field of lilies and lose myself there, sentient, watching the driveway until I could see him make his dramatic exit, more often than not with tires squealing. What was drag, what was lift? There was one more house after that, and then we were back in Georgia in the big old white house with the green shutters, interminable unused rooms to hide in, and the whole Alapaha River to myself, anytime I needed it, which was often until my father defected.

Was I hiding from him or from the cries of my mother?

—*I am tired of always hiding,* I said at last to Madeira, annoyed at how childish and irrelevant it sounded. She was silent. —*Sometimes I feel like we have all become the Ik,* I said. —*I don't want to live like that. Do you?*

—*Oh, love,* she sighed, burst into tears, and came to hold me.

My wife and I began to touch each other in the shared darkness, as if the situation required some greater caution than either of us had ever imagined. At first I couldn't stop thinking, couldn't stop the sentience. *WHEREAS,* I thought, holding out my arms to her, *WHEREAS* . . . love might only be a word in the language, and *WHEREAS* . . . human souls might possibly always wander restless, like the Upanishad swans, hoping someday to go to Friendly Village. And *WHEREAS.* . . . sometimes one can't tell drag from lift; *THEN:* human souls can agree on one point: the need for perfect tender regrets about saidsame predicament.

Thus we rode, past the untenable places where love has almost left the language, toward the friendly village, maybe toward our own deaths. In the moments before she could make me stop thinking, I thought, *Look at me . . . Colors of the Lord . . . Perfectoreno.*

YOUR PARTNER IN
PYROTECHNICS

*T*he little town in Georgia I had moved to was one you'd never stop in if you were driving through. The whole populace stays shut up in air-conditioned houses because coming out will cause others to feel uncomfortable about you and ask you if you are all right. They don't want you to be outside your living quarters at night; they like it better if you just sit in front of the TV like they do. They don't want you to stop if you're driving through, and their stares alone would send you on your way soon.

It began my first night in my new apartment, one of those cheap copies of elite row houses, very solid-looking on the outside, but walls so thin you could hear everything next door. That night, through the left wall of my bedroom, I heard the sounds of a woman being loved by a man: *Oh . . . ah . . . oh.* Then there was silence, while I lay wide-eyed in the darkness, feeling rent by her pleasure, with my heart beating too fast.

A few hours later, from the right—the opposite apartment—I heard the sounds of a woman being beaten by a man: *Oh . . . ah . . . oh,* then there was running upstairs, then silence. *People use the same sounds,* I thought as I lay on my back on the floor, my heart beating too fast, to the rhythm of those sounds, *Oh . . . ah . . . oh. The same sounds for love as for being hit.*

I phoned my father, who was fishing in Georgetown, Florida, to have someone to talk to—and I lay there on the floor in my empty bedroom because I couldn't afford furniture yet.

—*Job okay?*

—*Yeah, fine.*

—*You getting out? Making friends?*

—*Well, not really.*

Silence. Then, —*Well, that is unacceptable. You got to get out and explore the terrain.*

I promised I would soon, and hung up the phone. But I had always been as alone in the world as some tiny walleyed embryo afloat in a womb I could never seem to find my way out of. Tight membranes between me and the rest of the world, always. All the things I could never find permissible to say to myself, much less to anyone else.

The distillation of my life always seemed to come down to one date, my fourteenth birthday. In everyone else's mind, that is. No matter what town I lived in, I always seemed to end up across a desk from somebody talking about that night. Even in this town. I was talking to a therapist one afternoon early in the spring, and we arrived at that point: *Allie, when your father was hitting you, were your clothes on or off? Did he do anything besides hit you? What were you thinking about when he was hitting you? Why did you continue to see him after that?* I wanted everyone else to put it behind them, like I had done.

—*Why do you want to know if my clothes were off or on?*

—*It's important.*

—*I had on his girlfriend's nightgown.*

—*His girlfriend's?*

—*I had gone to her apartment. The policeman took me there.*

—*Why the police?*

—*I didn't have money for a cab. He didn't like for me to carry money.*

—*Why not?*

—*I think he liked to be asked for money. I think he felt more like a father that way.*

—*So how long did you wear the nightgown?*

Nice try. No dice.

—*Can we talk about something else for a while?*

He frowned at me in much the way my father does—*That is unacceptable*—and wrote in his notes for a while. He had a bank of files against a wall, and it made me tired to think of him sitting there every day of his life while people came to him to figure out something to confess to him, hoping to please him by being suitably screwed up. While he was writing, I had this moment of confusion, like I couldn't remember what town I was in or which man writing in a notebook was listening. This was one problem I always had: I always felt solicitous toward the therapists, as if there were whole worlds of meaning that I should shelter them from.

—*All I could think about was that I was ruining the nightgown, there was blood all down the front of it.*

—*Blood?* He was very eager, that one.

—*My nose was bleeding. I had bent over, balled up, and so the blood went on the front of it. It was a pink lace one, and very expensive.*

—*Oh,* he said, and settled back in his chair, like he could not quite figure out what direction to go in.

—*Why did he hit you?*

—*It's not important,* I said. —*Really it isn't. When you love someone, you love him.*

—*You have lots of work ahead of you, Allie. Lots of work.*

It was like the times when they call you into the office to tell you everyone else has scored better on their achievement tests.

—*I'm tired today,* I said. But the little black womb around me was whorled with silent sounds: *I do not violate my father, I do not violate my father.*

—*What is your sex life like, Allie? Are you satisfied with it?*

I got my purse and left, walked out of the belly of that whale. Not even a little lie about see you next time.

Progress, no? No one gets inside Fortress Allie.

I TRIED TO CONCENTRATE on my trouble at work with a kid who always came to the school library where I worked. Coaly black with dreadlocks. Kunta Kinte Washington, from a home where they slept in shifts because there aren't enough beds. The mother was a crack dealer named Queen Elizabeth Washington. He always did something to get at me, within minutes of coming into the library. Rip a page out of a book, steal some younger kid's homework and dance around holding it over his head. Every day it was something. I'd taken three knives away from him, and one ice pick.

The real problem is he's fourteen years old and he can't read.

The knives and the ice pick, it's all to compensate. I know this, and he knows this.

I called my father on the phone sometimes when my job got to me. I called him about Kunta Kinte Washington, thinking the name alone would cheer him up. He liked to hear about my life, and to give me advice about all the parts of my life that were unacceptable to him.

—*Allie, Allie. You don't teach the boy how to read, he's going to be the one coming in your window some night for your TV.*

—*I don't have a TV.*

Silence.

—*Well. He needs to learn to respect the chain of command. You are the quarterback in that library. He's the water boy.*

So I went back to Kunta Kinte Washington and I told him, —*From now on, you will act like a member of the species homo sapiens human being in my library. You don't, you will not get your lunch.*

I had him. They didn't eat at his house. His free lunch was his only real chance to eat.

He tested me the first day, of course, and so he lost his lunch. I parked him under the picture of Atlas holding up the world and went to the lunchroom myself, but I didn't have the heart to eat, so I went back and sat in the chair across from him. He could hear the others going to eat, and was getting madder by the minute. He wanted to get back at me, but he knew I had him. I had control of the only food he could count on in this world.

He stared at me, waiting for me to give up.

—*I'm going to cut your tires*, he said.

I smiled at him. —*You want to give me that in writing? You'll have to learn to write.*

—*I'm going to find your house, white bitch. I heard you live on Pecan Skreet.*

—*Well, you'll have to learn to read street signs, don't you think?*

—*You got a boyfriend?*

—*What's it to you?*

—*He beat you, don't he?*

He thought he had me. In his world that was the lowest common denominator—a man somewhere who beats you.

—*Listen, you. I'm the quarterback here. You're just the water boy.*

But he had me, he *had* me.

I was forty years old and I'd never made love to a man.

Oh, I had my share of fumbly high school heat in backseats, and I lost three boyfriends in college because I wouldn't be intimate with them. One of them nicknamed me Fortress Allie. I have, in my adult years, run through a succession of lukewarm suitors who never made it into the batter's box, much less to first base with me.

The last one, I just looked over at while we were sitting on my front porch, about to go out on our first date together and knew I wasn't even going to walk to the curb with him. There seemed no point in continuing, him with his bright exuberance, his bow tie. He was an accountant, and I thought that I was going to do something that would hurt him, like lean over and ask him, *—Why don't you just cut to the chase? We could eat a little Chinese at seven, marry at nine, save ourselves the trouble of the intervening years, and drive straight to the cemetery to pick out our plots. Lovebird special.*

The heat of that little town could make you a little daft like this. But you had to keep it to yourself. I had been feeling very strange, hot and dizzy and sad, and thinking wild thoughts, and then I found a folded note on the library floor one afternoon as I was leaving, the kind of things that the kids throw down with gum wrappers. I opened it up:

> *Dear Petey,*
> *I love you.*
> *Please check one:*
> *Yes____ No____*
> *Carol Ann*

Such a tender little transaction—but I began to cry, sniffing into a Kleenex, pretending allergies.

One night I walked out into the tall grass behind my apartment complex, and I lay down to look at the stars, to which I have always been partial. When I was a child I used to lie on my back in a field behind our house in Bermuda, and pretend they were jackstones I myself had flung up there. I would bounce an imaginary ball, and scoop them up in my hand.

That night I thought no one could see me, so I pretended again. Onesies, twosies, threesies.

Someone called the police. An officer came and stood at the

edge of the field and called to me, as if he didn't want to get too close.

—*Ma'am? Ma'am?*

I stood up and brushed the grass from my skirt. —*It was just such a beautiful night,* I said to him. —*It seemed like such a crime to stay inside.*

I felt hot and dizzy for days after that, so I went to a doctor, a man I graduated from high school with. The nurse was much younger than I, barely out of school, and she made me feel like a big old child when she stood with her clipboard asking me questions: —*Date of last menstrual period—you do still menstruate?*

That one was like a kick by a horse. What, did I think it would go on forever?

—*Make a fist,* she said, before she took a sample of my blood. What an ineffectual odd sight it is, the fist of a woman.

And the upshot of it all was that there were no clues in my blood about why I would wake up at night, or why, even if Atlas *were* holding up the world, did he have to stand on *my* chest to do it?

I left that weekend to go to a librarians' workshop at Tallulah Falls for the summer. I wasn't exactly delighted at the prospect of the trip—seven hours in the car with two other women who could drive me insane inside of ten minutes. Denise wouldn't say more than six words the whole trip, probably. Suzanne would make up for that by bending our ears nonstop, prattling off every little fact she could glean from brochures and pamphlets she'd stuffed into her purse, for events she would never attend. It's like a sickness with so many unmarried librarians. I have vowed that it would never happen to me. Frenetic, vicarious life.

Suzanne was notorious for conducting torrid but harmless one-sided love affairs with helpless victims. The married football coach at school had been barraged with home-baked bread. The band director had withstood it the Christmas she was teaching herself to do brioches. I'd seen her do some weird things at work: one day in the library she started reading aloud an old Dickinson poem:

> *Heart! We will forget him!*
> *You and I — tonight!*
> *You may forget the warmth he gave—*
> *I will forget the light!*

This for the edification of black teenagers with Nike Airs and gold chains and beepers.

In the car she read to us from the brochure about the place we were going, about the Women's Conservatory that used to be a hotel back in chautauqua days, the weekly fireworks displays on the lake, the lure of the mountains in one's quest for a summer of self-discovery. I saw her in the rearview mirror and thought that she was already *in love,* she just needed someone to inflict it on.

I just gripped the wheel until my nails were touching my palms, and drove on.

— *"Many women confess they have their most erotic dreams when they're pregnant,"* Denise retaliated, reading from the *Ladies' Home Journal,* and I caught a glimpse of her blithe face in the rearview mirror. Forty-three years old and her life still looked like a half-full glass to her. —*Sodium is essential to the diet,* she opined. —*Necessary for the transmission of impulses in the synapses.*

HELP me, God, I thought. —*Is this my life? Give me one good reason not to sling this wheel to the right and throw us all into the river.*

I think God spoke back. I had a vision of us all, zooming along in that car, and it seemed to me we were just bags of inert flesh being carted from one place to another, much like sacks of salt with the alphabet all over us. Sacks of salt have use, and so might we.

WE WERE ON OUR WAY to the Tallulah Falls Folklife School to learn how to preserve the old ways and teach them to the young. You had to pass along one old art and take up another. I knew how to make marionettes, and I wanted to learn to weave baskets. I was already imagining myself alone in the woods gathering weeping willow and honeysuckle vines, soaking it, weaving it. Far from the Kunta Kinte Washingtons of the world.

WE SAW THE CONSERVATORY on the side of the mountain as we drove along the lake. No Victorian spires, just crude cedar turrets with a beaten copper roof that had gone green in the mountain mist. Denise had to lie down the minute we found our cabin, and Suzanne was ecstatic that we were so near the water. There was only one cabin closer. I could already see Suzanne in the fall in the teachers' lounge, her hand fluttering to her throat: *—You know, we were right down on the water.* I had the sudden absurd thought that we should just get back in the car and drive home, and save ourselves the time and trouble of getting through the summer.

Denise had a big black Pullman suitcase and I was trying to figure out how to get the wheels to go down on it so I could drag it across the gravel and into the cabin. They wouldn't come down, so I had to try to carry it.

—Can you handle that yourself? a man called over to me. I noticed there was a man on the porch of the other cottage, with his chair leaned back against the wall, his feet on the rail. He was cutting lengths of thin rope, and winding them into coils.

He had sandy hair and pale eyes, and he was smirking at me, or maybe at the monstro suitcase. And why not? The stickers on it: *Epcot, Silver Springs. Fort Fredericka, St. Augustine.* World-class traveling, for sure. He thought it was mine. He was wearing a polo shirt and white shorts and he looked like he'd be more at home at some country club than way out here. He was looking at me like he thought he knew something about me—wrestling with a tacky suitcase, doomed to the company of other maiden ladies.

—This isn't mine, I explained. Not my luggage, not my life. I refuse it.

THE CABINS HAD TIN ROOFS, and we each had our own bedrooms, spartan little army cots with two sheets and a flannel blanket folded on it. Suzanne prissed in and said, *—Allie, they cancelled your basket-weaving class. Not enough interest.*

—Well, damn, Denise said, though she didn't really mean it. *—There's an opening in my class. Sallie Baker Newcombe. How many chances in your life do you get to study with a renowned woman painter?*

Perish the thought. Nine months of daily encounters with Denise in the teachers' lounge was enough. I could see it now: we'd return to work in the fall and she would hold forth in the teachers' lounge, with her hand fluttering to the base of her throat: *—You know, I studied with Sallie Baker Newcombe.*

I was looking forward to the little marionette shows I would do across the lake, every afternoon in the Carnegie Library, for the local children.

There was a little ferry I had to take each day to cross the lake. I always had my marionette case with me, and I liked to do stories that I thought they needed to know. Jason and the Golden Fleece, Perseus freeing Andromeda from the rock—things every kid should know. One afternoon I looked up from my marionettes over the tops of the heads of the children and there was the man from the cabin next door standing at the back of the group of children, holding an old leather-bound book. Watching me. He looked away quickly. I don't know how long he'd been standing there.

Later, when he and the children had left, I went over to see what book he had been looking at. It was old and rare and really should not have been just out on the shelf like that. *The Art of Pyrotechny*. Something about the firing of ships and sending them down upon one's enemies. Risky and sometimes fatal to the *capitaine de brûlot*. I liked that—*capitaine de brûlot*.

One afternoon Suzanne and Denise took the ferry with me. As we were waiting for it, Denise looked around the marina. The buildings were all old clapboard, half on the land, half on tall pilings in the water. One was an old AME church, still had the steeple. Over it a sign, "Caution: Ordnance." Denise and I noticed it at the same time.

—*Ordnance,* she read. —*What on earth? That's a military term. Did anyone think to pack a dictionary?*

The other sickness of librarians is the incessant jockeying for the world's most obscure fact. You could see it in her face: she *needed* that dictionary. Suzanne had a big English novel under her arm, something she'd been reading for days, and she seemed quite drugged on it. Title something like *The Minotaur*, with a picture of a woman running from a bull on the cover.

—*Allie, if you had to choose, what would you take—one night of untrammeled passion that might backfire, or a lifetime of deep abiding friendship?*

—*Christ, what a question, Suzanne,* I said. —*I never thought about it.*

—*I've been thinking about it lately,* she said. —*A lot.*

I looked over her shoulder and saw the man from the other cabin standing about ten feet away with a parcel marked "Explosives" under his arm. He'd overheard it all, and he was smirking a little.

—*Why don't you ask him, Suzanne,* I said, and pointed behind her. He grinned at me, and his eyes were like a little gift meant only for me. It had been a long time since I had been looked at by a man, so I looked back. I liked the way his eyes could make me account for myself.

That night we all trooped out to watch the fireworks from our deck. That alone made it all seem unreal, that we could just take the kitchen chairs out from the place we were living and wait for the show to begin.

Suzanne was deep into a monologue about her precious English book when we heard *poom poom poom* and saw three bursts of silver against the night sky.

They seemed to come from across the lake, so we watched that way. There was nothing but black night sky over the water for a few seconds and Suzanne resumed her monologue—*They're wearing bell bottoms again this year*—and I wanted to push her off the deck and drown her.

It had been a long time since I'd seen fireworks, and I forgot everything but what I was seeing. I thought of all the words it would translate into: *rosaries, rubies, aquamarines, palms of gold* that seemed to burst, then flickered, then faded. Generous booms, big rich gifts to my eyes, trailing off into showers of small sparks. All seemed lobbed up into the sky like a trail of burning offerings. Purple plumes, cavorting starfish, comets the color of champagne. I felt humble as a child, and I wanted it never to end.

I had forgotten about the human sound effects that happen between the bursts or fireworks. The arpeggio of light goes up, off, and fades into tiny disappearing sparks, and then there follows that soft human gratitude that comes after: *Oh . . . ah . . . oh.*

That night the sounds seemed to come from in the star-leaved sweet gum trees that grew all the way down to the shore. People so close? Lovers in the trees? This discomfited me. I thought I had taught myself not to feel that way, lonely in the presence of lovers, but now with each burst, those *oh*s and *ah*s hurt as much as if I'd been standing outside someone's bedroom window, listening to the sounds of love being made.

I went inside, watched the rest from my closed bedroom window so I could not hear those sounds.

Snowballs that burned, blue peonies with gold spangles, pink chrysanthemums with bowed heads. I could hear the whistles and *pooms*, but not the sighs in the trees. I liked that better.

THE NEXT MORNING AT BREAKFAST somebody was reading aloud from a brochure about some *other* women's art colony: — *"I come to the cottages to heal myself. Sometimes I cry."* It was enough to gag a maggot.

I was sitting there remembering something my brother Field told me once. His newspaper had sent him out to photograph a turkey farm, and somebody told him that turkeys were so stupid that if it rained they would look up into the rain until they drowned.

I saw the man from next door headed our way with his breakfast tray. There was a murmur, and I thought of the expression "rooster in the hen house." There is something that *happens*, some collective quickening of the hennish hearts, when the male comes into their midst.

—*Good morning, ladies. Everything copacetic up at the Conservatory?* *Copacetic.* I hadn't heard that in years.

—*We're here to learn how to get in touch with our inner woman,* Suzanne burbled.

I winced. Suzanne thinks people who paint by numbers are "creative," and she perked up at having been listened to. Her face was rapt, and she patted at her hair.

—*The inner woman,* the man said, smiling at her. —*How do you do that? Hold a mirror up to your crotch, or what?*

It took a few seconds for the smiles to drop off everybody's faces, but I laughed out loud.

—*Have fun, ladies,* he said, and was still smiling pleasantly as he walked on.

—*Who on earth?* Denise sputtered. —*Who does he think he is?*

—*Marshall Lambright,* somebody said. —*The fireworks man.*

—*Oh,* somebody said.

So *he* was the one out there in the dark, launching the Roman candles, inducing those *oh*s and *ah*s in the trees. That's when I got the crush on the fireworks man.

When I sat out on the pier waiting for my ferry, I could sometimes see him at work inside the old AME church through the windows under the "Ordnance" sign. The whole building charmed me instantly, and I felt like I knew something about the man to see the place he chose to work in. It had double screen doors on the front, a tin roof, and a deck all around. One time he looked up from whatever he was bent over and caught me looking at him. I looked away out of reflex, despising myself a little. Another kind of woman would have simply waved back, maybe walked inside to talk to him. I wasn't like that. When I got a crush on someone, I possessed all the charm and grace of a marsupial in his headlights.

The deck all around the water side of the little church had steps leading down to a dock. Tied to the dock was an odd old pontoon boat with tall metal racks on it, a kind of no-nonsense grillework that made the boat look like a silent dragon. It seemed very low in the water. Dangerous and risky to take out, even. I was leaning over the rail looking at this when Marshall came down the steps with some wooden crates in his hands.

—*What's on the menu for the kiddies today?* he asked, and he seemed halfway interested. I shrugged, careful not to allow much about myself. I was remembering he wore his wit like a serious barbed-wire fence around himself, and that I'd never met anybody who knew how to light up a whole sky before. The ferry was docking and I had to go.

—*Aesop's fables.*

—*You're pretty good at that,* he called as I left, and I heard his voice all day, all day.

The next day he was working on the boat when I was waiting. I walked over to say hello to him. There was a welder's mask beside his feet and the air smelled like hot metal.

—*What is all this?* I said, and reached out to touch one of the racks.

—*DON'T,* he said. —*It's still hot. These are finale racks. For launching the works.*

—*The fireworks.*

—*Yes.*

—*You do it from this boat?*

—*That's right,* he said.

The thought of him in that boat: those bursts of color across the sky: that anyone would *opt* to do that when he could have been

safer on the shore, a spectator: I blurted it out with my heart beating too fast: —*I think you're wonderful to do that.*

He looked at me for a minute, and there was something in his
face, like suspicion or disgust. He reached down to pick up the
mask, and I saw his hands then. The palms of his hands seemed lat-
ticed with black burn marks. From the arc welding? From the fireworks? I felt ignorant.

—*You're going to miss your boat,* he said, nodding toward the ferry
and pulling the mask down, but he was smiling. I watched him
from the back of the ferry, watched the sparks he made with the
acetylene torch. I was pretty far gone on the pleasure his smile
could bring me.

Sometimes at night in our cabin I would go into my room to get
away from Suzanne and Denise, opening the curtain of my bedroom window to see if Marshall was next door, but it was usually
dark. I think I wanted to catch his silhouette against his curtain.

He seemed so alone in the world.

I *wanted* to see him as alone in the world.

Like me. Like something I could comprehend.

Two mornings after that, the water was choppy and gray as I
waited, thunderheads gathering. But the Ordnance church was
well lit. The fireworks man came to his door.

—*You want to wait in here? The ferry's always late in bad weather.*

There was the momentary awkwardness. What to do with me,
where to put me. I put my marionette case down and sat on a crate
that said "Titanium Bombettes." There were crates stacked to the
ceiling, and I'd read several before I realized I was reading them out
loud. —*"French Violet. Precious Pearl. German Baldachin. English Pleasure Gardens."* It had not occurred to me that those flashes I'd seen
in the sky had names. —*"Taiwanese Silver Coconut,"* I read out loud.

—*It sounds like a candystore, doesn't it?*

—*Oh, it's just beautiful,* I gushed. —*The names are just as beautiful as
what you make them look like.*

—*Elevator music,* he said. —*These weekly shows.*

The wall beside his table was stacked to the ceiling with tiers of
little oak drawers like you used to see in old hardware stores. The
drawers were labeled in an elegant calligraphy on faded cards, *Aluminum, Antimony, Arsenic.* Alphabetical order. He put his tools
down and came over to stand beside me. I kept reading. *Naphtha-*

lene, Nitroglycerine. He was standing close, and I felt hollow in my knees. I couldn't remember the last time I had stood so close to a man, or the last time it had mattered to me.

—*This is for the real stuff. Tomorrow.*

—*Real stuff?*

—*The Fourth of July. I do my biggest show then. These little weekly things* . . . he trailed off. —*Look,* he said, and reached around me, brushing my arm, and my head went hollow inside. I couldn't even see what he was reaching for, his presence seemed to roar into me so.

Another woman might have known how to make something of that moment.

Another woman might have known what to do, what to say.

I only knew how to stand there, marsupial in the headlights. He moved away.

—*Come look at this.* He was rummaging in a box of explosives. He laid a Roman candle up on the table and slit it open like a long fish, making a deft cut with a penknife. He laid it open for me to look at.

—*Little bit of naphthalene, a little paraffin. Not much to it when you really see it, is there? It's mostly timing and balance. How much to let loose, how much to hold back.*

Why was he bothering to show me these things? I guessed that if you are one of a handful of people in the world who know how to do something, like making dulcimers or caning chairs, you don't run across that many people you can talk to about it. I was reading more boxes: *Gold Arabesque with Red Pearls. Treasure Chest.*

Then I saw on the wall a picture of a monkey with a nose like a basketball, captioned, *Never Be Ashamed of What You Are—But What in the Fuck Are You?* My eyes took in a radio, a hot plate, an old army cot.

—*Why don't you just get them from the factory?* I asked. —*Seems like less trouble.*

I had myself cocked and primed for an answer that would satisfy my taste for the poetic, like about how he longed to puncture the sky. Something along those lines.

—*What else is there to do?* He shrugged and piled some gray dust in a little conical pile on a slab of marble. —*Hold out your hand.* He put some yellow powder—sulfur—into the palm of my hand. —*Sprinkle it on there. Now.* He lit it with a Bic cigarette lighter.

There was a small fizz and flash, and I moved backwards quickly, straight back into him. His hands were on my shoulders just a moment, and we watched it burn turquoise.

—*Theater fire. The first thing you learn to do.* He pulled a long cylindrical casing out of a box. —*These are tourbillions. Every time I see them go off I think that must be what love is like.*

Nothing hooks me faster into a man than to have him seem a little needy. The lion in the nets that needs a mouse to get the thorn out of its paw.

—*Come out on the boat with me tomorrow. You can do the salutes.*

—*What?* I blinked at him. I'd been lost in imagining his lonely dinners, his holidays on the outer perimeters of, say, a sister or brother's family. His hurting paw.

—*On the boat. Tomorrow. I'll teach you how to do the salutes.*

I barely heard him. I was watching his lips move and thinking that I wanted him to kiss me until I couldn't stand. I was thinking that I wanted him to lay me down somewhere and we could put our heads together and figure out what love must be like.

There wouldn't be any holding back with a man like that. No Fortress Allie allowed. He wouldn't put up with it.

—*You're going to get yourself killed,* Denise said to me as I was getting ready the next afternoon. —*You don't know the first thing about fireworks, and I've heard HE doesn't know the first thing about women.* We'd spent a desultory day inside our cabin, simply waiting for it to be time to do something, anything.

What did one *wear* to do fireworks? I cut off the legs to my one pair of blue jeans. Did one carry a purse? I tucked a twenty into the left side of my bra, and my driver's license on the right. Denise was staring at me from the doorway to my room. —*So you can identify the remains if I get blown up,* I explained. I remembered the time my brother teased me about my flat chest: —*Some men LIKE brussels sprouts, Allie.*

—*You made it,* he said, and he had his hair slicked back like a boy's. I realized that there was something about him that made me feel older than him, though I probably wasn't.

—*Yeah.*

—*Life jacket,* he said, opening a compartment and pulling one out. —*It's the law.* But he was not wearing one himself. I pretended not to see the revolver in the storage compartment. He had a helper, a young black boy. —*This is Kareem Roosevelt,* Marshall said, and they both frowned when I laughed. —*Kareem, this is—what the hell is your name?*

—*Allie. Allie Durrance.*

The boat had a raised aft deck, and I wondered how many women had preceded me on it. He steered the boat out onto the open water, and the shoreline began to shrink. It was like riding in a floating fortress, snug inside all that grillwork.

—*Don't stand too close when he gets going with the fuses,* the black kid said. That was his sole piece of advice.

—*I heard that,* Marshall yelled back at us, and laughed. When the shore was out of sight, he cut the engine, let down the anchor, and said, —*Now we wait a bit. Ma and Pa Kettle got to get their lawn chairs in place.* He began sliding tourbillions into a rack and checking all the fuses at the tips.

—*You in with all those women?*

—*Women?*

He looked up the mountain at the Conservatory. I shook my head.

—*They fear love,* he said. —*What they really want is death. What do you do, anyway?*

—*I'm a librarian.*

He laughed. —*Jesus, a librarian.*

I laughed, but I felt very diminished. He didn't seem so needy out here, and I thought I was mistaken about the lion with the thorn in its paw. He seemed in perfect control of everything, even me.

When darkness fell, he lit a cigarette. I was uneasy at the prospect of someone smoking a cigarette in the dark around crates marked "Explosives." I had to watch him to see what the modus operandi was. He didn't seem to care, so I tried to stop caring. He adopted a slightly ruthless air out there on the water, so I imitated that. The wind was picking up, and the water was choppy, bobbing the boat up and down.

—*Let's do it,* he said, a signal to Kareem. —*The salutes,* he said, holding out the lighter to me. —*Five-second intervals.*

I lit the first fuse and he counted with me.

One bright booming aster of light. By the time the second one went off, I was so entranced at the sight of what I had done, I forgot to light the third. He guided my hand to it. —*It's a troublesome taste to acquire, I tell you. You like?*

—*I like. Very much.*

—*These things are just big guns in little tubes. The recoil—you'll have to hold on sometimes.*

He and Kareem seemed to have worked together before; they began with the racks on the foredeck. Their movements seemed choreographed. Sometimes they looked into each other's eyes silently, and I knew they were counting.

First there were a few small stars, exploding amethysts, Catherine wheels. I'm sure that I imagined it, the *oh-ah-oh*s that would come from all the lovers in the trees of the shoreline. I looked to see.

The shore was nothing now but a tiny chain of gold at the edge of the universe, and we were floating in black silk.

Then they got off a series of Roman candles, fountains of tinsel and sparks, shooting stars, tiger's eyes. I had never heard such booms and my ears were ringing. With each report the boat rocked a little from the recoil. I saw him look back at me once to see if I was holding on, then he seemed to forget I was there. There was a flash and I thought, *Tourmalines, tourmalines*—exploding into gold rings like the markings of a peacock's tail that dissolved into silver dust. The boat lurched, and I heard cursing from Kareem.

A whole rosary of bright orange poppies ripped across the sky, flowered, faded. I tried to guess the names of others from what I'd seen handwritten on the crates. *Crystal Snapdragons, Blue Electric Storm, Emperor's Gemstones, Corsairs.* Catherine wheels rotated like burning ice. I looked at Marshall's face. He was barely seeing the bursts, intent on the next series of fuses, barely able to stop long enough to see the results of what he had wrought.

—*So this is what a man is,* I thought. Whole sentences popping in my head, explosions of things I'd never thought of before. —*So this is who he is.* His eyes were half-lidded, and something about the curve of his lip—I felt like I was looking into his face during lovemaking. I felt like I knew what it might be like to know him. A little bit tender, maybe, and a little bit terrifying, but not inclined to make me feel like a Martian if I wasn't, well, *experienced* as he. I was gone on the idea of what he would be like in love.

He paused a minute while Kareem got off a rack. He held out the lighter. *—Do a rack. I dare you.*

That is how I ended up with the lighter in my hand. What if I dropped it overboard? Was there another? Would the show stop? I didn't like this much responsibility.

I lit one fuse, and a big tourbillion rose and twisted, burst into sheaves of gold wheat. Did I do that? I stood frozen, watching the black space where it had exploded and evaporated.

—Go on, go ON! Marshall was shouting, sounding very far away because my ears were ringing.

—Wait, I need to THINK, I yelled back. The fuses were linked and loopy and I didn't know where to start.

—Don't think! Jesus! Just light! Just do it!

I tried to be intrepid like they were, unafraid of the tangled fuses, unafraid of the booms. For a few moments there, it was like being queen for a day, as the other tourbillions rose and burst. *Ssssst . . . fweeee . . .* BOOM . . . red, gold, silver, blue. I counted and timed my thoughts with the rockets as if they were splashy valentines I was lobbing up there:

I . . .

think I . . .

love you . . .

Marshall Lambright . . .

Please . . . Check one . . .

Yes? . . . No?

I looked over at him to see what he thought, if he'd read my mind. Did it look like love to him now?

He had a preoccupied look on his face and he was looking over my shoulder up at the mountain. I remember seeing his hand come up toward my head and I thought, *God, he's going to hit me.* I stepped back too far too quickly trying to get out of the way, leaning against the back gate. The gate swung open—it hadn't been latched—and I was overboard, seeming to hang one minute and then drop like a cartoon character into the drink. The only shooting stars I could see then were the ones in my head as I fought my way back up to the surface to breathe. I was hearing my mother's voice when I was a girl: *Nothing is trashier than hanging around where a man is trying to do his work. Getting in the way.*

So while the Ma and Pa Kettles were snug on the shore, watching the finale, I saw it all by treading water as long as I could, then clinging to the little aluminum ladder at the stern of the boat. The report was deafening, like cannon, then machine-gun fire. Cascades of meteors, pools of blue minnows, strings of pink pearls, hives of a hundred bees. There was a moment of darkness, and I heard the two of them counting together, then the sound of screech owls, and a nest of snakes overhead. The snakes all seemed to contort and blossom into dragons with hollow eyes that broke into cascades, a finale of falling water.

It made me fear death and want love.

I looked toward the distant gold lights of the shore, imagining that I could hear the *oh*s and *ah*s. Even though my shin was scraped and burning in the water and I was getting cold, I wouldn't have been anywhere else in the world. I wanted to do it all again. I had had the best seat in the house.

The lap of the water on the sides of the boat, and the pounding of my own pulse. The sound of footsteps above.

—*See her anywhere?*

—*Nawsir.*

—*Goddamn women.*

—*I'm down here.*

—*What are you doing down there?*

I saw his face when I climbed to the top of the ladder. He didn't help me, he just held the lantern for me to see. He didn't have much to say. He started the boat and headed back to the shore. Kareem threw me an old towel. I was cold and the floating fortress seemed all hollow and sad to me. I looked back at Marshall's face in the lantern light. The curve of his lip no longer looked tender to me, and I wouldn't let myself think that it looked ruthless.

He wouldn't look back at me.

Here's the daft part to explain.

I knew I loved the fireworks man. When I knew that he was ruthless.

There was a large crowd of people on his dock in front of the AME church, a tumult on the shore. People were running and shouting, chaos. I got some peculiar looks as I got off the boat, and there were some men who acted like they knew me when they saw me get off that particular boat. Two patted me on the back and tried to put their hands around my waist in familiar ways. As if there were assumptions to be made about my slatternliness now. Friends of his? I didn't like it. Marshall had disappeared into the crowd, and one man kept following me, trying to hold my hand.

I saw what the tumult was about: the Conservatory was burning. The air smelled like gunpowder and cedar smoke and lake mist, and an antiquated fire truck was hauled out from somewhere. It has always been my policy to stay out of mayhem, so I simply went to the AME church. The door was open, and I went in. There were no lights on, and I didn't turn any on. I lay down on the cot. In the dark, I thought of what it had been like down in the lake water with the fireworks going on above me.

The door opened and there he was. He didn't know I was there. I didn't know whether to speak or not. What if he had the gun and I startled him? He was quiet for a minute, and he didn't turn any lights on.

—*You missed your ferry*, he said, finally. He sounded a bit annoyed.

I didn't know what to say next. So I said nothing.

He turned on a small light.

—*Jesus. You look like hell.*

—*Is that why you almost hit me?*

—*What was I supposed to do? Your hair was on fire. You'd rather I just stood there, maybe?*

I went over to a little cracked mirror over a chipped china sink. The hair on the right side of my face was gone. On the left, it fanned out ripply and red as usual.

—*Oh, God.* I wasn't only thinking of the odd sight of myself, I was thinking of those moments down in the lake water. I was thinking of those hands on my waist when I got off the boat. —*You didn't tell me it would be like this. You made it sound like all fun and games.*

—*It happens*, Marshall said. —*You lean in too close, you start thinking you're invincible, whatever.*

He looked lonely and tired, and I didn't know if he wanted me to go or stay.

—*It was very beautiful*, I said. —*I've never seen anything so beautiful.*

This seemed to bother him, as if I had failed some kind of test.

—*People don't know it, usually, but the original purpose of fireworks was to incite terror, not beauty. But, then, you're not a careerist, are you?*

Forget Claudette Colbert and Clark Gable—the blanket between the beds, the witty repartee. It didn't happen that night. He gave me a musty sleeping bag, took the cot himself. He seemed to tolerate my presence. I didn't sleep for a long time. I tried to imagine what the thorn in his paw really was, why was he so alone in the world? Couldn't I just somehow contrive to get the thorn out and wrap myself around him like soft bandages? There was a kind of intimacy now.

I wondered if *that* was what it was like to have a lover.

Before I slept I thought of something remote: my fourteenth birthday.

MY FATHER had taken me shopping. He always had it in his mind that he could transform me, on my semiannual visits to Savannah, into the daughter he *wanted*, not the daughter I was, which was red-haired and freckled. The clothes he bought for me to wear would have been more appropriate for Lolita. He liked having me turn around for his inspection, he liked instructing some gum-chewing beautician how to tease my hair into an approximation of Tuesday Weld's or Marilyn Monroe's, and he liked to take me out to dinner afterwards, in the new clothes and the new hairdo. Then he would watch me anxiously for any sign of bad table manners, ready to indict my mother.

That was the summer that lipsticks were "frosted" and my first lipsticks simply erased my lips, made them as pale as my face. There had been an uneasy moment for me in the beauty salon, when he was fingering some samples of hair color. I was afraid that he was going to tell the woman to dye my hair blond, which is what all the other women in the world seemed to be doing. My mother had instilled in me a great contempt for this. But the woman had told him that it didn't do well with redheads, and my skin color was too fair, and there was the problem of my eyebrows.

He always seemed to have this clear idea of what he wanted to turn me into.

We went to the Boar's Head Tavern afterwards, which is in the old Cotton Exchange Building, underneath where one of his old girlfriends had a studio. I felt a little like a drag queen in the frosted lipstick and the teased hair—I could just imagine what sarcastic thing my mother would say—but Daddy was happy with me, and it was worth it to be getting the best out of him—the best jokes, the best smiles. He was getting a little drunk.

—*You and me are compadres, eh, compadre?*

—*That's right.*

—*Forever?*

—*That's right.*

—*I worry that your mother is not teaching you how to be a real woman.*

That stymied me, but I let it pass. The waiter asked me how I'd like my steak, and I said, —*Cut*. This seemed to embarrass my father, but the waiter laughed.

Then a soldier from Fort Stewart asked me to go dancing. Just walked up to the table, just like that. He had Vietnam patches all over his uniform.

—*I'm fourteen,* I said, as if that ought to get me off the hook.

He grinned, as if that made things even better. —*Well,* he said, —*ask your old man here if you can dance with me.*

He was kidding, he just didn't know *who* he was kidding. Colonel Harrison Durrance, USAF, retired, and don't you forget it.

My father stood up slowly and ominously, and two waiters and the maître d' came over. He said something to the soldier—I remember it as a streak of obscenities. They seemed to back down from each other, but my father began to drink more seriously then.

At eleven he was still drinking, and the juices of his own rare steak had long since congealed on his plate. He ordered another scotch, and the maître d' came over and asked if he could phone us a cab. This infuriated him, and he began cursing them all.

I picked up my little new purse and ran out, and there I was, in the middle of Savannah at night. I stopped a police car and they drove me to the other side of town, up and down the avenue until I found Olivia's. She wasn't there, but I knew how to let myself in. That's where he found me later.

—*You don't walk out on your father,* was what he kept saying when he took off his belt, but I knew that wasn't what was bothering him. It was bothering him that I had seen him in a moment when he felt his own wretchedness—*Ask your old man . . .*

I remembered something my mother had told me—that she

used to pretend it was happening to someone else. So I did that too. So I opened my eyes and looked at him, and I saw that he was miserable. He hated himself, he hated his life, and possibly me, but most of all he hated his own wretchedness. But it *hurt* when he hit me, and the thought burst in my mind, *There has to be something to make him stop.*

—*Daddy, I love you,* I called out to him.

This was no lie. I never understood love more than I did in that moment.

And he stopped. He stopped in the middle of it and held me in his arms, blotting at the blood with a green scarf he'd just bought me, then rinsing it in cold water in the sink so the blood would not stain it. The intimacy that is impossible to explain, the tenderness you can't talk about. I wondered where he'd learned that trick of the cold water. Probably from my mother, because she had taught me that when I had my first period. This was at least *one* link we all three had, I thought.

And I felt uneasy. That I'd seen the tears in his eyes when he dabbed at my face. The shaking of his hands. I might have to pay for seeing him in his wretchedness. The thought crossed my mind that he might apologize to me, but he didn't.

One month later, my mother sat without touching me as I told her why I was covered with fading brown bruises. She took a long drag off her cigarette. I thought that she would throw her arms around me, that there would be one human being on the earth who would hug me, but she didn't. She had this way of acting like we were somehow closer now, like I could be admitted to some secret sorority with her, because I knew what my father's rages were like.

—*You know when he would hit me?* she asked. This was her way. All the crises of others were interpretable only in the context of her own life. —*When I told him the truth about himself. That's when you're in the most danger, when you tell the truth.*

What truth had I told him? I puzzled over this that night, and the answer came to me as I waited to go to sleep. The man who asked me to dance had told him the truth about himself—*Ask your old man*—and I had paid for it.

I have spent the rest of my life paying for that.

· · ·

I sat up straight in the dark in Marshall's place. —*I can only love what makes me fearful.* I said this out loud. There was no answer. Marshall was gone, as if he no longer wanted to be where I was.

The next day I cut off the other side of my hair so the sides would match. Denise was oddly pleased; she felt vindicated. Suzanne fussed over me and bought me a little book, *Ways with Scarves.*

Nobody seemed to know Marshall very well. Somebody said he was a lapsed Jesuit who only spent the summers at the lake. No matter, my poor head spun out long fantasies of him unabated. I dreamed of him at night, sheet-tangling erotic interludes in the AME church that woke me up with their power. Thank God for the privacy of the human mind. If Suzanne and Denise had had any inkling of the scenarios spooling around inside me, they'd probably have had me committed somewhere. Always I dreamed of being sweetly impaled by him, as if his wanting *that* with me would somehow make me into someone worth something more than a sack of salt with the alphabet on it.

I didn't want to go out of the cabin much, but I got through the marionette shows somehow. Every time I ate anything, it seemed to make me ill. The days were hot and made me nauseous, so I came out at night mostly. I was in the mall in Toccoa one night and I found a whole shelf of books about men. It had never occurred to me that I needed to *learn* about men. As I was flipping through one on *How to Talk to a Man,* there were two black women behind me, giggling over something.

—*Why Do I Feel Like I'm Nobody Without a Man?*

—*Because you ain't, chile.*

I was in the open-air market one night—I went then because I attracted fewer weird stares while my hair was growing back. I felt comfortable only in loose cotton dresses, and sunlight did not agree with me. I saw a hugely pregnant woman pushing a cart, and I began to follow her, interested in what she would choose to eat. She was getting things like white bread and Spam and tuna. The nausea made me barely able to walk, and I knew I better get to a doctor.

· · ·

—*MAKE A FIST*, the nurse said when she sampled my blood. —*Date of last menstrual period?*

I couldn't remember. I couldn't remember.

The doctor closed the door and talked to me alone. —*You have all the classic symptoms of*—he paused and I dug my nails into my palms—*pregnancy.*

—*Excuse me?*

—*Let's take a look,* he said, and smeared cold jelly on my stomach.

There was nothing there, of course. Nothing but gray staticky lines on the screen.

—*Have you been under a lot of stress lately? I'm going to refer you to a counselor.*

I was already thinking that I needed to get my clothes on and go. Get the purse and go. They had given me the name of a psychiatrist but I threw the card into the trash on the way out.

Suzanne and Denise were solicitous of my health, but they were more interested in going home. I had begun to feel at home in the cabin, and found it hard to imagine ever going back to that little landlocked town I'd never liked in the first place. I got a job in the public library at roughly half the pay I'd been used to. By the end of August, there were some brown leaves curling on the deck every morning and I swept them away as if that would lengthen the summer a little.

I stitched puppets for a new show: Mouse gets thorn out of lion's paw. I would stand at my bedroom window on the nights of the fireworks displays, coming out to the deck for the finales, which were always humbling. I would imagine him and Kareem out there on the fortress boat, laughing and cursing and lighting up the sky without caring who saw or why. They seemed to do it for *themselves.* Sometimes when I stared out across the lake water, I could see the dark shape of the boat, with the two little gold dots of the lanterns, and I missed him, I missed him.

> Heart! We will forget him!
> You and I—tonight!

Very hard to do with the ruby-tailed comets coursing across the night sky outside your window.

. . .

ONE EVENING, the edge of autumn seemed to have entered the air, and it was cool enough to walk outside. Dusk has always been a scary time for me, when I feel like the walleyed embryo floating in the black womb. I walked up the mountain to see the remains of the Conservatory. There were some shards of pottery and twisted metal, much broken glass.

Much had been destroyed. Sallie Baker Newcombe had set up shop in the Best Western in Toccoa, and soldiered on, tunneling toward the inner woman. They announced the day's topic in black plastic letters on the white plastic marquee: *Make a Fist*.

Turkeys in the rain, I thought, turning up the shards of an exaggerated ceramic breast. A thought went off in my mind like a titanium salute: *Capitaine de brûlot, capitaine de brûlot*. The ships of fire, raining ruin down on his enemies. How I loved him. Even if I never saw him again.

—O perfect love, I sang to myself one night when it rained and Marshall's fireworks were over. How perfect. It all began to make sense, Denise with that picture on her nightstand, that image in her head that would seem to suffice for a lifetime. Maybe it was better this way. Playing to an empty house. So full of the presence of an *absent* man that you were daft with it. At night when I went to the market, I felt like I was floating, smelling all the cinnamon and cloves and gardenias, the willow baskets filled with peaches and plums.

It felt like I was ripening endlessly toward him, for him. Hadn't he been more husband to me than all those tired distracted men I saw in the market could possibly have been to their lumbering wives? Wasn't I just as gravid as they?

I was hungry for foods from oceanside places. Limes, fish, crab. Where had he *been* all my life? Where had *I* been all my life?

But I ran into Marshall in the market one night, and my first instinct was to run away. My hair had not quite grown back, and I wanted to flee, but stood there holding a coconut in one hand, snow peas in the other. I felt guilty, as if I'd been caught stealing something.

Stealing life. From him.

—Hello, I said.

—How're you? You look like a little boy, he said, and moved on.

I was daft, daft, and playing to an empty house.

I bought silks and needles, plain stout muslin, remembering something my sister Phoebe had said about how impending new life had made her want a needle in her hands.

I started stitching an old Emily Dickinson poem that I seemed to remember from somewhere.

> *These are the days when Birds come back,*
> *A very few—a Bird or two—*
> *To take a backward look.*

I couldn't remember what came next, so I started on the border. It was all tourbillions, Catherine wheels, spindles of silk thread that made me remember him. One night I was working on this out on the deck during the fireworks finale, and the report was so loud that my sternum rattled. I walked over to stand by the window and placed my two hands on the place on myself where the baby would be if there were a real baby, looking down at the flatness there. I felt very bogus.

—*You old fraud,* I laughed at myself, and then remembered some more of the poem:

> *Oh fraud that cannot cheat the Bee,*
> *Almost thy plausibility*
> *Induces my belief.*
> *Oh Sacrament of summer days*
> *Oh Last Communion in the Haze*
> *Permit a child to join.*

What was I going to do with the sampler? Who would ever see it? I thought of mailing it to Marshall, but then I thought of poor Suzanne and all those breads and brioches for the football coach. No, mine would be the airtight Tupperware-sealed love that Denise had going with that photo on that nightstand. The kind of harmless little lunacy that the world will allow.

I stitched away happily, stuffed with secrets I couldn't tell. No one would believe: that the night in the cold lake water with those arpeggios going off over my head—it had made me a sweeter woman.

Why had no one ever told me it could be like this?

Why weren't there any books about men—for women to study—in the stores, simply called *Sit Down and Shut Up*? It seemed to me that that ought to about cover the subject.

I was stuffed plump as a partridge on all these sentiments, counting my stitches, when I heard a boat. I knew the sound of that boat.

I walked to the window. It was Marshall Lambright's boat. The two gold dots were moving closer. The *capitaine de brûlot* was headed my way.

A rakehell Jesuit headed your way—it gives you pause.

What were his intentions toward me? Dazzle me with tourbillions or blow up my house?

I walked out to the deck. It was coming to my dock. I didn't know what to do, so I walked halfway down the steps and sat down. I still had the muslin in my hands, clutched to my milkless breasts.

I watched him tie the boat and walk toward me.

My summer of self-discovery: I was incorrigible. I didn't care whether he was a Jesuit or not. I wouldn't have cared if he had a wife and children or not.

Something about how the breadth of his shoulders was very dear to me—it made me think of being sweetly impaled by him, of how it probably would hurt a little at first, just like it always said in the books, but at least then I would be free to *move*, to induce something in that face much like the *oh-ah-oh*s I had heard others utter. He didn't say anything at first, just sat down beside me. It was a peaceable kind of silence.

—*Your hair's coming back,* he said, and I felt a little lost in the headlights. He leaned back a little and looked at me, like maybe I should never be ashamed of what I was, but what in the fuck was I? Then he went on. —*I've been wondering how you'd answer that question that woman asked you.*

—What question?

—*The one about whether you'd take one night of untrammeled passion that could backfire, or something long and abiding, et cetera.*

I was too shy to look at him. Marsupial in the headlights.

—*Are those the only choices?* Ever the librarian chasing the obscure fact, my mind predictable as a Möbius strip.

He laughed. I had made him laugh.

—*I have been a disappointment to every man I've ever met,* I warned him.

—*Well,* he shrugged, —*I'm a Jesuit, but* . . . he stared off across the lake. —*It's supposed to be the first frost tonight,* he said, —*and it makes me want to* . . .

Kiss me until I can't stand, I hoped, my heart beating: *oh, ah, oh.*

He held his hands out palms up, as if he were trying to read his own fortunes there, not mine.

I wanted to kiss those palms, one after the other. But I did not understand what he wanted me to do, so I sat on my hands and stared out at the shimmer of the water. I closed my eyes a minute and the shimmer stayed. The black womb around me whorled with spangles of hot soundlessness—*may I never forget this warmth, may I never forget this light*—and when I opened my eyes, Marshall was staring at me fiercely, as if he didn't know if he loved me or hated me. I understood that it had to do with his being a Jesuit.

I wanted him to finish the sentence but I thought, *Oh, I get it: nobody gets inside Fortress Marshall.*

FLIGHT PATTERNS

*M*y earliest memory of my father? It's 1958. I'm three. He stands in the doorway. I'm next to my mother, with my cheek pressed against her gray wool skirt. —*Go . . . go . . . go . . .* is the word I keep hearing, and they are angry. My mother is crying, so I cry also, afraid of things I don't even have the words to name yet. My name is Phoebe.

When they fight at night, I run away across the street, open the unlocked screen door, and slip into my grandfather's big brass bed. In the mornings he sits with me in the front porch swing and we play the train game.

—*You want to take a ride on the Alapaha Star?*

—*Yes.*

—*You got your bag packed?*

—*Yes.*

—*What's in it?*

—*My red dress.*

—*What else?*

—*My red pocketbook.*

—*What else?*

—*My red flip–flops.*

He will never drive a train again. One of his legs has been amputated, he is an old man. But in the swing with my grandfather, I forget about those screamed words: *Go . . . go . . . go!*

My father goes. The boards of the walls seem to relax. Now we all sleep in one room, and my baby bed is beside the fireplace. We seem to eat crazily: cornflakes for lunch when there is no money and steak for supper when there is. I learn that it is terrible that I need new shoes. It makes my mother tired and tearful. Needing anything is bad, so I stop needing anything.

My red–haired sister, Allie, seems to be in charge of what I learn about the world. One day we steal eggs from a nest she has found across the tracks at an old black woman's house, and we learn how they will smash in our coat pockets if we ride the iron deer in a white woman's yard. Under Allie's tutelage I learn who in town has new puppies or old dirty magazines in their tool sheds. There is a strange roof on the ground at our father's mother's house; we break into it once and play among the old radio parts there. Once on a summer morning she discovers our father's car parked at his mother's house, which is two blocks from ours. His mother will not speak to us, but she lets us in. He wakes up to find us staring down at him. We are wearing matching playsuits with giraffes on them.

—*Don't you like our new clothes?* we say, but we cannot get him to say they are pretty. Because our mother bought them. I am three by now, my sister is five. I sit in a chair by the door while she sings him piano lesson songs and makes him laugh. He has a nickname for her, "Red." I feel safer being an observer than a participant.

Another day my sister takes me to a little room in our house that has always been padlocked. She has picked the lock with my mother's nail file. —*Look,* she says, opening a tall North American Van Lines crate, strewing the floor with the bright confetti of shredded comics. She hoists out a brandy snifter as big as her head. It has a circle of roses etched around its rim. When she lets me hold it, I drop it. Its shards will remain there on the wood floor for several years.

This becomes our secret, that we burrow and tunnel through boxes stacked to the ceiling. There are golf clubs in a leather bag fuzzy with mildew, and a rotting brown-leather bomber jacket. Light, airy watercolors of the villages of Bermuda, fringed with oleander and hibiscus. Uncountable long-stemmed cocktail glasses, which we break having imaginary tea parties. We're more accustomed to the cheap, thick crockery from the local grocery store.

We pass the summer ruthless in the wreckage of our mother's former life, piratical. We break the tortilla holder shaped like a floppy sombrero. Abundant booty: a box of evening dresses, tulle-festooned, satiny-slippery. We fight over a green paisley one studded with green brilliants. I settle for the strapless pink and blue one with the rustly skirts. Damask napkins down my front: instant bosoms. Black lace mantilla over my head: Bat Masterson's girlfriend. Sometimes we play office with the stacks of old Air Force photostats, black pages with white print.

We venture outside in our regalia, carrying champagne glasses for effect. The kids from the housing project in what used to be our grandfather's peach orchard are not amused.

—*That ain't yours,* one little boy says. —*And it's a sin to drank.*

—*Well, you don't even own the house you live in,* my brother Field says. —*We do. You live in the projects. My grandaddy sold that land to the government. It used to be my grandaddy's land.*

We know that we are poor, and that they are poor, but we live in a big white house with green shutters, and they live in cramped little dark ones. We know that we are smarter than they are.

Our secret seems to be out. Field investigates the room. By sundown he has used three sterling silver platters for BB gun targets, brittle 78-rpm records for flying saucers. Tommy Dorsey, Glenn Miller, and Benny Goodman: *fling, zing,* over into what used to be our grandfather's peach orchard.

—*This is mine,* my brother says, pulling out a heavy wooden propeller. —*It was on my wall in Bermuda.* He drives the propeller into the soft earth, like a conquistador staking claim. It seems to me that he has a bigger claim on the earth than I do, partly because he can remember more of the time that is prehistory, when our mother and father were capable of talking to each other. Our mother, when she finally notices, simply makes us throw everything back into the room and tells us to stay out of it. Of course, we don't. A teak and bamboo teacart makes a terrific entry in a soapbox derby, and a burgundy damask and lace tablecloth is just the thing for a mongrel to have her puppies on.

Some months later, Field calls me to come listen to a record he is playing on the record player my father left behind. I hear music playing, and what I remember to be my father's voice talking.

—*Listen, Phoebe. Daddy's talking about being shot down in the war,* my brother explains, and I look into his face and wonder why he has bothered to notice me. —*He fought against the Japanese. This is when they gave him the Silver Star.*

There is a big red book in our living room, with black-and-white photos of soldiers in it. Once my brother thumbs through it and shows me our father, sitting in the front row of officers, his legs crossed easily, squinting into the sun. For a long time I am confused when I look in the book by myself. I can't find him. They all look alike to me in their uniforms. I think that World War II is still going on, that my father is there, and they play a lot of saxophones in the background there.

My grandfather dies, and I understand that I am alone somehow now.

By 1963, SOMETIMES MY FATHER COMES from Savannah to get us to take us to a town nearby to eat at a restaurant called The Purple Duck. I love these times, because I can sit in the back seat of his Rambler station wagon, smelling his old fishing things in the back, hearing the conversation of my older siblings pass over my head. Their presence deflects his attention from me, and I feel safe, watching them. I like being in his warm car.

One early fall afternoon I come flying out of my third-grade classroom at 3:10, and I see the Rambler station wagon. I run up with my sister, and she explains that she has a piano lesson for the next hour. His smile fades, but he says he will take me fishing. He takes me to his brother's pond, out in his little brown wooden boat with green trim.

When I speak, he hushes me. He doesn't give me a fishing pole to hold. I sit facing him, my hands in the lap of the green party dress bought a few years earlier to go with my sister's red hair. I am worried that he is angry at me for wearing the dress. I study the whorls in the varnished wood of the seat between us. *Alapaha Star,* it says, and I want to ask him about this. I would like to think that if he doesn't love my mother, maybe he loved my grandfather the way I did. It begins to get dark, and my back begins to hurt.

On the way home, he stops at an old well. —*Bet you've never had well water before,* he says, registering a mild rebuke of my mother. He draws up an old metal bucket, reaches behind the well, and takes a dinged-up metal dipper, which he hands to me full of cold water. While I am drinking it, he says in his clowning-around voice, —*You'll never drink water this good anywhere else. I'm tellin' you like a friend. I used to haul so many buckets of water for my mama when I was your age, I felt like Paul Bunyan's ox.* He studies my face for a re-action. *—I've had water from all over the world, but it was never as good as this.*

When I'm getting out of the car, at our house, he hands me the string of small fish he caught, slick-slimy and walleyed dead. *—Give these to your mother,* he says, and closes the door and drives away.

This excites me. A string of fish is a joyous thing in the houses behind us, and I have seen the men come home and hand the fish to the women, who float them in red-rimmed white dishpans, then cut off their heads, slit open their bellies, and throw the little orange hot-dog-looking things to the cats. Then they cook the fish in big deep black skillets. I have even seen a big deep black skillet in the secret room of my mother's house.

My mother scowls when I hand her the fish. *—MORE work for me to do,* she hisses, and throws the fish, still on the string, out into the backyard. She curses our house, our clothes, our life. *—He could have been a general.*

My mother decides to dose us with more truth as we get older: my father is not with us because he doesn't love us. He loves to drink and dance with lots of different women. He once told her that he had better things to do with his life than to raise children. He has sudden unexplained absences, and he hangs around Navajo Indian reservations when he disappears. He was given the choice of retiring from the Air Force, at the age of forty-one, or being court-martialed; and that was the year we all crash-landed in my grandfather's house in Georgia, in the little town where he and my mother both grew up. In a drawer in her bedroom are manila en-velopes of old Defense Department photos: my parents greeting Eisenhower, Churchill, and Anthony Eden as they step onto the tarmac at Kindley Field in Bermuda, my father accepting golf clubs upon retirement. My father is saluting and serious in these, my mother's face is seraphic as she beholds Eisenhower.

My brother and I press my mother for information. She tells us that she used to read the Bible when he was in the air. We ask her about my father's separation and retirement papers—and all the details, such as the women he was seen with outside bars and hotels, in addition to the empty tanks in the planes when he flubbed an alert as deputy base commander at MacDill Air Force Base in 1957.

—*Sounds like he was set up to me,* my brother comments. He is a draft counselor at the University of Georgia. It's 1968, and I'm thirteen. My brother has a deep, instinctive mistrust of military men. This is a time when Vietnam was writhing in all our minds like a sly oriental dragon.

—*The alert came through and they couldn't get the planes off the ground.* My mother shrugs, as if that is the only explanation one needs.

My brother and I look at each other: the imaginary enemy was coming, and there was imaginary fuel in the planes: off with his head.

Field is 4-F. He lost an eye setting off a cherry bomb, while my mother and father were attending the Army–Navy Game. Now it is summer and he is home from college. He and the one other long-haired boy in town spend evenings on our front porch facing Main Street, discussing the act of war. My sister is in Savannah with my father for the summer. She is the only one who sees him. I am happy to be sharing the front-porch swing with rebellious long-haired young men, and I wish I had my own draft card to burn.

One night our discussion is interrupted when a young man with short hair runs shirtless, shoeless, and shrieking down Main Street and into the woods. We begin to hear screen doors slamming up and down the street—the men coming out from their suppers and TVs to go see who is screaming in the woods. So my brother goes, too. We can hear voices in the woods for a while, calls and shouts. Then my brother comes back.

—*It was Pierce,* he says. —*He got drunk and thought he was back in Vietnam.*

—*These people,* my mother snarls, and takes a long drag off her cigarette. —*They don't know what a REAL war is. World War II. Now there was a real war. This war is a moral atrocity.* She retires to her bedroom, with stacks of the Atlanta *Journal* and paperback Faulkner novels heaped in the place where most women would have installed a new man.

By the end of the summer my sister has returned, wearing long sleeves and pants, even in the swampy south Georgia heat. Her first night back, she and my mother sit in the kitchen crying and talking long after I have gone to bed. The next morning my mother explains to me privately that my sister's legs and back and arms are covered with old brown bruises. She had been out in an elegant Savannah restaurant with my father, who became drunk and combative with the waiters. She became afraid of him. She called a policeman to drive her to his house. He found her there, and beat her. When he sobered up, he bought her a new wardrobe and took her and his girlfriend to Hilton Head, to let the bruises heal.

—*Don't talk about it,* my mother tells me. —*We are not going to talk about it again.*

By the time school begins, the incident is buried beneath others. The schools are integrating. The first day of school finds my mother, an English teacher, standing in the elementary school yard, taunting some farmers armed with shotguns, like she must have taunted them as children.

—*So do you feel like a BIG MAN now? Showing your gun to a six-year-old child?* This man is on the local school board, and is a big deal in the Klan, if you can judge by the fear of the blacks. But the little black kids are more wide-eyed at my mother's wrath. One night there is a knock at the door, and my mother answers it, telling us to stay back. There is one of the farmers there. His gun is in the gun rack in his pickup truck.

—*I just wanted to see the pitchers of the niggers.*

—*What?*

—*They sayin' at the cafe you got pitchers of niggers on your walls. Just wanted to see what you teachin' your kids.*

—*The picture is in my classroom,* my mother said. —*Winslow Homer, The Gulf Stream. Come by and see it sometime.*

The townspeople stop speaking to us. My mother has causes instead of friends.

Books are what I have instead of friends. I read *Soul on Ice,* by Eldridge Cleaver, about his ambition to rape a white woman, to avenge all his oppressed ancestors. For one week in the summer, my brother makes me read the "Rime of the Ancient Mariner" to him in the afternoons, before he will agree to take me swimming.

My sister goes to a Methodist revival that fall, the kind where for one week out of the year everyone is fixated on the idea of being saved from something terrible. She goes down the rabbit hole of religion, never to surface again in quite the same incarnation that we knew her.

One day as I am leaving school, I see my father's new silver Chrysler parked in front of the school. He is waiting outside for us. What will it be this time, I wonder. A forced haircut just to show our mother he has the power to leave his mark on us? Expensive clothes that she can't afford to pay the dry-cleaning bills on? A two-hour wait in the car while he goes into a bar to drink? My sister runs to meet him. I hang back by the holly bush that grows outside the book room.

I can see my sister chatting with him, animated. I step between two girls I hardly know, and I walk right past his car, pretending to be so interested in what the girls are saying that I have no time to notice that he's there. And so he is out of my life for a few more years.

Now I'm twenty-one, and I neither smoke, nor drink, nor take drugs, though I hang with a crowd that does, daily. I still hang back like the junkyard dog, because that is what I am good at. I live alone in a little rented house on the edge of a cotton mill district, with the scrawls of previous tenants' children still on the bare pine walls, and the apparently stolen tombstone of one James T. Hughes, killed in the Spanish-American War, as the front stoop. I support myself by waiting tables. I managed to get the job when my predecessor, an Air Force wife, cut her feet to ribbons running across broken glass to get away from her husband.

I come home from my waitress job and stay up all night sometimes, listening to music and reading, the poetry of Yeats, visions of Byzantium wheeling in my mind like some sugarplum mandala. I rarely see my mother.

My father has cruised into my college town in his new Winnebago, towing his old silver Chrysler for me. It is his one rite of fatherhood to give each of us a used car when we become seniors in college. It's my turn now. My mother has coached me to identify him with Nixonian politics, the military-industrial complex, male chauvinism, and all the other bugaboos of the decade. I have seen him perhaps three times in the previous ten years, and always within the safety of my brother's or a boyfriend's presence. But now my brother is a newspaperman in Atlanta and I am a college senior. And our father has remarried, a woman I don't like.

He and his wife have invited me out to dinner. It's as nice a restaurant as can be had in the town, with a lengthy wine list. His wife waits for him to tell the waiter what we will all have for dinner. I order a cheeseburger, so I can offend him twice over by ordering something inelegant, and ordering it myself. I am waiting for him to give me the line that he always gave my sister, that real ladies always wait to have men order for them. If he does, I will walk out.

My father makes a big issue out of ordering the most expensive wine on the list. I make a big issue out of not drinking any. I keep a closer eye on his highball glass than the waiter does. I know the precise number of blocks to the little mill house. I know the precise number of blocks to my boyfriend's apartment. I know the drill that seems to have been dormant in me for a long time. I just don't know precisely where the line is that my father has to cross before I will walk free of him forever. I even know the precise objects in my house I would crack his head open with if he ever so much as lifted a hand to hurt me. It is a fantasy I have had ever since my sister's bad summer with him. But for the moment, in the restaurant, I'm navigating under a different plan: always know my precise position: where the available exits are in relation to how drunk he is getting. Keep money and keys in pocket, not purse. Like any good guerrilla, I know how to watch and wait.

He drinks prodigious amounts, but he doesn't seem to get drunk. They drive me home and we say goodbye. I assume that it will be for quite some more years, and that the next I hear from him will be his elegantly scripted postcards from places like Tempe or Gallup.

He shows up at my door the next morning, toolbox in hand. *—I have work to do here,* he says, and proceeds to nail weird shelves around. Bizarre places: thereafter I will think of him when I crash my head after brushing my teeth. He makes a pretty lamp out of a dimestore basket, hangs it over my garage-sale table, and puts a dimmer switch on it. My mother's anger is also in me: that he would think a dimmer switch to dine by is a necessity of life, when most nights I come home alone to wash the waitress smell of grease and nicotine off me.

He bumbles around my house, recognizes my refrigerator as one that used to belong to my mother's mother and hails it like a long-lost friend. I notice that he is not drinking. He quotes poetry to impress me, now that I am an English major. He used to be an English major, at West Point, he says, and this shocks me.

Nobody ever told me that. I tell him about finding some old textbooks of his in my mother's house, with fold-out maps of Civil War battleplans. He quotes poetry that I don't know. He has to identify it for me. —*Ever read Wilfred Owen?* he asks. —*Siegfried Sassoon?* I shake my head. He continues to tinker with the catch on the refrigerator door while I hold the handle he's removed. —*That's okay,* he says. —*"They also serve who only stand and wait."* He glances back at me to see if I know what I'm hearing and I don't. It's final-exam week at the university and I am cutting class as we stand there.

—*Uh, Dryden?* I say. —*No. Alexander Pope.*

—*Nope,* he says. —*Don't you do your homework?*

That night I pick up a box of greasy fried chicken and we shove my books and papers aside to eat together, dirt-smudged and tired. I feel good, I feel easy with him. I feel like I am meeting myself coming and going. He grew up in the same schoolyard that I did, played basketball in the same circle of daffodils I did. —*I used to raid your mother's acorn piles and shoot them in my slingshots.*

We both learned to swim in the Alapaha River, by diving off the same cypress stump. We bicycled over the same sidewalks, bought penny candy in the same grocery store. We both breathed the same air as my mother as long as we could, and then we left.

By the second nightfall I have cut another day of exams, to accompany my father to the hardware store while he indulges in an orgy of shopping for me. Jumper cables, gas can, pliers, hammer, fire extinguisher, deadbolts, window locks, fly swatter, hibachi. All the things he seems to be appalled that I don't possess. His wife joins us, bearing a Porterhouse steak. He goes down the block to buy scotch. She produces linen napkins, silver, and crystal that travel battened down in the Winnebago with them from Nova Scotia to Vancouver. —*He won't eat with paper napkins,* she says in her martyr's whisper. —*He gets very angry with me if—*

—*He ate greasy chicken last night off paper towels,* I answer, slapping my cheap forks onto the table. —*And he seemed to like it okay.* She looks puzzled and betrayed.

—He just drinks too much and I don't think I can go on—

—That's why my mother threw in the towel, I say. *—He broke her nose twice.*

—The sun is now retreating over the yardarm, he grins from the doorway. He begins to grill the steak, making great effort to show me the correct way to do it, out of some need to impart something useful to me. There is something in him that is wooing me. Now that I am no longer the little girl in the hand-me-down dress helpless in the boat, he wants to be friends. He wants to show me that he is a connoisseur of fine steaks, wine, and women. *—Look at this woman,* he says to me, pointing to her. *—Doesn't she look just like one of those fine carvings on the prow of a Swedish ship? This is no ordinary woman you're looking at. This is my mate.* He pulls her up to dance around the room to a Mills Brothers record he has fished out of his Winnebago. He sings along. *—Be my life's companion and we'll never grow old; I'll love you so much that we'll never grow old.* I understand that he delights me in some way, though his music enrages me. Those silly little love songs, *Picture you upon my knee, just tea for two and two for tea . . . Oh can't you see how happy we would be?*

I watch him drink his way into the late hours, though I have another final exam the next day. His speech becomes grandiloquent. He tells me fantastic stories: how he delivered a baby in a taxicab on the New Jersey turnpike, how he lifted a tree off his Uncle Artie after a tornado ripped through Alapaha before I was born. I no longer keep my eyes on his glass and the door simultaneously.

But you vanished when I was being born, I think.

But I have become a connoisseur of fine lies and a sucker for fantastic stories and grandiloquence, so I listen amiably, sifting out who he is by seeing what it is important for him to lie about. *—Tell me about when you were shot down over New Guinea,* I say, companionably. Tell me how things fall apart.

—Ancient history, he says, waving his hand, deflecting the thought.

Soon they depart, the Winnebago like some grounded zeppelin with a bass boat in tow, out of my life again. My whole house seems to sigh and relax. I am tired. I have had little sleep in three days. I go to see my professors whose classes I have been AWOL from. I explain that my father, an alcoholic, had showed up unexpectedly, and that I chose to spend the time with him. They let me make up my exams.

I get a postcard from my father some months later, in hand-writing so stark, lean, and elegant that it makes me ache to know the person who produced it: *The sight of 13 Winnebagoes belly up in an arroyo can give one a healthy appreciation of the value of the left turn signal. How you doin' down there in radioland?* —*Dad*. On the front: the Hotel del Coronado, resplendent in sunshine, clouds, and air-brushed stucco.

IN 1985 I GET HOME FROM WORK and my answering machine tells me: *Beep*: my not-quite-ex-husband loves me and will never consent to divorce. *Beep*: my boss wants me to work harder to per-suade the Pentagon that it is in the interest of national security to buy us a new podium. *Beep*: my not-quite-ex-husband tells me that he wishes he'd never met me and if he sees me again he will kill me.

How can he say this to me? He couldn't hurt a fly. He is some-one almost old enough to be my father.

I made the decision to leave the marriage in a moment when I seemed to understand my father. I was in a motel bar in Eufaula, Alabama, wishing my husband would ask me to dance.

He shook his head, annoyed. I seemed to have consigned my-self to a life of no dance.

After a moment there was nothing but this weird padded silence in the air. His long, thin fingers looked like foreign objects to me. Then a song cut through like an announcement in an airport:

> *Stay on the streets of this town*
> *And they'll be carvin' you up, all right.*
> *They say you gotta stay hungry.*
> *Hey, baby, I'm just about starvin' tonight.*

From some old memory, two images roared up across the synapses at the same time: me in my married kitchen with the window cracked and the radio on low; the Jews in the gas cham-bers looking for the cracks at the last minute: *Air, air*.

I looked out the window of the bar, across the river to the blinking bridge lights, and the steadier lights of the little fishbait stores across in Georgetown, and I saw it: *radioland*: right out there in the black air: the messages that crisscross and occasionally connect, hovering over the softness of the rivers and the unyielding cities. Amazingly simple statements, hanging out there to be intercepted and confirmed:

—*SOS* . . .

—*Are you a believer?*

—*Prepare for liftoff* . . .

I kept creasing my napkin and sipping my drink, until, toward the bottom of the glass, I swallowed one molten swallow that seemed to slide like shooting silk, *down down down*, until I could feel it glowing somewhere deep, like a heavy golden pear, and hanging by a thread. It was all quite simple. There are certain unalienable rights in this world. One is to dance to the music of one's rightful radio tribe, and another is to form a more perfect union.

I had not yet found the man I belonged to: someone who could accept it with equanimity if I ever confessed that I sometimes lie awake in the dark feeling like a cyclops, wondering if radioland is not some holy huge place where it all ends up, melded into one soft sussuration: the protests of the sheep as Noah led them into the ark, the cry that Shakespeare's mother made, and the patter of Navajo code talkers blending with stray drumbeats from the first time Benny Goodman did "Sing, Sing, Sing." And I wanted someone who could face with courage the prospect of stepping barefooted in the dark on a Tinkertoy or a cold mashed banana. And so I knew that I must never, ever touch the man across the table from me again, that it would be wrong to do so.

Which brought me to this stage of divorce: I need an air-traffic controller in my life telling me that it's time to eat or sleep, and that I am going to survive. My lawyer's secretary has watched me delete possession after possession on my divorce papers, the way someone might watch a fox gnaw its leg off to get out of a trap.

—*Do you drink?* she asks.

—*Not really,* I joke. —*Is it too late to learn?*

—*Well, come with me tonight. I know a guy you'd like a lot. He's divorced, too.*

But I'm avoiding men. They might sense how I am like an ex-con recently sprung from the slammer: suspiciously gaping and blinking in the sudden light of their presence: *Gee, when did they take the tailfins off the Cadillacs?*

I prefer to go to a little cafe around the corner where the men have learned that I will drink my two margaritas in solitude. I sit there wearing my first bikini tan in six years, still the junkyard dog who needs to be quieted by the proximity of the human species. But no real contact, please.

Then I go home.

I sit there in my first divorced dusk.

I remember that it was dusk that did me in in the first place, made me marry so I would have a man to cook for at dusk.

I sit like I'm washed up on an empty island somewhere, waiting for the Lilliputians to arrive.

I call my mother. She can't understand why I would leave a man who is neither a drunk nor violent, so she tells me about her new dahlias. —*I don't give advice,* she says, —*especially about THAT,* avoiding the word *marriage* as if it were an epithet.

I call up my brother; he's working late at his newspaper. —*Shit, shit,* he repeats like a mantra. —*Oh, little Phoebe.*

I call my sister and ask her to tell me about Jonah and the whale, like, what exactly did Jonah *do* with himself once he got out of that belly.

—*He praised God,* she says, without missing a beat.

My own personal guess was that he found a small tight cave and stayed there curled into the fetal position for a while.

After several calls around the country, I find my father. He is at something called the Trophy Bass Lodge in Georgetown, Florida, where he goes when he and his wife have had enough of each other's company for a while. I can hear a jukebox in the background, a heavy honky-tonk beat, and the rich human complaint of the saxophones.

—*So, how you doin' down there in radioland?* I ask. *Radioland* has come to mean the little backwater towns I have always ended up living in, or the places he goes to hide.

—*Doin' fine,* he says. —*They got bass big as Spanish mackerel here.*

I want to *be there*, with all the old men and their fishbait. My father's voice is all scotch-warm and wise through the eight hundred or so miles of telephone cable.

—*In a divorce,* he says, —*the potential for holocaust is real. You can't spend too much time lollygagging around in the wrecked fuselage. You got to explore the new terrain. But who you are has taken you this far, and who you are will take you any place you want to go. Just cultivate a sense of ironic detachment.*

He squires his sentences around like Gene Kelly dances with women: a masterful turn here, a droll pause there, an incremental repetition of the fun parts. —*Bitterness is a form of mental laziness,* he says, and I know that he is referring to my mother, who has nursed her wrath along with her dahlias for years. —*It means you can't grasp the big picture.* He lets that sink in. —*There is a young woman here that I watch,* he continues. —*She gets out in the middle of Lake George in the biggest goddamn boat around. And she is the mistress of her own vessel. The rest of us old geezers just get out of the way. You got to be like that babe in the Bayliner boat. You can't pay too much attention to that skinny cat playing the sad violin offstage—it'll mess up your sense of comic timing. You got to be like that babe in the Bayliner boat. Ironic detachment.*

He offers to meet me for a visit at Warner Robbins Air Force Base, in Georgia, on his way to a West Point class reunion. He blows into that place in a slightly smaller Winnebago, his old one having been declared too large to be legal. He and his wife meet me outside the gates, to get me in. The sentry does not salute him; my father chews him out, indicating the colonel's star on his windshield. The kid knows the drill and apologizes profusely.

My father is ready to hit the bar at the officers' club as soon as he has checked us into the VIP Suite. —*He's not well,* his wife whispers to me as we both stand at the same bathroom mirror applying makeup, dressing for dinner. —*We should never have left Savannah. We talked about divorce all the way up from Winter Park. He just drinks entirely too much, and I don't think that I can go on—*

Shit, shit, I tune her out with my brother's mantra. I am nervous. It has been many, many years since I have slept under the same roof as my father. I notice where all the exits are. I remember that my brother always parks his car head out when he visits my father, ever since the time he offered my father a joint rolled in flag paper and had to make a fast retreat—not because of the grass, because of the desecration of the flag. I put my car keys and my money in my skirt pocket and we head for the bar.

I explain to my father the problems of my job, of milking the federal government for strategic-studies money when you are located a thousand miles from the Washington Beltway think tanks.

—*All you need are the ideas,* he points to his temple. —*Nobody has a monopoly on the truth.* He has had three scotches to my one margarita, and his words are attaining that drunk cadence that can mesmerize me on the phone. I drink faster, to catch up to where he is.

—*Ideas,* he says tapping his temple. —*Go do your homework. Wars don't start in Washington. Wars begin out in radioland. Do you know that? Do you know what I'm talking about? You know why I went to West Point in 1935? Because I was tired of giving my mama my shoeshine money to feed me with.* Olivia's face softens, and I wish in that moment to know all the things about him that she knows.

—*You don't need Janes, just get a map. Look for the places where the people are fed up with being unfed. Look for where the malcontents mass along the borders. Look at that dude out in that jungle, homo sapiens human being, and he suddenly starts digging Dallas on his neighbor's satellite dish, and his baby needs a brand-new pair of shoes. War. Two, five, ten years down the road.*

—*But I work for people who just want to make speeches about rivet patterns on Japanese Zeroes, planes they flew forty years ago.*

—*A Zero is a worthy topic of study,* he says. I sense that he is tired of the discussion. He waylays a group of pilots coming into the bar. —*Lissen,* he says to them, at that stage of drink where you are open to whatever might flower around you. —*I have a lady female member of the species homo sapiens human being here who is bugging the goddamn hell out of me with questions about aircraft. Would you care to field the questions for a while?*

It turns out that they know a tad about aircraft. They are the Thunderbirds. My father has to find out all their names, ranks, and hometowns. Only one of them is drinking, the one from Red Cloud, Nebraska, who almost bought it this afternoon when a bird flew in front of his intake vent right before he chandelled.

—*Lissen,* my father coaches him, leaning forward. —*Lissenamee, Lieutenant Thackeray Phillips of Red Cloud, Nebraska.* My father points to the band. —*You hear those funny noises in the air? Those little ruffles and flourishes and beating of tom-toms? That stuff is called music. Take a lissen to that stuff, man. That is the sound of a human soul that knows the difference between drag and lift.*

The lieutenant leans backwards, enduring his second indignity of the day, being told how to act by an old geezer. His politeness is standard Air Force issue.

My father is in his element, eloquent in the altitudes of alcohol. *—And it is imperative that when you hear that stuff in the air that you get up and dance, shake a leg, trip the light fantastic. What are they teaching you in flight school? Get up and fly, man. There are females in the world languishing.* He gets up to demonstrate, pretending to pat the fanny of a stout woman dancing with her back to us, escorted by a dignified old general-looking fellow.

Olivia shoots me a look—*Help*—and I go dance with him. I am at that stage of drink where I can't tell which is the soft-petaled thing opening, the universe around me or me. My father is portly, but graceful. We dance, pausing only to have new drinks. The band does a cover of Springsteen's "Pink Cadillac," and we find that it is a magic thing, to dance to a saxophone joke about Adam and Eve. If nobody can touch us, it's because we've become the same person. I am him, young; he is me, old. We circle each other, smiling: *Hello, me. Long time no see.*

He can boogie like a college boy, or samba like a sailor, or float around as graceful as the *Hindenburg,* no feet, nothing to tie him down to earth. His wife sits patiently, looking exactly like something carved on the prow of a Swedish ship. The club is closing down; the waiters have all the chairs upside down on the tables. Not only have we skipped dinner, we have closed the place.

My father and I sit down a minute, oblivious, admiring each other's funny freckly hands. *—I have your hands,* I say, and there is a very thin membrane of something tough inside me, holding back a lifetime of tears waiting to spill on his calluses. We vow that if all else fails in my life, we will simply go into the fishbait business together in Key West.

—Can you do this? he calls when we are walking back to our rooms. He jumps up on a three-foot-high retaining wall that scallops the sidewalk we're on. He walks it all the way back, agile as an alley cat. He is seventy and has had more scotch-and-sodas than I could count. I am thirty, have had three margaritas, and I want to curl up on the sidewalk and lay me down to sleep. When he kisses me goodbye the next morning, I smell the fresh scotch. He's still cruising along, holding altitude, coasting over the tops of the heads around him.

Later I describe it all to my mother over the phone, omitting all my margaritas.

—He used to do that every weekend, my mother says. *—He broke my nose one time because I asked him for money to buy groceries.*

I cut her off before she can get to the part where I am conceived in what essentially amounts to an act of rape, and where he disappears for three weeks when I am due to be born, and how she almost dies having me, and how he beats her up when I am two weeks old. I know it all already, and keep it filed in the same place in my mind where he, in perpetuity, beats my sister Allie in an elegant pastel Savannah apartment, or burns my brother's hand with an alabaster cigarette lighter, to teach him not to disturb the symmetry of the coffee-table items. It's what we have in our family instead of a photo album.

—I really feel for Olivia, my mother surprises me. She's been doing a lot of that lately, now that I have joined the sacred sisterhood of divorcees. *—I always felt like marriage was just legalized prostitution,* she said, as if she suddenly needed to confess a past felony. *—I used to pray that he would die,* she says. *—I used to pray that his plane would crash.*

I want a drink, I think. *The potential for holocaust is real.*

My father mails me a photocopy of a letter, dated June 1942, that he wrote to a woman in Santa Fe, as printed in an Albuquerque newspaper. It described to her the last moments of her husband, his navigator, one Winston Fite, after they were shot down by a Japanese Zero off the coast of New Guinea in the Battle of the Coral Sea. He told her how much the man had loved her, and named the precise latitude and longitude where the plane went under.

I want a drink when I have finished reading it. I have several. I sit in the wisteria and drink my margaritas and listen to Benny Goodman. Pretty soon I feel like I've got squatter's rights to the stars, and I can handle the massive dose of history that I have been given. He knew the drill. Know your latitude and longitude the moment you begin descent.

Soon after, on a bright summer morning, I read a tiny box in the Memphis newspaper. Lt. Thackeray Phillips of Red Cloud, Nebraska, crashed into the desert outside Las Vegas, to the horror, amazement, and edification of a cheering crowd that had paid to see the Thunderbirds perform, applauding even as the flames erased him from the earth.

• • •

WHEN I WALK INTO my mother's hospital room in 1986, my brother, Field, takes one look at my face and thinks up a phony excuse to walk with me down the corridor. We wander without really knowing where we are, and I tell him that the doctor used the word *terminal,* and in that moment I understand what it must be like to bayonet someone who's been trained not to flinch. I tell my brother everything the doctor has told me, everything from the futility of surgery to the availability of little old polyester ladies who have no better thing to do than come keep the deathwatch and plump the pillows. He takes a long, even breath. —*We better get in there,* he says, —*or she'll start getting paranoid.*

We weave back through the sterile honeycomb of labs, gurneys parked in hallways, waiting rooms. —*Look,* he whispers, eyeing a shrunken old white lady asleep in a wheelchair, twisted into the fetal position. She is clutching a pink plastic baby doll. They have matching lipstick, fire-engine red, and matching wildly thatched hair. —*Dada art,* he whispers to me. I love him fiercely, proud to be breathing the same air that he breathes.

Back in my mother's room, he turns in a passably good performance of the man he was a few moments before. —*Jesus, Mother,* he teases, rummaging through a Whitman sampler someone has brought to her, —*you've hogged all the goddamn Brazil nuts.*

A few days after Christmas, when I am trying to answer my mother's mail, I find a lush, expensive Christmas card from my father. To her. The first time in my life I can remember his writing to her.

Wishing you a joyous and peaceful Nativity, the card reads. No note, just a signature. I study the illustration on the card, a blue and silver and green sketch of a Bayliner hauling a fresh-cut fir tree across a frothy glittering lake. Maybe ten seconds elapse before the scream makes its way up out of me.

She can't hear me, though. She's already floating on Demerol. The phone rings. She is oblivious, enchanted by the antiquity of her own hands.

It is my father. *Ah,* I think, *nice little bit of closure here.* He will talk to her. He will tell her he is sorry. She will tell him she is sorry. They will not die hating each other. He will be a father to me, and say the grandiloquent words that will help me live through this.

—There are certain documents I must have, he says, breathless at some automatic-pilot alcohol altitude where the air is thin. *—Photostats. You need to know the truth. Ask and it shall be opened unto you. Ye shall know the truth and the truth will set you free.*

Nothing will ever set me free from the knowlege of the world he is giving me in that moment. *Ironic detachment.* It means getting *yourself* out of the wrecked fuselage, forgetting the rest of the injured.

—You have not always been told the truth by your mother, he says and I look over at her. She is smiling beatifically at "Wheel of Fortune," the only show she recognizes anymore. "Sentimental Journey," she guesses correctly, without benefit of most of the consonants.

—I have to go help Mother, I say. This is no lie. She is picking at the buttons of her gown, convinced they are pills she needs to take. I am afraid she will fall off her high bed. *—Nobody has seen those papers in years.*

But he hasn't heard anything I've said, because he hasn't stopped talking. He is still talking about the truth setting me free as I put the phone back in its cradle.

I try to persuade my mother to lie back down, and the phone rings again.

—This. Is. Your. Father. Speaking. You. Do not. Hang up on. Your. Father, he is saying, full of what registers in my mind as rage and hatred of me.

I slam the phone down. *Come on, come on, old man. Your moment with me has come.*

The phone rings again. It is his wife, ever sweet-voiced. *—He asked me to see if I could get you on the line. There seems to be some problem with the line,* she says.

—It's not the line, I snarl.

I write my father a letter that night, my kamikaze rage burning me up before I finish: *Last time I heard, phone conversations were intended to be dialogues, not monologues. If you want conversation with me now it will be sober, and you will do me the courtesy of listening when I tell you something. You never stuck around long enough to notice it, but I am the toughest and meanest of your offspring. I am the most like you. If you give my mother one moment more of grief during what is left of her life, one of us will live to tell about it, and it won't be you.*

Soon I go next door to my aunt's and ask her to come show me how to give a bath to someone who can no longer move a muscle.

—*I'm not asking you to do it for me,* I say. —*I am asking you to show me how.* She is a nurse. She says, —*I remember the first time I saw you. You were nineteen days old. You all were a sorry-looking sight when you stepped off that plane. Your mother had a black eye from where he'd gone after her—*

—*Why?* I ask.

—*Some trouble they had in Bermuda. He didn't think that you were his baby.*

I want a drink. I want altitude, solitude. Solid alcoholtude.

My brother and I take shifts, spooning liquid Demerol into her, sleeping in turns. In the final days, my mother goes back in her mind. She welcomes Winston Churchill, she has tea with Queen Elizabeth. The pain intensifies and she goes back to 1921 or so, calling for the old local doctor who took her tonsils out. —*Go tell Dr. Moore,* she beseeches me, her face full of bewilderment at the war that is being fought inside her. —*He will fix me.* She goes further back: *A, B, C. One, two, three.* She goes back to an infant's rosebud-mouthed whisper, and then she's gone.

The funeral home man shows up within an hour. He has a pink carnation in his lapel. He is none other than Most Popular Boy in my brother's high school class. He is carrying his little music stand with the little satin-covered quilted book, all white and lovely like an albino Valentine. He used to sit in my mother's office and nego-tiate for graduation. She sat in his a month ago and selected her coffin from a brochure. She chose the cheapest one. She never did like Mr. Most Popular.

The farmers and their wives come with dishes of food, sign the albino Valentine book. We have to get the pallbearers together. My mother has managed to yoke together, nonviolently, and in public, the white racist mayor and her black yardman. Over her dead body. My brother and I break the seal on the bourbon bottle before we ride out to the cemetery to show Mr. Most Popular where to dig.

The sheriff, one of her students, comes to lead the entourage to the little Alapaha cemetery. The physician stands amazed, maybe at the knowlege that he lost thousands of dollars in her decision to ride out the cancer at home, or maybe at the knowlege of how she ran forward in her mind to greet death like a long-lost lover.

. . .

MY EARLIEST MEMORY of my child?

I come to, in my hospital room, to the sound of my new husband's voice. He is cradling our newborn daughter in his hands, crooning to her, *—What are we going to do? Your mother can't stay awake, and she walks like an old Chinaman*. I know that I am smiling at him, but I don't know much else, except that I have recently acquired some horrific memories, and there is a thin, thin membrane of drug between me and immense pain and those memories.

I swim up out of the Demerol long enough to hear him singing to our daughter, easing her troubled passage to earth because Mommy is momentarily blotto. The nurse is holding her out to me. My first sight of her: tiny hands clasped together, like a mezzo-soprano in a mouse opera might. It's like they are giving me my very own papoose to have, and from it are issuing whimpers of bewilderment at being born into the species *homo sapiens* human being, the bright lights, the big loudspeaker. But she seems to know who I am, and where to go for lunch.

My husband stands by to catch her if I am too woozy to hold her, and I push the blanket aside to inspect her fully.

She has my father's face.

It's like a slow fist of love slamming up through me. It's like the heel of God upon my neck, to give me back the same configuration of face I've always feared, to give it to an infant I love with ferocity. It's like being inducted into some secret chapter of species *homo sapiens* human being.

I uncurl the little fists. The thumbs are my husband's, a familiar arc in miniature. *—Look,* I say. *—She has your hands.* I am quite relieved by this, as if this gives her some greater purchase on happiness than to have hands like mine.

My husband calls my brother and sister to tell them of the birth. He does not call my father, because I don't want him to. In the first year of my daughter's life I don't want to see or talk to my father, for reasons that don't have anything to do with me. I have this child, and she is too helpless to know where the exits are. Every time I look into her face I also see my father as an infant, and I feel as if I am learning to love him from his own infancy. But I feel an obligation to my daughter to filter my father out of her life, the same way I stopped drinking coffee and alcohol.

I do not question why I must do these things, and my husband doesn't question it. I seem to be flying on instruments anyway. I can hear some other woman's baby cry in the supermarket and the milk will rush into my breasts, staining my blouse. I can no longer read newspapers; they will pipe wars and rumors of wars into my house. One night after several weeks of awakening every hour or so at night to nurse the baby, I dream I have become the ragged mother coyote, mother superior I saw once, milk-swollen, trotting oblivious alongside buzzing traffic in Wyoming, in transit either to her babies or her next meal, or lost.

MY LAST MEMORY of my father? Olivia calls a few days before he dies. —*Don't let him know that I called you,* she says. —*But can you please call him? He has talked and worried about you all day. But don't tell him I suggested it. He gets so angry if . . .* she trails off.

My father has ripped out his IV tubes a week before, and thrown his TV through his window. I dial the hospital number that she gives me, at the appointed time when she will be there to act surprised and hand the phone to him.

Who is this weak old man I'm talking to? He acts like we just saw each other days before. The truth is, we've each been locked into our respective aeries of outrage for so long, we hardly remember what the original fracas was. There is something in him that is still wooing me to be his daughter.

He tells me he understands why I haven't brought the baby to see him. —*You've got a good thing going,* he says, already sambaing with the angels at 30 milligrams of morphine a pop. —*I didn't want to spoil things for you,* he says. —*Man. Woman. Baby. Winter. Fire. There is probably nothing else, sweetheart. Nothing else but love.*

He mentions the time I walked past him in the schoolyard. The tears are like acid in my eyes.

I keep waiting for something that feels like apology from him, for what he did to my sister. He seems to be fishing for what feels like apology from me. He tells me through gritted teeth how he used to park his car a few blocks down from the house to watch me ride my tricycle up and down the sidewalk.

I do not believe this. I am no longer a sucker for a good story.

—*You used to stop and make imaginary phone calls in the crepe myrtle bush,* he says. —*Up and down the sidewalk you went. Up and down.*

The crepe myrtle bush.

There is no choice but to believe, the cold floes of old anger loosening, creaking. Almost like making it out of a wrecked fuselage, being frightened by the new terrain.

Within days I'm sitting with my brother and sister in a cemetery in Savannah, and even though I am expecting the salutatory gunshots, they give me the confusion of fight or flight. I want to rise up and gore the enlistees with their own bayonets. A military funeral is a cold, dead thing, even if you are basically a raging heathen. I come away from my father's funeral feeling like his life has not been celebrated in the manner he would have wished. It ain't over till the saxophones complain.

—*The sun is now over the yardarm*, Olivia says, back at the motel where we are staying. She produces a silver flask of scotch. I keep trying to get my brother and sister to listen to a tape of Clifton Chenier doing "In the Mood." As if that will evoke our father's presence. They don't want to hear it.

So I hang back like a junkyard dog in my expensive dress and my high heels, sorry that my father was not around to take it all in. He would have loved the spectacle: the opportunity to chew out the soldier in the honor guard whose left shoe was not spit-and-polish perfect. He would have marveled at the nicest piece of Dada my brother and I have ever seen: a funeral wreath of red, white, and blue carnations, shaped like a B-17. From the old geezers at the Trophy Bass Lodge, Georgetown, Florida. I am sorry that he is not here now to have a drink with us after we have taken off our shoes.

It wasn't a B-17, was it, I would tell him. *It was a Flying Fortress. Oh, really?*

Well, your brother told me that your name is in this book called Heroes of World War II, and——

I made that up.

I figured. Never could locate it. So I looked up the Battle of the Coral Sea, matched your dates and coordinates with what I found, and figured out that you were one of the scouts sent out looking for the Zeroes. You were three miles out of Port Moresby at eighteen thousand feet when one came at you. He wrote in his bomb report later that he knocked out your tail and your left wing. All of the crew were alive when the plane pancaked, so he kept strafing you. You told a Melbourne newspaperman who interviewed you that every time he came back over, you would dive as deep as you could, and think of all the women you had to get back to. When the Zero left, you swam to shore, alone. The natives passed you from tribe to tribe until you made it to base. It took two weeks. You weighed ninety-eight pounds and had dengue fever.

On the morning that your father got the telegram saying you were missing in action, your brother, a C-240 transport flyer home on leave, just happened to read in the Atlanta Constitution that you had made it back. That was the first time he ever saw your father cry. The second time he saw your father cry was later when your baby brother, a tail-gunner on a B-25, was shot and killed by MPs outside a Negro nightclub in Montgomery, Alabama, for refusing arrest after going AWOL. He was sixteen. You all called him Red, and he had enlisted by lying about his age. When they found out his age, they sent him home, but he just enlisted again in the next county.

You were given the Silver Star for gallantry in action. Red was given a quiet soldier's burial, with none of your other three brothers present. You all told your mother he'd been killed in combat, and she never knew the difference. You were all flying bombing missions or talking airplanes down out of the sky on radios, or trying to fly food into the Pacific Theater. You were a local luminary, the light of which blinded you and Mother both to the fact that the potential for holocaust is real. Did you know that she used to read the Bible and pray while you were in the air?—

How do you know all this?

I do my homework.

Then you ought to know that a B-17 and a Flying Fortress are the same animal. Not bad, though, for a dame. It was more like ten thousand feet than eighteen. I musta lied.

Tell me about the time you threw the TV through the hospital window.

Ancient history. Lissen at that music. Mercy. I refuse to believe that a child of mine cannot learn to samba. Come here.

And I'd come there. And I'd look at him and say, —*Hello, me. Long time no see.*

And he would forgive me.

ONLY HANOI KNOWS

*I*s the moon full or what? I haven't had time to look. My head feels like Grand Central Station. I'm getting too old to be doing all this missionary work they keep looking to me for: *Adrienne, can you check my blood pressure? Can you help me fill out this Medicaid form?* Every time I'm all set to be dead and gone, I keep wanting to stick around a while longer. I guess that's to be expected at seventy-five.

I make lists and lose them. So I keep the list in my head. It keeps me on track.

> *Motee and the refrigerator problem.*
> *The check to the League of American Families.*
> *My niece Phoebe. Reads too many books.*
> *The Methodist minister's wife and their new baby.*
> *The stray cats I feed at the cemetery.*
> *Toy Elliot. She's got her nerve.*

Bald curiosity. Now there's a *raison d'être* for you. Sometimes I just sit out on some old railroad ties at the cemetery and rest. Hell, I know more people out there than in town anyway.

I have to check on Motee to see if he can make it a little while longer until I steal back the refrigerator I gave to the church two years ago.

The League of American Families wants a contribution from me thirty years after my son Jim was listed as missing in action.

My niece Phoebe reads too many books.

The new Methodist preacher's wife and her sick baby. She thinks I was telling her to commit adultery yesterday. Or did that happen today?

I have to outrun her husband on two of the above counts.

I have to feed the cemetery cats.

I have to find it in my heart to put up with Toy Elliot and her so-called railroad museum.

I park my car up in the trees off the highway so nobody can see it and stop. They all know my car; it's the only one with the "Only Hanoi Knows" bumper sticker. There's no body under that marker over there with my son's name on it. That was a mistake I made some years ago, thinking that if there was a stone with his name on it, it would seem over and I could sleep at night.

But that's not why I come out here. There's a litter of kittens living under Artemus Elliot's marble slab and I come check on them because lately I have seen an old owl at dusk in the oaks, scouting out his supper. And I sit here on the old railroad ties they stacked up here when they ripped up the tracks.

It's already Thursday and I still haven't made it across the street for the girl to do something with my hair, so this morning I just put on my fishing gear, which consists mainly of the baseball cap that says Sheboggy Bait and Tackle on the front of it and the pants to that nice navy pantsuit I bought when Nixon was president, and an old blouse that the cuffs have frayed to ribbons on. I always have a bit of a start when I see myself in the mirror, to think that this is *me*.

You rock along for years and years, and then one day you look and think, *Damn, who IS that old biddy?* And then you see that the grim reaper would not mind at all homesteading in *your* house. Forget your former attempts at winsomeness and glamor—the best you can do is hitch up your stretchpants and try to be formidable.

They warned me at the post office that the Methodist preacher was looking for me, so I skipped going to the cafe for coffee. I didn't want to listen to that damn gaggle of farmers anyway. They belly up to the front door in their big-ass Lincolns so they can complain about how poor they are. The government lends them money not to farm and they sink it all back into CDs at higher interest.

They don't know what poor is around here anymore.

Motee is poor.

Old nigra who lost both his legs in a pulpwooding accident, and he now lives on the floor of a one-room house that used to be the concession stand at the Little League field down behind the schoolhouse. They were going to tear it down. I made them move it down across the tracks for Motee. They weren't even going to wire it for lights, but I made them.

I *made* them do it. People can be shamed into doing what they should do.

Another lady and I take turns paying Motee's bill. If we could prove he'd ever been born, maybe we could get him on welfare, but as far as they're concerned, no birth certificate, no help.

I'm determined to get him a refrigerator, and I'm sure that's what the minister wants to talk about. I gave an old refrigerator to his church two years ago, and now I want it back. They already told me in the post office that he wants to give it to that so-called Christian academy across the river. I want it for Motee.

The Reverend Everett Hardemann is what the minister calls himself, and he rang me up at seven-thirty yesterday morning and said that he wanted to make an appointment to talk to me.

Appointment, my ass.

Him with his little calendar *crying out* to have something inked onto it. Just like he is not some backwater preacher in a four-fire-hydrant town, and I am not an old lady with nothing better to do than save fish-heads and cornbread for the cats out at the cemetery.

—*Let me check MY calendar,* I said. —*I got things to do. How about late this afternoon? And I don't want any foolishness.*

He knew what I meant. I haven't darkened the door of a church in almost twenty years, and he is not going to be the one to land me on the front row for all to see what a good fisher of men he is.

We got that straight the first week he was in town.

First time I saw him he bopped up there on my porch in his Ray-bans and his madras shorts, his legs looking like rattails in fruit jars. His wife had on that kind of lipstick that is almost purple. She was pregnant out to here, all bird legs and belly. Looked like the municipal auditorium for the hookworm convention. This little boy child with them—an adopted one, they said—standing there in cutoffs and a striped T-shirt just like my own boy used to wear.

Just like my own boy.

—*This is* . . . Birdlegs said, and I was gawking at him so I missed the name. —*The Lord delivered him to us from perdition.*

I remembered my Jim at that age, standing just like that at Savannah Beach: —*Mother, ain't that the biggest pond we ever saw?* Then he grew up and crossed that big pond and disappeared into a jungle in Laos, and the government lied to me for twenty years about it. The bitterness rose in the back of my throat when I looked at the little adopted boy and I thought, *Just who do you think you are, standing on my porch like this?*

MY MIND keeps wandering.

Motee and the refrigerator.

The League of American Families.

My niece Phoebe and her books.

The preacher's wife and their new baby.

Toy Elliot. Sending word to me through other people. She wants my father's things for her so-called railroad museum. After all these years, she's got her nerve.

TODAY IT IS JUST THE MOTHER CAT out here at the cemetery. I don't see the babies anywhere. The mother is a calico—looks like somebody sharpened ugly crayons and flung the leavings in her face. The first time I ever saw her she came sidling out from behind a marker, pregnant as you please, and I said, —*My aren't you the little hussy?* She wouldn't let me pet her—still won't—but I've got her kittens to the point that they'll stroll right out, tails in the air like scraggly flags, ready for their cornbread or whatever I save from my lunch at the cafe.

I guess if I just set the cornbread down, the kittens might get it when they come back. Under the slab where it's washed out makes a nice little dry spot for them. That's where they were born. I had come out here to sit—there's that old owl that I like to watch sometimes at dusk—and I heard a little yelp, and went to look, and there was Miss Hussy herself, with one kitten already born and another arrival imminent. I figured I was upsetting her, so I got up to leave. She came waddling out from under there, crying to me. I said, —*Look—you can't do this. You'll have babies strung out all over the place.* So I walked back and sat down and she got herself all settled in with the other one, and every time I tried to walk away, she jumped up to follow.

Well, I have done crazier things in my life than this, I thought, and I sat there well into dark, that owl hooting over by the fence, mosquitoes having a heyday on my arms and legs, me presiding over the birth of those little balls of wet life. The mother in there with her four babies, lounging like Sheena, Queen of the Jungle. I said, —Bless *your hideous heart. You just needed somebody to make you feel like it all matters, didn't you?* and I reached in to give her a pat on the head, and she raked her claws across my hand. Drew blood.

THE SEARCHLIGHT SCHOOL is what they call that bunch of trailers sitting out there on a naked clay hill across the river.

Searchlight, my ass.

They *need* a searchlight to search with. Search and re-search some *more*, if you ask me. I have a bad memory, and I ramble on about things that happened before most people here were born, but I do sometimes have a feel for what is right.

In my book, if a man—black or white—has lost both his legs in a pulpwooding accident, and is probably a diabetic to boot, and the welfare lady won't even step up into his little concession stand and shake his hand, well, that man needs himself an *advocate,* and he needs himself a real refrigerator with the freezer on the bottom, so he can keep his banana popsicles in it. It does not need to be in some holy roller school where they'll just use it to keep pimiento cheese and ice in.

THE LEAGUE OF AMERICAN FAMILIES wants more money from me to keep up the search for my son. They sent me a postcard with boxes where I can pledge twenty-five, fifty, or a hundred dollars. I send them a little now and then—I am on a fixed income. The phone rang and it was the minister's little wife, and she said she was having trouble taking the baby's temperature, and she had heard that I was a nurse.

I thought the minister put her up to that. He was trying to flush me out.

I got over there to the parsonage, and I could not believe it. The house looked like somebody bombed Walmart. Dirty diaper up on the kitchen table. No milk in the house, not a drop. Baby had a fever of 102 degrees, little elbow skin standing to a pinch, so it was getting dehydrated. The mother was a wreck, standing there in sweatpants it looked like the goats had chewed. Looking, mind you, at *me* in my baseball hat and my stretchpants, like she was writing herself a mental note to never, *ever* let herself turn into an old lady like *me*, like if you crack me open you'd get useless old silver driftwood with no feeling anymore.

She said she was having bad cramps, and I said, —*Do you know what the best thing for cramps is?*

—*Hot water bottle?*

—*No. Just get a warm man to just hold you a little while. It's one of those endorphin things. I heard about it on the Discovery Channel. Where's your husband, anyway?*

She got this funny look on her face.

—*Where is he?*

—*He's writing a sermon over in his study at the church.*

I said, —*Is he nuts? You need him here.*

She began to cry. The little boy was sitting there in front of the TV with the cartoons on, zoned out like he was used to tuning real life out.

I said, —*Look. I'm going to call the gal that cleans for me and we are going to get this house under control. How long has it been since you've been out of this house? Give us two hours, and you just get in my car and go somewhere.*

She commenced to cry again.

I thought, *What? What did I say?*

—*I need to leave my husband.*

I said, —*You do no such thing.*

—*I do.*

—*You've just got the baby blues, is all,* I said. —*It will pass.*

—*No. I'm going to leave as soon as I can.*

—*Why?*

—*He called out another woman's name.*

I just looked at her.

—*When we were . . . you know.*

—*Whose name?*

She told me, and it was all I could do not to laugh.

She stared at me like she had just disclosed some great shocking truth only *she* knew. Kind of on the order of finding out the pope was a queer or something. It's a hard thing to learn, what she had just learned. It can make or break a woman when she learns it.

—*You know what it means when a man calls you by some other woman's name?*

She shook her head.

—*It means he's still alive in there.* She looked like she was trying to hear me over a lot of background noise, but couldn't. —*That's just the way they are, honey. I know, I've had two husbands.*

Now she was looking at me like she hated *me*. What was she, thirty?

—*That's not what you want to hear, is it?* I pressed on. —*I left my first husband for just such as this. I listened to my mother when I should have been listening to myself.*

Wrong thing to say to a preacher's wife, but it was too late to call it back.

—*But I loved him,* she said.

—*Who says you have to quit? You sure you're talking about love? Sounds to me like you're talking about a lobotomy. God MADE him in his own image, honey. Think about it.*

She was talking to a woman who'd seen dying men call out the names of women their wives had never heard of. Hell, I'd heard women in labor calling out the names of men, and not necessarily the one out there in the waiting room. There has to be a reason why the young are often so blindered. Has to be. This makes me want to stick around another few hundred more years, to get this figured out. Bald curiosity will keep you going when love is gone.

—*What's the matter with that boy?* I said. —*He never talks.*

—*It was trauma. They found him in the bottom of a boat. All his family had been killed. He has an imaginary family now. He only talks to them.*

I saw the problem. He knew very well the truth about which family was imaginary and which was real. I looked into those little eyes and wanted to know what they had seen. I wanted his eyes to speak it all out to me, little fellow, like a movie projector, as if I could find my one familiar face, my Jim, in his memories of death. He looked at me, skinny and pitiful in his Batman T-shirt, his Wal-mart flip-flops. And I decided right then and there that if somebody plucks you out of eternity like a room full of skulls and your new imaginary daddy is a royal jackass and your new mother is not much help, you have to have an *advocate* in this world.

—*Let me take him with me,* I said. —*Give you some quiet. We'll run my errands.*

I needed to talk to Solomon Herod, the nigra funeral director. He and I usually manage to be in cahoots about some thing or another. Solomon and I go way back. His sister Melvina used to work for my family.

—*Just let it ride, Miz Adrienne,* he said. —*I'll get one them college re-frigerators like my boy had at Spelman.*

—*No, dammit,* I said. —*It's my refrigerator and I want it back.* We both knew I was being a big baby, but I didn't give a damn. —*I'm calling in that favor you owe me, Solomon.*

He knew what I was talking about. I was the one who gave him the money to send his boy to Detroit, to get him out of town when everybody thought the boy was after that white girl and the farmers were carrying on about how somebody ought to take him out in the woods and settle it that way.

That was 1972. Nobody knew I bought the bus ticket. The two of them showed up at my door one rainy night, scared. It was the biggest case of cahoots Solomon and I ever got into. It was my opinion that he'd be safer staying in my house than in Detroit, but they wanted to send him anyway. It all worked out. The boy got a basketball scholarship later on.

I didn't bring all this up with Solomon. I was staring across the tracks at the depot. Toy Elliot had come back to "retire" in Alapaha, they said. No trains came through anymore, the tracks had been ripped up. She was living in the depot. I'd even heard she had showed up at the cafe. I had a fair amount of bald curiosity about her.

—*I'll think on it,* Solomon said about the refrigerator. —*Who you got here?*

—*This is the new preacher's boy,* I said. —*I'm going to teach him how to talk.*

The boy was looking at the white hearse, running his hands along the chrome. It wasn't his way to smile much, but I knew he was having an adventure. I could see it in his eyes. If he was going to have conversations, we'd better get rolling on the talking lessons.

—Say "hearse," I said. *— "Hearse?"*

He squinted at me a minute. Hand on that hearse like it was a hot rod.

—Go on, dammit, and say it, and we'll get you a banana popsicle later on.

—Hearse, the boy said.

—That's the ticket.

Little boys must have adventures. They need to touch hearses and be offered banana popsicles by old black men with no legs.

Banana popsicles. Now there's a *raison d'être* for you. Motee way-lays the littler nigras on their way to school and gives them money to go buy them for him. I gave up years ago trying to explain to him why he feels so bad after he eats them. Borderline diabetic. Now I just go check on him every day after I leave Irene's cafe at lunchtime. Most people think that he's off, but it's the banana pop-sicles.

The boy looked a little relieved, and interested, when we got to Motee's. I saw his little eyes pop when we stepped in; it takes a while to get used to the darkness. Then he looked up at me, almost as if I'd given him some kind of treat. Slight horror: a language he was familiar with. I took Motee's blood pressure,

—Evenin', Miz Adrienne.

—How's it hanging, Motee?

This is an old joke from the days when the nigra women would fight with knives over Motee on Saturday nights. And his eyes still pop when I ask it, old white lady with no shame, got it all sucked out of me in emergency and operating rooms long ago.

—Doin' awright. Yourself?

—I'm makin' it. I ain't dead yet.

—No ma'am. Me neither.

—You got a cold popsicle to give this boy?

He pointed to the Styrofoam ice chest. I looked in it, and there was a sad little mass of white paper and yellow gunk stuck to the bottom.

—What you doin' with him?

—I am teaching him to talk, I announced.

I didn't say how I'd come to be hooked up with the boy. I never tell all my business.

This is Motee's occupation, the little plot of black dirt and compost at the back of the concession stand. He started himself a little flower garden of his own volition. There is not much pleasure left on this earth to Motee, but I like to think that one is this. He saves his milk cartons and always has some nice fishbait ready for me.

The boy was taking it all in, wide-eyed. He comprehended the popsicle situation and looked at me like he'd been gypped. My credibility was on the line with him.

–*"Worms?"* I said, holding a squirming one up to the light. –*Lemme hear you say "earthworms."*

He stared at me.

–*We'll get you a popsicle, you little huckster.* I coaxed a little. –*"Worms." Say it for Motee.*

He wouldn't say it for hell.

–*I'm still working on the refrigerator situation,* I said to Motee. My credibility was on the line with him, too.

–*Yes ma'am,* Motee said, waving his arms. –*I thank you.*

IN THE 7-ELEVEN, I puzzled over the refrigerator situation while the boy picked out his popsicle. I thought about it so hard I was lost a minute, standing there at the cash register with my bill-fold in my hand, trying to remember what we had come there for.

–*Fifty-nine cents,* the girl said.

–*Fifty-nine cents for a popsicle? That's robbery. You used to could get a popsicle for a dime. Hell, a nickel.*

I didn't mean to go on like that, especially to some girl who doesn't know shit from Shinola about the economy, but it does give me a jolt sometimes, to think that we're all just hurtling into nowhere, into outer space, the whole mess of humankind just playing leapfrog, just playing leapfrog. *Me first, me first.*

That commercial on the Savannah TV station that I hate. The young man with his wife and kid standing in front of the bank: *I'm your Anchor Banker.* My blood pressure skyrockets when I see that commercial. That tight-ass standing there all clean and wholesome as if he never lost a night's sleep lying awake figuring out how to do people out of their money.

That wife with that Nancy Reagan smile, and on my set her lip-stick is just about the color of the nether end of a bluejay that's been into the pokeberries.

That child with that idiot smile like he's got it made in the shade because he's on TV and his daddy is the Anchor Banker.

Men in five-hundred-dollar suits talking about the economy like it's their own secret algebra that the rest of us don't have access to. You don't have to be an economist to understand human greed, in my book. Human greed as a motivator. The League of American Families. Supposing I did send them another check? How much of it would ever go to what it was supposed to go to?

But suppose they did find him? I think of this often, in spite of almost thirty years since I saw my boy. Boy, hell. Would he know me? Would he care? Would he even be able to stand up?

I had forgotten where we were going.

Plop, plop. I heard the dripping on the car seat. Sticky popsicle all over the boy's bird legs, little vitamin-deficiency legs. He was holding out his popsicle to somebody in his imaginary family who was sitting on the seat between us.

—*Hold it out the window,* I said. —*Let's go check on Phoebe.*

I parked the car at my house and we walked next door, and thought of how odd it still seemed to feel the freedom to do that, now that my sister was dead.

Close to ten years we didn't so much as pass the time of day, the weather.

My sister's youngest child was sitting all alone on the floor in a bedroom with nothing but books in it. I should say that they were all like that, my sister's children. Bookish. Don't get me wrong. Reading is a refinement I couldn't live without, like my *American Heritage* magazine and my *Reader's Digest,* but they all had this way of substituting books for human company. Marjorie used to do that even when we were children. Hole up in the house and choose books over people. Taught it to her children, too.

I looked around, stood over by the bay window.

—*Where's the furniture?*

—*We divided it up. It's gone.*

—*What are you doing with all these books?*

—*I'm going to see if they want them for the library at that little school across the river.*

She waved an old paperback, big fat book. —*The Second Sex. Si-mone de Beauvoir. Mother made me read this when I was eleven, when I had my first period.*

—*What's it about?* I asked.

—*It's a Frenchwoman's idea of being a woman. How it's supposed to feel,
I guess.*

I raised my eyebrows. —*Don't believe what the French tell you
about themselves. They lie to make themselves look good. That damn de
Gaulle—*

The boy had found a falling-apart book on aviation and was
poring over it. *The Wonder Book of the Air* in circus-sized letters on
the cover.

—*I believe you got yourself a customer right here. From what I remember
about your mother's reading habits, they won't want those French books at
that school.*

Phoebe put on some water to make tea. I looked around. There
were ceramic spoon rests everywhere. Little stalks of celery, rooster
heads, or asparagus. Hanging all over the walls. So this is what my
sister was doing all those years holed up in this house by herself,
her children all fled. Merciful God: how many years did it take
Marjorie to get these things nailed up?

Forty-two spoon rests. I swear to God.

Now there's a *raison d'être* for you.

If I ever get to that point, just back the car over me and be done
with it.

—*You been down to the depot to see your dear relative Toy?* She just
rolled her eyes and smiled.

—*She's nuts,* Phoebe said. —*She's got all these old handbills tacked up
in there. Toy Elliot, Child Performer. She told me she was a vaudeville star.
She said my father named his boat after her, the Alapaha Star. And they
even named a train for her.*

—*That's a lie,* I said. —*I heard you'd been married.*

—*Not anymore.*

—*What happened?*

She just shrugged it off.

Phoebe was doing the dishes, and when she finished, she started
wiping down everything in the room, cleaning it.

I said, —*You didn't learn that from your mother.*

—*Nope,* she said. —*I learned it from being a waitress.*

We smiled at each other.

—*Did she ever learn to cook?*

—*Only when we were all gone off to school and she could get a three-
month running start on Christmas.*

—Bless her old heart, She never had a chance to learn to cook or clean. It was all those Air Force years. She always had mess cooks or Melvina.

—One time she took us to supper at Burger Chef every night for two weeks running. One time we ate out every night for three months. Sometimes she would forget that it was time to eat, and she'd send me to the store to get tuna fish. Everything was always so uncertain. I was so glad to leave when I was seventeen. Phoebe said this like she'd been waiting all her life to tell somebody.

—Well, you've been running away from home ever since you were four years old. Nothing irritates me more than a young woman who has not yet had her comeuppance in the world. Phoebe was like that, twitching around in that kitchen. Dressed like some soiree was imminent. Middle of the afternoon, middle of nowhere. I thought I'd take her down a peg or two.

I said, *—You need to eat more.*

She looked earnestly at me, as if she needed to tell something urgent to someone.

Bald curiosity yields rich rewards. The only way not to end up as somebody else's missionary work is to pitch in there and do some yourself. The wall of human misery is like a slow tidal wave you can never quite outrun, like in one of those old Japanese horror movies. What do they call it? Satsumi, surimi, matsui?

I said, *—Phoebe, do you remember the time when you were four and that truck driver found you in the street at two in the morning? He banged on my door and said, Is this Grandaddy's house? I said, Yeah, but Grandaddy's been dead for a year and she's still dreaming about him at night.*

Phoebe just nodded, like she's heard it a hundred times before, and she probably had. She had walked back into where she was packing some books up.

I thought, *I can crack you like a papershell pecan.*

I said, *—You used to run away and say, Adrienne, can I come to live at your home house? That was what you called it. Home house. Four in the morning, like a clock.*

I decided to cut to the chase.

—You know, you and I have something in common, I said.

—What's that?

—My mother didn't want me to be born either.

She looked at me like I'd pulled a knife on her. I plowed on, figuring I would have to finish what I'd started.

—She used to tell me about it. She told me she drank turpentine to kill me. She told me terrible things.

That crumpled her, that cracked the shell. She'd been waiting a long time to run across somebody else who knows what that feels like.

—I used to think that your mother would snap out of it, and begin to pick you up more or hold you on her lap. I used to think if we waited long enough, she'd get more interested. And I used to look at all the little red crinolines in the stores, and I'd think why couldn't I just TAKE you? I was going to name you Julia Rebecca. And I always thought that the reason your mother was always so mad with me was because you were always trying to run away to my house.

She shrugged, kept creasing the dishtowel over and over. She wouldn't look at me. I said, *—You and I are going to be friends from here on out, understand?*

The boy came in about then with his dinosaur book clamped under his arm. He pulled it out to show me something, pointing with his sticky fingers.

—What's this? he said.

—You little shyster. You do know how to talk. I believe that is a Zeppelin. You just only talk it when it suits you, don't you? Phoebe, are there any more books about airplanes or trains in here, or is it all French liars? Put them in a box for this boy and we'll come back later and go to the cafe for supper. Right now we have to check on those old sorry cats at the cemetery.

So I parked up in the trees in case the minister drove by. It would not occur to him to come spend a quiet moment of meditation in the cemetery, so I figured I was safe. I laid some cornbread out on Atlee Redding's slab. The boy got out with his dinosaur book. It had been a long time since I'd been around a little boy. I didn't even have peanut butter in the house. I was sitting there checking my list in my head:

Motee and the refrigerator? No progress.

The League of American Families? No progress.

My niece Phoebe? Some progress.

The minister and his wife? God only knows.

The cats. Where were the kittens?

Toy Elliot, Child Performer. Alapaha Star, my ass. Does she think we're all provincial fools here? Does she think we don't know about the years she was a low-rent Hollywood whore? Does she think she can just move back into my town, MY town, and be forgiven for what she did to me?

About that time I saw Solomon Herod drive up in the white hearse.

Dammit to hell. If that didn't flush the minister out and unleash him on my head, nothing would. Shiny white hearse parked as big as you please. What a start it would give the preacher, whizzing down the road to his next appointment, see that Negro hearse in the white cemetery, and almost run his car off the road thinking that some act of God had occurred without him being in on the show. I was smiling when Solomon walked up jingling the change in his pockets.

—*You got it figured out yet?* I demanded, grinning at him. I love to be in cahoots with that man.

—*Done done it.*

—*Say what?*

—*I went by the church to get a bier of mine they used for that lady's funeral.*

—*And?*

—*And my helper already been by in the other vehicle.*

—*Solomon, tell me.*

—*And I figure if I take off the coil and lay it on its back, I got just enough clearance in my vehicle to get it in.*

Sometimes life itself bellies right up to me, big and grand like an ocean liner up to a dock. My laughter boomed so loud that the boy looked up from where he was squatting over across the way, over in the Durrance family plot. He was poking at something with a pine branch, holding deep consultation with the imaginary friends.

—*Well, is it running okay?*

—*Yes ma'am.*

—*Motee like it?*

—*Motee real proud.*

—*Well, I reckon I be bailin' you out the jailhouse any day now, Solomon.*

—*Nome. I got my cousin to help move it. We left a note saying you ax us to move it, and where it is, and what have you.*

—*Oh, Jesus. So they'll come after me.*

—*Might. But I doubt it.*

We sat there and thought about it a minute, like there was a cartoon balloon over both our heads: the church people in their big air-conditioned Buicks cruising up to Motee's concession stand to claim a refrigerator that should have quit running fifteen years ago. We were laughing together when we saw the minister whiz by, hit the brakes, back up slowly.

—*Merciful God,* I said, and wondered when did I get to be such a baritone old lady. —*You and that damn hearse like Moby Dick on wheels.*

—*I best be movin' on, I believe,* Solomon laughed.

—*You best be staying right where you are.*

The minister walked toward us like we were an interesting new wrinkle on his horizon. He was rummaging in his rag-bag of Bible verses in his head.

Out of nowhere I felt a cold fear clamp on to my mind, and it was hard to shake it off. It can hit you in broad sunny daylight sometimes, that horror, and makes you want to cry out to know what there *is,* if anything, to hold on to. You think, *Who are these people and what have they to do with me?*

Those are the times when I was most likely to remember Austin. When I got scared. For years and years: deep, deep consultations in my own head when there was no one else there. The reality was more like this: I might bump into him in the grocery store, and we might smile like strangers clutching their purchases—*Hello, so nice to see you*—and then flee in our respective directions, each of us with about as much purchase on this earth as a beggarweed has. And at these times I would think, *Let me die. Right here. Now. If this is life, I abjure it.*

The last time I saw him he had only weeks to live. I heard he was sick, and I thought, *I will see him.* And *she* answered the door like I was some Jehovah's Witness that wanted the gold out of her teeth. I had not seen him in five years.

He was in his library, an afghan across his knees. He was ripping pages out of a ledger and throwing them into a fire.

—*What are you doing?*

—*What the hell does it LOOK like I'm doing? I'm getting ready to die.*

—*Look, you can't do that,* I said, meaning *die.*

—*You watch me,* he smiled, knowing what I meant. But there was something foreign and preoccupied in him, like he had battened down the hatches already and Grace and I were just skin-covered sticks running up and down the shoreline watching him set sail. He was readying himself for a journey that had nothing to do with us.

What will I call out when it's time for me to die? What names? What will remain from it all? Who will even be there to hear or care? I envision eternity as some big room stacked full of parched, grinning skulls, and mine thrown into the general, speechless pile.

SOLOMON JINGLED THE CHANGE in his pocket to call me back, I'm sure of it. The sun seemed too bright, and I thought, *Merciless God, am I bored with you—same old sun, seventy years of you.* The pendulum swings; sometimes I am curious about what is on the other side. The other side. Do I believe?

—*Solomon, promise me that minister will never preach my funeral.*

—*Shit, you gonna outlive me.*

The boy saw his adopted daddy, his REAL imaginary daddy, and the funny thing is, he just stood there. He didn't run right over. I had the thought then: that poor man has to spend his whole life outrunning his own irrelevance.

—*What are you doing?* he said. He seemed genuinely confused, as if the work of the world could not be carried on without his initiating it or giving it his blessing.

—*What the hell does it LOOK like I'm doing?* I said. —*I'm getting ready to die.*

I regretted that instantly. Here would come the foolishness.

—*Well, it's been weighing on me a lot too, Miss Adrienne. I would love to talk with you about it. Your plans. The true nature of your soul.*

I was popping and snapping inside. He'd rather sit around farting words like *redemption* and *grace* than offer a dying man a drink of cool water. If he'd lived in Puritan times, he'd have had to burn me for a witch.

—*You got a little missionary work to do under your OWN roof. You go see about that wife and baby under your OWN roof, and then you'll be qualified to come talk to me.*

And he hemmed and hawed and sputtered a bit, but there wasn't much use in talking. I was just an old lady to him. Then the boy came up with his hands and pockets full. He held out his hands and there were some baby wigglers in one hand, kittens' teeth in the other.

So that's what went with the kittens. The owl got them—god-dammit to hell.

—*Hearseworms*, the boy said, just blurting it out.

Nobody could think of what to say for a minute. He could talk when it suited him.

—*Well, in a manner of speaking, yes, they are hearseworms*, I said. —*You could say that.*

The boy went home with his *real* imaginary daddy, who would figure out in due time that we got the refrigerator. I went to check on Motee and take him some lime sherbet. Dietetic. The refrigerator was humming nicely.

—*This is going to send your light bill through the roof, Motee. Fifteen, twenty dollars a month.*

But his eyes were like warm coals that glow.

I ate supper with my niece Phoebe and she told me the only story she had to tell: about herself.

—*Why did you marry him?*

—*He said he needed me.*

—*So what went wrong?*

—*We lived in this big redwood and glass house on a high hill. We chose it for the view. It was one of those neighborhoods where if you built a dog-house, the doghouse had to be expensive and match the big house. Or the neighbors would have a meeting about it.*

I must have looked odd. I didn't get it.

—*I would sit by the big windows sometimes waiting for him to come home, and I'd see other couples out walking together, and I'd think, The prisoners are getting their exercise. He would get angry if I didn't hate everyone as much as he did. He would say that since he put the roof over my head and the clothes on my back and the food in my mouth, he would decide who we would hate. It was making me not want to live anymore. I started feeling bad, and I hated for him to touch me. I ended up with this weird stress condition, like the Jewish women got in the concentration camps.*

She was looking at me like she wanted sympathy, or agreement. She needed to believe that her little catastrophe was somehow grander than anyone else's.

—*Phoebe, you can't just take yourself on like a cause célèbre. You got to take everybody on like a cause célèbre.*

That was not what she had her ears all set to hear.

—*You don't understand.*

—*Don't tell me what I understand. You don't want to feel like you have to fuck for your supper. No woman does.*

She blinked like she couldn't believe what she'd heard. Like maybe that word was only invented specially by her generation.

—*That's it. That's right*, she sputtered.

— *Last time I took money from a man was 1947. You got a good job?*

—*It's not a real one. I still feel like some camp follower waiting for the soldiers to throw me some hardtack. I don't make much, but my car is paid for. I don't have to ask anyone for money. The clothes on my back I bought myself.*

She made a big deal out of paying for my supper. I let her.

I listened to the eleven o'clock news and then smashed it off when the Anchor Banker came on. I went to bed.

My list floated over my head in the dark, the way the face of a lover's would have in my younger days.

Motee. Definite progress there.

League of American Families. No progress.

The minister situation. He feels irrelevant.

My niece Phoebe. Progress? Can't tell.

I hate going to bed. Even now I have dreams of my grown Jim lying on the jungle floor, calling for a drink of water. I still wake up wondering where I was the precise instant he perished, what banal or useless thing I was doing. If I were a praying woman, I would pray that he did not understand the banality and uselessness of my life before he died, I would pray that it was all an orange flash of red-hot righteousness to him, death. I've figured out within a week of when it could have happened, and I have gone over and over it in my mind like those trucks the high school boys drive out to the river flats with those enormous wheels. Bogging, they call it. You burn a lot of gas, you get nowhere.

But tonight the moon is indeed full, round, and comforting, like an old traitor I have long since granted forgiveness for its sins.

The moon gave me my Jim.

I ran away from home in the middle of just such a full-moon summer night, wearing a pink eyelet dress and not much else underneath. Pink lipstick. Nineteen forty-two. Just stood up with a twenty-year-old marine in front of a justice of the peace in Jacksonville, and his wife in twisted paper hair curlers, in a peignoir and gown as if *she* were about to embark on the honeymoon, not me.

We must have looked like stunned birds. They gave us each a stiff drink of bourbon to get us through it. Later we climbed up onto the roof of the Ponce de Leon Motel so we could see the stars on our wedding night. Star-bathing, he called it.

—*You will be my life and my wife,* he said. Just like that!

I was fifteen. My life looking to me like blank perfumed parchment stationery that I would write his name on a thousand, thousand times a day. My sour mother a thousand, thousand galaxies away.

Sweet Jesus, the things men say to us to get their babies born. Do they *mean* them? And the things we say back to them, *meaning* every word? Is it real or is it all just stagecraft, overseen by the man in the moon, who could very well be just another shyster in an elegant pair of spats waiting to sell each of us a used idea that the odometer's been rolled back on.

Sometimes in the night I rummage through those old ideas. Memory stew. It's one of the chief pleasures left to me now that I am an old woman, believing that men and women *mean* the things they say to each other when they love each other. And if I rummage patiently enough, through the years and the men and the children, it all becomes a fuzzy catholic pleasure, there in my private dark.

I moved in with my young marine's parents, and his mother put me in charge of the laundry. She annexed me like the housemaid she'd been waiting for all her life. Then I was sixteen, pregnant, and anytime we went anywhere, he would walk just fast enough that I couldn't quite keep up with him. As if he could not quite believe he had any connection with me, this creature whose belly went from flat and firm to obscene with life, right before his very eyes.

—*You better watch out for yourself,* an old woman in the church said to me. I wondered what she meant, not knowing that my private life was all pasted up in the big billboards of their minds.

Then one day I picked up his shirts to wash them, and I held them close to me for his smell that I loved, I could smell perfume, *perfume,* and it was some other woman's smell, not mine.

The moon gave me Jim, but it stole his father from me.

Took me close to *forty years* to quit crawling out of the wreckage of that moment and understand that I was never again going to be a star-bathing girl again.

You are never that girl again, trembling under a man but trusting him, and believing only *his* touch can make you live.

That time does not come again.

The square root of the world's misery is what women are taught to expect from men. The square root of the world's misery is what men are taught to expect from women. Each of these statements is true.

Who is responsible for this? I want a culprit.

I'm bogging.

Fix the world. I have to do this sometimes. It's the only way I can get to sleep.

I wish I could teach a childbirth class. Not that nonsense they do now about how you're not a *real* woman unless you do it without drugs. I'd tell them the things what they really needed to know. *Don't worry about the baby getting here,* I'd say. *The baby will get here.*

—You don't belong to yourself right now, I'd say. *—You're on loan to the tribe. It's not the arms of your man that hold you up during this time, it's ours. He's doing good to hold himself up right now.*

A pregnant woman is an ugly hunk of blue-veined human scrimshaw for a while, temporarily *hors de combat.* No man can look at her for very long and not be filled with disgust for all life. But I wouldn't say that in my birthing class.

I'd do some deep spiritual lying, clean and holy. I wouldn't tell them about the cruel part. Somebody else do-si-dos your partner, promenades him home.

You give a gift that may never be returned to you. It's the only way to survive.

I'd have the girls lie still and breathe deep, and envision their husbands in the arms of other women. I'd say, *—That other woman's the one giving him the will to live right now. Not you. It all evens out for the good of the common tribe. So breathe in the so-called abundance of life. The pangs of birth are nothing compared to what awaits you if you don't learn this little breathing trick of mine. You also have to give birth to your new self, your true soul.*

And they would look at me like I was the most pompous and most interesting old lady they ever ran across. The truth is, I lie here on my back like a seventy-year-old sequoia, full of concentric rings of memory that might be of use to someone once I'm felled.

A lonely man is a winged quail.

The woman who sees is a stunned canary.

Snared, both.

The man in the moon rolls the odometer back.

The woman is then the scrimshaw belly on the birdlegs.

The baby with the puppy's breath that needs schooling in the habits of the tribe.

The man is then lonely twice over, like a twice-winged quail.

Comes the name of a new woman. Whispered to you by old women: *Toy Elliot, Toy Elliot, Toy Elliot.*

All are now the snared canaries.

She took my husband from me, her and her spangled vaudeville dresses, and he came back from California a broken-spirited man who died of drink, angry and alone.

In my own mind I've Fixed the World. I've run up and down the streets of my town in my nightdress, throwing open all the doors and windows, covering a span of seventy years. I've seen bewildered, stunned birds cringing and cramped from imagining that they are all starvelings in the avenues of love, in these houses.

—You don't have to live like that, I've told them. *—I am freeing you tonight. You will be loved tonight.*

I've freed the men, freed the women. Led them all outside into a star-bather's dance, naked as newborns, able to *look* at each other with something better than mutual suspicion. I've choreographed the whole dance: *man, woman, man, woman, man, woman*—holding hands to make a circle around whoever needs protection the most at that moment, like some wreath of life readable from the air.

By whom?

The other side. Do I believe? I look at that bunch of holy rollers out across the river, their faith a safer stupefacient than any drug you could ever hope to devise. I think, *Why not?*

Never worked for me. I've always thought that if God would quit prissing around in drag like Mother Teresa, he's probably got the soul of P. T. Barnum. *He's* that shyster in the spats rolling that odometer back, beckoning us all into the big top. It's the only way to insure that a new sucker is born every minute.

What is it all *for*? I made the mistake once of thinking my new-

born boy belonged to me. He was on loan from the tribe, and the
tribe took him from me. To guarantee that I would have the pleasure of watching the Anchor Banker get richer every night.

That song that everybody thought was so cute in 1945: *Ev-ry . . .
boy should . . . learn to . . . be a . . . military man.*

I should have been putting my *own* boy on a bus to Detroit.
Canada just on the other side.

—*Son, do you WANT to die?* I asked him that last time.

—*I am a soldier,* he said, as if it were a calling.

Memory stew.

Tomorrow: my list:

Phoebe to meet Motee. Take her down a peg or two.

Motee and the electric-bill problem. Well, we'll just see if the Searchlight School can search its own pockets for a change.

That damn owl that ate my kittens. I have no right to wish him evil.
He's just making it from day to day, too.

The League of American Families. I'm thinking, I'm thinking.

If I don't send them any money, I ought to have just enough left
over this month to take the preacher's boy down to the hardware
store and pick out a big Western Flyer wagon. If they still make
them. If you want schooling in the ways of the tribe, and your
imaginary mother's lounging around in that wrecked fuselage like
she's got a whole lifetime to burn, and your imaginary daddy's irrelevant, you need yourself a Western Flyer wagon. That red-metal
kind with the wooden slats you can take off when you're out there
having your adventures and hauling your box of wonder books or
hearseworms and what have you.

Toy Elliot, Child Performer.

That's a tough one. I could ignore her for the rest of our lives.
Or maybe if you are an ugly little old woman with nothing but
your old handbills and your whore's memories, maybe you need
yourself an *advocate* in this world.

I could go down there and thank her for opening the door to
my cage so long ago.

IF YOU LIVED HERE YOU'D
BE HOME BY NOW

*I*n the neighborhood where I grew up, there was a ramshackle fortress that I loved, built on a bluff, cobbled together from objects pilfered from construction sites. Some older boys started it by building a hut of two-by-fours at the base of a big tree, and it evolved from there. One wall was an oval of translucent plastic that said "Exxon." If you needed a good view of the city, you could climb out onto its roof, an old real estate sign that said the same thing on both sides, whether you were lying on your back inside the fort, or sitting on the roof: "IF YOU LIVED HERE YOU'D BE HOME BY NOW." At night, there was Atlanta, off on the horizon like an oncoming arc of light, a gold glacier inching its way out to us in our subdivision named for birds that do not inhabit the North American continent. I grew up on Nightingale Lane.

There was a time I was playing behind our house at the edge of a field of wildflowers. I had pressed down the flowers in a small circle to make a playhouse for my Barbies, making Ken and Barbie kiss, and this gave me an odd feeling. Like warm sunny secrets inside me. Then the bully from next door was there, and he said, —*Tory, take your clothes off,* so I did. You always defer to them, even at that age. Partly out of fear, partly out of reflex.

—*Tory, do you know how to kiss?* he said.

I pecked at his cheek.

—*That's not the right way,* he said. —*You have to put your tongue in my mouth. Parents do it that way.*

—*Do not.*

—Do too.

—Do not.

—Do too. I'll show you.

—Ick, I said, and pushed him. He punched me in the chest as hard as he could. I fell down in the wildflowers and cried.

—I can't believe you fell for that trick, Graham said, and touched one of my nipples softly, then ran away.

Our parents have snapshots of us naked as downy ducks together in a wading pool with his little brother, Lyle. There are videos of my second birthday party—they had been picking at me to make me cry, and you can hear my mother's voice in the background, *—Love the boys, Tory,* and I reach out and hug them through my tears and say, *—Wuv boys, wuv boys.*

I hate that video, I *hate* it. I hate my tear-streaked face, and how everyone *ooh*s and *ah*s at how cute it is, the toddler dispensing love to the little hellions. Like some pop-up dummy that keeps coming back for more. I hate how I squint into the camera after I hug them, searching for approval from the adults offstage.

But Graham was my favorite human being on this earth. Sometimes he led me on expeditions around the yard, showing me the robins' nests and rabbit holes. Sometimes he ignored me. One time he tried to teach me to play tennis but hit me so hard in the mouth with the ball that I just sat down dumbly on the court, eyes stinging. After that, I didn't play with him anymore. But we grew up side by side. He had a few years' head start.

Then at school they took all the girls out of homeroom one morning and piled us all into the auditorium. A girl had committed suicide—they wouldn't tell us where. They talked to us for two hours: *Remember that you are a person and you have value and worth, and yatta, yatta, yatta.*

Our subdivision hired an architect to design a fence to match all forty-six houses, and you had to know a security number to get in. It's called a gated community. I was fifteen when this happened, and so I was still young enough to be running around on my bike. It didn't take anybody very long to figure out that there was a way to get in and out. Behind those houses where Nightingale Lane turns into a cul-de-sac, you could lift the bottom corner of the cyclone fence and step through the privet and ivy out onto a little bluff of land left over from the bulldozing below.

Sometimes when my boyfriend's parents were out for the evening we would go upstairs to his room and lie together in his bed, his music booming too loud, and I'd look at all the warriors and wizards and guitarists on his walls and try to figure out what was important to him. He had these posters of nude women all over the walls. All the boys had them. It was an understood thing that I was what he had instead of those beautiful blondes in bikinis. I was a slightly less than adequate substitute.

Sometimes it was like walking a dangerous line with him, kissing and learning the nicest places to touch, to see how far we could go before one of us would chicken out. Usually it was me. He was, I'm sure of it, always relieved when his fingers would slide past the elastic of my panties and I'd tense up.

The fastest way to get him to tense up was to tell him I loved him. The first time I did it he sat up, like, *Okay, game's over, you can go now.*

He had a little basket on his nightstand that he kept his pot in, and he started hoarding my earrings there. It started one night when I had taken them off so it wouldn't hurt to lie with my head on his shoulder, and I put them in the palm of his hand. He dropped them in the basket and turned out the light before reaching for me. I forgot about them. Then another time, and another, until he had several pairs. Even some diamond studs that belonged to my mother and she didn't know that I had them.

—*Hey, give me all those back.*

—*Nope, not until.*

—*Until what?*

—*Until you give me what I want.*

I didn't say anything. He liked to tease, I liked to be teased.

—*What do you want with a bunch of old earrings?*

—*They are my payment.*

—*For what?*

—*For not raping you.*

It was a little game we had together. I knew I was perfectly safe in his arms. I learned that you can buy a little time. I learned how to take off my earrings while he was driving us to the mall theater, and to press them into the palm of his hand, like, *See you later, alligator*, and we'd both smile because we both knew how hard he'd get the minute those earrings touched his hand. And that he'd probably stay that way until the moment came when I could coax him out of his young-man pout, appease him by kneeling between his knees and taking him into my mouth, musky family jewels I liked very much. Sometimes we never made it to the mall.

Then, when my grandfather Durrance knew he was dying, he got me to read to him every time we went to Savannah to see him. I would take down the big blue leatherbound book he liked and sit in a chair beside his bed. The deal was, he would quote a line, and I was supposed to find the poem it was in.

He was like a formidable old baby with a mottled hawk beak. —*"Nothing can bring back the hour of splendor in the grass,"* Tory. *Do you know what that means?* he'd said once, and I dutifully started rustling the tissue pages. There was always a folded map of a battleplan for a bookmark: the Somme. I couldn't find it. So much of my conversation with him was always like that, a cloud of words hovering over my head, without meaning to me.

—*You got a boyfriend?* he demanded.

—*Yes,* I said.

—*"What is it men in women do require?"* He said then, my cue to start page-rifling. —*"The lineaments of gratified desire." This is important, Tory.*

His wife, Olivia—she's not my grandmother—brought him some bouillon to drink once, and we had to help him sit up.

—*What is this swill?* he said, smiling at her. —*In the old days I would have thrown it at you, baby. I will not be tyrannized by women.*

—*In the old days I wouldn't have fixed it for you, baby.*

He whined a little, but he liked being babied. —*"And here we are as on a darkling plain . . . with neither hope nor joy nor certitude . . ."*

—*That's right, love,* Olivia crooned softly to him absentmindedly, and dabbed gently at the beads of sweat on his brow. —*No joy. No love. Whatever you say, baby.*

—*Tory, I want you to have my old camera,* he said one night. —*Treat it with respect. Incredibly sweet power of aperture.*

The Leica was so old you had to put it in a black bag to load the film in it. The first time I opened the film compartment, a note fell out in his wobbly handwriting, like an afterthought: *Available light is enough.* The lens had a nick in the top quadrant. My art teacher at school loved the Leica, then peered into my face as if it had been squandered on me. It was an odd-looking thing next to the Yashicas and Minoltas the others had, and I learned to keep it out of sight. It attracted attention and made me feel like a first-class nerd.

Then I got a postcard of Namu the Killer Whale, telling me to come back to Florida. —*You forgot something*, it said in the birdtrack writing. That was all.

A ruse to get me to come back for the tripod, I thought.

My grandfather sent me a letter rolled up like a scroll. His handwriting had gotten wobbly gothic there toward the end, like Art Deco bird tracks:

1. *You are an unofficial ambassador of the United States of America.*
2. *We are not without our vestiges of civilization here.*
3. *Sometimes the only true believers are the infidels.*
4. *Who you are has taken you this far, and who you are will take you anywhere you want to go.*

That was his way. Cryptic sayings that came off like some kind of corny intergalactic double entendre.

My father made the last trip to see him alone. He got back home and there was this long bundle attached to his car. My mother wandered out in her robe and then shuffled back off to bed, saying something about how my grandfather's epitaph should have something about boats and trailer hitches in it. We all ended up down in the driveway looking at the big bundle, like a giant baby had just been put on the doorstep.

—*That is definitely not a tripod,* I said, warily.

Graham, the boy next door, stepped out into his driveway and I saw him look over. I didn't have any robe on, just my football jersey and those big wool socks. I had my hair in Velcro curlers and the old Leica around my neck like I'd just won the doorprize at some geek convention and I thought, *shit!* and stepped around behind the boat.

—*He wanted you to have it. It's his little catboat.*

Nobody in my family knew how to sail, not even my grandfather. I stared at it as my father uncovered part of it. —*Alapaha Star,* he said. —*Good God, I'd forgotten about that.*

—*But where will we keep it?* my mother asked. They decided that my father should back the car down the driveway, and slip the boat, trailer and all, into the garage.

—*Perfectoreno,* my father laughed, looking at how it fit perfectly. Bald stares from people out walking their dogs.

And the catboat stayed there through the winter.

By the summer, my parents were worried about me. I stayed in my room listening to music all the time. I didn't read enough books to suit them. My father had tried to show me how to use the camera, and I had lost interest in it. One Saturday he seemed very hurt about this. So I loaded the film in it and sat across the room from him while he watched a football game. The older I got, the more he treated me like he treated my mother, controlling me with his brooding silences. So that the only way you can get over that sudden feeling of worthlessness is to start coaxing him back out of the man pout.

I snapped his picture while he was watching a football game. Three, four times during the game. I noticed that his face seemed different as the game went on. Sometimes his face was full of light, like a little boy at Christmas, sometimes his face was like a faded, blank ocean, so tired. He looked a little annoyed at me, but he said nothing. He knew what it was like to try to learn to use a camera. I do not know why I wanted to photograph him instead of my mother. I did take one of her, in the bathroom, grimly trying to pencil her face back into existence with her expensive makeup.

—*You were really pretty once,* I said, and knew immediately that this was another one of those terrible slips.

She stopped, eyeliner in hand.

—*You did this to me,* she said decisively. —*I used to have a figure and a face, and then you came along. I could have studied at the Cordon Bleu if you hadn't come along.*

Attention from her was like that—critiques of me by conducting a postmortem on her own life.

—*Well, why did you marry him?* I said one time when she said that she should have gone to Antioch instead of marrying my father.

—*Because he was so comme il faut,* she said.

—*Comme il faut? What does that mean?*

—*When it feels like he hung the moon,* she said. —*You'll know it when you see it.*

To please my parents, I enrolled in a Water Safety Instructor class. The teacher turned out to be Graham, the older boy next door. I'd never thought of him quite as a Water Safety Instructor. I kept sneaking looks at his legs, which I liked so much that it was often difficult to hear his words.

On the first day of Water Safety instruction, Graham had six of us perched like sparrows on the edge of the pool, and he did not seem to be exactly pleased at the prospect of a few weeks with us.

—*I'll show you what you have to do to get out of this course,* Graham said, treading water, and I could see the palms of his hands and feet flash white underwater. He swam out to the center of the deep end, his hands cutting cleanly. He paused, piked down so quickly there was barely a ripple to prove he'd been there, and we could see his shape toward the bottom.

—*What's he doing?*

—*Showing off.*

—*No, I mean, what's the point? Anybody can hold their breath.*

He'd been down long enough that I was uncomfortable. Too long. We all started holding our breath. The surface broke, and there he was, pulling something.

—*Jesus, he's got the fucking drain cover.*

The drain cover, a circular, cast-iron grille that always appeared to crouch on the pool's bottom like a dark toad monster. We were all still quiet, and he brought it over to us with a kind of graceful, but dogged, sidestroke. He hauled it up in front of his little brother, who'd been the cockiest, and said, —*Take it.* His brother smirked a little and reached for it, but the minute his hand closed around it, Graham let go and he was gone, sunk, sputtering up a few seconds later while we all watched the drain cover go down, to the ripply shadows of the bottom.

—*You trying to drown me, man?*

—*Any other questions?* Graham said, and we were all humbled a little.

I remembered those words, *comme il faut,* which I still had not bothered to look up.

The first time it was my turn to practice saving someone, Graham pretended to be the drowning victim. He swam out to the center of the deep end and flailed a little, teasing me, —*Come on, move your ass, I could have drowned by now.* I swam out warily. He moved into a dead man's float, as if he were going to make it easy for me. It felt oddly foreign to cup his chin and tip him back. I felt the rasp of his beard and he passed in my mind into some new category—*them.* Men.

His chest was so broad that I couldn't get my arm across him, but he went completely limp and I actually swam a few strokes back to the edge before he came to life, put his hand on my head and pushed me under.

I came up sputtering and coughing, and he was already on the other side of the pool, a swift swimmer.

—*You held me like a teacup,* he said accusingly, so he could justify humiliating me in front of everyone. —*It's a good way to get yourself drowned.*

The second time it was my turn to save someone, the victim was Lyle. There was a bit of confusion, we scuffled in the water, as if we couldn't quite get it straight who was saving whom.

—*I'm saving you,* I sputtered. —*It's my turn.*

—*Is not,* he said.

—*Is too,* I said.

I did not fare very well in the Water Safety Instructor class.

Forget raising the hundred-fifty-pound drain cover. I couldn't even pike down to touch it. I would tense up on the edge of the pool, feeling dread weighing me down. Then I'd swim out until I could see the outline of the drain cover down there: black toad monster crouched on the bottom. I'd pike down okay, but I could feel the weight of all the water on me on top of all the heavy dread, and I'd give up. Sputter back up to the top, where Graham would look faintly amused. As if nothing were to be expected out of me anyway.

It was a relief to know that it was all just a game, this Water Safety Instructor bit, to keep girls busy and occupied on summer afternoons. It would never be incumbent upon me to actually *save* anyone. There would be men around to save people's lives.

I sat one time on the side of the pool with all this still in my mind. I didn't even have my suit on, had no intention of getting in. I had the Leica with me, and I took pictures of everyone, but the only person I really wanted to watch was Graham. I snapped his picture as he moved, more patient with light and shutter speed than I had ever been before. This pleased me very much. I took pictures of him so intently that I forgot the time, forgot that I was supposedly there to learn to save people. I was reloading the film and somebody splashed water in my face. Graham.

—*Aren't you going to get in?*

I shook my head miserably.

—*It's not as scary as you think,* he said, and I looked up sharply at him. It usually made me uncomfortable to have anyone notice things I thought were private. —*You're not going to pass the course if you don't learn to do this.*

I shrugged.

—*Stupid cunts. I don't know why you even come here.*

I quit going to the Water Safety Instructor class, maybe because I knew I'd never be able to pike down. I was even having nightmares about it: I'd get all the way to the bottom and the drain cover would not be there, and then I'd push off the bottom, scissors kick, and never seem to make it to the surface. I'd wake up with my temples sweaty and my pulse crazy, and a memory, a sure knowledge, of fear.

When my parents went out to see a movie, my boyfriend came over with a video he'd found in his parents' bedroom drawer—he made me lock the doors so my parents couldn't walk in while we were watching it. It was about these guys who meet women out on the street and take them somewhere and tie them up, then do whatever they want with them. I couldn't believe what I was seeing.

—*I'm not watching this sicko stuff,* I said, and got up to go into the kitchen.

—*It's not what you think,* he said. —*It's not real. It's the way adults play.*

Cheap stupid-looking women who just happened to be wearing G-strings under their jeans. I couldn't get into it. First I kept thinking about the actresses and wondering what their lives were like. Some looked like Waffle House waitresses trying to pass for college girls. The clothes were okay, but the genes were not. Then the men were tied up and the women had the whips. This was the worst. I grabbed the remote and zapped it into fast forward and the women flailed comically.

—*Christ,* I said. —*How totally fraudulent. Fake people sitting around watching other fakes.*

—*You don't understand. It's a ritual about trust. You can stop it at any time.*

—*You meet someone, and then you ask them to hurt you a little, and then you ask them to please stop?*

—*Safe words,* he said. —*You have a safe word that can stop it all.*

· · ·

ONE SATURDAY AT THE END OF THE SUMMER, my father told me to clean out the garage. I was stacking some old boxes of magazines out by the curb when Graham walked out with some old crates of records. We didn't speak to each other straight off, but we noticed each other's throwaway stuff. He was looking at the *Baseball Weeklies* we were throwing out. I was looking at the albums they were throwing out. The catboat had caught his eye.

—*What's that?*

—*Something my grandfather gave me when he died.*

—*Cool.* He was already in there, looking it over, and he slid the tarp over it the way I'd seen men slide their hands under women's dresses in movies. I was feeling a little defensive, had myself braced for some snide remark about how old and shabby it was.

—*Alapaha Star. What a sweet little old boat. Have you ever taken her out?*

I shook my head.

—*Do you know how to sail?*

I shook my head again.

—*Christ. You own a fucking sailboat and you can't even pike down in twenty feet of water.*

He pulled the tarp off. I'd never really looked at the boat before. It was dark varnished wood with green trim.

—*There's a bunch of junk in the front*, I offered.

—*You just think it's junk because you're a woman.*

Woman. Nobody had ever called me that before, and I started sneaking looks at his legs again while he looked at the stuff in the boat.

—*Lines, sail, anchor. All the amenities. Does your dad sail?*

—*No.*

He shook his head. —*What a waste.*

We ended up spending some evenings in my parents' garage together. All our conversations centered around the boat, the only thing about me that interested him. I mean, these times weren't, like, *dates.*

On a date you know why the guy is there and what he wants with you. He showed me how to raise the mast and rig the sail. All in the garage. He told me the only way to feel more comfortable in the boat was to spend more time in it. One rainy night after school started I was sitting in the stern doing my algebra homework. I looked up to see him standing watching me.

—*You need to know about tacking.*

We played this little game, sitting in the boat with the imaginary winds churning around us. —*I'll show you how to come about.*

—*Come again?*

—*Come about. The wind shifts, you come about.*

The boom swung around and I ducked.

It was a game I liked very much by then, watching him move for me while his words hung above us like clouds.

Always when it was time for him to go home, it was like a spell had been broken, and I had to step out of the boat and back into the ordinary air. I'd go upstairs to my room and look out across the elm trees to the light from his room, my head so full of him that I couldn't do my homework, couldn't do much more than listen to the radio and send up wishes like invisible flares that only I could see. I caught a snatch of song once, rather plaintive.

> *Oh mama, there's this Spanish dancer—*
> *Steps I follow when he's near—*
> *The red dress of temptation—*
> *Over a long black slip of fear.*

I phoned the radio station to see who it was and what the name of it was, but the receptionist wouldn't put me through to the DJ. I could still hear the end of it when I hung up the phone.

> *Just like a Spanish dancer I*
> *Throw my roses down for him.*
> *Across these beds of darkness he*
> *Opens his arms and gathers—*

I couldn't tell what the rest of it was. Gathers *them* in? Gathers *me* in? *Gathers me in* was more to my liking.

I almost walked in on a discussion of my parents' one afternoon before I left for a date. It was the sound of my mother's voice that made me stop. I'd heard her cry only once or twice before, but I recognized the sound of it now.

—*Don't even think of it.*

—*But we could try,* my father said. —*Forty-five is not so old to be a father again.*

—Forty is old to be a mother again.

—Madeira.

—I'm not going through that again. It's like that Chinese proverb—you fool me once, shame on you; you fool me twice, shame on me.

It was like having a ringside seat to something that surpassed pornography in making me feel naïve. I put on my father's parka and went out the back way. I didn't want to see anyone. I knew my boyfriend would just shrug when I didn't show up to meet him, and he'd go home and watch a ballgame.

I had nowhere to go. I went to the fortress.

Graham was up on the roof, noticeable first by a little orange dot, the end of the joint he was smoking.

I climbed up with him. He was the kind who would not ask you what in the hell you were doing in a place like that at a time like that, partly because he would then have to explain what *he* was doing in a place like that. I made a mental note again to look up *comme il faut*.

He offered me the little orange dot, and I shook my head. I could hear my father's voice, like my conscience, like Jiminy Cricket: *—Never underestimate the tactical advantage of sentience.*

—Just say no, Graham mocked a little. He was like that. He held people at bay by the hint of ridicule, bringing about a cowed obeisance that seemed to satisfy whatever need for friendship he had. The crowd he ran with was pretty vicious sometimes, like they had this little collective fiction going: they were better than everybody else. It seemed to give them a reason to live. The girls could vamp their dads for money to get the clothes and nose jobs and breast implants to snag the guys; the guys could suck up to their fathers to get the cars to acquire the girls. Warm-up acts for adulthood, I guess.

So I knew what he was doing at the fort. He was feeling free of everything.

Graham wasn't one of those people who get stoned and say only stupid things, as if they should be entered into the cosmic historical register—*Baby Wipes are cool, man.* Graham was the kind who bloomed like a dark velvet lily.

—All those poor sons of bitches, he said. *—Everybody's looking for a little oasis of tenderness.* The orange dot flared. *—Sometimes I wonder what it was like to have been the first one to arrive, you know, like Cortez*

going into Mexico, like before it all got so fucked up. He burned his boats so his men could not turn back. He fucking burned his boats.

Graham was watching the car lights go. To me they looked like colored shuttles in a big loom, everything a gold net woven together by light. I always felt ashamed of how beautiful things could look to me when I was around Graham, as if I couldn't see all the hidden things he could.

I was trying my best to be cynical and *comme il faut*, too. —*So we could live in little ticky-tacky houses on streets that are named for birds that do not inhabit the North American continent,* I said, and there was this bad silence before Graham spoke back.

—*You know, I can predict your whole life,* he said. —*You'll marry some ordinary guy, and your ass will spread, and your whites will be brighter than white. You'll only listen to music with no words. You'll quit reading books. And then you'll wake up someday wondering how in the fuck you ended up on some street named for some bird that does not inhabit the North American continent. You'll go to the Caribbean for Christmas and try to remember who in the hell you used to be. You'll feel so invisible sometimes you'll run away to the city and go into secret rooms where some stranger will have to hurt you to make you feel alive again.*

It was like when he shoved me under the water. Sink or swim. I couldn't say anything for a while, just stared out at Atlanta, the cubes and quadrants of light, all the little gated communities. I wondered what had *happened* to him since the wildflower and robin's egg and rabbit-hole times His world: one was either the predator or the prey, take your pick. Always assume the worst. When in doubt, lash out.

Telltale signs that someone has been mistreated in his life, I decided.

—*I have to go feed my father's lab animals,* he said. —*My parents are in the Caribbean. You have to go home now.*

—*Not yet.*

—*You can't stay here by yourself. Are you crazy?*

—*Crazy would be going home,* I said, and this caused him to survey me a little differently.

—*Come on, then,* he said.

We drove all the way into Emory.

He had a key to his father's lab. There were these monkeys in cages, with little wizened faces. They began to chatter, glad to see him.

—*God, how cute,* I said, and ran over to them. I'd never been that close to real monkeys before. Then when I got close enough, I saw that each one had something that looked like a tiny sparkplug sticking out of its head.

—*Shit,* I said, and jumped back. Electrodes.

—*It doesn't hurt them,* he said, defensively. —*It's just a way of retrieving information.*

—*How do you know it doesn't hurt them?*

—*They don't feel it.*

—*How do you know they don't feel it? They can't talk back.*

He was filling some water bottles and putting them on a tray. I saw another tray with syringes with long, curved needles.

—*What is that?*

—*It's how they eat. Gavage. Portion control. Otherwise, they'd probably eat themselves to death. Or fuck themselves to death.*

There was a cage with two monkeys in it, but they were strapped to opposite walls of it. They had electrodes, too. They were positioned and restrained so they couldn't do anything but look at each other without touching.

—*What's the matter with these?* I asked.

—*Nothing's wrong. Just a different experiment.*

—*What's your dad trying to find out?*

—*If love is an instinct. Or if it's, you know, imaginary.*

—*It's horrible,* I said. —*It's a horrible way to find out.*

—*You just think that because you're a woman.*

Woman. The word now hung in the air like a gossamer pear, a blown glass tree ornament in his mind, something totally removed from the room we were standing in, some oasis he needed to believe in.

I didn't feel much like a grown woman. I just felt lost, like if anybody could ever journey to the center of me, I'd just be a howling baby in a white christening dress. —*But what happens to them? When the experiment is over?*

—*They have to be destroyed, I guess. I never really thought about it.*

Their eyes were terrible, as if that is the part of us that dies first. No wonder the world looked grim to him. No wonder he was tougher than anyone else I knew.

Comme il faut. I didn't have to look it up. I knew. I fell in love with him then, that instant.

—*Hey,* he said, —*we got real possibilities here. We got your prototype for your space-age state of holy matrimony here. Future couples can meet, misunderstand each other miserably, and die, all from the safety of their own armchairs. Think of all the trouble it would save everybody.*

He looked a little wistful when he said this, and I wanted to homestead in his heart, spade under every bad thing that had ever happened to him, and plant bright zinnias.

He nodded at the monkey couple. —*Night-night, lovebirds.*

I laughed, irascible as he.

It was quiet in the car driving home. I wanted the road to go on and on. We drove past some hookers. I snorted, said something derogatory.

—*You know, for somebody who looks like she fell out of a Walker Evans photo, you sure are haughty. Whores are the few holy women in the world. In some Eastern societies they don't even let a woman marry until she can go into a temple at night and persuade a stranger to fuck her for her supper. They don't consider her qualified to be a wife until she can do that.*

That F-word again, only he made it hang in the air like some kind of sacrament. I looked at his knees and had this dizzy, dizzy wish to be between them, kneeling the way I did with my boyfriend.

He stopped the car in front of my house to let me out. I looked at the dashboard. He had an index card taped on the glove compartment: *It is a fearful thing to fall into the hands of the living god.* I couldn't remember where I had read that. He had his arms cradling the steering wheel. Lucky steering wheel, I thought. His hands were beautiful. Then he reached across me to open the door, studying me in the darkness.

—*I don't know why,* he said, —*but the world looks ugly to me a lot.*

I needed to touch him, but I sat on my hands. The rule so old that nobody knows where it came from: never touch him first. He has to touch first.

—*You know, I could make a complete whore out of you if I wanted to.*

It didn't shock me that he would say this. But I'd never been afraid of him before, so I ran inside.

I lay curled in a ball in my room with the cat curled on my feet. I had my headphones on, flipping the dial on my radio till I found the song. I knew it would be out there somewhere.

Oh, Mama when you were a young girl
Did you ever love a man so much
As if he were some fantastic jewel
You could never be worthy of?

This was *my* song.

RIGHT BEFORE the Christmas holidays a girl at our school got beat up by her boyfriend and they piled us all into the auditorium to show us a film about boys who are abusive, and *yatta yatta yatta.* How if someone is pressuring you, drop him. The usual.

I would have loved it if Graham had pressured me.

—*So can you sail this thing yet?* He said this one time when he stopped over. I was sitting in the boat, loading film into the Leica.

—*No,* I shook my head. I snapped his picture and he frowned a little.

—*Can you even do knots?*

—*What knots?*

He picked up some old frayed rope in the stern of the boat, looked around, then at my wrists.

—*Half hitch,* he said, looping, then knotting. Then he undid it, one hand holding my wrists while the other wound the rope again. —*Clove hitch.*

My eyes widened at the touch of that scratchy rope. I looked up at him, and he seemed to let me have his eyes for a long, long time, seeing right into me. The haughtiest me inside stumbled to its knees. I wanted him to push me up against a wall somewhere, anywhere, and make me belong to him, make me believe.

—*You like that, huh?* He smiled.

Another time I was doing my algebra homework. I looked up to see him making little cuts on his wrists. I jumped up and rocked the whole boat on the trailer and knelt in front of him. There was a scratch on his wrist, a little bead of blood forming, the play of a sad smile on his face.

—*Stop it,* I said.

—*Why?* he said, and he sneered at me. —*What do you care?*

—*Because.*

—*Because why?*

—*Because I love you,* I blurted out. Because it felt like he was cutting me.

—*Love is a dead language,* he said. —*I don't speak dead languages.*

The wind can shift, and you can come about without understanding what has happened until it has.

WE HAD THIS DANCE inside our own gated neighborhood because our parents didn't want us to go to the high school dance. Too dangerous, they thought. But the big deal to me was that Graham was there, leaning against the wall, watching everything. Totally cool. Not even dancing. Just watching. I wanted to be out in the dark with him, up against a wall somewhere. The rest of us were like monkeys on short leashes that our parents could retract at any minute. There was this song, an old one, something about if you can't be with the one you love, love the one you're with.

But when it's *you* in the backseat of some car on a cold fall night, dressed in some fritzy dress that was never intended to keep you warm, kneeling between the knees of someone who doesn't need you or even *know* you, it doesn't feel like love. It feels like gavage, like portion control.

—*Jesus, Tory,* my boyfriend said the night after the dance, when we went parking, pulling my face up from his lap to face him. —*It's like you're not even here. You're like a zombie. We can't go on like this.*

Major lightbulb going off in the head: *I don't have to take this from you.* I grabbed my denim jacket and ran out of his car, picking my way home across backyards of the ticky-tacky houses.

It seemed to me that I had entered a new kingdom of candor in my life. I asked my mother one night at dinner, —*When did you lose your virginity?*

She paused, salad fork in midair.

—*It wasn't something I just lost,* she said, looking at my father. —*It was a gift I gave.*

—*It has to be with the right person,* my father offered. —*Otherwise . . .*

—*Otherwise what?*

—*Otherwise you might end up with your name scrawled on the boys' bathroom wall,* my mother finished for him. —*It has to be someone you trust.*

—*How do you know who's the right person?*

My father looked at my mother. My mother couldn't look at him.

—If you have to ask, then he's not the right person, my mother said.

Later she came into the garage, where I was sitting in the cat-boat, listening to my Walkman. I took my headphones off.

—What is it?

—I just need to tell you, she said. *—Don't give your gift away too soon.*

I stared at her. She looked like she'd been crying.

——And you always have to let him make the first move. He'll think you do that with just anyone if you don't.

I must have looked blank.

—It changes everything, she said. *—Everything.*

Then my mother wanted to take me shopping the Saturday before Christmas. She let me have a glass of wine with my lunch, while we waited for my rolls of film to be developed, and she made a big deal out of making me feel grown-up. It felt pretty fraudulent, this quality-time stuff. To be suddenly a person, especially now that you have to be handled carefully, like a bomb on a timer, some illegitimate-baby factory waiting to explode.

She was looking at the pictures we just had developed. She raised her eyebrows at me when she saw the ones of Graham. Then she saw the ones of my father and she burst into tears.

I wanted to give Graham some pictures of himself for Christmas. It had to be something special. I thought of the photographs I'd taken of him, one off the high dive, one piking down, and the one he never knew I took, sitting alone by the side of the pool with the water streaming off him, looking desolate.

We were walking down along the lake when I pulled them out of my jacket and gave them to him. Even though I knew it was a much bigger deal to me than it was to him, I had the idea that if he could see himself through my eyes he would understand it: no world with him in it could ever be ugly.

He didn't say anything for a few minutes. I made the mistake of feeling close to him, that whatever was mine was his, the shirt off my back, the words out of my mouth, the blood out of my veins if he needed it, no questions asked. It felt inviolable, and it felt like enough. I understood that he would never love me. It had to do with how gypped he would feel because I was not the beautiful blond oasis he was always making his way toward across the sand. I could never be those pictures up on his walls.

—You don't have a clue, do you? he said, staring out across the water. *—You don't understand how the world really works, do you?*

—I think I understand some things, I said. I was thinking of my father and the football-game pictures. *—Some terrible things happened in my family,* I said. *—Well, look,* I said, and I pulled out the photos of my father and mother as if they were some proof of something. *—Do you know what available light means?* He looked at them silently, and handed them back to me like they were dead fish. Other people's family pictures are boring. I was boring. Where did I get off thinking he needed anything from me? He had a whole family who loved him.

—You think you care about people, but what you really care about is taking pictures of people. It's not your fault. People just do not care about each other, per se. It's just a lie that dumb losers like you need. He was saying something else, but I couldn't seem to hear it for the buzzing in my ears. That is the way it is with older guys. Everything you feel deeply is just some tacky phenomenon they've already survived. I remember how the Leica looked as it flew out of my hand, in a slow arc, into the water.

—Jesus, he said. *—What did you do that for? Women are nuts. Women. There is no such thing as a safe word.*

Boy, you don't have a clue, do you? I was thinking. I was imagining him in my room, surrounded by my votive candles. I was seeing myself kneeling before him, taking him into my mouth like warm, welcome fruit. Private cinema: how to make him helpless in the firelight, calm him somehow. I had read about it in books.

—Can we continue this conversation, like, in some bed somewhere? I said, and the bitterness in my voice surprised even me. Utter it out like that and it sounds like root canal.

—You can't be serious, he said. *—What would all my friends think?*

There was this sense of an experiment, of his being snapped shut, of lab things being put away. He kept talking, forced small talk, but I couldn't hear it, *or* what I was saying back. I was already running down some abandoned road in my mind, like that old Vietnam photo—the little naked girl running fast to get away from the napalm that has burned all her clothes off—*I understand nothing, I will trust no one.*

Pike to the bottom of yourself and—*surprise*—there's no baby in a white christening gown at the core of you. There's a thing

that just blunders on, mantis-like, eyes bulbous, forelegs raised beseeching, doomed to derive its life from its imaginings that others
need it.

Was this what my dad meant by *sentience*?

I WAS THAT INSECT for months and months. We all looked like
an armor-plated species to me, eyes bright with grim purposes to
live, waving hinged appendages as we creaked out communicative
noises to each other. I could smile and carry on as if everything
was normal, but I kept looking dumbly at my wrists, as if I could
peel back the skin there and see my basic insectness, the underly-
ing horror of me. The whole world looked ugly to me, no matter
what light was available.

I wanted to talk to Graham, as if that would make me human
again. I phoned him every day for a week, and he wouldn't talk
to me.

—*He's busy,* his little brother told me.

—*So how's school,* his mother asked me, all icy politeness.

—*He doesn't want to talk to you,* his father said bluntly. —*What is it
with you and this phone thing?*

His mother mailed my mother a clipping about aggressive
teenage girls that phone boys compulsively all the time. They got
an unlisted phone number, and I had a note in homeroom telling
me to talk to the counselor. Graham's parents had talked to my parents, and they decided that if I couldn't stop phoning him, I would
have to go to one of those places where they get you off drugs or
whatever.

—*I can't believe you threw that Leica in the lake,* my father said that
night at dinner.

—*I don't know what's got into you,* my mother said. —*Why are you
embarrassing us like this? What are you thinking?*

—*I'm thinking I wish I were dead,* I said to them, and my father
threw his napkin across the table at my face. I slammed the door
and walked outside.

I went to the fort because I didn't want to go back home again.
There was another orange glow in the dark. *Graham.*

—*Hey,* I said, but there was this ominous silence.

—*What are you doing here?*

—*It's a free country,* I answered.

—*That's what you think,* he said, before he pushed me up against the wall.

Did he rape me?

I don't know. I don't think so.

It is a fearful thing to fall into the hands of the living god.

I opened my mouth to speak—I think I meant to whisper, *Don't hurt me, I already love you,* but his thumb slid into my mouth. I didn't know what else to do; I sucked his thumb. He seemed to see me then. He liked the feel of my mouth, but he didn't like the way he was reacting, like, *Wait—you don't understand. I need to torment you, it makes me feel like a man.*

I probably looked surprised, too, like, *No—YOU don't understand. I need to love you. It makes me feel like a woman.*

Does not.

Does too.

My inititation into the basic argument.

I don't remember if it all hurt or not, the slap and rasp of flesh that was not lovemaking. We could not seem to synchronize our movements. He didn't seem to need pleasure, he needed power.

I could see through his skin, into the netting of anger that held him together. He hated me. It was like looking into the place where murders and atrocities and war begin, where men can only understand their own power by being mean. I remember the moments when his eyes flared and I saw *into* him, like a deep place trampled by people who had preceded me. He saw me looking, so he closed his eyes. That was the part that hurt, when he closed his eyes to me, and chose his own survival over mine.

—*I love you,* I said. It seemed like the only thing necessary to say.

—*Jesus,* he said when he was leaving, —*are you some kind of sicko, or what?*

When I could, I walked home. All the lights were out, but I knew that my parents were probably lying there listening to every sound around the house, like chirrupy, sentient insects themselves. I climbed into the little catboat and curled up, closed my eyes. I thought, *Graham? You were like a stranger in a temple to me. Does that make me holy, or just a whore?*

The voice of the suicide girl was pretty strong to me then. It was like she was calling me, patting the seat beside her on the big bus to a quiet place: *Come here, we've saved you a place, it's all quiet here.* But why should such a voice be trusted? Suicides probably have the same need for vindication that the living do.

I curled up under my gingham bedspread in the boat. I decided to keep it all inside me. I decided that if no one knew what I knew about Graham, it would be contained. The hate would not pass from me and contaminate others. I decided to remember Graham's voice, pretending he cared what became of me. In my own head, the place where I was in control, he assured me, *You can only keep moving if you learn to tack . . . the wind shifts . . . you come about.*

You can need governance from a man so badly that your mind will just *make it up.*

—*Tory.*

I opened my eyes. My mother. Standing there with a cup of hot tea. I closed my eyes again, ignoring her.

—*This will all pass. You'll see.*

—*You don't understand anything.*

—*You'd be amazed at what I understand, baby. We all have one we just have to try to forget. You'll grow up, and you'll have all you want—Mr. Right, the laughing kids, the schoolbuses, and baking cookies.*

I opened my eyes and stared at her in horror. *Liar, liar, your hair's on fire.* She went away.

I always felt tender and angry toward Graham when I saw him later, like, *What next? You're supposed to show me what comes next.* There was always this tension, like we couldn't get it straight in our minds who had violated whom. Each of us liked to move through the world with impunity, so each of us was apt to play the victim, howling mad at the world.

I heard the end of the song, finally, one night in my room.

> Just like that Spanish dancer I
> Throw my roses down for him.
> Across these beds of darkness he
> Opens his arms and gathers them in.

Gathers *them* in, not *me.* Big difference there.

My parents went to the Caribbean one spring weekend, to try to remember who they used to be. It was the first time they'd left me alone.

I pulled the catboat out into the driveway and hitched it to the car. I piled some magazines and newspapers in it, and the gasoline can from my father's lawnmower supply. I cut school and drove to a small man-made lake. It was deserted, mostly. I backed the boat trailer into the water. Some old men fishing in a boat watched me.

I stood there looking at the boat with the matches from my mother's rose-trellised kitchen. I felt a need to say something that would give poetry or meaning to the moment, but I could only re-member the line about throwing down the roses. I didn't like that anymore, it reminded me of some awful insect noise: *Need me need me need me.*

—*Yippee-ki-aye, motherfucker,* I said to the old boat. This was my favorite line from a Bruce Willis movie.

The catboat turned to tinder with a *whoosh* that terrified me. I got afraid, suddenly, that people would run out and stare, perhaps take me away to the place they take kids to get them off drugs. Magazines and newspapers curled and flamed like I was burning the person I used to be, the old insect needful one, the one always like some magazine-ad beggar-child with hand outstretched: *Love-hunger is all little Vientiane has ever known. Can you please give?*

I pretended the next day to have had an accident at the lake. *Geez, I have no idea what went wrong.*

My father was incensed, though he had never had the slightest interest in the boat. Maybe it reminded him of his father. He lec-tured me about drugs.

—*Sentience is the desired effect, Tory,* he said. —*I don't know what you're doing or whose company you're keeping, but never underestimate the tactical advantages of sentience.* I dreamt deeply of Graham, for long afterwards drugged on remembering him. Waking and sleeping. Always I was looking for him in broken orchards that dripped with soft rain. I would always say, *But you DID hang that moon! I saw you!*

If my mind tarried too long in that dream, he would turn into a bully, putting my name on the boys' bathroom wall—*If you're des-perate, call Tory Durrance*—and then I would wake up sweating like the scalded girl running down the road, her love all burned off by the napalm: *I understand nothing, I trust nothing.*

But it would not be correct to say that I was ever raped.

What became of Graham? I don't know. I heard he went away to military school.

What became of me?

I woke up one day in a place purportedly so uninhabitable to all life forms that some of the bravest men in the world refuse to live there. Many of the women there have to be drugged into staying: ticky-tacky houses on streets named for birds that could never have survived on the North American continent. My husband and I worked hard during the day and fell into bed too tired to touch each other at night. Sometimes I cried for no good reason over stupid things, and we talked about going to the Caribbean to try to remember who we once were. My husband sent away for catalogues for small boats. We whispered in bed sometimes, trying to navigate through the plenitude, wondering if perhaps our children would murder us in our sleep some night because we didn't have the wherewithal to buy them Porsches.

Sometimes after dinner I was filled with a kind of votive rage I couldn't talk about, while I did the supper dishes to the accompaniment of piped-in wars, gunshots, women screaming, cars crashing, glass breaking. It was as if our bearing silent, nightly witness to these things was more important to my family than talking to each other.   Sometimes it seemed to me that people do not care about each other, per se.

I had trained them to need me, to be hostages to my care, and it was suffocating us all. We figured out that I could have thirty minutes of solitude at night, in between the supper dishes and the youngest child's bath, but it took an offer of divorce on my part to negotiate this.

So I made little apologetic jokes about my belly and ass as I laced up my shoes to go walking. This my family understood and excused, and I became safely unnoticed by them again.

One's womanly worth depends on her maintenance of the illusion that that no new soul has begun its transit through the gates of her hips.

I walked in the same paths wearing the same black tights and white T-shirt that the other women walkers wear. I passed other walkers, mostly wives, most of whom must fuck for their suppers. We came out mostly at night and walked with our heads wired to listen to private music, navigating by strangers' voices in a colloquium that never quite connects with the outside world.

O sisters make my wedding bed, and tie a wild thorn crown around my head.

Love me tender, love me true.

Why don't you love me like you used to do?
Yatta, yatta, yatta.

I walked right past the bookstore where sometimes I could see the men and women standing up in there reading things to each other, the men not understanding the women, the women not understanding the men. *How I suffer, yatta, yatta, yatta,* travelogues for the darkling plain, offered to the deaf. I fell out of the habit of buying books. It felt too much like paying strangers good money to close their eyes and choose their own survival over mine.

I listened a lot to the Pachelbel *Canon.* It didn't have any words, so it felt safe. Listening to it under a starlit winter sky was one of the deepest pleasures I knew. Like eavesdropping on some forbidden old experiment to see if love was a real instinct or imaginary. But even music with no words is not safe. The body's penchant for falsehood is almost as great as the mind's: sometimes the muscles and veins go all gold—*perfectoreno*—with something like the memory of a real love.

One night, with nobody but the moon looking over my shoulder, I took a shortcut through an alley so dark and empty that the music made me dream of Graham and me, naked as downy ducks in the wading pool again. It made me want to believe that if ever the cuts across his wrists became more than games, I would somehow feel it myself, and could get to him in time, heroically across years and miles. I need to believe the accidental and unrehearsed forms of bondage are more authentic.

But that night I passed an ordinary man, a stranger to me, whose shoulders seemed stooped with the weight of his life. What ever could have happened to him? I imagined that in the slump of his shoulders I could read it: he was no longer a believer. Ordinary man, the kind on whom so many depend.

The thought crossed my mind that I should accost him, whisper to him, —*Up against the wall, thou disbeliever. We are not without our vestiges of civilization here.*

It was like some maverick dream that came unbidden: I should kneel there before him in the alley, and welcome him into my mouth like warm fruit. I should make him speak forgotten words in the dead language, make his face go votive with belief in something, even if only his own power to humble me.

Which may be the only power I will ever know.

I imagined doing it the way the whores on the bridges of London did, without even confessing their names, in the last days of the crumbling empire. I read about this, horrified, as a girl. It was not so horrifying anymore. It made perfect sense.

Simply to give oneself, without demanding lifelong servitude of the other as payment, in perpetuity, of the gift. Without even confessing one's name.

But I walked on, and he did not look up. I understood then: I was an arriviste in the realm of invisibility.

It was as close to a secret sortie into the city as I could manage in a thirty-minute walk. It was as close to being fucked in a temple into shame at my own whoredom as my wifehood would allow. What is it the world in women does require? The lineaments of a steadfast, cheerful liar. Is love any less real because it is imaginary?

$\mathcal{A}$CKNOWLEDGMENTS

If there was any one moment when this book began, it was during a phone conversation with Charles Verrill, who advised me to write about history and families. My friend Leigh Feldman sustained the life of the book for a number of years with her indefatigable enthusiasm and energy. Dan Frank's editorial instincts shaped the course of my thought profoundly, and I am indebted to him for his belief in the book. I am also fondly indebted to others: my teacher Barry Hannah for his unconditional encouragement, Ann Abadie and Richard Howorth for exposing me to prodigious amounts of caffeine and good judgment.

Marc Smirnoff read an early portion of the book and saw potential in it; Jimmy Faulkner and Jeff Meaders were game enough to talk at length to a woman about airplanes and wars. My fellow curators Scott Higginbotham and Dan Kostopulos contributed much to the book's completion by showing support for it. And to Charlie Simic, whose book on Cornell kept me from tossing this one in the rubbish heap, *thank you*.

VINTAGE CONTEMPORARIES

INDEPENDENCE DAY
by Richard Ford

Independence Day is a moving, peerlessly funny odyssey through the American commonplace—and through the layered consciousness of one of its most interesting representatives, Frank Bascombe.

"As gripping as it is affecting. . . . Ford has galvanized his reputation as one of his generations most eloquent voices." —*The New York Times*

Winner of the Pulitzer Prize

Fiction/0-679-73518-6

SNOW FALLING ON CEDARS
by David Guterson

This enthralling novel, set on an isolated and ruggedly beautiful island in Puget Sound in 1954, is at once a murder mystery, a courtroom drama, the story of a doomed love affair, and a stirring meditation on place, prejudice, and justice.

"Compelling. . . heart-stopping. Finely wrought, flawlessly written."
—*The New York Times Book Review*

Winner of the PEN/Faulkner Award

Fiction/0-679-76402-X

THE JOY LUCK CLUB
by Amy Tan

For almost forty years the members of the Joy Luck Club have met to play mah jong, eat Chinese delicacies, and brag about their children. Now one of those women has died, and it is up to her daughter to take her place—to learn her mother's secret story and those of the women who left China with her.

"Vivid . . . wondrous . . . what it is to be American, and a woman, mother, daughter, lover, wife, sister and friend—these are the troubling, loving alliances, and affiliations that Tan molds into this remarkable novel." —*San Francisco Chronicle*

Fiction/0-679-72768

VINTAGE CONTEMPORARIES
Available at your local bookstore, or call toll-free to order:
1-800-793-2665 (credit cards only).